Shattered Bonds

Broken Legacy Series, Volume 2

R.A. Vincent

Published by R.A. Vincent, 2024.

Prologue

"Enough of your insolence!" Queen Kisandra punched the air, and the rafters fell from the ceiling.

"Dominic!"

They collapsed on him—twisting and twining like writhing snakes. The break in concentration dropped the hellfire barriers around the twins. They piled on Dominic—lashing him with vines. Holding him down. His shouts cut off as Ormr cast a wind shield around him. No sound. No air.

His hellfire petered out.

No fire. No escape.

"Let him go!" I thrashed against the clinging, liquid stone, plumbing my depths for something. Anything! To trigger my magic. "Come on!"

A boom shook the palace once, and twice as Reyna rammed the window.

This is my magic. I use it when I decide! Absorb her living magic. Free yourself and Dominic. I strained, screaming for him. *Do it now!*

"Treason," Queen Kisandra shrieked. "Insolence. Mutiny. Violence against your queen. That disgusting whore's spawn has poisoned your minds as her mother did my son's. Kill them," she ordered. "Every last one of them. Their life is forfeit by order of their queen."

The chairs and statues were only too willing to comply. Bodies hit the ground—their necks snapped. I struggled harder as Keely turned blue, the chair arms squeezing the life out of her.

"Stop!" General Roark broke free of his executioner and kicked it away.

Boom! Boom!

"There is no need of this, my queen." General Roark dropped to his knees, bowing before her. "That boy does not speak for us. The royals, nobles, and soldiers of this kingdom are your loyal servants, and have always been." He swept out a hand. "It's been my honor to serve this kingdom until a time as you were ready to return."

"Yes," voices cried out. "Kill the Druk bastard."

"We serve the one true queen."

"Slit her throat."

"Break her neck."

"We never trusted that Druk's spawn."

"Is that so?" Through the eye space, hers narrowed to a slit. "You're a general now, Ladon Roark. High commander of the Royal Riders." She snapped her fingers. "In my time, the general carried out the execution of traitors."

The doors opened. Dragged in by chairs, wooden beams, twisting rope, and binding metal... were Sister Aven and the children from the orphanage.

"No!" I broke my body in half, clawing and bleeding on the stone. *Magic, do something! Steal her power! Help!*

The last to be dragged in was Rosaleen.

"Ainsley," my best friend cried. "I didn't tell them anything, I swear. Ormr came to the Veil. They asked all these questions about you, but I refused to answer. So my aunt did instead." She burst into tears, cutting through the already running face paints on her bruised and battered face. "She told them everything for ten fucking ryus! I'm sorry. I'm so sor—" The vines climbed her neck, lashing around her mouth.

"Let her go!" I screamed. "Don't do this. You don't have to do this! I'll leave Golden City. I swear I'll never come back." My Ilemka, my Niamh, my Colm. All my brothers and sisters there in clothes that were clean and sandals that were new. I did all this to give us a new life. It would not end here. "Please! Let them go."

Boom! Boom!

Queen Kisandra gave no sign she heard me. "I ordered that abomination dead, and instead, that woman harbored the enemy of my blood," she said, leveling a finger on Sister Aven. "She fed and housed the worthless thing when she should've drowned it at first sight. And that harlot," she spat, swinging to Rosaleen. "Refused to give up the betrayer and attacked my heirs when they sought to carry out my rightful justice.

"Execute them, General, oh loyal servant. All of them. Orphans are cursed children and drains on society. For all we know, she's harboring another demon's spawn in that brood. Prove you will carry out my will."

"No!"

"As you wish."

"Noooo—!"

General Roark waved his hand, and my family crumbled to dust.

I collapsed on the ground—jaw cracked on a choked sob. No... not a sob. A scream. I screamed and screamed, calling out for people I would never see again.

Boom! Boom! Boom!

"See, my queen?" Roark bowed. "It is my honor to carry out your will."

"Hmm. Then, you know you're not done yet." She pointed at Dominic.

"Don't touch him!" *Break free, Ainsley! Stop this. Save him!*

"Your son committed violence upon your rightful ruler and incited a mutiny against her."

Ormr released the air shell and Maili's vines lifted him free. His head fell forward, unconscious.

"Kill him."

General Roark dipped his head. "Yes, my queen."

"Roark, stop. He's your son!"

The general looked right at me and said, "I have plenty more." He touched Dominic's ankle.

Wither magic consumed him greedily—eating his legs, pants, belt, and everything away.

My mind broke.

I clutched my head, shrieking under ferocious, unforgiving pain. The ceiling collapsed under the dragon's final strike. Glass fell like rain. Pouring in, their bonds ripped my mind apart one by one. Kenna, Cadmus, Suoh, Mireu.

Tizor.

Their minds, thoughts, and feelings rushed into me, sending spasming agony throughout my body.

"Tizor?"

"Cadmus? Cadmus, love, what are you doing!"

"I can't feel your bond, Kenna. Kenna!"

They became mine. Mine to command. Mine to love. Mine—for I finally knew what I was, and as Kai said, it was so much more than I thought possible.

I roared as I drained General Roark of power, undoing his vile, twisted magic on Dominic. The man collapsed in a heap, unfortunately not dead.

Ripping my hands apart, I tore Maili's vines to shreds, dropping my love whole and alive on the floor.

I looked to the shadow of the podium. Just a single look and I was there, standing tall and free of the queen's magic. I raised my hands to the heavens. To my dragons.

"What have you done?" the queen bellowed. "This is forbidden magic. Usurper. Usurper!"

There was nothing forbidden about my magic. Deep in Elder Tizor's mind, he held the true name for my magic—revered and feared throughout time, my abilities were the origin. Named forbidden to keep the truth of what my kind could do hidden.

"*Dragon mother,*" six voices said at once.

"I am not the usurper," I said with a calm that wasn't mine. "She was a failure. I won't be.

"Kill them all."

Unhinging their jaws, my dragons set the throne room ablaze.

Chapter One

Fires blazed all around me, engulfing all in my sight.

"Destroy our enemies."

"Avenge the hatchlings."

"Protect our mate."

"Kill. Kill. KILL!"

I screamed, and a gush of wind blew out in all directions, blowing flaming mounds that used to be people across the room until my wind found the people that mattered.

Wind barriers surrounded Poet, Keely, and my mate, Dominic. In there they would be safe, while our enemies burned.

"What have you done!" The would-be queen of Adalinda raged as hellfire consumed her robes, greedily devouring all in its path as hellfire did. "Beast! Monster! Usurper!"

"Kill her." "Burn her." "Avenge the hatchlings. Avenge the lifemate. Avenge them!"

I stalked toward her, a strange sensation rippling over my skin. "Die."

Hellfire lit my hands aflame, awaiting my guidance to their next meal. All around me, people screamed, shouted for their dragons, desperately flung around magic, and perished.

"Die!"

Hands seized me from behind. An outraged roar had barely left my lips before a vicious blow struck my head.

Black bled into my vision. The last thing I saw was the throne room wink out.

Cold air smacked my cheeks—the only hint that I was not where I should be.

The hands released me and I fell, darkness claiming me before my face hit the ground.

***

Four Moons Later

I walked through the marketplace, my presence cutting a path without force or words.

People were shouting, running, cursing, and throwing everything from fruit to magic at me. The fruit passed harmlessly off my wind barriers. The magic absorbed into my skin, filling me past the brim.

"Leave this place, you monster!" A man rushed me, a shovel raised over his head and eager to come down on mine. "We'll have no trouble here!"

I flicked him away with a twitch of my finger, blasting him back onto his manure cart.

"She's there. I smell her. I hear her." "Up ahead." "Right there." "Blue door." "Avenge the lifemate. Avenge the hatchlings."

"Kill her."

"KILL HER!" they shouted, ripping a snarl from my lips.

I rounded the corner, leaving the marketplace behind. I had a trailing mob behind me—trying and failing to stop me.

A blue door appeared at the end of the dirt street. The stone house it defended was similar to the other stone houses on the row. It boasted a rooftop courtyard decorated with hanging laundry, and a walkway that connected the rooftops together.

"Kenna."

My sky dragon swooped down. Lighter than air, she landed on the roof, cutting off that escape route. She would not escape me.

I blasted the door off its hinges, beckoning a scream from inside.

"Leave them be!"

Waving my hand, a wall of hellfire erupted behind me, trapping the mob on the other side. We would not be disturbed.

I crossed the threshold and breathed deep—sensing, searching, waiting.

"Kill her."

"Kill her," I growled.

"Avenge the lifemate."

"Avenge the hatchlings."

Noise sounded to my right, snapping my head around to the staircase. I dropped on the floor. On my hands and knees, I climbed the stairs, narrowing in on my prey.

I reached the top step. A pan whizzed through the air, striking the spot where my head would have been and bouncing off the stone.

"Stay away. Leave me alone!"

I looked to her fallen shadow and I was there—behind her.

"What—? Where—?"

I struck the back of her knees, making her crumple to the floor.

We were in a dining room. The table set for three people—plates, mugs, spoons, forks.

A metal mage had attacked me. Today? Yesterday? In the marketplace, or no place at all. It mattered not. Time was a human shackle. Dragons lived long enough to become its master.

I felt the metal mage's magic swirling within me, waiting until I sounded the call. With a thought, the metal plates, mugs, and utensils rose in the air. Their— *My* magic bent, twisted, and shaped it. I jerked my head and the daggers flew through the air, piercing her hands, legs, and feet—pinning her to the wall.

"Ahh," she screamed. "P-please! Spare me!"

"You were the one," I hissed, dropping back on my hands and knees. "You betrayed my lifemate. You killed the hatchlings. Die." I drove the daggers deeper. "Die!"

"I didn't want to!" said Rosaleen's aunt.

She looked even worse than I remembered. Bloodshot eyes from a night of heavy drinking filled with useless tears. She had more lines on her face, holes in her dress, and dead teeth in her mouth. Months on the run hadn't been kind to her, as I wanted.

I saved her for among the last for a reason. Terror sweetened the blood.

"Please," she sobbed. "I had no choice. They came to me and said they were the true heir to the throne. If I didn't tell them everything I knew about you, and what Rosaleen had to do with you, I would be executed for crimes against the throne right along with you both!"

"You're to blame!" Uma shouted. "You stole a dragon, then came up with that insane, treasonous lie to cover yourself. You dragged Rosaleen into it, and you're the reason she, those brats, and that pious bitch were killed. This is all because of you!"

"No," I said, tone calm. "It was you. You resented Rosaleen from the minute she arrived on your doorstep. Young, beautiful, happy, and so much to look forward to. She had everything you didn't.

"No matter how hard you tried to make her feel worthless and miserable. She had me, Sister Aven, and the orphanage—always there to give her love and a safe place to get away from you. Sister Aven even petitioned the magistrate countless times to get custody of Rosaleen.

"You hated the sister for seeing through you, and fighting to take your punching bag away. And you hated even more," I hissed, "that Rosaleen suddenly had coin. When Ormr came to you, telling stories of a rider that sounded suspiciously like me, you knew where she was getting those ryus from.

"Soon, Rosaleen would have enough to buy out of your bullshit contract, and live the happy, free life that you never would. So you took it all away. From her. From Sister Aven. From my brothers and sisters."

Uma shook—her whole body trembling as blood streaked down the wall, marking the final resting place of a cold and selfish bitch.

"Admit it," I growled. "Admit it!"

"Okay! Fuck's sake— Yes!" She tossed her head, flailing to get free. "I hated her! I hated all of you! Worthless, cursed orphans, and you dare to look down on me? I gave that little cunt a home, but who did she love? *Sister Aven*," she mocked. "Sister Aven this. Sister Aven that.

"And *you*. You dared to stand before me, not even ten years of age, and claim that one day you'd buy Rosaleen out of the contract, and I'd never see her again." Uma laughed—a wild, shrieky sound. "How did that work out for you? Maggots are feasting on that holier-than-thou sister, right next to her favorite little whore, Rosaleen. So go ahead and kill me."

She spat on my head. "I'll see them both beyond the veil. It'll please me to laugh in their faces, as I wish I could've done when they were stepped on like the cockroaches they are."

I weathered her rant, lips peeling farther back from my teeth. Not a trace of remorse lived in her rotted soul. She had my lifemate, hatchlings, and borrowed mother murdered. There was only one recourse left to me.

"Go on," she bellowed. "Kill me!"

"I'm not going to kill you."

The cry trapped in her throat. She blinked, surprise stilling her. "You're... You're not?"

"No."

I blasted a hole through the roof, my hellfire shredding through stone like a fist through paper. Kenna was ready.

She stuck her head through, ripped a screaming Uma off the wall, and tossed her into the air.

"They are."

My dragons descended and ripped her limb from limb. Uma's head plummeted back down at my feet—a cry of surprise still frozen on her lips. Rising up, I kicked it away and went down the stairs.

"Lifemate avenged." "Let us leave." "We stay. It is safe here." "Find our mate. Where's our mate?" "Hungry." "Tired." "Too bright! We return to the dark." "We stay." "We leave!"

"Argh!"

Something hard bounced off my leg. I looked down at the empty chamber pot rolling at my feet, then over to the person who threw it.

A small, dirty face poked out of the closet. Three places were set on the table. Uma, the man she seduced into hiding her, and *her*.

The girl glared at me—brave even as her knees knocked together. She picked up a shoe and threw that too.

"Go away!" Stringy, greasy hair hung in lanks around her bony shoulders. "Leave us alone."

Turning, I closed the distance between us—growl leaking through my teeth. I picked the youngling up by the arms, paying no heed to her kicking and screaming. Focusing hard, I channeled Mireu's healing power through me, letting it pour into the child.

The lurking pneumonia in her lungs cleared away. The sores and welts from evil and abusive beltings vanished. A badly healed broken wrist reknit itself, setting perfectly.

The youngling ceased her crying, gaping at me as I set her down.

"Come," I said. "We're leaving."

I stepped through the gaping hole where the door used to be. The girl didn't move.

"Or would you rather stay with the beast who did those things to you?"

"Who are you?" she asked, voice small.

"I'm someone who will never hurt you."

"But..." She gazed at my outstretched hand, then at the wall of hellfire surrounding her home, keeping the villagers back. "But aren't you the dragon thief? The traitor? Everyone says you're a monster."

"You and I both know people don't recognize the true monsters. Even when the bruises aren't hidden."

Her fist balled. Glancing back inside the home, she stepped out and ran to me.

***

Cadmus let us both off in front of the gates.

Mira, my new companion, drew close to me, clinging to my leg. Whipping, icy winds were twice as bitter that day—stealing warmth from all they came across.

I led her up the steps of the mansion, shielding her best I could with my voluminous skirts. Throwing open the front doors set off a cacophony of noise. Children streamed out of every entrance.

"Younglings." I plucked Mira up and placed her in front of the children. All of them varying ages, ethnicities, and sizes. All of them mine now. "Meet your new nestmate, Mira."

"Hi, Mira."

"Welcome, Mira."

"Nice to meet you."

I checked them all over, but they were fine. Of course they were fine. I left Tizor behind to guard them.

"Show Mira to her new room. Get her some clothes and food. Then show her to the baths."

"Yes, Shaya."

Shaya. Big Sister. One of the Hyelongan younglings named me that, and all the children took it on.

"Don't worry, you're safe now," Haza said.

"But what is this place?" Mira asked.

"This is your home now, but it's okay. It's a good place. Shaya is kinda weird. She growls, and crawls, and talks to herself sometimes. But she gives us all the food and clothes we want, and we're even learning how to read."

"We get our own rooms too."

"And there's a whole room filled with toys!"

"And books!"

They led Mira away, chattering in her ear.

"*The younglings are safe,*" Reyna said.

"I will protect the younglings," I hissed, head jerking. "No one will hurt them again."

"*They are not yet avenged,*" Suoh shouted. He shouted everything. "*The soulless one still lives. You will kill him. Dragon law is absolute.*"

"His death is absolute. It shall be as I say. My will is law."

"*Dragon mother,*" they said as one.

"Tell me where he is."

"*He hides in the dark and forgotten places. We will find him,*" Tizor said. "*All of dragonkin obeys your will.*"

Nodding, I left through the gates. The path my bare feet cut through from the mansion to the forest was quickly blanketed by snow.

Chapter Two

I walked through the empty town square, the soft whispering of my skirts the only sound piercing the quiet.

It was such a beautiful wedding dress. Nothing more than rags and shreds now. And my mate? Where was my mate?

Approaching the fountain, I gently sat down on the rim, getting comfortable. They streamed out of every house, shop, church, and pub. I was surrounded in seconds.

"Don't move, aberrant!"

I flicked up, landing upon dozens and dozens of archers, leaning over the rooftops.

"There's nowhere for you to run."

"He comes." "He's here." "Avenge the hatchlings." "Carry out your will."

"Why would I run?" I said lightly.

Royal Watchers, Royal Renders, and Royal Riders alike. Every one of the kingdom's forces was out, and after me.

"I've been waiting for you."

The frontline moved back, their swords shaking in their grips. They weren't nearly as confident in my presence as they wished to be.

"Hold your nerve. The witch is trying to unsettle you. Don't let her." Exiting the double doors of Tenille Cathedral, General Roark stepped into the morning light.

A growl rumbled low in my chest. It did not lessen my ire to see the crown gone from his curls, or the vicious burn scar claiming one side of his neck and part of his jaw. He was King General Roark no more, but what did it matter? He wasn't a king when he killed my predecessor the usurper either. One didn't need power to be powerful—something General Roark should've remembered when he let me get too close.

"You were clever, girl. Retreating to Edjer and hiding out in Awnan Elsher's township." General Roark moved through the crowd, parting the ranks. "Awnan fled into hiding to escape justice, then his parents, the regents, abandoned this town lest the Watchers take them into custody too. Their home has been sitting empty all this time. You moved right in. My only question is..." He looked around. "What did you do to the people who lived here? Where are their bodies?"

I cocked a brow. "I did not kill them. I gave them each two hundred gold ryus to relocate. The Elshers have been pocketing their taxes instead of putting it toward the betterment of the town. They amassed quite a fortune, that I gave back to the people who earned it.

"That's all. I didn't even tell them to keep it a secret that I was here. Seemed they did that on their own." I shrugged. "No surprise, commoners prefer the monster who returns their money, over the monsters who steal it."

Anger ticced a muscle in his jaw. "You lie. You gave nothing to no one. You slaughtered the innocent people of Vallo, and their deaths will be added to your sentence. Each and every one."

Of course Roark would rather believe I massacred the whole town than the plain and terrible truth. The people of Vallo chose a side... and it wasn't his.

"Look around you, witch." He swept out a gloved hand. "Manmade weapons of steel and wood. Not a single person here will use magic against you, leaving none for you to steal. Scan the skies," he said, tipping his chin. "No dragons for you to steal and forcibly bond. Your reign of terror ends today."

I hummed. "So your pets have finally learned after the twelve times they tried and failed to kill me. Good. These little play fights were getting quite... tedious."

"Silence!" Roark brandished his sword and charged me. The tip stopped just short of my chin. "Where is Tizor?"

"*Kill him. Kill him. KILL HIM!*"

I rolled my head, temples pounding. "My dragon... is none of your business."

"Tizor is my dragon." Fury rattled his voice. "My bonded. He will return to me if I have to take you apart limb by limb. I will wash away your forbidden magics in a sea of your blood."

I rose, making him step sharply back. Visions of Rosaleen, Sister Aven, Niamh, Colm, Ilemka, and all my siblings danced through the square—their faces frozen in fear. That was the general's final parting gift for my innocent family. Filling their last moments with terror and helplessness.

"Thank you for coming to me," I said, holding out my hands. In a blink, they were consumed by Reyna's hellfire. Tizor's magic would kill him quickly, but Reyna's would do it painfully. The right choice was obvious. "I had gotten tired of chasing you."

"Uh-uh." Inexplicably, Roark smiled. "You've forgotten I've fought and killed one of your loathsome kind before. I know well you've stolen the dragon's abilities as easily as you steal magic. As easily... as you've been stealing children all over Adalinda."

My eyes narrowed.

"Most assumed you were killing them, but that didn't make sense. You didn't need to whisk them away to kill them. You'd have left their pieces where we found the rest." His smirk widened. "You and I know better. You have a soft spot for orphans, whores, and the dregs of society. Which is why we stopped by an orphanage on the way here, and brought this..."

Hairs standing on end, my hands fell to my sides. Roark had even more men and women hiding in the buildings, and they all came out, holding knives to the throats of their crying, frightened captives.

Children no older than ten years and as young as three. The supposed heroes of our nation stood ready and willing to slit their throats.

"You beast," I rasped, the dragons roaring in my mind. "What's wrong with you? They're children!"

"Yes, they are, which makes your choice simple. Surrender," he barked. "Break the unholy, wretched cursed bonds you forced on those dragons. Return Tizor to me. Then, come quietly to your execution. Do so, and they'll be returned to their beds. Refuse and they die."

I looked from him to the faces of the children. "No. Release them, or you all die."

His grin tightened around the edges. "Do not test me, witch. You know well that I do not hesitate."

I didn't react.

Roark's smirk faded fast. "Return Tizor!"

"No."

Bellowing, he sliced the air. "Execute them!"

The Renders and Watchers hesitated, clearly believing this move was meant to be a bluff. They were never going to actually kill innocent children.

That hesitation was all I needed.

Vines burst through the cracks in the cobblestones, wrapping around their wrists—tearing the daggers from their grips. But my vines weren't quick enough to stop them all.

Soulless, obedient soldiers struck on his very command... and bounced off my air barrier. Throwing my hand up, I encased the children within a protective bubble and sent them flying two miles north, where Elsher Manor had become a safe home for hatchlings.

The small army stared at me—eyes wide and jaw hanging. "What is she?"

"Wields two magics at once."

"She's impossible."

"We can't win." A pack of Watchers broke ranks and took off running. "Stay away from us. Usurper! Usurper!"

"I told you," I said lightly, speaking to everyone but looking at General Roark. "I'm not the usurper. She couldn't win. I will."

"You will not." He leveled the sword between my eyes. "If it takes every last one of our lives, we will bring you before the might and justice of the people. For Adalinda!"

"Adalinda!"

"Attack!"

They charged me. Swords raised. Arrows notched and sent flying. The combined forces of Adalinda's best and strongest attacked.

I cut the air, and dozens of hellfire balls hovered above us. I tossed them at every man, Watcher, Render, and Rider—ripping holes through their chests the size of watermelons. They dropped where they stood. Dead.

"Nooo!" Roark cried, bringing his sword down on my head.

I rained hellfire down on him, watching him overtaken in seconds. He fell to his knees—screaming, thrashing, dying. Finally, he collapsed at my feet.

Sniffing, I kicked his body away. If only ripping this terrible, vile man from the world was enough to convince Calthoon to return his victims to this side of the veil.

I turned to leave, then stopped. Snapping back around, I narrowed on the bodies—disbelief chilling my scales.

"What is this?"

They weren't bleeding. No organs spilled out of the holes in their chest. The screaming corpse kicked and flailed as it crumbled, not burned.

They were fakes. Created by someone with earth magic so impressive, they easily fooled me. But what was the point? Keeping the true force at a safe distance so they wouldn't die along with the others who foolishly faced me? Did they think these dolls would succeed where all the others failed?

I snapped the air, anger rising up my forelegs and burning my whole body. They mocked me. Wasting my time with silly little—

I froze. *Wasting my time. That is what they did. They kept me busy here while the real attack happened elsewhere.*

"Tizor!" I was running before my body registered the movement. "Reyna! Suoh, Cadmus, Kenna, Mireu! They're coming. You and the children have to get out of there now. They're coming for you!"

Nothing.

"My dragons? Are you okay?"

Deep and terrible silence trickled down the bonds.

"No!"

I wind-blasted the ground, propelling myself into the air. I'd done the one thing I learned so many moons ago that I should never do. Underestimate General Roark.

Panic filled my lungs, forcing out air. My roars trumpeted the sky. Bloodlust dripped from my claws. If he hurt my dragons, or dared to kill my younglings, it didn't matter how many dirt dolls stood in my way. I'd kill him.

The mansion crested the horizon, easily seen on the barren hill. Another reason this was the best spot for us. No trees or mountains obscured our view. A dragon knew how important it was to always see your enemy coming, but what I saw...

My concentration broke, cutting out the wind. I plummeted—heart jumping into my throat. Vines shot from the ground and caught me, saving me before the thought that I needed saving penetrated my shock. They held me in the air, partially concealed by the clock tower.

Impossible...

Reyna towered over the mansion, hellfire blasting from her maw, wings blocking out the sun... and she wasn't moving.

How? Why? Who? Questions and impossibilities tumbled through my head as I gaped at my beauty—frozen and unmoving in the air. Above her, Kenna reached for the clouds and fell short, hanging still in the empty space. Mireu clung to the tower—her claws mid-swipe at a target that was no longer there.

Cadmus was on the ground beside the gates, twelve younglings on his back, and clearly having been in the process of evacuating them. Suoh was nowhere to be seen. My shadow dragon vastly preferred the dark, dank dungeon beneath the mansion, but by his lack of response, he was no less trapped by this impossible magic. Trapped by the real army that came to destroy me.

"Ryuku squad."

Dragons flew through the air, they just weren't mine.

Lieutenant Colonel Phiala rode an earth dragon not dissimilar to Cadmus. Except she was a deeper shade of mottled green and had the telltale horns of a female. She sat patiently while Phiala commanded the army of dirt warriors, lifting my frozen younglings off Cadmus's back and putting them on hers.

The squad was everywhere. Trampling on my territory. Breezing past my immobile dragons. Carrying my younglings out of their home.

"Get off!" Bahaar pummeled her captor's face with her little fists. "Let me go!"

"Hey— Would you—? Stop that," he cried. "I'm rescuing you! I'm one of the good guys."

Pebbles flew off the walkway and attached to her fists like sticky paper. She punched him dead on the nose, breaking it.

"Argh! Little brat!" He tossed her in the wagon as quickly as he could. "What is wrong with these kids?"

"The dragon thief," a short man wearing the black uniform of the Ryuku replied. He skipped fighting with the children and brought them out in cages made of sand. The bottoms hardened to keep them in, while the ever-flowing sand bars allowed their useless swipes to pass right through. "The beast must've done something to them. Addled their minds with forbidden magic. We'll undo whatever she's done when we get them back."

"Hurry up, you stupid shits!" Phiala's dulcet tones carried on the wind. "She already destroyed my warriors. I feel it. She'll be back any minute."

"What? Why didn't you say!" Bloody Nose charged into action. "We have to send the dragons out of here now. They can take the kids we've got. They'll come back for the rest after we've killed her."

"No one leaves!"

Hatred curdled my heart by his voice alone, heralding his arrival as General Roark stepped out from behind the wagon.

"Retrieving the children is secondary. Our primary mission is and remains Tizor."

No sooner did he say his name than Tizor's head rose from behind the mansion. Frozen with the same unknown magic, he was in the middle of snarling, with his wings up and shielding the three dragon babes on his back—Sarcany, Scartha, and Ur.

I didn't know what was lifting them into the air. A type of air magic was possible, but not even in the dragonkin hive mind did I witness an air mage strong enough to carry a full-grown dragon.

A rider flew on dragon-back to the floating Tizor. From where I hovered all I could make out was their blond hair, and their hands. They waved and sliced the air as if conducting a symphony.

An object appeared in the sky. Then two. Four. Eight. I quickly lost count. Hundreds upon hundreds of strange little black balls hung over my Tizor.

The rider clapped and the balls suddenly shot together and flattened. Understanding couldn't follow what I was seeing as pieces broke off, and reattached in a different spot. Broke off and reattached. Broke. Reattach.

I didn't know what it was until it separated into four pieces. Three small. One big.

Nets.

"Hurry up and get them out of here," Roark ordered. "Carefully. If even one of their scales is scratched, on your head be it, Rider Niran."

"Yes, sir."

"General, something isn't right," Phiala spoke up. "She defeated my warriors some time ago. The square isn't far from here. Why isn't she—?"

Vines burst from the ground, lashing around their wrists, legs, stomachs, and throats. I appeared behind Bloody Nose and touched his neck. He slumped in the vine's hold—dead.

I looked to another trespasser and youngling thief. Looked to his shadow. In a blink I was behind him. In another, he was dead. Tizor's death touch flowed through me, unhindered by whatever magic held him captive.

His power was one I rarely called on. Dragons preferred to be at full ability when focused on rearing their hatchlings. If I drained him and something happened and he wasn't strong enough to protect Sarcany, Scartha, and Ur, he'd never forgive me.

But in this case, he'd have no objection. I would slay them all for daring to enter our territory, and kidnap our hatchlings. The corpses of this once proud Ryuku squad would fertilize this land for a millennium.

I moved from shadow to shadow—killing one, three, five too fast for them to stop me.

"Shaya!" one of the children cried. She ran to me. "Shaya, help."

"Inside!" I stopped on the spot, exposing myself. "Everyone, inside now."

"There! She's there. Stop her."

My prey thrashed in the vines. Their magics summoned to their aid, as impressive as expected. Lightning crackled off one of my prey, striking the vines holding her. I was already gone before her lightning struck the spot I was standing in, and she was dead before she got another try.

"Your shadows," Phiala shouted. "Protect your shadows. Don't let her get behind you!"

Dirt warriors. Water scythes. Bronze lances. Sand swords. Icicles. They rained down and defended the three-sixty perimeter around them, not allowing me close. There was no reason they should make it easy for me. Honestly, it was no fun when they did.

I swept my hand, gathering the children in the wagon and the ones still running, into my air cocoons, and inside where they were safe. Drawing deep into my bonds, I threw my head back and roared—exploding magic.

Kenna's wind magic. Reyna's hellfire. Cadmus's earth magic. Stolen water magic.

Ground softened beneath my prey's boots, sucking them down into the dirt. I raised my wind barriers left and right, deflecting their desperate attacks. High above, my borrowed scattershot knocked the riders off dragonback. They were flaming bones before they hit the dirt.

Water filled their lungs—drowning them on dry land. Their desperate clawing ended when my wind scythes separated their heads.

The symphony was mine. I moved, spun, waved, and danced on my toes—commanding the elements like Tenille of the heavens. No one would ever hurt the children again. General Roark would not take another person from me.

I spun, snarl twisting my face as the general climbed atop the wagon, avoiding the sinking ground.

"Agh!" I opened my hands wide, then smacked my palms together, sending vines, wind scythes, water, and hellfire on the spot.

The mass of fire and weeds that used to be him, tumbled onto the ground.

"So much power—"

I whipped around, landing on a whole and living General Roark stepping out of the manor. A figure in black stood at his side.

Another fake!

"—for such a stupid girl," he finished. "Take her."

I screamed. Raising my hands, I—

"Xremya."

The world stopped.

Birds stopped their cheeping. The wind ceased blowing. Frozen flames clung to the ground. The Ryuku riders suspended between the edge of life and death. And General Roark...

All I could and would see until the end of time, was that triumphant smirk.

Chapter Three

"Pashkan."

Visions tumbled through my head one after the other. My dragons captured and flown away. Surviving riders carrying my younglings back into the wagons. General Roark smirking as Phiala's dirt warriors carried me into an iron wagon just for me, but not before she punched my still face.

Darkness. Darkness. Darkness.

A long journey going by the gnawing hunger that built in my stomach even while I couldn't feel it. We stopped after too much time, then a hooded figure climbed into the wagon, put a hood over my head, and I was carried again.

The memories whipped through my head too fast for me to grab on to one and make sense of it. It all ended with the cold bite of steel around my wrists and ankles.

"Release me!" "Insolence." "I will bite you. Free me, or I'll kill you all!"

That last shout could only be Reyna, my harsh and ferocious beauty. Her cry jangled my aching head, calling me to action. My dragons needed me. My younglings? Where were my younglings? I had to find them. Help them. Free them. Protect them.

"My dragons," I rasped. "I'm com—coming... for you."

"I wouldn't be so sure of that."

The hood was ripped off my head, bringing me face to face with... I did not know. A stranger gazed back at me.

An ageless face set within the safety of his black hood. Umber eyes shone clear and steady under thin brows. He was handsome in the way you could only be handsome when the gods themselves reached down and sculpted your sharp cheekbones, and blessed your dark, shadow-kissed skin to never know a blemish. But his face was sorrow—the way it could only be when you were without hope.

"Hello, Ainsley. Forgive me, but you'll have a headache for a while. Having all of lost time caught up to you in an instant will do that to you."

"Free me!" "My hatchlings!" "Dragon mother. DRAGON MOTHER!"

I growled, snapping at the air.

"Hmm." He moved away. "I'm not sure if that's a threat. Either way, I strongly suggest you don't do whatever it is you're thinking of doing."

My head lolled back. Iron chains bolted me to a stone wall. We were in a windowless room— No, a windowless prison. This dank, cold hole in the earth wasn't meant to be anything else.

Four stone walls and a single door on the opposite end. There was nothing there to tell me where I was, or how long I'd been there.

"No, not those," he said, penetrating my aching head. "Those manacles are merely iron. They assumed if they magicked them, you'd simply drain the magic and make it yours. No, they had something more brutal in mind to keep you in line."

The man knocked twice on the door. It opened right away, and three more hooded figures backed into the room, each pulling a cart. They turned around, giving me a full look at who they wheeled inside.

"Dominic!"

I threw myself against the chains, straining to get to him.

Dominic stood on the cart, frozen with the same odd, unidentifiable magic. His arm pulled back over his head, like he'd been in the middle of throwing his fireball. Two stiff and silent statues stood on either side of him.

Poet and Keely.

"Those two swore up and down that they didn't know anything about your treasonous attack against the crown," he said, pointing to Keely and Poet. "But of all the people you protected that night, you chose your lover and those two. That was enough to condemn them."

"Argh agh ag!" I roared, wrenching in the chains. I'd kill him. I'd kill them all for hurting my mate and my clan.

I looked for them. Even in the midst of my single-minded revenge against everyone who hurt Rosaleen, Sister Aven, and my brothers and sisters, I searched for Dominic, Poet, Keely, and the unknown person who snatched me away that night, forcing me to leave them behind.

They were nowhere. Not even the dragons knew where they were, and I tapped the entire dragonkin hive mind to find out.

"What have you done to them!"

"They were questioned," he calmly replied. "Brutally. Everyone wanted to know where you disappeared to that night. You and the dragons you stole. They wondered for all of a week. Then, you and the dragons showed up in Hyelong, where you murdered Laelia of House Xenar.

"Why, may I ask?" He shuffled at the corner of my vision. I looked at nothing but Dominic. "Every report said she never left Hyelong, and you've never been anywhere other than Ossian and Golden City. Why did you murder a woman you've never met?"

I forced the words through gritted teeth. "Sister Aven's nestmate. She killed her mother, then allowed her to be tortured by Faynari. Everyone who harms the clan dies."

"Avenge them." "Free us." "Dragon mother."

"The clan," he repeated slowly. "You're referring to the sister of the order who raised you and the other orphans? Nestmates, you said..." His brows shot up. "You mean they were sisters? We have no record of Laelia having a sister. Did you kill the wrong person?"

"Argh!" I shrieked, making him lurch back. "I avenged the borrowed mother! Everyone who hurts the clan dies. You're next!"

"Once again, I urge you to hold that thought." He gestured to Dominic, Keely, and Poet. "They're held in sway by my magic. You got a taste of it yourself." The stranger approached Dominic, ratcheting my growls louder. "It isn't that I stop time. That would be impossible. It's more that I slow down one's perception of time. In that moment, everything stops. Your heart, body, brain.

"All of it freezes in that instant of time while the world goes on around you." He pointed. "Their world stopped two moons ago, after you slaughtered your twenty-fifth victim, then blew through an entire battalion of Royal Riders. You blasted all their magics right back at them, destroying them without breaking a sweat.

"On that day, Queen Maili and Their Royal Highness Ormr decreed that all unique mages shall forfeit their rights, and be bound in service to the throne."

Talking, talking, so much talking. Why did this human insist on chattering on? I needed to get to Dominic. The only thing the stranger said that mattered is that Dominic had been waiting too long.

"The general must've had people watching us. Spies throughout the kingdom that reported every unique mage they found, and their power," he continued. "It's the only explanation for why none of us had a chance to run. The day after the law was passed, Watchers dragged me out of my home... in front of my son." His eyes unfocused, gazing off into the distance. "They drew their swords on my crying, terrified boy—demanding he perform magic and prove he wasn't one of the *aberrant scourges*.

"I guess you could say he was lucky to have inherited his mother's fire magic. If only we hadn't lost her two years ago."

I rolled my head, wincing. They were shouting so loud. Their tangled voices came together with difficulty, telling me they were being pelted with magic by mages trying to break the bonds I *forced* on them.

"Calm, my dragons. I will come for you soon. You and the younglings. Then, they will pay for this."

"—put my son in an orphanage," the chatty human continued. "Even though he had a living and loving father, my child was ripped away from his home and shoved into an overfull and underfunded hovel while I was carted off and clapped in chains."

He ripped off his cloak, revealing gold manacles around his wrists, legs, and throat. I knew what I was looking at immediately. The gold that bound him lived in my skin. Queen Kisandra's living magic.

"My boy hated it there," he spat. "They shoved twenty children in a room barely big enough for two. They barely fed him. There was no running water for the children to bathe and brush, and there hadn't been for months. He lived in misery... until you rescued him."

Brow crumpling, I narrowed on him. He had my attention.

"In the midst of your spree, you wound up in Nehebkau and crossed paths with my son. You freed him," he said. "Not just him. You took all the children out of that terrible place, and brought them to the Elsher mansion."

He laughed mirthlessly. "Imagine my surprise when my son was one of the children kicking and screaming as they brought him out. He loved it there with you and the other children. He had his own room again. Clothes, toys, books, and food. He said the best part was when you carried them up to the skies, letting them fly with you and the dragons.

"Command is saying you bewitched them. Used more forbidden magic to addle their minds and make them sing your praises, but I know my boy. You, of all people, showed true care and kindness to him during the worst time in his life."

"Orion," I said, finally seeing the resemblance. "A bright and clever boy. He spoke of his father, Claudius, often. Said one day you would find him and we'd all live together." Claudius's eyes softened. "Of course I took him out of that horrid place. It's an abomination to harm younglings. I will protect them. I'll protect them all."

He studied me. "You're not what I expected. I see that now. Truthfully, I hated you. We all hated you," he claimed, gesturing to the other robed figures. "The laws enslaving unique mages were put in place because of you. Though, I see now that they have you as wrong as they have all of us. I may have even started to see that a while ago when I was given the task of connecting your victims.

"Xandar Graylick—accused of rape by multiple women. Never convicted because of lack of supposed proof. Gaia Juno—people seller. Nero Gottfried—the owner of that awful orphanage. I saw the link between your victims early on, but command disagreed. A number of your targets were nobles and royals who were *above reproach*."

Sighing, he rubbed his temples. "You're not a monster, are you, Ainsley Boreen? You're just a girl who's been kicked around your whole life, and when you finally had power, you made them pay. On the way, you rescued and protected those like you. The ones... who have no one at all."

I said nothing. Claudius was speaking strangely again. I avenged my clan and cared for younglings, as was the dragon way. I did what must be done under dragon law.

"Here's how it is, Ainsley. You were kind to my son, and I'd like to show you kindness in return," he said. "At this point, I'm supposed to tell you exactly what it means that your lover and friends have been under my time magic for two moons.

"I froze them in time. I do so by maintaining constant control of the magic. If you drain or kill me, in that single millisecond, the magic is released, and all that time will catch up to them in an instant. That is two moons that they didn't eat, didn't drink, didn't sleep." He met my eyes.

"That's two moons they spent starving to death. That death is waiting for them."

"Argh!" I flung myself against my chains, gathering my dragons' magic like standing beneath the gush of a waterfall.

"But I don't want to do that," Claudius shouted. "I don't want to kill them or hurt you, and I won't. Not if you help me."

"How can I help you? I'm the one in chains!"

"They sent me down here, along with three mages skilled in determining the truth, to interrogate you. If you lie one time..." He slid a look to Keely, Poet, and Dominic. "You only have two more chances to tell the truth."

It was an awful and broken person who thought that up. Which could only mean General Roark.

"We can skip all that unpleasantness and just talk," Claudius said. "Tell me the truth, and no one here will hurt you or them. I give you my word."

"What good is the word of a man in chains? It lasts only as long as the person holding them allows." I rattled my own chains. "My bargained agreeableness lasts just as long. I'll talk, but only with General Roark. Take off that stupid hood," I said, narrowing on the silent man behind Dominic. "Ask your questions from your own lips."

Chuckling, the man in the middle lifted his head. Claudius shot back when he dropped his hood, revealing none other than the general. I assumed Claudius wouldn't have said any of the things he did if he knew who was really in the room.

"Very good, girl," Roark said, tossing the robe aside.

My first time looking upon the real him in moons, and my disappointment was heavy. Very few walked away from the destruction of Golden City without a scratch. Hellfire raged through the castle and beyond until everything, and nearly everyone was consumed. By all rights, the destroyer of my family should be ash.

There wasn't a single new scar on him.

"How did you know?" he asked.

"There's nowhere else you'd be. You've been waiting for this for a long time."

He hummed, inclining his head. "It's never a good thing when a strategist becomes predictable, but I can't deny it's true. There's nowhere else I could be."

One of the other people still wearing their hood, stepped forward. "Is this wise, sir? If she drains your magic, she'll wreak unholy havoc through the entire estate. She'll wipe us all out. That's why you yourself ordered that only Claudius and mages with harmless magics be allowed near her."

He waved that away. "I said that to satisfy you cowards. Truth is, now that she's completed the stolen bonds, there is no safe distance. The dragons can find her wherever she is, which means her aberrant power can steal from the bonds at any time."

"What?" she cried. "But if that's true, what is she waiting for?"

The general's smirk mirrored by own. "Simple. She's a dragon, and dragons aren't hasty or impulsive. She humored you, Claudius, because you very easily gave her information she needed. Most important of which that she can't act until she figures out how to save my son and safely get him out of here. Until then, she's happy to pretend she's helpless to make us more comfortable."

"Mother Zaeah," she breathed, backing to the door.

Roark's smile didn't waver. "Isn't that right, young Ainsley? You believe you're a dragon?"

"I am a dragon," I snapped. "Are you going to ask a lot of stupid questions?"

"See?" He waved a hand over me. "The psychosis has already begun to set in, but she has held on to some of her reason. She was able to plan and carry out the murders without collateral damage. And she successfully cared for those whelps for months. By the end of the usurper's reign and life, she was quite insane.

"She crawled on her belly and kept jumping off of things, believing she could fly. Not to say she wasn't a fierce opponent." Roark absentmindedly rubbed his thigh. "She commanded the magics of thirteen dragons. If she hadn't been so greedy, she wouldn't have broken her mind into so many pieces, they were commanding her in the end."

"The usurper, sir?" The final man dropped his hood, letting me see the freckled, lined face beneath. And the gold manacle around his neck. "She was like this too?"

"Oh, yes," Roark said softly. "If six bonds are too much for a weak mind, a strong mind should have no issue. Even seven could be possible."

I frowned. *A strong mind?*

"So they are one and the same," the woman remarked. "They had the same magic."

Roark scowled, appearing irritated that she was speaking. "Of course they don't have the same magic. Do you think me a fool? If some girl with the same magic as the usurper walked into my citadel, wouldn't it follow that I'd have suspected her sooner?"

"Of course, sir." She shrunk, retreating into her hood. "Forgive me, sir."

"The usurper was not an aberrant mage. She stole dragons, but didn't steal magic. Although, her ability was rare. She was a light mage." Roark seemed to be talking to the room, but I had a feeling this conversation was purely for me. "She wielded pure light, fashioning it into anything. Weapons, clothes, transport."

He held up his hands. "She could take the light from these torches, turn them into daggers, and plunge them into our hearts without moving a muscle. She could make a key to unlock her from these chains. She stole the dragons, but she wasn't able to steal and wield their magics. Even so, she didn't need to. They obeyed her without question. Killed whoever she said to kill. Without the dragons she was formidable, but with them, she conquered five kingdoms. A goddess among us... until insanity drug her down to the mortals."

He drew nearer to me, ripping a growl from my lips.

"There are forbidden magics that let you bond with a dragon, but it isn't a true bond. More accurate to call it mind control," he said. "It allows you to control the dragon. You can ride them, or force them to defend and fight for you. But the true bond between rider and dragon where two beings share a mind—nay, a soul. That cannot be forced or replicated by any human magic.

"As of six hours ago, when we exhausted the list of cancelling magics that free a dragon under mind control, we were forced to accept that young

Ainsley did not lie. She performed no forbidden magic. The bond between her and those six dragons is true. They cannot be broken unless the dragon wills it, and"—he stiffened—"Tizor refuses."

The three captured mages shared incredulous looks.

"Twice in my lifetime, I've had the misfortune to cross paths with a mage possessing this impossible ability. What many don't know about me is that I believe in fate. The first time I went looking for it, but the second, you came to me. Stealing my son's dragon, then mine. Setting off the events that forced me off the throne, and now setting in motion grander events that will shape this country.

"I should be angry. I should despise you," he said mildly. "No matter what you may believe, I don't. There's no need for anger, because destiny is patient. If you allow her the time, she will show you the correct path.

"Because of you, laws I've tried for decades to pass have finally been put through by the High Council. I have amassed in mere months the most formidable aberrant force that five kingdoms and beyond have ever seen." He pointed. "That girl forces everyone in her vicinity to speak the truth. That boy there calls himself an empathic mage. Can sense the emotions of those around him.

"But young Claudius..." Roark tossed his head. "A chrono mage. Such magic couldn't be thought of when I was a boy. Now he and his aberrant brethren are all under my command. With them under my control, and with you." He smiled. "I will be restored to my proper place."

I flicked from him to the truth mage. The explanation of her powers explained why Claudius and the general were being so forthcoming, but that didn't mean I liked what they had to say.

The dragons were roaring in my mind, sounding a warning that came too late. I forced my voice steady under the pounding in my skull.

"Hmm. Obviously your truth mage doesn't force the truth. Only the truth as we want it to be." I gestured with my chin. "Because they're not under your control. Those are golden chains on their wrists. They serve House Boreen. And if I know anything about my lying, scheming sister and sibling, they don't trust you," I hissed. "They'd never allow you to have any true power that'd let you overthrow them."

His jaw clenched. "No, you're not stupid." Stepping back, Roark rolled up his sleeves. Two golden bands wrapped around his wrists. "As you say, they don't trust me. High Queen Kisandra bound me in service before the fires stopped burning in the palace. I exist to serve her.

"But I told the truth," he said. "Destiny gave me the means to reclaim what I've lost. She gave me you. So this is my question, young Ainsley." Roark closed the distance between us. "Where and how did you acquire the magics to bond with multiple dragons?"

I didn't speak. I didn't have to. My snarl told him what I thought of his question.

"Silence won't be tolerated. There is something different about this ability. Both times, it was acquired later in life. Once by a woman who was not magicless. Another by a girl who is. Was this gift given to you by someone? Did you stumble on an ancient, unknown text that revealed the way? Is there something special about you that sets you apart from other humans? Something dragons can see, but others can't."

Silence.

Roark straightened. "So be it. Claudius, kill the girl."

"No," I cried, throwing myself against the chain—halting Claudius as he raised a hand. "Fine. Fine! I'll answer your stupid questions, because my response is the same as everyone else's. I don't know how I got this ability. I must've been born with it."

"You were born from the unholy union of a prince and a Druk. Was your mother truly changed before she had you?"

"I don't know. All I know is that she's a shadow Druk. Or she was. I don't know if she survived the attack on Golden City."

He raised a brow. "She was there? Among the filthy creatures who all bowed and obeyed your every word. Is it your ability that forces them to serve you?"

"I don't know."

Roark looked to the girl and the empathic mage. They both nodded. I told no lies. "You don't know much. Further proof that this gift is wasted on you. You're nothing but a poor, talentless bastard shouldering a destiny that shouldn't be yours."

The general spoke like he wasn't insulting me. He was simply stating fact.

"Nonetheless, you are special. No female Druk in history has ever fallen pregnant, but here you stand. You've died countless times, and walked away from the veil without a scratch. You've formed true bonds with powerful dragons. Bonds that let you speak to them, and they speak back. There is a reason. Tell me what it is," he gritted, eyes bulging. "Why did Tizor abandon me for you?"

"Because I am dragon mother," I blurted. The words tore out of me. They'd been pushing against my lips, waiting to be spoken since he said the word *dragons*.

My bondeds raged in my mind. It wasn't for humans to know our secrets. But nowhere in the endless knowledge of the hive mind, did a dragon meet a human like the quiet woman in the corner.

"Dragon mother?" Roark's eyes sharpened. "What is that?"

"It is what it is. Dragons know me. They know I am dragon mother. They know they are safe with me."

"Tizor was safe with me."

I scoffed. "You knew nothing of Tizor. You didn't know that with his species of death dragon, the fathers raise the hatchlings, *not* the mothers. He raged and threw himself against the cage every day while you ignored him."

Roark shook, balling his fists.

"For more than half a century, he stood by you. But you wouldn't give him a measly five years to rear his children."

"I would've! If I had known— He only had to tell me!"

I looked him in the eyes. "He did tell you."

Roark's hand shot up like he was going to slap me. Taking a breath, he dropped it. "Forgive me, I forget myself. I asked for truth. You gave it. You're right," he said, surprising me. "Tizor did not hide his wish to be with his offspring. I should've given him that wish. I didn't and he found me lacking. This explains much."

He nodded to himself, coming to understandings I couldn't follow. "Dragons leave their bonded for a *better* option. I lowered myself in Tizor's eyes. Maili and Ormr are sniveling children nipping at the high queen's heels. Keir Stryker is an impulsive, violent boy. And Dominic was always weak when it came to women. We all were unlucky to be too close to you when your ability called on their bonds, so they broke them all too easily.

"Somehow, they sense that you're different. A natural affinity that calls to them, like the usurper. Dragon mother." Roark rolled the phrase around on his tongue. "This ability can't rely on magic, because you have none of your own. Tell me, was it entirely their choice, or is there something you do to trigger this dragon mother ability?"

My hands opened and closed, longing to wrap around his neck. I could kill him at any time, but a second after he died, Poet, Keely, and my love would die too.

No more.

"It's not what I did," I rasped. "It's what you did."

His brows snapped together, then smoothed out just as quickly. "I see. Yes," he said, pacing the floor. "I understand. You were trapped, hurt, scared, so your soul called out for help. This isn't magic. It's evolution. Just as Tenille of the earth and heavens saw fit to change all that we know, bringing about the arrival of aberrant mages. The bond between dragon and rider must change too.

"Gone is the era when dragons bonded only when they needed humans. Now, a human can bond when they choose. When they need the strength and power of a dragon. Such a human would be so rare and unique, of course they'd give you a name.

"Dragon mother."

I couldn't tell what my dragons thought of that. Their voices were so loud and jangled together, nothing made sense, though one thing couldn't be mistaken. Their fury.

Roark raked me up and down. "The question is how do I unlock this ability within myself. There must be a way. Fate would not have given you to me otherwise."

"Sir?" Claudius spoke up. "Unlock the ability? You said it was evolution. A gift given to her by Tenille. Surely it's impossible—"

The general held up a hand, silencing him. "You are young, boy. You haven't yet learned that there is no such thing as impossible. Within this estate is a copy of every text on forbidden magic written, along with every aberrant mage of worth. The girl herself is the first key.

"Once her borrowing magic is mine, I'll strip her of the dragon power. Then, I'll send her beyond the veil for good."

I never thought the day would come that I'd wish for lies. A blunt and truthful General Roark was more terrifying than the cold, silent man I knew.

"But we have orders, sir," the freckled mage said. "Queen Maili said we're to publicly execute the four of them after we capture and question her."

"And so we shall obey," he said, sweeping out the door. "After I've questioned her."

***

"We have to try the blood rites again."

"We did that three times," Osman snapped. "It doesn't work."

"But we know it does." Junia struggled to hold the heavy book one-handed while flipping the pages. "This forbidden spell steals magic. It worked on that poor soul they dragged in from the village, it should be working on her."

"The only difference is *she doesn't have magic.*" Osman's freckles darkened amidst his frustrations.

Many days we'd been together. Many days they poked, probed, magicked, and tortured me.

It was only natural we were on a first-name basis.

"She only has magic when she steals it, so there's nothing to take from her blood. We have to move past the blood rites."

"We can't move past the blood rites," Junia forced through gritted teeth. "The blood rites were our last hope. If we move past the blood rites, we have nothing left to try. Will you be the one to tell General Roark we failed?"

I slumped against the wall—a still, silent shadow in the corner. I barely heard a word they were saying. Only roars and pain existed in my mind.

"Why do you wait?" "Free yourself." "Kill them!" "Destroy Sire. Destroy them all."

"Dominic..." I croaked. "Dominic."

"—have no choice. We need her to use her magic, so the spell can take it."

"Are you insane? She can use magic. She always could. It's only the threat of killing her friends that's protecting us," Osman said. "Take that threat away, and she'll kill us all."

"Do you have a better idea?"

"We tell him it's not possible. We don't have a choice. The general gave us two weeks. That ends tomorrow. We've run out of time."

"We haven't. There's still... this."

Junia turned the book around. Osman's cheeks drained of color.

"No."

"It will work."

"It requires a sacrifice." He dropped his voice, hissing in low tones. "A sacrifice from the general. Every rite in that book requires vile, irreversible sacrifices to achieve your goal. There's a reason these texts are banned, Junia. The general would never do it. This solution is no solution at all."

"We leave the choice up to him. He told us to find a way to steal the power from this girl." She looked at me, lips trembling. "This is the way."

Osman followed her line of sight. He dropped his gaze the second he met my eyes. "This is wrong."

"It's more than wrong," she whispered, but not low enough. "It's the worst kind of hypocrisy. When he was king, the general slaughtered anyone found using forbidden magics. Now that it suits him, he'll engage in treason and force us all to be his accomplices, just to get what he wants."

"How do they do it?"

Osman and Junia froze. They stared at me like they forgot I could speak.

"You— You're not allowed to speak, dragon thief. Keep quiet or I'll—"

"How do those manacles control you?" I asked Osman, ignoring Junia. "How did they turn you into... this?"

He reddened as though I insulted him.

I did.

He looked to Junia. For a second, I thought he wouldn't answer.

"The same way the high queen cursed the throne when the usurper took over. If anyone not of her bloodline sits on it, they die." He held up his wrists. "If we disobey the high queen's orders, we die."

"What are her orders?"

Junia advanced on me. "What does it matter to you?" she snapped.

"Is it not obvious? I need to know what could happen when I free you, Osman, Claudius, and all the other unique mages."

Her lips parted, brows blowing up. She wasn't expecting that response. "Free us?"

"Dragons don't believe in slavery. That is human vileness. Every creature is born free. They should live free." I let my head drop. They were starting to spin. "What are your orders?"

I couldn't see them, but I sensed them exchanging looks. Hushed whispers echoed off the walls, bouncing back only a few words.

"...trust her..."

"...got to lose..."

"...no choice..."

"You would really do it?" Osman tipped my chin. "You'd help us after everything we've done to you?"

I nodded.

"What do you want in return?" Junia asked.

"Insolence. These younglings are so stunted and short-sighted. They can't conceive of doing right for right's sake."

"Did I ask for anything in return?" I said, chiming in with Reyna's indignation.

The dragons were nothing but angry and indignant about our capture, but none of us could leave without Dominic, Poet, and Keely. I'd spent four moons hunting down the betrayers and abusers of my clan. I would not fly away from the last three of my clan left.

"Tell me your orders. Can I take you all away from here with the bands on, or will they kill you immediately?"

"Immediately," Osman said, ignoring Junia's hissed warning. "If we leave the estate without permission from one of the High Command, we die. If we use magic without permission, we die. If we try to remove the manacles, we die."

"Are any of you bonded?"

"No."

"Osman," Junia cried. "If you can't fight my magic, you have to gag yourself. I've told you that a dozen times. She's not going to get us out of here, and you know that. What did the general say? She could've gotten away the minute Claudius freed her. She's only enduring this until she can figure out a way to free her friends. Leveraging our freedom is a good try, but it won't work," she said, turning to me. "Claudius is the only chrono mage alive, and only his magic can help you. Exactly why he's being kept far away from you." She shook her head. "Didn't help that my magic made him say that he would help you if he could.

"You're never getting anywhere near him, and yes, we've been ordered to make sure you never try." She slammed the book shut. "Don't waste your time filling his head with false hope. If we're freed, it won't be by the traitor who got us imprisoned in the first place."

I heard her speech but not easily. My dragons argued their outrage over her disrespect.

"Freeing you all is very simple," I said. "You could walk out of here just as easily as I can."

"We can?" Osman leaned in. "How?"

I put my face in his, dropping my calm exterior. "Me. So ask yourself if you really want to help the general steal your last chance of escape? Or will you give it away because you're angry at the wrong one? I didn't pass any laws or put gold chains around your wrists."

I lurched against the chains, making them both jump back.

"When will you start fighting back against the ones who did?"

"You say that like it's simple and we're being cowards," Junia replied. "He told you that if we fight back, we die."

"Yeah." I sat back and rested my forehead against the cool stone. "If you fight back with magic."

She blinked. "What—?"

The door banged open.

The general and two riders walked into the room, driving Osman and Junia to the opposite corner. They always got as far away as possible from him. Not that it did them any good.

"Aberrants," he greeted.

General Roark slowly walked the length of the cell, inspecting. I wasn't sure what he expected to find, but all must've seemed right to him, because he nodded as he planted himself in front of me. "Have you found what I needed?"

I saw them share a look over his head.

"Yes." Sounded like the word was dragged out of her. "And no."

"Explain."

"There is a forbidden blood rite that steals the magic from one and gives it to another, but only because the magic lives in their blood. In her case, it doesn't. She only has magic—"

"—when she steals it," Roark finished. "Interesting. Seems Master Whelan's assessment was correct. She truly is an empty vessel, waiting to be filled."

"It also occurred to us that even if we allowed her to channel magic while we performed the blood rite, all you'd get is the stolen magic. Not her ability to steal it, or dragon bonds."

He inclined his head. "Fairly reasoned. So why did you say yes?"

Junia looked to Osman... who looked at me. A battle raged behind his eyes. His hatred for the one who put him here clashed against his bitterness towards the one who put him in chains.

Osman flicked away, releasing my stare. "We found reference of something called the siphoner's blade. The text said it first appeared a thousand years ago in a small Hyelongan village. The village was under rule of a tyrant who slaughtered villagers at random to keep them all in line.

"A poor farmer had lost both his wife and his oldest daughter to his cruelty. The farmer got down on his knees, and prayed to a god of wrath for the means to take away everything the tyrant loved. The god told the farmer he hadn't lost everything... not yet."

Roark frowned. "Skip the bedtime stories. Get to your point."

"The god demanded a sacrifice. His youngest and only surviving child. If he pierced his heart with a silver blade, that blade would be imbibed to carry out his wish, and take away the only thing the tyrant loved. His power."

Osman picked up the book and handed it to the general. "That farmer became Gaius Daoud, the greatest blood mage in history."

"What?" Roark snatched the book, roughly flipping through the pages. "This book claims the origins of Gaius Daoud? Nonsense. I studied Daoud and all the great mages in the university. Nothing about a siphoner's blade was ever mentioned."

"Because his origins are of cursed blades, forbidden magic, and the murder of his own son," Junia remarked. "It does not surprise me that it was stricken from the history books."

Roark glared at her, but I could tell, he was listening. "Why should this work when the blood rites failed?"

"The text doesn't speak of blood," she replied. "It speaks of power, strength, and what's loved above all. Seems to me if there's anything a poor, magicless whelp would've wished for all her life, it's all of those things. Power, strength, and incredible magic to defeat her enemies. Miraculously, she was granted all of those things. She loves this power, General. She loves those dragons. Taking what she loves—"

"—is to take away the dragon mother. Yes," he whispered, nodding to himself. "It's perfect."

Roark snapped his head up. "A story of a farmer cannot be all there is. What is the name of the god he called upon? Can it be any silver blade? What other rituals and magics are required?"

"But you—" Osman stepped forward. "We assumed this wouldn't be an option for you, sir, so we didn't look any further. One thing the text was clear on is that you must cut out the still beating heart of your love. To take away everything, you must lose everything. Surely you could never, sir."

Roark held up a hand. "Calm yourself, Aberrant Osman. There will be no cutting out of hearts. Magic is never simple or straightforward. Just because Gaius—if this was indeed him—interpreted the instruction to lose what he loves as the murder of his son, doesn't mean that was the only way to create the blade. It's possible the heart of his prized horse would've done as well." He shoved the book at him. "Find every scrap of text and reference to the siphoner's blade. You have one day left."

He went on to say more to Junia and Osman. He pointed at the books and seemed to be rattling off instructions. But I couldn't see him.

I couldn't hear anything over my dragons' desperate roaring. They didn't need to read the texts, or study a thousand years of whispered legends and passed-down tales. Floating in the dragonkin hive mind was the knowledge of the equally great blood dragon who bonded with Gaius Daoud.

He did call upon the forgotten god of vengeance, Titana. She did tell him the only way was to cut the beating heart out of his beloved son's chest. So consuming was his rage and grief, he did so. Gaius plunged that cursed blade into the tyrant, and stole the only thing he loved—his power.

The tyrant was left magicless, and dead, while Gaius went on to become one of the greatest mages in living history. He ruled Hyelong for two hundred years, bringing out a golden age that turned a tiny, swampland country into a strong, enduring kingdom.

He never used the blade again, because he didn't have to. Bonding with a great dragon boosted his power to unimaginable levels. No one was stronger than him, so why bother siphoning their abilities?

But none of that is what made my dragons scream. They knew what the Elder dragon Maaza knew. That blade stole more than magic. Cursed by a goddess, it stole the essence of who a person was.

The siphoner's blade would work on me where all their other attempts failed. It would take my thief magic. It would take my right and soul as dragon mother.

In twenty-four hours, I would be a poor, magicless whelp once again, and General Roark would become a being more fearsome and dangerous than the usurper ever was.

Chapter Four

Two silent hooded figures unlocked my chains. I resisted the urge to bite, scream, and claw their eyes out. The general was ready with three strong reasons for me to behave.

"The first sign of resistance, and the girl dies." Roark stood beside Claudius and three carts, all bearing Poet, Keely, and Dominic. He wheeled them in just for me. "Try again to flee and Aberrant Claudius will be forced to kill the son of an old friend. If you continue to fight and I'm forced to kill Dominic..." He gazed down his sharp, wrinkled nose at me. "I swear to you your escape attempt will fail, because I'll strike you to dust where you stand."

"Don't pretend you care about him!" I screamed over the screaming in my head. "He only lived because I saved him from you!"

"He needed saving because you addled his mind like your Druk whore mother bewitched the crown prince. If only I'd seen it in time. If only I ran a sword through your chest the first moment I laid eyes on you.

"But destiny is just. As much as it takes from me is as much as it gives." He jerked his chin at my captors. "You will return the power you've stolen. Power you never deserved. It shall be wielded by someone worthy."

"You're insane!" I shouted, but I didn't fight.

I did nothing at all as they led me from the dim, musty hole that had been my home for two weeks. There wasn't a single doubt in my mind that Roark would carry out every single one of his threats against the innocent Keely, the son of the man who saved his life, and his own favorite heir.

The guards released me as soon as we crossed the threshold. Quickly they put distance between us, no doubt wishing they could get even farther from the magic-stealing mage who easily evaded their best and strongest forces for moons.

I remembered bits and pieces from my first introduction to the estate. I knew we'd left Edjer long behind and were somewhere in Old Adalinda—the strip of country that stood before the usurper conquered Ghidorah, Edjer, Nehebkau, and Hyelong.

As much as I traveled the nation in search of my clan's betrayers, I never had reason to venture this deep into the Ossian Forest. On every map I'd seen, Ossian sat between Golden City and miles and miles of thick, tangled forest that went on forever until it spilled over the Dark Border.

The threat of Druks lurking under cover of the forest stopped anyone exploring it, let alone building the massive, sprawling estate that fell before me as we passed an open window.

A courtyard ringed in by four castle walls claimed my attention. Standing in twenty rows were upwards of two hundred silent, robed figures. If not for the occasional shuffle or turned head, I would've thought they were living statues—too much like the ones that used to stand in the general's throne room.

Something glinted at the edge of my vision, tearing my eyes up. I squinted, slowing down.

Is that—?

"It is us." "We're here." "Free us, dragon mother." "FREE US!"

I flinched, my head swung around like I'd been dealt a physical blow. That glint was a cage not unlike the citadel's hatchery. That's where they were keeping my dragons.

"Why have they kept you so close to me?"

I had to ask the question a few times before they heard.

"My former bond demands your immediate execution," Cadmus replied. The others quieted for a few blessed moments. *"She wants you dead so that I will return to her."*

"My boy's sire is hiding you and us in this place," Reyna continued. *"His queen refuses to come here. Once your nestmates discover he's captured us, they'll know he's captured you. He'll give up his victory only after stealing your ability as his."*

I clenched my jaw tight, fighting everything in me that screamed to jump my captor, latch on to Roark's throat, and rip it open. Maili and Ormr were right not to trust him. If only they'd carry that mistrust all the way, and executed him.

"Move." One of the guards prodded my back, making me continue on.

"Why are you doing this?" I rasped. "What do you think will happen, former king general Roark?"

A vein in his brow twitched.

"Do you think you will steal my power, my dragons, and then storm the castle? Is your plan to become the very person you risked your life to defeat? A usurper."

"Silence."

"The people thought you a hero then. They gave you a crown and a throne." I scoffed. "What will they think of you now?"

He spun on me so fast, I ran into his chest.

"You will not be told again," he gritted. A glance over my shoulder at Keely drove home his warning.

I gave him the silence he asked for. There was not much choice for anything else.

Satisfied, General Roark marched on. Someone shoved my back, forcing me to follow.

Not a scrap of paintings, decoration, or even paint graced the gray stone walls. The only thing the hallway boasted was half a dozen closed doors.

I wondered where we were and who owned this place that they would build it within such a treacherous forest. Why did the general feel safe to hide me and the dragons here?

Not that the whys mattered. He clearly was safe to hide us here. Two weeks and Maili and Ormr didn't know the dragons they didn't own and had no right to claim, were in his cage.

My minders stopped before a door at the end of the hall. Shoving it open, I was allowed a look down the long, winding staircase. Every muscle in my body went rigid the further I descended.

It wasn't possible Junia and Osman discovered all the general needed to know about the siphoner's blade in a single day. Was General Roark truly prepared to call upon a goddess I'd only heard of in Tizor's mind? The hive mind didn't know the particulars of the ritual Gaius Daoud performed, but I had to believe it wasn't as simple as cutting out someone's heart with a silver blade. Was this madman so desperate for power, he was going to throw my life away to get it?

Of course he is, a dark, desperate voice chimed in my mind. *Either I die and he gets my power, or I die and Tizor goes back to him. Either way, he is the unstoppable General Roark once again.*

I felt something for the first time since they locked me in that useless, paper cell—fear.

I was not afraid for myself. My fear was for Keely, Poet, and Dominic. Even if it was possible the general held a trace of affection for the son he tried to kill, Dominic would always be the one who blasted the mask off High Queen Kisandra, setting her on fire. While Poet and Keely were nothing to her at all. When they could no longer be used to keep me in line... they would die right along with me.

After all I'd done to avenge my clan, protect my new hatchlings, and become stronger than my enemies could ever dream of, it would all come to nothing.

They shoved me off the bottom step. I tripped and sprawled on the floor of a large, circular room. Rough, uneven stone pushed back on me as I sat up. Sweeping the space, I didn't know what to make of dozens upon dozens of candles glowing within the recessed spaces in the walls.

In the middle of the room, strange foreign characters were painted in black on the floor.

"Stand inside the circle," Roark ordered.

I looked back as Poet, Dominic, and Keely were floated down behind him. My heart stirred gazing at Dominic.

Haggard lines froze on his face. Dark circles under his eyes. Tattered clothes. A snarl on his lips like he was preparing his last stand, and still he was the most handsome man I would lay eyes on in this life and beyond the veil.

My mate was perfect in every way. A dragon and a human. Our love was impossible. Mother Zaeah knew how our hatchlings would turn out, but if there was one thing I knew, our story wasn't meant to end in this dirty room. I had to get us out.

But how?

"Stand inside the circle, girl. Now."

Stiffly, I got to my feet. My dragons screeched at me as one foot set in front of the other, carrying me to the small, round space amidst the strange symbols. I turned and faced a small table carrying a large clay bowl, a silver dagger, and the book that started this all.

"Leave us," Roark ordered. "Only Aberrant Claudius and Aberrant Rufina are allowed in this room. No one enters for any reason. Am I understood?"

"Yes, sir."

One by one, they filed out—leaving me and my three trapped companions with the general.

I heard movement behind me. Roark kneeled down at the foot of a symbol that looked like a dog standing on its hind legs. He began removing his hood, jacket, boots, nearly everything until he was down to nothing but his pants.

"Rufina, bring me the bowl."

The cloaked woman crossed the room. Two small arms weighted down by golden manacles slipped out and picked up the bowl. She walked the rim of the room to deliver it to him.

Roark dunked his head directly in the liquid. Murmuring words I couldn't make out, he did it over and over again as the water—or at least I thought it was water—ran down his neck, back, and torso.

"Bring me the blade."

I fixed on Dominic. The dragons were absolutely feral, demanding that I end this charade, channel their power, and reduce General Roark to dust. He could not have my ability to steal magics, or break bonds and make them his own. The destruction he'd wreak on Adalinda was... unknown.

Truly, I did not know what Roark planned to do. Did he want the throne back? He battled so much with the loyalists before the royal family turned out to be alive and thriving. What would they do if he attacked the royal family and stole the throne?

He'd have the power to bring them all to their knees, but that wouldn't make him a true king. It wouldn't make his children legitimate, or win the support of anyone unless they wanted to latch on to him for power.

He strived for so long to sink his hooks into the five nations. It made sense that what he wanted above all was this kingdom back under his control, but if he tried, he would surely receive war in return.

His barked order for me to lie on my back barely registered. This was it. This act would mark the first day of war, and an end to a fifty-year peace. Unless I stopped him. Fought back. Let my love and my friends die.

"—Titana, I call on you." Roark dropped his knees on either side of my head. He held the blade high. "This creature is a monster born of a monster. She's murdered countless innocents in her insanity, ripped children from their homes, and poisoned the minds of men in her quest for power.

"Because of her, fear and suspicion have spread through the land. Decades of peace and harmony through the five nations crumbles around us. All that I've achieved has been wiped away with the arrival of this magicless chit.

"I ask you, great goddess, fill this blade with your power that I may strike down my enemy." The blade rose higher. "I am a servant of Adalinda. The day I bonded, I swore an oath to protect this country from all who seek to tear it apart. I will not fail in that mission. I will not be weak while my enemy dares to grow strong."

He reared back. The blade dropped in a swift and sudden arc, piercing flesh and bone and severing it straight through.

"Ahh!" Rufina screamed, clapping her hands over her mouth.

A dragon would never utter such a sound, but I came close. Eyes wide, I gaped at the fallen hand lying beside mine. Roark severed it at the wrist without blinking.

"T-to you…" He clutched the stump to his chest, face purpling. "I give th-this sacrifice. What I love—my strength, my ability, my position as general—I give it all up… to take what should not be hers."

He raised the dagger again. "Titana! Curse this blade. The siphoner's blade!"

I dropped my head. The noise, the roaring, the shouting—it all stopped, and it was only me and Dominic. I could fly away from all this and leave him behind.

But I never will.

I closed my eyes, seeing Dominic and me in the most wonderful, peaceful place beyond the veil.

See you soon, my love.

"Stop!"

My eyes snapped open. It was the black, gold-trimmed boots I saw first. A style favored by one person I used to know.

Ormr stepped into the room. The look on their face could only be matched by the shock on General Roark's.

"Tenille, bless us. What the fuck is going on here?"

I could only imagine what it looked like to them. Walking into a candlelit dungeon with their greatest enemy and sibling lying on the floor next to a severed hand, and a half naked man holding a dagger above her.

"Your Royal Highness." Roark snapped agitatedly at Rufina. With a wave of her hand, his flew up and reattached to his body.

My stomach heaved.

"This is easily explained—"

"I doubt it," Ormr snapped.

Wealth and royalty suited them. Gone was the stressed-out uniform of the Royal Riders. Ormr wore a long, expensive coat of the finest leather, over pants the same shade of gold as the crown woven in their hair. That was not the only thing different about them.

Half of Ormr's jaw was disfigured by a burn scar.

"You were ordered to inform me the moment you captured that thing." They flapped a hand at me. "How long has she been here? How long has Kenna been in that cage!"

Roark rose, expression placid. "Your Majesty, your orders were to turn her in after capture and questioning. I wasn't done questioning her, nor am I now. If you permit me more time—"

"More time to what?" Ormr's eyes narrowed to slits. "Perform forbidden magics on her?"

Roark stiffened. "You dishonor me, Your Majesty. I would never do such a thing."

How anyone alive could be such a lying, scheming bullshitter, I would never know.

"I've interrogated her for weeks and gotten nothing but lies. I had no choice but to take drastic, harsher measures. This is all in service of you and the kingdom."

Silence smothered the room as they stared each other down.

"You can repeat your excuses before the high queen," Ormr finally said. "After she commands that manacle around your throat to choke you if you lie."

Roark bowed low. "As you wish, Your Royal Highness."

It was only my position on the floor that let me see the disdain dripping from his curled lips.

"After," Ormr continued, "her execution."

Roark slowly rose. "Of course, but if I may. I believe it wise to discover all we can about her abilities before we do so. Twice in a century a disgruntled commoner has risen up, stolen dragons, and gone on a rampage. We need to understand why these two, and how they did it."

Ormr waved that away. "Forbidden magics. Magics that will cease its terrible hold on my dragon once she's dead. There's no more I need to know."

"You kept me on as general because you trust my—"

"The high queen kept you on." Ormr picked up the water bowl and smashed it on the symbols. Black ink bled onto my dress. "I don't trust you, and I never will."

"I am sorry to hear that." Roark's face was unreadable. "I hope one day to prove to you that I have only Adalinda's best interests at heart."

Ormr turned their back on him. "You and you. Clap her in chains, then carry her out to the courtyard. Her execution is now." They flicked to Dominic and my friends. "Bring them too. They're to be freed and fully pardoned if she goes down without a fight. If she doesn't, she watches them die slowly and painfully. This ends today."

"I'll take her," Claudius said, stepping out in front of Rufina. "Get the others to help you bring up the rest."

Rufina looked to the general for instruction. He stood stiff-backed and stoic—the picture of the obedient soldier.

Claudius helped me up. He held tight to me, practically carrying me up the steps under Ormr's and Roark's watchful eyes.

"I'm sorry." If it wasn't for the slight twitch of his mouth, I wouldn't know the soft whisper came from him. "Junia and Osman told me what you said about freeing all of us. We had to stop the general going through with the ritual. Sending a message to Their Royal Highness Ormr and Queen Maili was the only way."

Movement sounded on the other side of the approaching door. Our conversation was about to come to an abrupt halt. I had to speak quickly.

"The quickest way is for you to free my mate and clan. Can you do it without killing them?"

"If I didn't have these around my wrists and neck, yes," he hissed. "But I can't perform magic without permission. If I try, I'll be killed, the magic on them breaks, and they die anyway. If you drain me, my hold breaks, and they die in an instant."

My jangled mind spun. The dragons were all shouting suggestions, it was impossible to hear one for the other.

"If I drain you and then quickly put them back under until we're clear of this place, would that work?" I rushed.

"You must understand this." His grip tightened as boots rapidly clomped up after us. "In every way that matters, they are already dead. The question isn't if you're quick enough to outrun my magic, it's if you're quick enough to outrun death."

"I—" The door opened, trapping my questions behind my teeth.

What could I do? Wind barriers, wind scythes, shadow traveling, vine magic, death touch, and hellfire scattershot. I never truly learned to use my thief magic. After bonding with my dragons, their power flowed through me, and I used it the way a thief would—by copying the powers and techniques of their former riders.

Cadmus watched Maili practice with her vines a thousand times. Those memories were as mine as they were his. There was no need to practice when his memory showed me the way. That couldn't be said for any of the other magics thrown at me over the last four moons.

I either blocked it with my wind barriers, or stole it and threw it back. Unrefined and haphazard. No special knowledge needed to absorb a Watcher's sand magic, then toss it back at them—burying them under a pile before they knew what was happening.

How could I trust it was that easy with chrono magic? My dragons knew nothing about it. If General Roark was to be believed, no one alive knew anything about it. Was it as simple as draining Claudius, and throwing the magic back at Dominic, Keely, and Poet? Claudius said he had to maintain constant concentration to keep them under. Could I maintain that control while freeing hundreds of enslaved mages, my dragons, myself, and then getting us all out of here?

Could I gamble their lives on that chance?

Claudius handed me over to the three men waiting in the hall. Each one wore a leather coat not dissimilar to Ormr's, if not for the red insignia on their chests. A sickle and an axe crossed at the handles. Only one force bore that sign—the Royal Renders.

My execution wasn't today. It was now.

"Walk ahead." Three swords leveled at my chest. "Walk quickly, but do not run. Any sudden movements or hint that you're using forbidden magic, we will run you through. Understood?"

My answer was to turn away, and begin down the hall.

"*You must not allow this, my bond,*" Reyna ordered. "*Mortal weapons will kill you. You know this.*"

"I have to save Dominic and the others."

"*You cannot save my boy if you're dead. Free yourself. They will keep them alive to use against you in the future.*"

"They don't need all three of them alive for that," I whispered. "Roark will kill Poet or Keely just to punish me for escaping. I can't let that happen."

"*Saying it means nothing,*" Tizor growled. "*No plan is not a plan. All four of you die this day, or the dragon mother lives.*"

"*Dragon mother must live.*" "*Dragon mother must live.*" "*Dragon mother must live.*"

"*Dragons are not ruled by sentiment. We accept death as the natural part of the cycle, for no one is truly lost if they live on in the minds of the dragonkin,*" said Elder Tizor. "*You know what you must do. Free yourself.*"

"But even a dragon will do anything to protect their—"

"Stop talking!" A Render shoved me hard from behind. "Another word and your journey on this side of the veil ends here."

There wasn't another word to be said. My dragons had made up their minds. They had no advice for me, or a way the four of us could get out alive. Between me and my clan, their answer was me.

Hard prods and barked orders guided me through the winding, twisting halls and out into the courtyard. It was nothing like I saw earlier.

Gone were the silent rows of captured unique mages. They'd been shunted to the side by the construction of two platforms.

Stone and wood mages waved their hands bringing forth a stage, and placing three thrones upon it. Moving back, they punched the sky, and dozens of boulders erupted from the ground. I watched as the rocks moved, shrunk, grew, and formed into high-backed chairs set before the second platform.

An audience for an execution.

More shoving forced me up the steps of the platform. It had nothing for me to sit on. I was to stand before everyone as the Renders ended my life.

Standing above them, I saw the black orb appear in the air before the unique mages noticed. Whispers spread through the crowd as it grew long and wider. Light, space, and color repelled it. It hung between the fabric of the world, rejecting everything we thought we knew of magic.

Actually, everything they thought they knew of magic. I had seen this power once before.

The first heavily jeweled royal stepped out of the orb. They led the parade of people wearing ruby, emerald, and diamond rings on every finger. A cascade of necklaces falling down their necks to their chests. Earrings and cuffs climbing the shells of their ears, and burn scars somewhere on the parts of their bodies that I could see.

These were the survivors of the fall of Golden City. They'd all come to watch the one responsible die.

Last to step out of the orb was Maili and High Queen Kisandra. I knew Queen Kisandra from the familiar mask covering her face, and the red-and-gold robe covering everything else. Maili took longer to place. I almost didn't recognize her without the burnished reddish-gold hair that was one of her loveliest features. I didn't know why it was gone and covered with a chestnut-brown wig, but I'd guess it had something to do with the scars peeking out along the top of her forehead.

Dominic, Poet, and Keely were lifted up beside me as the royals and nobles took their place.

"Welcome, loyal friends." Ormr took their place before the platform. "Finally, after the destruction of our beloved home, countless unsensible deaths, and four moons of terror and tragedy, the nightmare is over.

"The dragon thief has been caught, the dragons she stole were recovered safely, and she stands before you today to face her rightful justice."

I flicked to Maili to see if she had any reaction to Poet standing up here, facing possible death. If she did, her blank expression didn't give her away.

"Many of you were afraid to come here. Her foul legend grew during months of rumors, whispers, and exaggeration," Ormr said. "Let me reassure you, she is not the usurper reincarnated. She is not a tool of the gods sent to punish us. Nor is she a great mage.

"Ainsley Nothing and Nobody is a peasant," they spat. "She's a worthless, cursed creature born from the monster who seduced and raped my father. Forbidden magics is her birthright, and it's forbidden magic she used to steal powers and dragons. Look at her now."

A hard shove threw me off my feet. I crashed on my back, head bouncing off the wood and stone. Raucous laughter belted my ears.

"She's nothing."

Footfalls, then I was roughly picked up and shoved onto my feet.

"You will see for yourself. She steals magic to save herself, so no magic will be used on her. Likewise, the only dragons within a hundred miles are the ones who will soon be freed from her. She will steal no more to make her escape, and she dare not drain the magic of the forcibly bonded dragons, lest she gets her only remaining friends killed like she got the whore and the orphans killed."

Fists balling, I tuned out the rest of their speech. It's hard to believe I didn't see their true nature before.

The real monster was always looking back at me.

A wooden block was set down before me. Grabbing my shoulders, the Render forced me to my knees. I refused to turn my head and look at the glint shining out of the corner of my eye.

Beheading was how they commonly dealt with commoners who illegally bonded with a dragon. Fitting that should be my end too.

"—will remember this day," Ormr called. "No matter who or what rises against us, Adalinda will prevail."

"Yeah!"

Flicking over their jumping, waving, and clapping, I fixed on the cage housing my dragons. How easy it would be to channel their power and break us out from this place.

And how easy it would've been for Keely to stop fighting and go along with Awnan's disgusting plan, so that he'd free her from her prison under the Yellowtail. How easy it would've been for Poet to chime in with all the royals shouting for my death when Queen Kisandra and the girl he thought he loved crashed my wedding. How easy it would've been for Dominic to shove his feelings down and forget about the throne-stealing dragon thief that blew into his life. Instead Keely fought for weeks to get a message out. Instead Poet shouted down the people calling for my death. Instead Dominic died alone in the snow all for the sake of protecting me.

Dragons didn't know sentiment, but they did know loyalty. My clan was there for me when no one else was. I would not abandon them. If we couldn't get out together... then none of us would get out.

"*What nonsense you speak,*" Reyna gruffed. "*Take my boy and the unnatural mage, and fly away.*"

"I can't," I said, standing up tall. "If I take them away without removing the manacles, Claudius will die, then Dominic will die."

"*Take off the chains!*"

"You know this, my beauty. To have the power to undo living magic, I need living magic." I fell on the seven guards standing around Queen Kisandra—their bows and arrows leveled at my head. "They'll kill me the second she feels the drain on her magic."

"*You will survive death. You will return.*"

"But Keely won't. Or Poet. Or whoever they choose to punish for my actions. I cannot risk the lives of the people who gave everything to defend mine. They have a chance if I go peacefully. I will give them that chance."

"*You are not allowed to die. Free yourself now. I order it.*"

The barest smile touched my lips. "*Goodbye, my beauty.*"

The Renders grabbed my head. Pushing me down, they stretched my neck over the chopping block.

"*Flying with you has been the greatest honor of my life.*"

The axe fell.

Chapter Five

"Open your eyes."

My lips drew tight, eyes squeezing shut. That voice? It sounded like—

"Wake up, Shenha. We have a lot to talk about."

I blinked open.

Kai stood outside the circle. His flaming red—sky-blue—lily pad-green hair flashed in the corner of my eye, taking the place of the glinting executioner's axe.

"What is this?" I shot up. I was in the same place, kneeling before the chopping block in the courtyard, but everyone else had vanished. "Where are Dominic, Keely, and Poet? Where's the queen?"

He shook his head. "I plucked you away from your life enough times that you should know the answer to that. They're right where you left them, but you're not as I left you. You've bonded with too many dragons, Shenha. They've overwhelmed your mind."

"What are you talking about?" I crouched on all fours, baring my fangs. "Bring me back to my mate. Now!"

"I will return you to your suicide mission shortly. But first, we have to talk. There's a choice you must make, and you must make it now before all is lost."

Confusion stayed me. It wasn't his words. It's that he was more serious than the fragments of my memory had ever seen him.

"A choice? Am I not dead?"

"You're not dead, Shenha. That's the choice." He helped me up. "You can pointlessly die here as a sign of misguided loyalty to save people your siblings will have executed ten seconds after you." Kai held up a hand, silencing me when I opened my mouth. "Or you can listen."

Stepping back, I considered him. Ormr would go back on their word and kill my clan? Why do these things keep surprising me? Dragons don't know lies and deception. There's no point when they all share a mind. But humans...

As I once told my love and my life, every second word out of their mouth was a lie.

"I'm listening," I said. "Are you going to tell me how to save them?"

"I'm going to tell you a great many things." Kai snapped his fingers, and a throne like the high queen's appeared. He sat and draped one leg over the arm. "My brothers and sister are occupied elsewhere, so I have time to tell you everything. If you want to hear it."

"I do. How do I save Dominic? Will I be fast enough if I steal Claudius's magic and put them back under to make our escape?"

"No. Not even if your mind and senses returned. You've played around with bone, silver, fire, and shadows, little thief. This is time. Time marches on relentlessly. Nothing stands in its way. Nothing holds it back. It must and will be free. Your chrono mage is holding back the flow of the universe with his will alone. One slip of the grip, and they're all swept under."

"Then what do I do!"

He gave me a hard look, all trace of his boyishly wicked grin gone. "You know what to do. Or you would, if you were my Shenha, and not a walking, talking puppet. You are not a dragon, Shenha. Let me rid you of that delusion now."

"What are you talking about? You're delusional." I held out my wings. "A full-grown dragon sits before you. Do you not trust your own eyes?"

"Do you?"

Another snap of the fingers, and a mirror appeared in front of him.

I gazed into it. Another time, I would've wondered at this strange magic. A woman gazed out from the other side. Dirty, tragic thing, her golden waves were greasy, tangled locks. Streaks of black covered her face, arms, and the remains of a red, shredded gown. She looked familiar but I couldn't place her. Wasn't my fault humans insisted on looking alike.

"How are you doing this?" I asked. "Have you trapped her in the mirror? Why show me?"

"That is you, Shenha. The real you." The mirror disappeared. "You were only just beginning to understand and control your bond with Reyna when you suddenly took on five more. You couldn't—*can't* handle it. There's a reason the Elders don't allow humans to connect with the hive mind. Thousands of years' worth of dragons living and dying, and sharing all that they are, think, and do with their kind.

"Druks are forever changed after consuming the heart of one dragon. Did you think you could take on all of them with no consequences?"

"I don't understand."

Sighing, he looked out over the distance. "Comparing the dragonkin hive mind with one human mind is like comparing the sun to a candle-flame. It's overwhelmed you like it did Zalina. And just like her, it has brought you to ruin."

"Zalina." I didn't have to ask who that was. The dragons knew. "The usurper."

"Dragons don't feel love in the same way humans do. The feeling that you tell yourself is love, is actually a mix of Reyna's affection, respect, and possessiveness over you," Kai said. "They feel such things for their bondeds. They feel much more for their hatchlings, but they feel nothing in particular for their mates. They're a means to an end and nothing more."

He sat up, leaning in. "If you were the same person you were before, the one who ignored my explicit warning and sacrificed everything to bring Dominic Roark back from beyond the veil, you wouldn't have stopped searching for him after you were taken away from the castle that night.

"If you had devoted yourself to finding him, you would've found all three of them in time, and there wouldn't be an axe swinging down on your neck."

"But—"

"But you couldn't do that," he said, slicing me off. "Because whenever you had moments of clarity, remembered how much you love him, and tried to find him, the dragon instincts, and their incessant badgering and roaring, crept back in again. Only fire dragons breed easily. All the rest struggle to protect their eggs, and then their young. They struggle even more under the relentless slaughter of the humans who want to be Druks. As such, they value younglings above all.

"There are so many things you need to do, Shenha. Battles to be won. Enemies to defeat. But for the last four moons, you've been consumed with hunting down every person who harmed your orphan brothers and sisters. Dragons don't know love, but they do know revenge."

I tossed my head, turning away. "Why are you saying all these things? What's the point? Are you going to tell me how to save Dominic, Keely, and Poet, or not?"

"Only you can save them. The real Ainsley Boreen. But if you're going to be her again, the laws that bound me say I have to give you a choice. You need to know what that choice is."

"Then stop speaking in riddles and tell me!"

He chuckled. "Always admired that short fuse. If you want me to tell you, why not simply ask?"

I quieted, studying him. If we truly had time, and he was truly here to tell me all that I had been wanting to know...

"What... am I?"

Kai smiled. I had asked the right question. "I will tell you what you're not. You're not a unique mage. You're not a curse. You're not the next stage in evolution. You're exactly what you've always been. A poor, magicless girl from Ossian."

"But I'm not. I have magic now. Like you said. Thief magic."

His smile stayed. "You don't have magic, Shenha. Magic is human puffery. It's tricks and games and look-at-me attention-getting. What you have... is power."

"More riddles," I scoffed.

"Then, let me speak plainly. You have the power of a god. One god in particular." He waved a hand over his face. "Me."

"You..." My brain stalled.

Kai sighed. "Seems I'm not speaking plain enough. Remember I told you that there are many more gods and goddesses that the world has forgotten?"

I nodded.

"Think of the gods and goddess that you do know. Zaeah, mother of dragons. Parthelan, father of man. Calthoon, god of the veil. Tenille of the earth and heavens. Zaeah birthed dragons. Parthelan created humans. Calthoon rules the land beyond this one. Tenille created the earth and sky, and gave humans magics that let them wield a piece of his creations. Did it ever occur to you, human, that this isn't enough?"

"Not enough? What do you mean?"

"I mean you humans do so much more than live, wield magic, bond with dragons, and die. And yet, that's all those four gods can give you the ability to do."

My lips parted, and nothing came out.

"In the short spans of your life, you live them. You sing, dance, tell stories, and write poetry. You create weapons for war, and tools for innovation. You learn, reason, and discover more than the generation before. You love, rage, lust, and suffer. You plan and hope for the future.

"The first incarnations of the human race were a failure. Parthelan, the fucking show-off, boasted about being the creator of new beings that would love and worship him forever. But they didn't. His humans were dull and stupid. They didn't know how to create, so they couldn't build shelters, or make weapons and tools.

"They couldn't lust, so they rarely mated. When they did figure it out and managed to give birth, they abandoned the screaming thing because they couldn't love. They had nothing to live for," he said softly, weaving me into his spell. "No hopes, no dreams, no light, no music, no fun. The ones who didn't die from hunger, animal attacks, or the elements, killed themselves."

"I... I can't imagine a world so bleak," I whispered.

"You couldn't *live* in a world so bleak." He shook his head. "None of you could, so the human race died out within two generations."

I was silent taking that in. "If that's true, how did we come to be what we are now?"

"Because the next breed of humans, we created together," he said. "The gods and goddesses. Everyone."

"Gods and goddesses of love, music, hope, and wisdom."

"Gods of war, suffering, hate, betrayal," he finished. "All that you are, we gave to you. And you worshiped us. All of us. Until they attacked."

I made to sit and found a chair underneath me. Kai had hooked me on his every word. "They. You mean Zaeah, Parthelan, Tenille, and Calthoon."

He nodded. "Zaeah and Parthelan are twins. Always one-upping each other. Zaeah birthed the dragon race, which made Parthelan want to be the father of his own race. But unlike humans, dragons didn't need power of the other gods to survive. Humans did. They needed the other gods, and they worshipped and called on the other gods often more than they ever did him."

"He was jealous."

Kai tipped his head, brows raised. "So very jealous. His creations were growing, thriving, spreading, breeding, and becoming one of the dominant species right along with dragons. But it wasn't him they called on to grant them love. It wasn't at his altar they fell upon to protect their sons as they marched to war. It wasn't even him they cursed when they lost everything. Parthelan was an afterthought to his greatest success, and he would have it no more."

"Okay, but what about Zaeah, Tenille, and Calthoon? Why did they join his attack?"

"Zaeah is his twin sister. At times they are rivals, but always they are partners. She was never going to stand against him," he explained. "Calthoon was lonely and isolated in the land beyond the veil. I mean, for fuck's sake, it's such a dreary, depressing place with a million poor souls wailing about their untimely death. Can you blame us for never visiting?"

"Seems like Calthoon did."

"Yes," he replied, heaving a sigh. "He did. When Zaeah and Parthelan offered him a throne next to them at the helm of the universe, he couldn't resist. To escape his hell, he condemned the rest of us."

"What about Tenille? What did they offer him?"

"They offered him nothing. They didn't have to, because he didn't care." Kai saw my frown. "Think of nature, Ainsley. Think of storms, mudslides, hurricanes, and wildfires. These things happen because they happen. Natural disasters strike and take out all in their path with no discrimination based on age, ability, skin color, or nation. It's not personal.

"Such is Tenille. He has no particular care or hatred for anyone or anything. He just is because he is. Calthoon, Parthelan, and Zaeah told him they were going to overthrow and imprison the other gods, and he shrugged and said why not? It's been a boring millennium, and that sounds interesting."

"Wow." I had no other words.

"Yes, wow." He gazed in the far-off distance. "Your human speech captures more than god speech can."

I hesitated. "How did they do it? You make it sound like there were a lot of you. How were you defeated by only four gods?"

"Easily. That's the worst part." His nails dug into the wood. "How easy it was. Whatever humans are, they were made from Parthelan. He is their ultimate creator. So erasing from their minds the names and knowledge of every single god barring him and his accomplices... it was all too easy."

"He erased our memories? But why? How did that lead to defeating you?"

"Gods are sustained by worship. We were much weaker beings before you humans came about. With nothing to do and no one to do it for, we slept within the eternal nothingness between all that was and all that will be. After we helped to create the humans, you believed in us. Prayed to us. Begged us. Cursed us. Called on us for help and favor. Every time you did, it made us stronger." He jerked a chin at me. "Consider how many times a day you say 'Calthoon, bless me' or 'Mother Zaeah, save me.' Those mere words are power to a god."

I nodded slow. "When Parthelan erased you from our minds, you lost that power."

"Not completely," he admitted. "There was still a part of us in all of you. Not to mention all the temples, paintings, and evidence of us around. Tenille and Zaeah took care of those."

"Zaeah had the dragons burn them and Tenille sent natural disasters to destroy them."

"Yes."

"My gods." I shivered. "To do something so terrible out of petty jealousy."

"No, Shenha. To do something so terrible for power. That's what it always comes down to—power." He leaned back in his seat. "Anyway, after we were wiped from your minds, we became a fraction of the gods we were. All that was left was for Parthelan and Zaeah to attack, snatch, grab, and drag every last one of us into the prison Calthoon created for us beyond the veil. We've been trapped there for over ten thousand years."

My brows popped. "Ten thousand years? But that— Are you still trapped?"

"Yes."

"Then how are you talking to me?" I looked around. "Are we there now?"

He shook his head. "We are in the place where I was born. The eternal nothingness between all that was and will be. I just decorated it a bit for you. A human mind cannot see it as it is. You'd go mad."

"I am going mad," I cried, clutching my head. "This is all too much. How could any of it have to do with me?"

"It all has to do with you, Ainsley Boreen. It's why you *can't* throw your life away. The fate of everything relies on you."

"It can't! How could it? This doesn't make any sense. I'm no one. Just the abandoned daughter of a murdered prince and a Druk. No one's fate could possibly rely on me."

Kai gave me a hard look. "Unique mages. Where is it do you think they get their power?"

My face crumpled at the sudden change in subject. "What? What does that have to do with—?"

"Answer me."

"I—" I threw up my hands. "I don't know. Some people are just special, I guess. Different. Like my brother who could do complicated math without ever picking up a book. Or my sister who couldn't walk, but could fly. It's impossible for us all to be the same."

"A fair answer, but the wrong one. If power over water, air, earth, and fire is born from the part of you that is Tenille, then it follows that magics that aren't from him—"

"—are from the other gods." I bolted upright. "Their magics aren't unique at all. The world has just forgotten where they came from, because we forgot the old gods."

"Your lover is right. You are incredibly intelligent."

I preened like Reyna would. My beauty does so love compliments. "But what does this have to do with me? You said I don't have magic."

He held up a hand. "Patience."

Inclining my head, I signaled for him to go on.

"I once told you that even a god has to obey the rules. Whose rules? Our parents."

"Parents? You have parents."

"All That Was and All That Will Be."

"What about it?"

"My parents," Kai said.

"What? Who?"

He laughed. "My father is All That Was and my mother is All That Will Be. Or if you prefer the names they were given by your ancestors, they are Father Past and Mother Future."

"Okay…" I said slowly. "Your parents are the past and the future. Does that mean they have form? They're beings who walk and talk like you?"

He shrugged. "I don't know. I've never met my father because he's past and the past is gone. I can't meet my mother because she's future and the future hasn't happened yet. They haven't even met each other."

"You do know you're speaking absolute nonsense, right?"

Kai barked a laugh. "I'm not, but I understand why it sounds so. Either way, you must know them, so you understand why they bound us with rules— Actually, with one rule above all. Whatever we do with the world and its creations, and we can do much, we can't interfere with your free will."

"Why? It's a good rule of course, but why that one?"

"Think about it. The past has no meaning if all of your decisions were decided for you, and the future is bleak without choice."

I thought about that. Truly thought about it. What meaning would my past have if I'd been forced to fall in love with Dominic? Forced to befriend Rosaleen? Or forced to protect my brothers and sisters? What made it wonderful and special was that it was real and true from my heart. As was the future I wanted to have with Dominic. It was worthless if we didn't build it together from our own wants and choices.

"Yes, I agree," I whispered, nodding slow. "That means when Parthelan wiped the memory of the other gods from our minds—"

"He took away your free will. Your right to worship who you choose. Your right for your mind and memory to be your own. The second he did, our parents acted."

"Did they? You said you've been imprisoned for ten thousand years."

"They can't free us, Shenha. The past and the future cannot directly interact with the present, and the present is where we exist."

My head was beginning to hurt like I bonded with a thousand dragons. Even simplified, this was difficult to follow.

"How did they act?"

"Father stole their past like Parthelan stole your ancestors. They know we are their brothers and sisters, and they know why they imprisoned us, but that's all they know of us. Severina, goddess of luck. Kenyatta, goddess of wisdom. Our names and power are gone from their minds."

"How does that help you?"

"It helps because of what Mother did. As we were locked away, a prophecy resounded through every realm. A prophecy that is and was written on the soul of every human born with Mother's gift. At some point in all of their lives, these fortune-tellers will recite this:

Born from enemies lost and love found, an impossible child will enter the world through destiny alone. Tested on a battlefield of strife, struggle, and pain, this crucible will forge her into the weapon of the fallen gods.

She will lead the forgotten. Wield the unthinkable. Overthrow the mighty. Topple kingdoms, and give peace to the suffering.

This child of vengeance and fury will rise.

She will rule.

Or she'll fall harder and lower than all before.

My eyes widened with every word. "No."

"Yes."

"No! That— That's not me!"

"It is you," Kai said calmly. "I chose you. A parent knows their child."

"You're not my parent," I snapped, shoving up. "Enough of this. I'm not a child of prophecy, or whatever nonsense you've made up. I'm a simple dragon who needs to save her mate and clan. Tell me how to do that, then let me go!"

"Shenha—"

"Stop calling me that!" I roared, lunging at him. My maw snapped shut centimeters from his nose. "Let. Me. Go."

Kai blinked lazily. He hadn't so much as twitched. "I cannot help you until you make a choice. You cannot make that choice until you know everything. As I said, you must decide your own fate."

I growled. "I am not the person you're looking for."

"You are, because I made you into the person I'm looking for." Kai snapped their fingers and I was back in my seat. I didn't see it happen. I didn't feel myself move. One moment I was in his face, the next I wasn't. "My traitorous brothers and sister destroyed my temples and removed my name from the minds of man, but they didn't get rid of every trace.

"There was still mention of me and the other gods in the ancient texts. The names mean nothing to you, naturally. Most of you wouldn't think to repeat them in fear of blaspheming the *true* gods. It was rare that one of you was so desperate, so lost without hope, that you'd scour all of known history searching for a way to gain power above your own.

"Power to make someone fall in love with you. Power to make a barren womb fertile. Power to avenge your loved one. After praying to Tenille, Parthelan, Calthoon, and Zaeah failed, they moved on until they found the few whose names still live on, and called upon us.

"Six times I've been summoned. The fifth was by a woman named Zalina. She heard the prophecy while out on a walk with her lover, Ladon Roark. She didn't think much of it until Queen Kisandra had her entire family put to death when she discovered her mother was Hyelongan. Mother, father, three sisters, her brother, and her nieces and nephews. All killed. Zalina only survived because of her magic."

He saw my horrified look. "Another thing you don't get to learn when you're not allowed to go to school. Adalinda's borders were closed back then. People from other nations were not allowed to cross, and vice versa. If you hadn't already noticed, your queen is obsessed with... purity."

My stomach churned. "Every day, Queen Kisandra becomes more disgusting to me, and the usurper more sympathetic."

"I certainly found Zalina so. When she called to me, begging for the strength and power to overthrown a queen. I gave it to her. I convinced myself she was the child of the prophecy. A child of two nations separated by walls and hatred. It shouldn't have been possible for her parents to meet and fall in love, but they did.

"I told myself everything fit, and imbibed her with my power." He shook his head. "But she didn't free the fallen or give peace to the suffering. By the time she achieved her goal of overthrowing the queen and uniting the nations, she'd bonded with so many dragons, she went insane."

"That was the fifth time," I rasped. "Tell me about the last."

"Ahh. My Shenha." He smirked— No, Kai smiled. At me. With a tenderness that unsettled me. "The first time I saw you, I knew you were the one I've been waiting for.

"The shock of your father's death sent your mother into early labor. Just like that, her hope of a happy future with a kind man who loved her exactly the way she was... disappeared. As she screamed and wailed on the forest floor, her heart cried out and *puullled* me to her," he gritted, putting out his fists, then snapping them to his chest. "No magic. No rituals. No sacrifice. She snatched me from bondage by sheer will. Nothing like that had ever happened in the history of the gods.

"There I stood before her," he whispered, and our surroundings changed. "As surprised to see her as she was to see me."

Grass grew beneath my feet. All around us, trees sprung from the ground, cloaking us in shaped beams of light. A woman crouched on the ground. Claws where her fingertips should be. Scales rippling over her skin. Black wings sprouting from her back. Sorrow twisting her soul as she sobbed beside the still and broken body of a dark-haired man with Ormr's nose and Maili's mouth.

"This woman—this Druk—asked me for the power to avenge her love... and I said no."

"No..." Tears ran down my cheeks. "Why?"

"Because it wasn't her destiny. It's yours, impossible child. I knew it as you kicked your way out into the world the same as you kicked your way into it—demanding to be born even though nature itself denied your existence. You were the one I've been waiting for."

Kai grew. Shedding the height and boyishness of youth, his legs, arms, and torso lengthened. His nose rounded, eyes softened, and skin darkened. Kai's color-changing hair found gold, kept it, and made more. I stepped back as his—her pants and tunic knit themselves together, melting into a tight, red-and-black bodice that flared at the waist, then spread to the ground in a riot of roaring flames and wispy black miasma.

"Titana." I fell to my knees. "Goddess of vengeance."

"Stand, my daughter." She helped me to my feet. "It is I who should bow. You are everything that I hoped for and more."

I swallowed hard. I wished to say I wasn't who she wanted, but it would be hollow. It made no sense. It was absolutely impossible. But... I remembered being in this forest with her and my mother the day I was born. It was me.

"How can you be proud of me? I didn't know," I said, tossing my head. "I haven't freed you yet."

"You may never free me, and I'll remain proud of you. You are my daughter. My child of vengeance and fury."

My head spun. I fell back and landed on my chair. Wincing, my twisting vision revealed the forest and my parents were gone. So was Titana. Kai gazed back at me.

"Forgive me," he said. "My siblings aren't looking this way, but they will if I stay too long in my true form."

"This is a lot," I croaked. "It's too much."

"It's destiny, Shenha. No one ever said it was easy."

"None of this makes sense. You say you're imprisoned, but you're here. I'm talking to you. You appeared before my mother, Zalina, and others when they called you. If you can leave your prison *and* wield your power. Why do you need me?"

"This is hard for a human to understand. You have one form. You have a body. I don't," he said. "The core of who I am is imprisoned. My soul—for want of a better word. But the rest of me still flows through the universe, and in the part of me that dwells in every human. Such is the same for all of us.

"There was a time when we walked among you. You spoke with us, fell in love with us, and knew us so well to paint our faces and build our statues. No more. Since you forgot us, we've grown so weak we can't so much as appear before you, let alone fight the most powerful beings in the universe—which is what my brothers and sister have become.

"It took immense power, irreversible sacrifice, and the invocation of my name to manifest enough of my form in one place, to serve the six people who called on me. The last time"—he stroked my cheek—"I gave you nearly everything I have. There is more of me in you than there is in me. That's why I can come to you at will. When my siblings aren't watching, that is."

I covered my face, shrinking from his touch. "But what am I supposed to do? Wield the unthinkable? Lead the forgotten? What does any of that mean?"

"You're already doing it. This gift I've given you isn't new. It's been used before which is why the dragons know and named it. But none of those people knew what it's like to stand apart in a world of magic. They didn't know how to make a family of the people you find on life's path, instead of the ones you're given. They've never so refused to bend to circumstance that they stole what they needed, and forced themselves to get up and forge on with broken bones."

"That's different," I cried. "That had nothing to do with being a prophesized child. I was just a poor orphan getting by."

"Were you? Shenha, you traveled the five kingdoms for four moons, wielding fury and vengeance like twin swords. That is my gift. But rescuing every lost, scared, and hurt child along the way. Protecting them like you never were." He grasped my hand. "That was you. Dare I say, that was you leading the forgotten and giving peace to the suffering.

"I didn't make you into our savior. I couldn't. It had to be your choice like it had to be your choice to unlock the god's power within you. But you did it, because this is who you are."

I was shaking my head. "I didn't unlock your power. I knew nothing about it!"

"You knew as those filthy boys dropped their pants that you wanted vengeance. You demanded it from your soul, and Reyna responded."

"I wasn't demanding vengeance. I was screaming for help," I cried. "I was scared. Desperate."

His eyes flashed. "Was that all you were?"

I tensed, looking away.

No, that wasn't all I felt. I was... angry. In the raging pit of my soul, I was furious that those shits believed my body was something they could take whenever they wanted—without permission or respect. I wanted them to know what it was like to be small, helpless, and at my mercy.

I wanted them to suffer.

"Yes," he whispered, snapping my head around. "You did. Because what does everyone who wants vengeance pray for? The strength, power, and wits to defeat their enemies. What being has that in spades? The dragon."

"But..." It was amazing to me that I had any *buts* left. "I didn't call to her. She came to me. She wanted to help me."

"I'm certain she did, but she didn't have to bond with you to do that. She's a fire-breathing dragon. She's lethal with or without a bond."

My throat tightened. "So I did, in a way, perform forbidden magic on her that forced her to break the bond with Dominic."

"No, Shenha. I assure you, it was still her choice. Dragons prefer to bond with the strong. In that moment when the 'dragon mother' power was brimming within you, you became the strongest being she's ever come across. She chose you. They all did. They protected you."

"I feel sick," I forced out. "Please, no more. I understand, okay. I understand everything. Just tell me the choice I have to make, so I can get my clan free of this place."

"You don't understand everything, but you soon will, because we near the end," he said. "The fact is this, Shenha. My brothers and sister cannot see us now because they're waiting. Beyond the veil. For you."

A buzz sounded in my ears, blocking out whatever he truly said. "Excuse me? Waiting for who?"

Kai's gaze pinned me. "Waiting for you."

"Me? Why would they be waiting for me?"

"They didn't know about you, Shenha. They know a child of fury and vengeance will rise to rip them from their thrones, but they don't know that god is me, or that they should've paid more attention when a grieving Druk summoned me.

"They know about you now."

I choked. "What? Why? Because I bonded with too many dragons? Did that draw Mother Zaeah's attention?"

He shook his head. "A human bonding with many dragons has happened before. She ignored it then, and would've ignored it now. But you made a mistake, Shenha. The mistake I warned you not to make."

"Warned me not to make—? Wait. Are you talking about that incredibly vague and useless warning to do the opposite of what is right?"

"Yes," he returned. "That one. I couldn't tell you more, but in the end it didn't matter. Your lover died protecting you, and in a rash, spectacular, wonderful, and terribly stupid move, you yanked him back from the veil while screaming your defiance to Calthoon. If that wasn't enough, you stole the power of Tenille to explode the earth and toss you both back on the cabin's doorstep. So yes, my dear. They are very well aware of you now."

My jaw hung open. "That was the warning you were talking about? You thought it best that I left Dominic for dead!"

He didn't blink at my shout. "I did not think it best. Whether or not Dominic Roark lives or dies makes no matter to me. It is you I care about. You wield my power. That in and of itself was nothing for them to concern themselves about. As you figured out yourself, your unique mages channel the power of the other gods.

"Even when you died and used my gift to yank yourself back from the veil, Calthoon paid it no mind. You're not immortal. Death will find you in the end, so for now, he was fine to let you play your games.

"But then you took Dominic from him."

My lips peeled back from my teeth. "Dominic isn't his. He's mine."

"Oh yes, you made that very clear to him while you shouted your blasphemous rant at the sky." Kai's amusement lit his face. "It was quite funny. I wish I was there to see his face." He burst out laughing, but stopped himself quickly. "That said, Dominic was supposed to die that day, Shenha."

"No."

"It was his fate. He was already in Calthoon's realm. Calthoon knows every soul under his charge, and he knew it the moment you pulled him back. It was because he dies for you that in your grief, you unlock your full power and rise stronger than you were before. And you do it *without* drawing their attention. At least until it was too late," he said. "Now they know you're the child of the prophecy. Now, they know they have to stop you before it's too late."

Something deep and small in my soul shrank into a tight ball. The most powerful beings in the universe were after me.

"But they can't hurt me, right? You said it was against the rules to mess with our free will. Including my will to save you. They broke the rules once and your parents punished them. They wouldn't do it again."

"They don't have to," he said forcefully. "Listen, Shenha. You're not listening! The dragons have so warped and strangled your mind, my quick and clever thief is nowhere to be found. Why should they trouble themselves when you are making enemies everywhere you go. Enemies who heard the prophecy and have no interest in a random girl becoming the ultimate power and toppling their kingdom. Enemies like—"

"General Ladon Roark."

My voice was barely a frog's croak. I was getting slow. Kai had told me. General Roark was right beside his lover when she heard the fortune-teller's prophecy.

"Is that why he tried to steal my power with the siphoner's blade?"

"No," he said, surprising me. "Roark doesn't know the prophecy speaks of you. He believed, and still does, that the prophecy was about Zalina. He wants your power simply because he covets it, but don't for a second believe this ignorance will shield you for long. Ladon Roark is a smart man. Eventually he will get over his stupid prejudices against commoners and aberrant mages, and realize no child could be more impossible than one of a Druk."

I wanted to deny this, but couldn't. General Roark would have to realize what I am soon... and how much harder would he try to cut out my heart then. It was true. Tenille and the gods didn't have to send an earthquake or something to kill me. They only had to wait.

Wait for the mere milliseconds it takes an axe to fall.

"What do I do, Kai?"

"I can't tell you what to do. All I can say is that the prophecy doesn't promise victory. You can fail, Shenha, and if you die here today, that's exactly what you'll do. Calthoon will not let you leave his realm again, and you will not like what they have planned for you when you cross over."

"Then we're back where we started." I pushed up, turning my back on him. "I can't die, and I can't let Dominic, Keely, and Poet die. There isn't actually a choice."

"Yes, there is." Urgency laced his voice. "There is but you can't see it as you are now. The Ainsley I know— The one who jumped off a dragon's back with an arrow in her hand. She would find a way out of this. You can be her again... but you'd have to close off the bonds to your dragons. Get them, and the hive mind, out of your head."

I made a harsh noise in my throat. "You're speaking nonsense again. I'm a dragon. I'm dragon mother. I can't be cut off from the hive mind."

I didn't understand the exasperation that darkened his face. "Trust me, Shenha. You can be, but it will be like before you died in that room in the citadel. You won't be able to speak to Reyna, or the others. You also won't channel their abilities with a flick of a wrist."

"Ah, I see. My options are to die now, or die ten minutes from now after I launch a useless, magicless attack against the most powerful mages in the five kingdoms."

I heard footfalls, then Kai was in front of me, grasping my shoulders. "It's not forever. Without six voices constantly in your head, and their dragon instincts shouting over yours, you'll learn to wield your power *the right way.*

"You'll build up your own walls to take in what you need, and keep out what you don't. And when you stop living under their influence, throwing brute strength and power around like... like a dragon," he said, "you'll plumb the deepest depths of what a goddess of fury and vengeance can do, because believe me, you haven't begun to tap into your potential."

My jaw clenched. Can it be said there was a choice when he was making it clear only one path was correct?

"Can I really do it?" I whispered. "Can I save them?"

He shrugged. "My mother tells the future, not me. I do know I've seen you tackle harder challenges than these."

I was quiet for a long time.

"I'll really stop hearing their voices? Reyna's commands? Tizor's sweet words to his hatchlings? Cadmus's grumbles for more cows and Kenna's singing as she soars through the sky?"

"Yes." He guided me back into my seat. "Having a god's power doesn't make you any less mortal. Your mind was only meant for one. They're tearing you apart."

That couldn't be true. I knew it wasn't true. My dragons were my strength. They needed me as I needed them. Together, we were a family.

But my family includes three more.

I couldn't agree that I had to be cut off from my dragons to save them, but as it was, I had no ideas. No plan. No hope.

I didn't know what else to do but drain Claudius's magic, and I didn't know what to do with it when I did. If there was a chance I could get us all out of here, I had to take it knowing I would work every day and night to return our bonds to how they were.

"Yes," I said without another thought. "Close the bonds."

Kai reached for me. His hands stopped just short of my temple. "There are two things you must know."

"You're telling me now?" I cried.

"First, the bonds will close in order of the one with the strongest hold on you to the weakest. I can't say how long that will take, so don't waste precious time."

I didn't have to ask who my strongest bond was. Of course it was my beauty, Reyna, who dropped out of the sky on my worst day and changed everything. My heart broke hearing our bond was first to go.

"Will I still be able to steal magic from mages who attack me?" I asked.

"As long as you do it without dying."

"Okay. For now that will do until I can put everything back how it was."

Kai still didn't move. "You understand that everything their dragon instincts have changed and suppressed in you will come back."

"I know who I am. I'm a dragon. That can never change."

"Everything, Shenha." His voice softened. "All that you so eagerly ran away from. Dragons understand fury, vengeance, loyalty, and even trust. But they do not know love. Not in the way you do. Not... in the way you will."

"I understand," I snapped. "Now isn't the time to start doubting me."

"This isn't doubt." An expression I'd never seen on his smirking, smiling face knocked me over.

Regret.

"I'm sorry, Ainsley. I'm so sorry. But you can't be a weapon of vengeance without someone to avenge."

"What does that—?"

He grasped my temples. In a blink he was gone...

...and my executioner towered over me.

Chapter Six

A wave of shouts, jeers, smells, and lights assaulted me, jarring me out of the peaceful place I knew with Kai.

I screamed.

The Render jerked back. Dropping the axe, it *thunked* in the wood inches from my nose as he quickly threw up a writhing, twisting wall of briars.

"What the hell are you doing, man! Kill her!"

"Kill her," the crowd screamed. The same blood-soaked chant they shouted... when General Roark murdered my family.

It all flooded back in. All that I hid from while cowering in the hive mind, believing I was dragon mother because human Ainsley didn't want to remember. She didn't want to live.

Soul-ripping, lung-shredding sorrow strangled my throat, holding back the sobs straining to burst free.

Colm, Ilemka, Niamh, my borrowed brothers and sisters.

So young, sweet, and trusting. They loved me. They came running when I topped the hill, shouting my name with such excitement in their voice. The only ones to ever be happy at the sight of a poor, magicless peasant drawing near, and they were everything to me. My reason for stealing, my reason for fighting, my hope in giving them a better future.

Sister Aven.

The kindest person you'd ever met was an abusive brute next to her. Every good memory of my childhood, she was in them. Singing to me as she brushed my hair by the fire. Chasing me under tables and through the fields when we played hide-and-seek. On the day my mother left me, she came to give me all the love she couldn't.

And Rosaleen. My best and truest friend.

Dragons may not know love, but they did know loyalty. Cherished even more than their mates, they honor the one who was always by their side through peace and war. The one they could always rely on, knowing not even the threat of death would make them betray.

A lifemate. That's who Rosaleen was to me. The one I was supposed to spend the rest of my life with as assuredly as I was Dominic. We were meant to gather together every Calthoon, and sing and dance our praises while our children played by the fire. She was meant to be my maiden witness and I hers. I was meant to save her. Rescue her from the life her disgusting aunt forced her into, and fly her away into a new and wonderful one.

I wasn't meant to be the reason they were all dead.

Pain lashed through me. A living, breathing animal rampaging and destroying all in their path. I tried to seize hold of it, but it burst through.

I caught fire.

Hellfire erupted from every pore on my body. My would-be executioners flung themselves off the platform, narrowly escaping certain death.

The chopping block blasted away from me, smashing into half a dozen people awaiting a front-row seat to my end. Snapping back, I screamed at the sky, crying under agony no one had ever known.

Something had gone terribly wrong. I was burning. I no longer had the protections I did when I wielded my dragons' magic. Reyna's unstoppable flame was consuming me, and it was no more than I deserved.

I was selfish. When Reyna first bonded with me, I should've taken her and run far away. Lived with the pain of the bond and let the people I loved get on with their lives. But I wanted it all. I wanted to be a dragon rider, soaring through the skies, and defending a country that was wrong to underestimate me. I wanted to be the hero, saving Rosaleen, Sister Aven, and the children.

Calthoon doesn't grant the desires of the selfish. He knew what I should've known then.

I deserve to burn.

"Tenille, save us! What is she?"

"Get us out of here!"

"Kill her— No, don't use magic!"

A blast of liquid knocked me back, smothering me in a torrent of water, flames, and steam. The sizzling hiss of magic fighting magic couldn't overcome my wailing cries. Through my haze, something glinted on my skin.

"Archers? Archers!"

I pushed up, struggling against the seawater pushing back. All I could see were their faces as they strained against their inanimate captors. My family, my surrogate mother, my best friend reduced to dust—

"Because of you."

I snapped up, eyes narrowing on the painted mask beneath a decadent cowl. Watchers swarmed around her, Ormr, and Maili, practically shoving them at another growing black orb, waiting to carry them far away. They would not get away from me again.

"No!" I flung my arm out, slashing the air. Something lashed over my head, blocking the water.

I stared, my foggy haze clearing for the briefest moment as shock blew in.

What is it?

Bright red and blinding, the strangely shaped thing curled around me. What it looked like was not nearly as confusing as what I felt from it. That I *could* feel anything from it. The water pressure blasting against it fed back to me, causing a peculiar feeling between my shoulder blades. Twisting around, I followed the thing around where it was... attached to me?

I swiped at it and stopped, eyes widening at my arm and hands.

Glimmering, red scales rippled down my arm, on the back of my hand, over my knuckles, and down to the fierce, deadly red claws where my nails used to be.

"Reyna..."

Reyna's claws. Reyna's scales. I had scrubbed, stroked, and praised my beauty enough times to know them better than I knew every spot and freckle on my skin.

Amidst the screaming, shouting, and archers setting me in their sights, I slowly turned to the other side, gazing upon the twin pair of flaming wings on my back.

"*When you stop living under their influence, you'll plumb the deepest depths of what a goddess of fury and vengeance can do, because believe me, you haven't begun to tap into your potential.*"

I flashed to the memory of Titana in the clearing with my mother, wearing bitterness and pain like a cloak.

"Child of vengeance and fury."

I shot into the sky, leaving the spot as three dozen arrows buried in the wood. High above the scampering, panicking mages, I saw the cage holding my dragons. They should be roaring at me, but there was silence. As silent as the overwhelming part of my brain that smothered everything and told me I was a dragon. Finally, my mind was clear.

And I knew exactly what to do.

"A Druk? How?"

"Where did it come from?"

"Get us out of here!"

I drew my hand back as the weapon formed in my mind's eye. A scorching trident made of pure hellfire appeared on my palm as if waiting to be summoned. Roaring, I flung it across the sky.

"A Druk! The unholy, beastly thing." High Queen Kisandra broke free of the blockade of guards, fisted the air, and punched the sky. The unique mages yanked across the courtyards by their necks and wrists. "Kill it! Protect your queen."

Narrowing on her, the faces of my terrified brothers and sisters haunted me. All I heard was her sentencing innocent children to death for being drains on society. Another trident appeared in my grip, destined for the twisted, hateful snarl beneath her mask.

I fell.

My wings flamed out. My scales and claws disappeared like they were never there. Shrieking, I plummeted to the ground.

"Cadmus!"

I hit the ground hard—the force reverberating through my bones, and snapping my jaw on my tongue. Blood filled my mouth.

I didn't move.

"Is it dead?"

"Archers, a hundred arrows in it to be sure—"

"Stop!" I knew General Roark's voice anywhere. "Don't kill her. We must capture her. We must understand—"

"Silence, Ladon," Kisandra barked. "That filthy stain on my bloodline dies now. Archers, you were given your orders."

Arrows flew from everywhere, blotting out the sun. They struck every inch of my body from the tip of my forehead to my smallest toes.

Silence reigned.

"Is it done?" someone gasped.

"Send the aberrants to check."

Cautious footsteps approached. I rose from my would-be grave, shedding broken arrow tips like fallen leaves.

"What is it?" Queen Kisandra shrieked. She fought against the guards trying to drag her to safety. "Why won't it die?"

What indeed. Where brilliant fiery scales once were was now replaced by hard, mottled bumps and ridges. My skin was rock to the touch.

"Kill it!" Kisandra screamed.

The unique mages cried out. Hissing, searing steam wafted from their manacles.

"Kill her now!"

"Don't!" the general roared. "Don't use magic. Please, my queen. She'll only steal it! Non-magic attacks only— I order you to stand down!"

It was no use. Magic came at me from everywhere. Types that I once believed impossible. Purple leopards rose from the ground—forming, growing, snarling as pure magic conjured them into existence. One mage screamed, and resounding, booming sound waves poured from her throat and incapacitated everyone around her. Magic to make me happy and in love. Magic to turn my bones to water, and transport my mind to a world of their own making. The greatest and largest force of unique mages came at me with everything they had.

"Enough," I hissed. "Out of my way."

I smacked my palms together. The earth rose up and tossed them off her back.

Mages tumbled like chess pieces in the earthquake, their wildly flung magic hitting some of their own, and many more of the royals and nobles who came to watch me surrender to death.

I ran through them, my footfalls steady and sure as I narrowed in on one target.

Queen Kisandra's mask slipped as she foamed at the mouth, shrieking she wouldn't leave until I was destroyed. She was steps away from the portal.

"My queen, please be reasonable. You must go!" The portal mage paled at the sight of me. She rolled and pitched off her feet, straining to hold on to her magic. "Go now!"

"How dare you order me—!"

My earth dragon armor vanished. I was ready as the earthquake stopped, already calling upon my jewel of the sky.

"Kenna!"

Wings burst forth from my back again. I glimpsed them as they carried me into the sky, such beautiful creations of cloud and sunlight, they would've made me weep if I wasn't already doing so.

Maili fought past her grandmother. Reaching the portal, her grasping fingers passed through—

I flapped my wings hard, buffeting a gale of wind and blowing the portal mage through her black hole.

It disappeared.

"Noooo!" Maili's scream echoed through the forest.

I drew my wings back again. The next blast would be a rain of wind scythes, tearing to shreds all in their path. The house of Boreen would die with me.

Boom!

Something whizzed past my head.

"You fool, you missed," Roark growled. "Again, and don't kill her!"

Before I could think to turn, a hard, unforgiving force struck my back, snapping my spine in two.

"Arghhh!"

I dropped—hurtling to the ground with two useless legs that had no hope of bracing my fall. I struck the earth, feeling every bit of the vicious pain. Cadmus's magic couldn't save me.

I lay there—crumpled and broken, blood pouring from a hundred wounds on my body, and all I could hear was Rosaleen's laugh—deep, smoky, and only genuine when she was laughing with me.

Voices floated to my ear, fading in and out as black crept into my vision.

"Is it finally over?"

"Hit her with another one, General."

"No, draw your swords," Kisandra ordered. "Stab the thing until I'm certain it's dead."

Footsteps closed in on me. I was too broken to cringe at the *zing* of a dozen swords leaving their scabbards.

"Su... Su..." I whispered. "Su... oh."

His power bled into me like creeping smoke, and spread through my body—turning my skin black as night. All I had to do was—

"It's changing again!"

"Kill it! Kill it now!"

Searing pain exploded in my side. Suoh's power vanished in the space of my scream—our bond snapping shut. I lay there trapped, defenseless, magicless... as they surrounded me.

"It's normal again," someone said. "Now!"

They attacked.

Dirty boots stomped my arms and head. Blades stabbed my legs and back, shredding my insides to ribbons. All I heard over their bloodthirsty roaring was General Roark's shouts for them to stop. I did not mistake this as mercy for me. He wanted my power. Ladon Roark wanted it more than ever. The only good thing that could come out of this is that he would never get it.

"Get back," Kisandra demanded after an eternity. "Hand me the axe. I will behead the disgusting thing myself. This shame on my blood and my son dies here."

Red blotted out my vision. I heard more than saw her. Heard her grunt as she hefted something heavy. Listened to the whisper of her gown coming closer to me.

"Mi..."

A shadow fell over me. "You should've been strangled by your demon cord in your mother's cursed womb. Today, I correct the travesty of your birth." She sounded her war cry as the axe fell.

"...reu."

Power burst out of me, blowing her off her feet and me into the air. I gasped as Mireu's healing magic spread through every corner of my being—stronger than I ever felt before.

My spine knitted together. My insides healed. My cuts, gashes, and wounds sewn together. I dropped down, collapsing on the ground. The only trace that I was ever hurt was the rips in my dress.

I swept the courtyard. Almost everyone was on the ground, knocked off their feet by the shock waves. I tensed as they stirred.

"How—? Something's different."

"It's gone. The pain is gone."

"My scars."

"My leg."

"My hair," Maili whispered. Her wig lay at her knees. Jaw working, she couldn't get another word out as the horrific scar tissue on her head faded away, and the brilliant red hair that was always her best feature, grew anew from her scalp.

Ormr clapped their neck. Feeling nothing, they ripped their shirt, tearing half off, and gaped at what they saw. Not only were their new burns gone. The mangled scar on their arm that they showed me that first day of training—gone.

"No," I gritted, slowly turning around. "No!"

High Queen Kisandra kneeled on the ground, partially concealed by a horde of buzzing guards clamoring to know if she was okay. She didn't respond as shaking hands lifted off her mask.

My stomach heaved. She was beautiful.

Only a touch of wrinkles at her nape and the corner of her eyes hinted at her age. Full lips parted in wonder, not a snarl. Stunning aquamarine eyes blinked—both of them. Pushing back her cowl, the raven hair she gifted my father grew till it fell in soft waves past her shoulders.

"How?" She clapped and pinched her cheeks, patted her regrown nose, and yanked on her hair as if believing it not real. "I went to every healer. Every one. They all said it was impossible. I can't— I can't believe it." She laughed—a light, joyous sound.

My heart ripped in two. I wanted to kill the evil, rotted bitch. Instead, I granted Queen Kisandra her most desperate wish.

My attackers rose to their feet. They were new people, rid of aches, pains, scars, and all ailments. They picked up their weapons with renewed vigor.

"She's just sitting there," one said softly. "I think she's out of tricks."

I glared, but didn't speak. My bond with Mireu hadn't broken yet. Even so, there was nothing I could do. The type of water dragon she was gave her the ability to heal, and only heal. Her gorgeous scales covered my arms and legs. Claws tipped my fingers, and sharp canines forced themselves past my lips, but for all I knew, they were just for show. I could scratch one of my attackers and give him more healing magic. That wouldn't get me out of here.

It wouldn't kill High Queen Kisandra.

"Go for the head, and only the head," ordered the Watch commander. "Let's see her heal from that."

They converged on me.

"Stop."

No one was more shocked to hear that voice than me.

Queen Kisandra, the famed beauty of the southern kingdom, rose to her feet. "Don't kill it." She beheld me, then flicked away—disgust doing little to cheapen her radiance. "You have new orders. I want it captured and studied. General Roark was right"—she nodded over my shoulder—"we need to understand what it is, then harness its power for the good of the kingdom. After doing so, it dies."

I bared my teeth. For the good of the kingdom, my ass. Queen Kisandra just learned her most hated enemy had the power to keep her young, beautiful, and healthy for as long as I lived. Now, I was valuable to her.

"Forgive my short-sightedness, Ladon," she continued. "You remain a calm, guiding voice in these troubling times."

"Thank you, my high queen." Something akin to satisfaction laced his voice. "It is my honor to serve you and the five kingdoms."

I tensed as the guards closed in on me.

"But we can't trust it," a royal shouted. "It could be pretending to be helpless. We have to get away from it now."

"Calm, everyone," said the general. "If you'll permit me, High Queen, I've been watching her fight closely. Her attacks and Druk-like armor and wings mimic the dragons she stole. I suspect she discovered a trick the usurper never did, and has channeled so much of their magic, she can wield it like a Druk, without killing the dragon. Every dragon rider gaining the ability to do this will change everything. It'll turn the tide of the war in our favor."

"How do we capture it?"

The two of them spoke like I was a hissing wild animal who wandered inside.

"It appears she can only use this trick with each dragon once. I imagine it drains them terribly."

As if to mock me and illustrate his point, my bond with Mireu disappeared. I crouched on the ground—all human, and completely defenseless.

"She's gone through five now." His voice hardened. "There's only one dragon left."

Tizor's name whispered through the crowd. The guards advancing on me snapped back, putting a mountain of distance between us.

"Capturing her is out of the question, then," said one of the Renders. "She'll wipe us out in an instant channeling the power of a death dragon."

"She won't," the general barked over the growing clamor. "Because she still wants them. She wants *him*."

A hate-filled gaze left the queen to meet General Roark's eyes. Yes, that was definitely satisfaction in his voice. He positively beamed with it as he pressed the dagger to Claudius's chest.

"You know how valuable this aberrant is to me." Roark spoke to me. Only to me. "He is the rarest find, but I will plunge this dagger in his chest, losing him and my own son... to get you."

I knew this man to be many things. A liar wasn't one of them.

"You will not channel Tizor. You will not steal a drop of magic from anyone. Even a glimmer of a pale scale, and I kill him. Understood?"

Neck stiff, I forced a nod.

"Good." He shook Claudius. "You, freeze her. Aberrant Galen and Aberrant Ari, create a cage to transport her.

"Does that suit, my queen?"

"No," Ormr sliced in. "Grandmother, she has to die to break her hold over Kenna and Cadmus. How are we supposed to rule with dignity when the whole world believes we can't protect our own dragons—?"

"Silence. I will not be questioned."

Ormr quieted.

"Do it," Kisandra ordered the general. "Now."

I got to my feet, causing a ring of guards to level their swords.

"Do it."

"Do not move, girl." Roark tightened his grip on Claudius. "You tempt fate, and she doesn't like to be tested."

"No," I said clearly. "I test you. Go ahead and kill him. Kill Dominic, Keely, and Poet too. I won't stop you."

Roark's expression froze between rage and confusion. "Excuse me?"

"This will never stop—"

"Silence, Druk's spawn," Kisandra snapped.

"You'll never free them," I continued. "Dominic and my friends will stay captive and be used against me until I die. Two minutes after, you'll kill them too."

"I told you to be silent! You do not, nor will you ever have permission to speak in my presence."

"Shut the fuck up, you hateful, old piece of shit. It's you who doesn't have permission to speak to me."

Everything stopped.

Maili's eyes bugged. The guards' sword tips jerked in surprise, and Queen Kisandra did not look beautiful then—standing there gaping like a fish.

"You— How dare— You can't—"

I turned my back on her sputtering. "Go on, Roark. Kill your own son for everyone to see. It's past time everyone saw you for the kin-slaying monster you are."

"Face me," Kisandra shrieked in the background. "Foul, wretched thing! Look at me!"

Roark's eyes were narrowed to slits. He paid her even less mind. "I take no pleasure in this. It's my duty to protect the five kingdoms. No duty is without sacrifice."

"Don't convince me. Just go on." I looked him dead on. "Kill them."

He looked from Claudius, to Dominic, to the watching crowd, and back to me. "What game is this!"

"—at me. Face me!"

"Fine," I said. "If you won't do it, I will."

Snapping around, I ran at Queen Kisandra—who let herself get a fraction too close to scream at me.

Watchers lunged at me—weapons raised.

"Tizor!"

Their blades broke on pale scales. Bony wings stretched over my head, made up of translucent skin that looked fragile to the touch. I whipped them back, striking the running guards and scrambling royals in my way.

They were dead before they hit the ground.

"Stay back!" Kisandra whipped her hand around, circling the air.

Stone became quicksand beneath my feet, sucking me down and trapping me.

Finally.

I sunk deep in the moving earth, and drew in the living magic until my body was fit to bursting. Bringing my fists together, I snapped them apart. All over the courtyard cries of shock and elation sounded. Gold melted to vapor. Manacles banged on the ground.

The freed mages didn't waste a minute.

A giant purple eagle appeared in the sky. Screeching, it swooped down low, scattering royals and nobles in every direction. No less than a dozen unique mages hopped on its back. They were gone and soaring away before Ormr's "No! Stop them!" hit the air.

Chaos broke out. Guards, Renders, and Riders couldn't decide if their duty was to protect the queen, kill me, capture me, or stop the escaping unique mages. It didn't help that Maili, Ormr, and Queen Kisandra were shouting for them to do all four.

"Protect me! Protect your queen!"

"Kill her!" Vines shot out of the cracks in the stone and encased my wrists, legs, middle, and throat. "Stop her before she attacks."

Maili's roots withered and died on my skin and scales.

"No one leaves," Ormr bellowed. "I order you to stay by royal decree—"

A blast of blue smoke zipped through the crowd and hit them over the face. Ormr blew off their feet and crumpled on the ground, tangling in their cloak.

"Ormr!"

Maili ran to her twin. Throwing off the cloak, she lurched back, choking on a scream.

A small, cherubic face blinked back at her. Rosy cheeks, tiny nose, bouncy curls. Where Ormr once sat was now a small child no more than ten years.

"Who did this?" she screeched. "Change them back. Change them back now or you'll die the most gruesome death I can think of!" Maili strained to see through the surge of bodies and fighting. "By order of your queen, change them—"

Blue smoke came from behind, narrowing fast on her. I saw no reason to sound a warning.

It smacked her over her newly healed head. In an instant, a small, wide-eyed child Maili trembled next to Ormr. She burst into tears.

The sight of my siblings turned into children was the least important thing to me. I searched for General Roark and found him where I left him—purple-faced, shouting, and his dagger trained. But Claudius was not where I left him.

He whipped and spun on the platform, freezing every person and bit of magic that dared to come for him. Next to Poet, General Roark stood trapped in time and locked in the instant of his most pathetic moment—threatening to kill four innocent people, one of them his own son, all so he could trap a young woman and steal her power for himself.

"Claudius," I shouted over the din. "You said you could save them. Was that true!"

"Yes! But not here in the middle of this," he called, striking a Render still. "We have to get somewhere safe, and I'm not going without my son!"

"Don't worry about your son. I saved him first."

"What does that—?"

Roars pierced the noise, shaking the castle to its foundation. Reyna, Mireu, Cadmus, Suoh, and Kenna crested the horizon with my younglings on their backs. Tizor winged close behind, carrying Scartha, Sarcany, and Ur.

Of course the first thing I did was free them and send a desperate command through the bonds to save the children. If I only had precious moments before our bonds closed indefinitely, I had to put right what I'd done wrong. A dragon wouldn't think like that, but the real Ainsley—who knew no child deserved to grow up in an orphanage away from the parents who loved them—she knew what she needed to do.

"Get out of here." I summoned all the living magic I had left, and poured into the stone and wood beneath their feet. Dozens of voices shouted out as they were lifted into the air—Claudius, Poet, Dominic, and Keely along with them, all following after my dragons. "Save them!"

I slowly turned, narrowing on one face. "I have unfinished business."

Her forces had organized themselves into a semblance of order. The riders shouted out for the dragons they sent away to protect them from me. They called on them—eager to give chase and pursue the escaping unique mages. The Watchers formed a protective circle around Queen Kisandra and the child rulers, while the Renders whisked them off... to the new growing black orb, ready and waiting to send them far away. The portal mage had returned.

"You're not getting away from me. Kisandra Boreen!" She snapped around, eyes finding mine. "You die today."

Her face hardened even as Renders grabbed her under the arms, carrying her faster away. "I will die, but not at your filthy, disgusting hands. You wait, beast. I'll soon have you in a cage."

I ran at her. Tipping my wings, I caught the air, and tucked them in. I shot into the wall of guards, plowing through like a canon blast—killing all who dared stand in my way.

Steel sharpened to sword tips appeared before me. I pulled up sharply, narrowly escaping death by a thousand impalements. Calthoon was waiting. The next time I crossed the veil, he'd make it my last.

"What are you doing?" Kisandra slapped one of the Renders across the face. "I said to capture it, not kill it!" She shoved him away. "Incompetence. I will do this myself."

Kisandra threw off her royal cape. It swerved before hitting the ground, and came straight for me. I tried to dodge but was too late. It covered my face, wrapped around my arms, and tangled with my wings.

I dropped out of the sky.

Striking the ground, I swallowed the pain and fought back, tearing the cursed thing to shreds. I threw it off. "Is that it, O High Queen? Pathetic!"

Inexplicably, she smiled. "Stupid, ignorant beast. That was just the distraction."

The queen flicked over my shoulder. I followed her line of sight. A shout sprung to my lips.

A piece of metal had taken flight, soaring straight for Claudius on literal wings.

"Claudius!"

It struck him over the forehead, knocking him off the stone carrying him away. The time mage hit the ground—out cold.

"No!"

Dominic, Keely, and Poet came to life.

I watched trapped and horrified as the last two months rushed back to them in a blink. They fell—gasping, choking, clutching their throats as they died of thirst.

"Dominic!" I cried all too late.

He slumped over—the emaciated husk of the man I loved.

"There." Kisandra's triumph pierced my grief. She turned her back on me, heading for the portal. "Grab it while it's weeping over its lover's corpse. And bring me the time mage too. He serves for the good of my kingdom, or he dies."

I whipped back and forth between Kisandra's retreat, and my lover and friends. It was a miracle my bond with Tizor lasted this long. Right then, I brimmed with the power to kill her with one brush of a wing. If she got away now, I may never get another chance to make her pay for what she did to my family.

"Dominic..."

Kisandra's laugh grated on the wind. A dragon wouldn't question. Potential mates were around every boulder. A chance for vengeance wasn't. The choice for them was clear.

"But I'm not a dragon."

I sprung up, flying fast to Dominic as Kisandra and her child heirs disappeared.

I didn't know how much time I had. I may already be too late, but I would hang everything on this last hope. I was the child of vengeance and fury. The power of a goddess flowed through my veins, gifted to me the day

I defied impossibility and demanded to be born. But above all of that... I was a thief.

I fell deep into the well of my power, drowning in the pain I pushed out. Rosaleen, Colm, Ilemka, Kwame, Silvia, Sister Aven, my brothers, my sisters, Poet, Keely, and Dominic. I demanded to be born because this was my destiny. To put right what is wrong in defiance of queens, generals, laws, reality, and the gods themselves.

Falling deeper than I was ever meant to go, I found the part of my soul that was him, and ripped it free.

"Calthoon!"

I cloaked myself in his power as my last bond broke, severing my tie with Tizor for good. Screaming, I tore through the fabric of the realm—reborn. Remade. Renewed.

As a goddess of the veil.

Chapter Seven

The world abandoned me, leaving me alone at the edge of a river.

Where am I?

I would never get an answer to that. Everything around me was gray and shifting. I sat in the middle of a swirling thunderstorm—clouds whipped past angry, hungry, and alive.

Who am I?

I wasn't to know that either. The reflection of a strange and terrible woman gazed back at me.

Skeletal, black bones shaped like wings rose over my back. How could they fly when they didn't look like they ever lived?

I said the same of the woman. Pale, sallow skin stretched over gaunt cheeks. Ebony, iris-less eyes captured me, holding an abyss within its pools that no one was meant to see.

I wasn't wearing clothes. Not in a real sense. The same swirling gray clouds cloaked my body—fine, delicate wisps that covered little and revealed all.

"Ainsley!"

I whipped around. Standing thirty feet from me at the edge of a cliff, were Keely, Poet, and Dominic.

"Dominic," I breathed.

He reached for me, and fell.

"No!"

The cliff edge crumbled, pitching my friends and my Dominic into the unknown.

I shot into the air. I didn't think or care how the bones flapping on my back were carrying me. I dove over the cliff.

"Ainsley, help!"

"Where are we?" Poet tumbled head over feet. "What is this place!"

We were falling into nothing. Just more spinning, wispy thunderclouds and a cliff that wasn't there anymore. I didn't know which way was up. I wasn't certain we were still falling.

"Leave," Dominic shouted. He reached for me even as he sent me away. "You shouldn't be here! You have to go. Now!"

"I'm not going anywhere with—without... you..."

A being broke through the smoke, stopping the breath in my lungs. Endless shadow eyes, a cloak of smoke and whispers, skeletal face, and bloodless lips. Whatever creature I had become, this was my creator.

Jaw cracking, he roared a terrible, soundless cry that struck my body stiff with fear. *Me.* This creature— This *god* wanted me.

His hand reached through the gloom, opening his palm to catch Keely, Poet, and Dominic. Somehow I knew if he caught them, I'd never see my love and friends again.

My impossible wings beat faster, struggling to close the distance. "Keely," I cried. "Use your threads. Wrap around the guys and then me."

"I can't! I've been trying." She kicked and clawed the air. "My magic doesn't work here!"

Of course it couldn't be so simple. We were beyond our realm, in the one the other gods themselves never wanted to go. Calthoon was in control here, and he had no reason to make it easy for us to leave.

They fell so far away from me, and closer to him. This couldn't happen. I didn't come so far to lose them now. Bellowing, I stopped flying and fell.

Tucking my wings and limbs in, I was a lance cutting through the smoke, shooting past a spinning Poet, I fell on Calthoon's palm. His fingers closed around me, pulling back from Dominic and the others to catch me. I was the desired prize.

Moving fast, I tucked, rolled, and propelled through his fingers—coming up beneath my friends. I grabbed Poet and Keely around the waists. Dominic bounced off me, encircled my middle, and tore away.

"No!"

Calthoon had him by the leg, dragging him down where I couldn't follow.

"It's okay, Ainsley." As Calthoon closed around him, he smiled. "I love you. I'm happy I got to see you one more time. You're still my perfect, sadistic beauty."

"Stop it!" I veered around, chasing after him. "Stop saying bye to me. Our story ends when I say it does."

He chuckled. "Pretty sure that's what got us in trouble the first time."

Dominic had no idea.

"Ainsley, who the fuck is that?" Keely cried.

"Someone who didn't learn the first time." I winged faster. "I didn't let you have him then, Calthoon. I won't let you have him now. Grab him!"

Poet and Keely grabbed Dominic's shoulders, wresting him free as I flapped hard, fighting to break us all away.

"Give him back! Give him—!"

Calthoon's gaze fixed on mine, trapping the shout in my throat.

"*I know you now, child of vengeance. You fight and delay the inevitable.*"

Dominic slipped through his grip... or did he let him go?

"*Death will come for you.*" Calthoon sank into the mist.

I fell hard and fast—fear a lodestone on my back.

"*It comes for you all.*"

***

Sunlight stunned me.

"Ainsley, look out!"

My vision cleared on a rapidly approaching pillar. I swerved, and their weight dragged me down farther than I intended. The impossible wings that flew so easily in Calthoon's realm were not meant for this place. They were weakening, and a crowd of Watchers, Renders, and Riders beginning to mount their summoned dragons, were waiting for me.

I whipped around, searching for—

"There!"

Three men carried Claudius, dragging his hapless body to the portal. One of them General Roark.

"Keely, you have to use your threads and grab that man. They can't have him. Of all the unique mages, they can't have him."

Keely was already moving before I finished. Dozens, or hundreds, or more threads than I could count burst from her fingertips. Roark bellowed as Claudius suddenly tore from his grip. He threw up his hands. I knew what was coming next.

I veered sharply up, snatching Claudius out of the way as half a dozen of the general's own people evaporated into dust.

We flew high above the estate, his echoing shouts chasing fast behind.

"Princess, put us down," Dominic called. "We're too heavy."

"No, we have to get farther away. Riders are mounting their dragons... to chase after us... as we speak." My lungs screamed for their effort. "Only when you're safe."

"If we have to fight, then we'll fight!" Dominic dangled over the trees, twisting in Poet's and Keely's grip. Their bulged veins and purpling faces proved how hard they were trying to hold on. "Put us down."

"Only you can argue with me when I'm saving your life!"

"Only as much as you argue with me when I'm saving yours."

"I'm not letting you die!" Tears stung my eyes. "Not this time. Not you."

"I don't need to be protected, Princess."

"Your track record with death says you do."

"Can you two have this lovers' spat when there aren't three riders on our tail!" Poet sliced in.

I twisted to see over my shoulder. Poet was wrong. There weren't three riders on our tail. There were four—six—seven riders and more coming after us every second. They weren't worried about me stealing their dragons anymore. Or maybe they were. They just cared what Queen Kisandra would do to them more.

"We're sinking closer to the trees," Keely said. "We are too heavy. How long can you keep this up?"

"Not long," I admitted. "This form wasn't made for this realm. I don't know how long—"

My wings vanished.

"Ahhhh!"

We plummeted to the ground. Blasts of fire, water, and earth blew through the spot we were in. My terrible timing saved our lives only to die seconds later with a sudden reacquaintance with the ground. Calthoon said it well.

Death always finds us in the end.

We plunged into a tree. Branches beat and tore at me, slowing my fall and punishing me for the trouble. I cried out as vicious limbs raked my back—opening bleeding wounds to match the bare remains of my wedding dress.

Thud. Thud. Thud. Thud. Thud.

We crumpled on the unforgiving earth, groaning.

"Fuck's sake..." Poet tried to stand and promptly gave up. "That was the worst rescue ever."

I almost laughed. It was funny, if only it wasn't so true. Riders were circling overhead. The rest of the general's forces were right behind. Something in my right leg had snapped.

We were done for.

"Dominic..." I arm-crawled over to him. My love was flat on his back, bleeding from a dozen cuts on his face. He squinted up at me. "We have to fight."

"Okay." He didn't sound like he fully understood what was happening. "But we can't... kill the dragons. We'll become enemies of dragonkin too."

He didn't have to tell me. Four months as a dragon, I knew how hard they held on to a grudge.

"Where are they?"

"They fell around there," someone shouted back. "Septima, rip the trees out of the earth. Those rats can't hide."

"Stand." Keely picked me up under the arms. She held me tight though I leaned heavily on her. "We're not dying on our backs. We're not killing our fellow riders either. They don't know who the real enemies are, and no one will believe it's not us if we become murderers."

"How did we even get here?" Poet staggered to his feet. He stumbled over to help Dominic. "The last thing I remember is finally escaping that fucking cell. I breathed air for the first time in two months, then everything stopped. Felt like I watched my life pass me by, and I couldn't do anything about it."

I glanced over at Claudius, who was beginning to stir. I didn't blame him for the things he'd done while his son was missing and those manacles were around his neck. I hoped the others didn't either.

Dragon legs broke through the trees, flattening them with their girth. They'd found us all too soon. Riders hopped off their backs, coming from every direction.

"What about Libelle, Valor, and Calliope?" I asked.

No one looked at me.

"What? What is it? We need help. Summon your dragons."

"I can't, Ainsley," Dominic said. "I felt it after we came from... that place. My bond with Libelle is broken."

"As is mine with Valor."

"Me too."

"Oh no," I breathed, eyes squeezing shut. "The bond between rider and dragon breaks when one of you dies. And, that's what you did. I'm so s—"

"Don't apologize," Keely sliced in. She threw me a furious look. "You saved our lives. Don't ever apologize for it. Calliope chose me once. She'll do it again. That's if we live past the day, of course."

Dominic stepped forward. Fireballs danced in the air. "We will."

Poet unleashed his fire whip. Keely's threads spooled from her fingertips. I reached down into my bonds, and found nothing.

The bonds were closed. Their voices were gone from my head. I dared not even summon them because they were protecting the children, and wherever they came from would reveal their location.

I was useless in this fight. Again.

"Get ready," Dominic rasped. "I'll strike the ground at their feet to keep them back. Keely, you do the same. Trip up as many as you can. Poet—"

"Or."

I jerked around, landing on an unfamiliar face.

She waved from across the bush, standing under another oak tree. I recognized the robe she wore as one of the captured unique mages.

"You can just come with us."

More people stepped out from behind the tree. Junia, Osman, and other freed mages.

"That would be nice, whoever you are," Poet said, "but we're in the middle of fending off an attack."

"No, you're not."

"We—"

A rider ran up on us, and kept going, skirting around our tree. "This way," she called. "They must've run in this direction."

"They can't see or hear you." Again, she gestured for us to come over. "I'm Akasha. A sensory mage. And you freed me from the poisonous queen bitch who put me in chains. You freed us all." She smiled. "Did you think we'd run away and abandon you after what you did for us?"

"I…" I stared at the army of riders walking right past us. "I wouldn't have blamed you if you did."

"Really?" She shook her head. "Seems the children were right. Their version of you is the correct one." She came over to help Claudius up. "We're a few miles that way. Many of the children are our children, so we followed after your dragons. But they won't leave, and they're growling at everyone who tries to take one of the kids away. We think they're waiting for you."

I said nothing as we followed the mages through the trees. I didn't know what to say. I'd never been more humiliated and embarrassed in my life.

I hung my head, lips trembling. I was no one's hero.

Dominic looked across at me. "Ainsley, your leg."

"It's fine," I whispered. "My speed healing will take care of it soon enough."

He came over and scooped me up, ignoring my protests. "I said I'm fine."

"You did say that. Your expression says something else." Holding me tight, he fell back, letting the others get ahead. "What's wrong?"

I looked away, lips pressed tight.

"Can I guess?" he asked softly. "You're blaming yourself for things that aren't your fault."

"No. I'm blaming myself for things that *are* my fault." My fists balled. "It was me, Dom. I was the unique mage Lemomi was speaking about all those months ago. I burned down Golden City, then went on a murderous rampage through the five kingdoms.

"I lost all sense of myself and thought I was a dragon. A *dragon*! Only in my lucid moments did I remember that I love and needed to find you. Those moments were few and far between." I tossed my head. "You suffered because of me. You—you were tortured and killed because of me. And my family... Rosaleen..."

"Ainsley." A soft kiss pressed against my forehead. "None of that was you. You can't possibly think I blame you for falling under the hold of your dragons. It's me you should blame for getting captured. You needed me and I was fucking around in a prison cell, playing the role of a statue. I let you down."

"How can you say that?" I cried, facing him. "You don't know what's happened. You don't know what I've done—"

"I do." Even disheveled and dirt-streaked, Dominic was the most handsome man I'd ever lay eyes on. "I heard and saw every second of the last four months. I know what my father tried to do to you, and why. I watched the cold and calculating bastard while he spun praises and promises in Queen Kisandra's ear, and plotted his retaking of the throne behind her back.

"You told me of the fortune-teller's prediction, and I didn't listen to you. I've known Maili and Ormr for years, but I didn't see what they were. After you told me the truth of your friend and the children from the orphanage, I should've had them moved somewhere safe.

"I didn't because I thought my father would have no reason to harm them after you abdicated." His jaw clenched hard, eyes shining. "I let you down, Ainsley. I promised in that cabin that I would protect you... and all I've done since is fail you."

Words deserted me. What could I say against all those blatant untruths? It was me who failed. Me who wandered around like a snarling, growling lunatic for months when I had the power to free him and my friends the whole time.

"It wasn't you who swore to give Rosaleen, the children, and Sister Aven a better life," I whispered. "The only broken promise is mine. I was stupid, Dominic. I missed all the signs. Maili and Ormr went out of their way to become my friends after Drake announced I was the princess. I wanted my amazing new life as a dragon rider so badly, I didn't question why two random nobles gave a shit about me.

"I made it easy for them to learn all they needed to destroy m-me." My voice cracked. "I handed them everyone I loved on a silver platter."

"So kill them."

I started. "Excuse me?"

"That's what you want to do, isn't it? That's what you spent the last four months doing." His voice was light. Impossible to read. "I assume there's a brutal and extra-cruel reason that you saved Ormr, Maili, my father, and the queen for last. I'm also sure the reason is going to make me love you more.

"So let's do it, Ainsley, because the dragons had one thing right. Everyone who had a part in the deaths of those poor, innocent children deserves what they have coming to them. We'll take away all they love too, then we'll send them screaming into Calthoon's grip."

"I..." My head spun. "There was a reason. I wanted them to be scared. I wanted them to surround themselves with more and more guards, dig deeper and deeper holes to hide in, and pass every law they could think of to protect themselves... and then find out that none of it was enough.

"Many people don't know that dragons like to play with their food."

He growled. "See? I knew it would make me love you more."

"How can you say that?" I cried. "How am I not disgusting to you? I was a monster, Dominic. A crazed murderer hell-bent on revenge. Children cried when they saw me coming."

"Then they stopped when you took out the real monsters and left them unharmed. If you remember what you did, then you remember who you did it to. Did a single one of them not deserve it?"

I wanted to say they didn't, but it wouldn't come out. "Murderers," I croaked. "Tyrants, rapists, people sellers, and child abusers. Everyone who did terrible things to the people I love and got away with it because they were rich and noble. All of them, Dominic. I had a list."

He nodded sharp. "You know who the real monster is, Ainsley, and so do they." He glanced at the unique mages. "There's a reason they're following you."

"They'll be disappointed," I said, tone dull. "All I do is get people killed."

Dominic gazed at me for a long beat. "That isn't true, my love, but I understand you can't hear that right now."

My chest squeezed.

"You're going to feel guilty until you don't. You'll take on the responsibility of their deaths until you can accept it isn't yours, and you'll despise me just a little bit every time I refuse to let you sink into self-hatred. I know because it's what I felt every day carrying the deaths of my siblings on my shoulders. I wasn't worthy of anything good, but you fucking refused to stop making me love you.

"You insist on not seeing me as the twisted, ruined piece of shit I am—"

"Don't talk about yourself like that! That was your father, not you."

The corner of his mouth quirked up. "See?"

My face warmed, in no small part because a tiny part of me did despise him in that moment. I wasn't interested in understanding the point he was making.

"We'll get through this together. I promise." He kissed me soft and sweet. "I won't leave you behind."

I turned away. I wouldn't respond to his words. I didn't respond to his kiss.

The dragons had many things right. The crushing pain breaking my chest open wasn't useful unless it was fuel for the power needed to avenge the people I loved. I wasn't doing that then, so I refused to feel the pain.

Climbing out of Dominic's hold, I shoved it down—hard. Weeping and wailing wouldn't bring Rosaleen, Sister Aven, or the children back. But fulfilling my destiny would give them peace in the next realm.

"There's more you need to know," I said. "The general had some things right. Many more wrong. But because of everything that's happened, I discovered the truth of myself."

I told Dominic everything Kai revealed to me. There wasn't a version of events where I kept the truth to myself. We traded lies and secrets for love and honesty a long time ago.

"I'm sorry, Dom." I hooked my pinky through his. "I did steal Reyna from you. She was in the wrong place at the wrong time, and all this set into motion."

Grinding to a halt, Dominic snagged my hand and tugged me yelping to his chest. "She was in the *right* place at the *right* time, Ainsley. Fucking hell. You told me that she saved you, but you didn't tell me from what." He tipped my chin. "I understand. If you had told me that first day when I declared I was going to kill you, I would've taken it back and given you both my blessing.

"Thankfully, Reyna is wiser than me and did the right thing. Actually..." His expression changed. "She did more."

"What do you mean?"

"Think about it, Ainsley. Reyna happened to be flying over your head at the exact moment you needed her. On the day she flew in from Ghidorah to meet me after I moved into the castle. Only a few moons after your twentieth year when you were old enough to start dragon rider training." Sunlight caught his locks as he tipped his head back, defying their obsidian black and tingeing his tips with gold.

"All of this. Meeting you, hating you, falling for you, loving you. Fate," he whispered. "You and I were meant to be."

I blushed stupidly. All the time we spent together. All the confessions of love that passed from our lips. I still lit up like a fireworks mage when he spoke to me like that. "Don't be sweet to me right now."

"I'll be sweet to you whenever I fucking want."

I heaved a sigh, covering the smile that tried to poke out. "Remember what you said in the cabin? That you wanted to be a writer, not a ruler. But the only way to honor your siblings' memory was to take control of the kingdom away from your father."

"Yes," he said slowly. "Why?"

Taking a deep breath, I let it out. "We can't speak of how wonderful it was that we met and fell in love... and ignore that there was a cost. If Reyna hadn't chosen me that day, I never would've entered dragon training with a desperate lie about being Queen Kisandra's descendant. A lie that turned out to be all too true."

"What are you saying?"

I'd gotten this far. I had to get the rest out. "I'm saying we can't skip around happy and in love, singing of our good fortune, while everyone I love is dust on the wind. At least not now." I stepped back. "I'm a weapon of vengeance and fury. The people I should've saved and ones waiting to be saved need me to be that now. But those two emotions are the last things I feel when I'm with you."

Dominic went very still. "Are you telling me to leave?"

"What?" I growled. "No! You're mine."

His brows blew up, grin returning. "I am, am I?"

"I— No— Yes—" I blew out a sigh. "That wasn't supposed to come out that way. Even with the bonds closed, I can't have six dragons in my head and go unscathed. Their instincts will still bleed through, but I won't forget who I am, or what I have to do." I met his eyes. "You can't think of your dreams until you've honored your siblings' memory and saved Adalinda from your father. It's the same for me now, Dominic.

"I can't be your happy and merry wife when everyone I know was murdered on our wedding day. I'm sorry, but we have to break up."

Silence stretched between us, deepened by the fading voices of the group leaving us.

I reached for his hand, then stopped. "Say something, please."

"I don't know what to say." He slipped his hand in mine—firm and sure. "I understand. No one but me could understand more, but... I want to marry you, Ainsley. I want to go on a grand honeymoon, bending you over to and from every major city in the land."

A soft laugh escaped me.

"I want to sing to our growing babe in your belly, and fly side by side through the skies until I cross to the other side. I see that life so clearly, and I'm so fucking tired of never being happy because twenty years ago, my mother spawned with a monster."

Tears spilled down my cheeks.

"But..." He slumped, that very happiness going out of him. "I understand."

"I'm sorry," I rasped. "I know it's not enough, but I truly am."

"What are we now?"

"For now we're Dominic." I pointed at him. "Ainsley." I turned my finger back on me. "When it's over, and I've freed the gods, avenged my family, and we've taken control of the kingdom away from House Boreen and House Roark, then we can be Dominic and Ainsley again."

"No. Then we'll be husband and wife."

"I don't know how long this will all take," I whispered. "But I do know it's not fair to ask you to wait. When I say we're broken up, I mean broken up. No kissing, no sex, nothing that friends wouldn't do."

His expression didn't change.

"I need you to understand that, Dom." I probed him for anger. Hurt. Something. "Do you?"

He tipped his head. "I understand that we're on a break until we've avenged your family and saved the kingdom. Nothing about that I don't understand."

"Dom, I'm not trying to downplay this as a break. It's a *breakup*."

Still, his face was relaxed. "Do you want to be with me when it's all over?"

"Dom—"

"Do you?"

The reply pulled out of me. "Yes," I whispered.

"Then, it's not a breakup. It's a break. I can handle that." His fingers laced through mine. "I can wait."

I didn't have the strength to correct him. It took everything in me to say the words in the first place. I didn't want to say them again.

We gazed at each other for too long, then started walking—for lack of anything else to do.

"Should we clarify what it means to be on a break? Since I remain yours." Teasing laced his tone.

"That's a good idea," I told the forest floor.

"Can we talk?"

"Always. About everything."

"Can I...?" Fingers curled through mine. "Hold your hand?"

It was ridiculous that after all the dirty, imaginative things we'd done to each other, simple hand-holding lit my face on fire. "Sometimes. If the situation calls for it."

"I'll makes sure it does often."

He's not going to make this easy. Although, when had he ever?

"Can we kiss on the cheek? Forehead?"

"Better that we don't. Friends don't go around putting their lips on each other."

"Okay, but will you consider something important?"

I tipped my head up to him. "Consider what?"

"That I really want to kiss you anyway."

A grin tugged at my lips. "That is very important, but if we cross all those lines, it'll be no different than it was before. I don't want to feel guilty every time we kiss."

"You don't have to," he cried, coming out in front of me. "My father and the queen are responsible for what happened, not you. Your family wouldn't want you to blame yourself."

"I am to blame. I wanted a new and better life so badly, I didn't protect them. A no-name bastard peasant who wanted to be queen. What a laugh!"

"Ainsley—"

"No, Dominic, because I know you realized the same thing I did. You're too smart not to. I can't be a weapon of vengeance without someone to avenge. This was *supposed to happen*. Every year that Druk attacked me, and then left saying I still wasn't ready. He was testing me! He was trying to provoke me into using my power, but I couldn't because I wasn't filled with hate, anger, or vengeance. Why would I be when I had a loving borrowed mother, the best brothers and sisters, and the truest friend I could ever ask for?

"It's just like Zalina and Gaius Daoud. Zalina didn't need Titana's power until Kisandra slaughtered her family. Gaius didn't call upon her until he lost his wife and daughter. This is what everyone's been fucking waiting for," I shrieked, throwing out my hands. "For me to lose them and finally be *ready*. So don't tell me I'm not to blame when fate herself demanded they die so I could be whatever the fuck I am."

I stomped off.

Heavy footfalls ran after me. I felt his hand take mine.

"Now is not the time to hold hands," I snapped.

"Then let go."

I huffed, jaw tight... but I didn't let go. After a beat, I let out a breath. "I'm sorry. I don't know why I keep yelling at you. Many are to blame, but none of them are you."

"It's all right, Ainsley. Yell at me. Scream, rage, and hate-fuck me. If I can take you breaking every bone in my body and negotiating our marriage contract under a knife's edge, I can handle a little misfired anger."

I almost cried. Dominic Roark was a good man. The best man I knew. But he couldn't know my greatest fear. He couldn't know his wonderfulness was exactly why I wouldn't bend.

We were broken up. It was just how it had to be.

"Rules," I continued. "We were talking about rules."

"Okay. Can I tell you I love you?"

I softened. "Only if you mean it."

He bumped my shoulder. "Are you going to have other lovers?"

"What? Why the hell would I do that?"

Dominic smirked. "Correct answer. I'd hate to leave a trail of burned corpses in your wake."

My lips peeled back from my teeth. "Are you—?"

"No."

"Correct answer," I forced through gritted teeth. "I wouldn't hate leaving a trail of bodies in your wake."

"Understood." He was entirely too amused over the unwelcome picture he put in my head of him with another woman. I couldn't blame the dragons for this. The possessiveness over Dominic Roark was all mine.

"Since you brought up lovers," I said, "we should talk about sex. We can't do it, Dominic. There also won't be any hate-fucking. Nothing I'd do with you could be hateful."

Figures and voices filtered through the trees. We were getting close to camp.

"I hear you, but can I give you another vitally important thing to consider?"

I bumped him back. "I know what it is. I want to." Desire stirred in my lower belly. "I really, really, really want to. But we can't. Friends definitely don't have sex."

"Okay."

"Okay?" I frowned. "That's it? You're agreeing just like that?"

"I am. Why argue? This vow of abstinence won't last three days."

My brows blew up my forehead. "I beg your pardon?"

"You can't resist me, Princess." Pulling ahead, he walked backwards, winking at me. "That's always been true, and it'll always be true. You could've dreamed of wealth, land, good health, or fame, but when Dervin looked in your heart, all you wanted in this life was to have your way with me."

"That's not— You're taking that—"

"This rule wouldn't last till the end of this sentence if other people weren't around. So no," he breezed, "I won't fight you, Princess. I'll just wait until ten seconds after we're alone when you break it yourself."

"Arrogant, self-assured, son of a dragon," I muttered at his back, watching him go off to join Keely and Poet. Despite his lack of faith in my self-control, I was more than capable of keeping my hands to myself.

My gaze drifted down to his backside. Was it firmer and shapelier than I remembered? There was really only one way to be certain, and four moons is such a long time. Soft mounds topped with hardening pebbles inside my breastband, imagining all the things Dominic had been waiting months to do to me.

I heated beneath my scales. Crouching low, my wings unfurled from my back in preparation of the mating dance—

I roughly shook my head, scrambling back up on my feet. I was out of the hive mind, and they weren't shouting in my head anymore, but their presence was still felt.

Slapping my cheeks, I grabbed hold of myself and walked into camp. Ten children broke off and ran to me.

"Shaya! Shaya!"

They were all over me—hugging, talking, squeezing, and grabbing my hands.

"Shaya." Little Mira wiggled through the pack and threw her arms around my knees. She trembled, the fear not yet leaving her. "You're back."

"Of course I'm back." I stroked her hair. A smile real and genuine beamed in the kids' eyes. "I would never leave you alone."

"Are we going home now, Shaya?"

"Yeah, let's go home." Orion spoke up from within Claudius's hold. The man was hugging the mess out of him. "I want to show Daddy my new room."

I made to answer, then looked up. All eyes were on me.

"No," I said clearly. "We can't go home. The people who found us would look for us there. They'll never stop looking."

"Then what do we do?" asked one of the unique mages. "I can't go home either. The Ghidorian Watchers posted a reward for turning in unique mages. People I've known my whole life gave me up."

"Yes."

"Me too."

"We can't go back."

"But you," Akasha said. "You're amazing. Your power is like nothing no one has ever seen. You'll protect us. You'll free us if the queen's guards come for us again."

I bit my lip hard, flicking to my dragons. They each took a post encircling the small meadow, providing more protection than I could. How do I tell these people that the incredible creature that freed them and returned the targets to their foreheads, was back to being a magicless nobody?

I raised my chin. "You don't just want protection. You want somewhere that you're safe. Where your children are safe, and you won't have to look over your shoulders. Right now, that place doesn't exist in Adalinda."

"What are you saying?" Keely spoke up. "That we can never go home?"

"I'm saying that I know a place where we can go where no one is going to hurt you, enslave you, or turn you over to the guards." My gaze drifted to Reyna. She was already snarling. "But you're not going to like it."

"Why?"

"Because we're crossing the Dark Border."

The blowback was immediate.

"No way."

"Are you insane?"

"They'll slaughter us the second we step a toe across!"

"And what do you think General Roark and Queen Kisandra will do?" I untangled from the children. "You know the new laws better than I. Either you're a slave to the kingdom, or you die."

"Because of you," someone blurted. "They passed those laws because of you."

"They passed those laws because General Roark had been waiting for his chance to use your power for his benefit, and the fear and paranoia he spread about how dangerous I am gave him the chance. You're vital to his plans, and Junia can tell you that herself."

Dozens of pairs of eyes flew to her. Pale and stiff, she nodded.

"Look, I'm not going to force you," I said. "You can make your own choices. But I am crossing that border, and joining forces with the only powerful group of people who want General Roark dead, and Queen Kisandra dethroned as much as I do."

"That's not all they want," Osman said. "There's the little fact that they also desire to slaughter all the dragons."

"I'd never let that happen. The killing of dragons stops now."

"Why are you talking like it's up to you!"

I met Dominic's gaze and a silent conversation passed between us.

Osman wasn't at the battle of Golden City, and it appeared word hadn't spread of what I'd done.

"You're asking to protect you," I finally said. "I will. I promise you that here and now, but either you trust me, or you don't. I'm crossing the border. The choice to follow me is yours."

With that, I marched on—leaving silence in my wake.

***

I made it all of twenty feet.

"I won't let anything happen to you."

Growls, snaps, and roars were their reply.

"I know the very existence of Druks is abhorrent to you, but there's nowhere else for us to go."

Reyna bit the air over my head. I didn't need her voice in my mind for her to make her point clear.

"I don't have all the answers yet," I said. "The only person who can give them to me is my mother. If she's alive. I have to find out."

Reyna turned her back on me, sticking her haunches in my face. That was the dragon equivalent of fuck you.

One after the other, Mireu, Cadmus, and Kenna did the same. Suoh and Tizor didn't bother because they were shading themselves and the hatchlings under the copse of trees. They weren't paying this conversation any mind. They weren't going anywhere near the Dark Border.

"You have to come with me. We can't be separated."

None of them moved.

I clenched my teeth, stifling a scream. I understood. I truly did. They were connected to the dragons when their hearts were cut out of their chests and consumed. They felt their fear, pain, and rage. Something like that couldn't be forgiven. But the seven of us roamed the five kingdoms for months, spreading no small amount of fear ourselves.

My dragons were known to all, and they were wanted by their original bondeds. More cages and experiments were in their futures if they were caught again.

A thought occurred to me.

"Nada," I said at Reyna's back. "Your nestmate. She lives somewhere across the Dark Border. Wherever she is, she must be safe. Will you go there?" I asked, knowing they all understood me well. "If I find her and confirm it's a safe, Druk-free place, will you follow me?"

Reyna sniffed. An emotion I couldn't place came through her bond.

I wasn't sure if it was a yes, but it had to be. We were out of options.

"Okay. I love you." I hugged her hind leg. "We'll be together soon. Until then, Reyna, hide in the Ghidorian fire pits. Suoh and Cadmus, find the deepest, darkest cave you can. Tizor, take the hatchlings to the ice caves. Kenna and Mireu, stay atop the Romanus Mountain peak. I'll call for you when I know it's safe."

They took off in half a dozen directions, dispensing with long goodbyes. I watched them go with a crushing weight on my chest. Nothing felt more wrong than us being separated.

I rejoined Dominic, Keely, Poet, and a group that had shrunk by almost half. Those gone had made their decision. They'd rather take their chances with the roving Watchers hunting down unique mages than put their hopes in me.

Junia, Osman, and Claudius weren't one of them. They were silent figures by the juniper tree—waiting.

"Waiting no more," I said, taking Dominic's hand myself. "Let's go."

Chapter Eight

"This is a terrible idea."

The trees closed in—snarling their branches, entangling their leaves, and blocking out the moonlight. It was nearly impossible to see, but we dare not use fire in case we drew the wrong attention. Single file we walked, climbing over massive roots and squeezing between trunks. It was as if Tenille himself erected this barrier to keep us away. None were meant to go this way and find the land beyond.

"It's the only one I have." I cut a look over my shoulder. "But you don't have to come with me. You're not a unique mage, Poet. The general wants everyone to believe I've been bewitching and brainwashing my allies. If you showed up on your father's doorstep, denouncing the forbidden magic I used on you, the nobles would take you back and you could continue on with your life. Even find Valor, get the bond back, and return to the riders."

Poet gave me a flat look. "You don't think I have any honor, do you."

"What? No," I rushed. "I didn't mean it like that—"

"Then, how did you mean it, Ainsley? Why in the fuck would I spread lies about you to save myself? I was a coward on the day you met me, so now that's all you see."

"Poet, no," I whispered. I stopped dead, holding up everyone behind. "Never. I'm sorry, I... None of that came out right. I only meant you have a family. I don't want to be the reason you can't be with them."

After a beat, his anger faded. "You're not the reason. After Golden City burned down, I was questioned for weeks, even though Maili and Ormr knew the truth and could've stopped it any time. They knew I didn't have any special knowledge about you, your magic, or your plans, but they assumed since you protected me that night, you'd come back for me. I was bait— We," he said, looking at Keely and Dominic, "were bait.

"As long as we are friends, and I very much consider us friends, they'll use me against you. I won't have that." He shook his head. "Especially not to fight for a kingdom I don't recognize anymore. Enslaving unique mages young and old. Throwing their children in orphanages. And the way I was treated for being half Nehebkan...

"The only kindness Maili did me was to shout at High Queen Kisandra to stop when she ranted that I was a half-breed mongrel, and no wonder a beast like you took to me."

Bile burned my throat.

"It's true," Keely said softly, closing the distance. "Of course prejudices like that died decades ago, but with a high queen like her back on the throne, she'll do her best to bring it back. She won't make it easy for us to rejoin the riders, even if our dragons choose us again. And I damn fucking sure don't want to fight for her even if she does.

"We're with you, Ainsley. So lead on."

Saying no more, I led on. I tried to protect them that night and did everything but. If only I knew who dragged me out of the castle that night, and forced me to abandon them. They would've been top of my list for revenge.

Hours passed as we trekked, and the grumblings got louder. Food, water, and rest. None of those were in heavy supply while we were held captive in that mysterious estate.

I squinted through the gloom, trying to separate wood from shadow. They didn't name this area the Dark Border to scare us. It was literal. "We can't be far."

"Not far at all."

I whipped to the side, calling on hellfire as quick as Dominic.

The tiniest spark appeared in the air and burned itself out before it touched the ground. My shame was hidden by Dominic's many fireballs blazing around and above the trees.

My brother stepped into the light. "Hey, Pain-in-the-Ains. Took you long enough."

"Velez?" The next thing I knew, I was running. I threw my arms around him. "It's you. What are you doing here? Were you following me again? How long have you been doing that, freak? Where have you been all this time? I—"

"Whoa, slow down." He laughed. The dark didn't hide his long, blond hair; crisp blue eyes; easy grin, and the scar cut through his beard. Everyone always said Velez was more handsome than a person had a right to be.

"I know you have a lot of questions, and I want to answer every one of them, I do. But first... you look terrible. What the hell are you wearing? And when's the last time you bathed? You're looking every bit like that toothless woman who stalked the marketplace, spitting on everybody and rubbing mud in her hair to keep the dark spirits away."

"Hey." Dominic came up on him fast. "Who the fuck do you think you're talking to?"

"No, it's okay." I shot between them. "Dominic, this asshole is my brother, Velez. Velez, this is—"

"I know who he is." A sudden and surprising chill burned his voice. "The useless general's spawn that suddenly forgot about being your enemy when you decided to hand him your kingdom."

A slow brow rose up Dominic's forehead, chiming the warning bells loud in my ears. "And you're the borrowed brother that ran off and abandoned Ainsley and all the children in your charge. How unpleasant to meet a walking, talking piece of shit in person."

Velez smirked. "I never abandoned Ainsley. Someone had to watch over her while you were a wall ornament in your daddy's dungeon."

"That's enough," I said, grabbing Dominic's balled fist before it came up. "You two are not allowed to hate each other two seconds after your first meeting. Velez, tell me why you're here and that it's a good reason."

"It is." He smiled at me, but glared at Dominic. "You're finally ready. You've come into your true power. It's time for you to go home."

"Home." My voice shook. "By that I assume you don't mean Ossian."

He shook his head.

"Is—" I forced myself to ask the question. "Is my mother there? Is she alive?"

Meeting my eyes, he nodded.

A tight ball of grief and worry unknotted in my chest.

"Can we all go?" I swept over the watching mages. "We will be safe? My dragons too."

"They will be if you demand it so. Normally we kill every invading pet that crosses the border..." I didn't miss the sideways glance he threw Dominic. "But those were the old laws. You make the rules now."

My mind couldn't comprehend that.

"Just take us to where my mother is. You can explain yourself on the way."

"I would, but it might get a little loud."

"What do you—?"

He snapped his fingers. Druks melted out of the shadows. Literally, out of the shadows they grew, surrounding us in seconds. I didn't get out a cry before clawed hands grasped me under the arms and lifted me up.

"Stop!"

"Help!"

"Get off me!"

Shouts rang out as the others were lifted off their feet.

The shadow Druks carried me effortlessly past the branches till my feet skimmed the treetops.

I gasped.

Carried on the backs of dozens of sky Druks were ornate wooden litters built like carriages, if those were missing wheels.

My carrier opened the door and plopped me in, placing me on a mound of soft pillows. Velez was brought in after me.

"Where's Dominic?"

Velez's response was lost in the *whomp whomp whomp* of half a dozen pairs of flapping wings.

I strained to see where everyone else was through the small window, but it was too dark.

Velez said they would be safe. Time was his word was all I needed.

I glanced at him out of the corner of my eye.

I trusted the brother I thought I knew. The one whose parents were murdered by Druks when he was two years old, and found his way to the orphanage after a neighbor dropped him off.

I trusted the guy who couldn't do much with his stone magic, but that didn't stop him from making me little stone animals, toys, and people for me to play with.

I trusted the guy who tickled my feet in the middle of the night till I woke up giggling, and always gave me the bigger half of the food he stole.

That guy didn't keep secrets from me. He didn't let me miss him for years, thinking the worst had happened to him.

I trusted my brother. This guy... I didn't know him.

Velez caught me looking and smiled at me. I smiled back for lack of anything else to do. He said he had answers for me. All I could do was wait until I heard them. Afterward if they weren't good enough, I'd kick his ass.

Velez pushed some pillows and unearthed three small packages wrapped in wax paper. He kept one and handed me two.

Curious, I unwrapped one and was hit over the face with the most heavenly smell.

Meat pockets.

Or that was the name we gave them because we couldn't pronounce the Edjerian word.

Different kinds of meat—all seasoned, cooked with rice, and baked into a sweet, flaky dough. I tried it one time when an Edjerian noble bought some for me and the kids one day when we were begging. I declared it my favorite right there on the spot.

Velez remembered. He remembered... and he gave me more than half.

I smiled at him—a real one. Maybe I did still know him.

I wolfed the food down, tossing politeness out the window. It didn't need saying that I wasn't fed regularly while General Roark kept me captive in the cell.

I was licking the paper clean when Velez gave in and passed me his. I made short work of that too.

I must've fallen asleep after because the next thing I knew, Velez was shaking me awake.

"Wake up, Ains. We're here."

Sunlight streamed through the window. I heard voices outside. One of them Dominic's.

"Where is here?" I asked.

"Itzala." Velez stood, dusting himself off. He was bursting with excited energy like a little kid showing off their new toys to their friends. "The colony of the shadow dragon slayers. Of course all the colonies are mixed now, but this one was built by and for them."

I craned around to see. All I made out were trees and moving shadows.

"Is my mother here?"

"Of course she is." Climbing out, Velez reached out a hand for me. "And she's been waiting a long time for this."

I didn't move.

The only one who waited just as long for this meeting was me, and I was showing up looking like a madwoman with mud in my hair.

I flicked down at the tattered remains of the dress I'd been wearing for four straight months. Dominic really did love me for not saying exactly what Velez did when he first saw me.

I looked terrible.

"I have to change first," I blurted. "And shower. She can't see me like this."

"What? Ains, she's your mother. She doesn't care how you look."

"Velez, please. I—"

"Ainsley..." Dominic's voice floated inside. "You need to see this."

Something in his voice burrowed through my self-consciousness. I stuck my head out, and fell over.

Velez caught and helped me out. He was saying something, but I couldn't hear it. It was like my dragons were all shouting in my mind again, but this time the jangled voices were mine—all clamoring with a million questions.

"Where are we?" I whispered.

"Itzala." Velez moved to the cliff edge, sweeping out a hand to the impossible sight below. "The first grand and bountiful city of the shadow dragon slayers."

My feet moved on their own power, bringing me to the edge and closer to the most beautiful city I'd ever seen.

Wide lanes big enough for four ox-drawn carts to cut through side by side, weaved around strange buildings with no doors or roofs. Everything from the cobblestones to the structures from glittering dark rock that shone like obsidian.

My wide eyes traveled up, following towering spires that reached for the sky and fell short, contained by a massive, tinted black–soaked dome that covered the entire city. The spires were riddled with entrances like a beehive. Druks flew on and off the perches, appearing through shadows, or flying high. Their stolen wings sliced through the air as they dove, zipped, zigzagged, and chased others.

"Fun," I croaked. "They're playing?"

"Sure." Velez fell in beside me. "Why wouldn't they be?"

I sensed Dominic come up on my other side. He was already reaching for my hand as I reached for his.

"Why is it so beautiful?" A stupid question, but all I could manage.

"Neither dragons nor humans like living in squalor. The union of them both wouldn't stand for it either."

"Ainsley," Dominic said. "Do you see?"

I nodded slowly—at a loss for words. Walking the broad streets, chatting with friends, and holding tight to the Druks flying them around the city... were humans.

Normal, unchanged, scaleless, wingless, and clawless human men, women, and children. Hundreds of them by my quick, guessed count.

"Those people." I couldn't take my eyes off them. "Are they waiting to make the change? Is that why they're here?"

"Some, yes. Most, no." Velez shrugged. "We don't all want to be dragon slayers. We just want to live in peace."

"We? How long has this place been here? How long have these people been here?"

Another shrug. "It was built centuries ago by the shadow slayers and the unchanged members of their family, so they've been here for generations."

I gave Dominic a look that continued on to Keely, then Poet. We were all thinking the same thing. It was written on our faces. Everything we thought we knew about Druks was wrong.

We didn't know a damn thing.

Emotions flooded me, drowning out my stunned wonder. *Anger, hate, sorrow, disgust.* They tumbled through the bond, filling my eyes. None of it so strong as Suoh's agony. All he saw here were the remains of his brethren.

It was a minute before I could speak. "If all these humans can live here, why do you have laws to kill anyone who crosses the border?"

"Kill any *pets* who cross the border," Velez corrected.

Keely peered around. "You call us pets because we respect dragons instead of slaughtering them?"

"No. We call you pets because you blindly follow a twisted, hateful, war-mongering queen, and the peasant-hating tyrant that came before, and after, her. Queen Kisandra passes a law to capture and enslave your fellow innocent countrymen, and you say 'oh, please, can I?' And that's not even the worst of what your rulers have done over the centuries. Yet, you take it and obey. Who other than a mindless animal is that self-destructingly loyal?

"Not you all," he said, flashing a grin over our slack and washed-out faces. "Not anymore."

"You..." Poet trailed off. "You're being kind. We should be called far worse."

"Come on." Velez walked off, forcing me to follow. With us out of the way, Junia, Osman, and other mages and children rushed in to see the city for themselves. "Dragon slayer homes take getting used to. Everything is huge and reinforced to accommodate the wings and claws. Plus they don't have roofs. Once we got word you were finally heading for the border, your mother had the stone slayers begin building human homes for you and your friends. You can bathe and change there, if you still want to do that before meeting her."

"I do, but I have to tell you now, I can't stay in that city."

He stopped short. "Why? I thought you'd want to be near your mother."

My chest tightened. After decades of wishing and wanting to know her, we were talking about my mother as someone finally within reach. "I do want that, but my dragons will go nowhere near that place. We need to be somewhere far from Dru—dragon slayers. Is there anywhere like that? Maybe somewhere a hellfire dragon would happily make her nest and live there undisturbed?"

He screwed up his face. "That's an oddly specific request." Velez sighed. "Well, I don't call you Pain-in-the-Ains for nothing."

"You can stop calling me that."

"Hmm." Velez scanned the landscape. "Hellfire dragon... Wait, the Gaia Curves. It's about seventy miles that way." He pointed past the city. "The Curves are a line of mountains and volcanoes that go on for miles like the bumpy spine of the earth's back. The volcanoes are active. Ten or eleven have been spewing lava for years, so there are no cities or settlements around it. Would that work?"

"Yes. That's perfect." I turned to the others. "Is that okay with you guys?"

"I go where you go," Dominic said, but my question was for my dragons.

Anger and fierce displeasure surged back at me. I was not taking that as a positive, even as ripples of agreement passed through the humans.

"I won't set foot in that place." Osman shivered. "It's too... weird."

"We'll make camp here until you come back." Claudius pulled his son close. "He talks of rulers who do terrible things while we sit back and watch. I've got something to say about people who kill innocent dragons for power. I'd be a terrible *pet* if I strolled along them side by side like it was okay."

Velez's expression was relaxed. "He says while relying on us to shelter him within our borders."

Anger and shame flit across more than a few faces.

Claudius was as neutral as Velez. "Touche. But I've noticed you're just as human as the rest of us. Seems to me you want something from them without having to be them too."

My eyes flicked between them. I could've stepped in, but I was more than interested in Velez's response.

Velez grinned. "I wouldn't say I'm *just* as human as the rest of you, but you make a fair point. There's a bit of self-serving bastard in all of us. Who am I to judge?" He threw out his hands. "You're free to camp here. As I said, guests of Ainsley are honored guests of ours.

"Get comfortable. I'll be back with food, clothes, supplies, and toys for the kids."

Velez set off and a few of us broke off to follow. Junia and Mira included. The little girl took my hand again, staying close.

He led us down the hill and to the gates of the dome. My eyes were huge stepping through. Seemed like a lifetime ago I was sitting in scholarship class, listening to our instructor tell us different kinds of Druks couldn't live together, so they formed separate colonies.

Were there cities like this all over this unknown land? For fire, ice, sea, earth, wind, and all the Druks in between?

We passed through and pulled up short when a group of giggling girls blew by.

"Hana, you're so slow," one called back to the girl lagging behind. "Hurry up, we're going to miss the fireworks."

"I'm coming!" She stopped, blinked at me and my strange appearance, then kept going. "Wait for me!"

We continued on, passing through a world bathed in artificial dusk. The sun fought to defy the dome, spreading its light through and soaking into the strange stone city. It took that light and cast it back, refracting a million billion glittering rainbows on this little slice of world.

"It's like—"

"—swimming in starlight," Dominic whispered.

"Yes." We shared a smile. "Exactly like that."

"This is where you would've lived," he said, drawing me in close. "This city would've been your home. It's okay if a part of you wishes it was. It's not a betrayal to your dragons. Doesn't mean you loved Sister Aven, Rosaleen, or your family less. And it doesn't make you a self-serving bastard."

Laughing softly, I laid my face on his shoulder, letting him hide the myriad of conflicting emotions warring in my soul. I loved this man so much it hurt. He saw me in a way no one ever would.

"Ilemka?" someone called. "Ilemka."

I lifted my head, looking around. "Ilemka?"

A Druk woman perched on top of her house, laughing as she waved to someone flying above. "Demka, say bye to your friends. It's time for dinner."

I swallowed through needles. Of course she wasn't calling my sweet little borrowed sister. Ilemka's gone.

I drew away from Dominic, moving to the other side of Velez. I didn't let myself look at the bemusement on Dominic's face.

Dark clouds stormed in my mind—raging torrents that slipped their lid with that sudden, crazy swell of hope. I shoved it back down, roughly wiping away a stray tear. Crying wouldn't solve anything. It wouldn't bring them back. It wouldn't make it right for me to carry on with Dominic like nothing happened. I didn't get to spit on their graves by being happy and in love when my selfishness caused their deaths.

"It's just up ahead," Velez said. "I'll leave you and get your mother while you're changing. She lives at the top of the hive."

I couldn't see what he was pointing to ahead of us, but I had no problem following his gaze up, up, and up to the top of the tower. All this time and my mother's location was close enough for me to see.

"...she is..."

"...it's her..."

"Ainsley."

I dropped my head at the sound of my name, and met their eyes. People were stopping, looking, whispering, and I didn't believe it was due to my appearance.

"Princess Ainsley." A Druk man broke from the crowd and fell at my feet. I choked when he kissed them. "You've finally returned to us. We welcome you. Our savior."

"Your what?"

The dam broke.

They surged at me. Druks dropped out of the sky. I pulled Mira close as they touched any part of me they could reach, and dropped kisses on my tattered hem.

The first Druk was still on the ground. "Child of vengeance and fury."

What did he say?

"Finally our wait is over."

"All right, everyone, give Ainsley some space," Velez said. "She's on her way to meet the Five."

These words had magic effect in clearing a path. They let us through, but they weren't silenced. Cheers and praises for the returned princess rang through the street.

"He called me a child of vengeance," I whispered.

"Yes, he knows who you are and about the prophecy," Velez said. "We all do."

"What? When—"

"Here we are."

I looked where he was pointing. "I don't see anything, Velez. Is it behind that courthouse?"

He laughed. "That's not a courthouse, Ainsley. It's your home." He twisted around. "Head inside, everyone. There are plenty of rooms, baths, and food prepared and waiting in the dining hall. Help yourself."

My jaw worked as Junia, Akasha, and the children cautiously passed me, heading inside. Only Keely, Poet, Dominic, and Mira stayed behind to stare at the place with me.

It wasn't unreasonable that I thought the place was a courthouse. It looked eerily similar to the magistrate's building in Ossian with its three stories of sloped roofs, columns, and a grand entrance to welcome someone more important than me. How was this my home?

"They built this place in less than a day?"

Velez nodded. "Consider it one of the many enticements for you to stay."

"I don't know about that. I do know I'll stay long enough"—I pinned him with a look—"to get some answers."

"I get it, I get it." He laughed, throwing up his hands. "I have a lot of explaining to do. We'll talk while you're getting ready. I swear."

"We can talk about why you're so happy and joking... when everyone we grew up with is dead."

The smile melted off his face. "Ainsley..."

I blew past him, hurrying inside. My friends and Dominic were quick to join my side. I felt a hand brush mine and slipped free, picking up the pace.

Bursting through the doors, I passed through a shining, marble foyer without really seeing it. There were rooms everywhere. I just wanted to get inside one, slam the doors, and hide until everything made sense.

The biggest shock of my life was common knowledge to the people of this town. They praised and kissed my feet while a brother I didn't recognize anymore, walked the streets of Itzala like this was his true home.

"Shaya, are you okay?"

I pulled up short, blinking down at my side. I hadn't realized I brought Mira along on my mad dash.

"Oh, I—" I kneeled in front of her. "Of course I am, sweet one. It's just been a long day. Why don't we find some food, then get you settled in your room. I bet we can find one with a huge bed."

She ducked her head. "Do I have to have my own room? I want to share with Gwen and Jennet."

"I'm sure they want to share with you too. Let's go find them."

Mira and I wandered the cavernous halls until we found the dining room. The near-palace didn't have much in the way of decorations or furniture, but that was to be expected for a home built in a few hours.

We found the girls where we found all the children—sitting around a grand stone table covered with food of all kinds and cultures, and trying to eat all of it. Mira ran to her friends. Only when she was eating and the smile returned to her lips, did I duck out to find a quiet spot of my own.

"—knew we should've said something."

"What were we supposed to say? Nothing we could say would make her feel better."

"So you say nothing? Gods, you're so insensitive, Poet."

"Me? I didn't hear any sweet words of comfort coming from you."

I stuck my head around a corner. Poet and Keely argued in hushed tones, their conversation bouncing farther down the stone hallway than they would've liked.

"I was going to tell her how sorry I am but there wasn't a good time while we were running for our lives," Keely said.

"Ah, so it's bad timing for you, and insensitivity for me."

Dominic came down the other end of the hall. He gestured for me to follow him.

Leaving Keely and Poet to it, I padded after him.

"I had a bath drawn for you, and found the only clothes in the closet that wasn't a dress or ballgown."

I sighed in relief. "Thank you. It'll be nice to be in boots and pants again. Plus this bodice has been strangling me for four months."

"I'm sorry. I intended to rip it off you and make it watch while I plundered you in the back of the carriage on the way to our first honeymoon spot."

Heat stained my cheeks.

"But we'll have to do that another time."

I cleared my throat and wisely decided to stay silent. I was honest with Dominic about the way things had to be between us. Despite his certainty that I would break my own rules, my self-control was stronger than that. I went without sex for years. I could keep my hands off him for longer than ten seconds.

Dominic led me to a massive room that again did not have much in it. A bed covered in massive, downy blankets and pillows. A small vanity beside a window that looked out onto the tower, and a small half wall that concealed the bath I was looking for. Vanilla-scented steam wafted off the warm and inviting water.

I reached for my back buttons, eager to accept that invitation.

"Let me."

Dominic was behind me before I could speak. I bit my lip under his touch, once more choosing silence as gentle fingers slid down my back, popping buttons as they went.

Slowly, deliberately, his hand found his way through the opening—gliding soft and caressing around my middle to the front of my bodice.

He popped it off, making me squeak.

"That's better."

The man was not talking about my relief at shedding the tight, dirty thing and we both knew it.

I was glad the builders didn't have time to put a mirror in the vanity. My scales had to be redder than Reyna's—

Skin, Ainsley. Skin.

Dominic continued down, taking my dress with him. The remains of the gown pooled at my feet, revealing me in my naked glory.

He hummed, lips pressing to the nape of my neck. "Can I say I love that you didn't wear anything underneath? Couldn't ask for a better wedding-night present. Only having to get through one layer."

"You shouldn't," I whispered, eyes fluttering shut. "Say it."

"May I join you in the bath, my love?"

I trapped a moan behind my teeth as he kissed down my spine, moving lower, and *lower.*

"We shouldn't. It's not a good idea."

"Are you sure?" He peppered a trail of kisses along my hip bone, taking him around to my front. My body was screaming when he kissed the apex of my thighs. The raging desire in my soul thought my rules were stupid. The stupidest rules ever established since Parthelan created humans. "It's been a long four months. All that time, you lost sense of your body and who you are. All that time, you haven't had what you needed." Warm, calloused fingers stroked my thigh. "Let me give it to you."

No. Say no, Ainsley. You can't—

"Yes."

We lunged at each other.

"Ainsley?" The door creaked open, and Velez's voice came through. "Are you in here?"

"No— I mean, yes—" I ran behind the partition, a blurred streak when he stuck his head inside.

"Can I come in?"

"No," Dominic barked. "Get the hell out." I heard it in his voice. I was too late. He already hated my brother.

"Who the fuck asked you?"

And the feeling was mutual.

"Ainsley, we need to talk," Velez said. "Alone. Please."

I opened my mouth.

"Did you not hear me? I said get out."

"Are we going to have a problem, general's spawn?"

"You tell me." The room lit up in a flash of hellfire. "We can solve it right now."

"Enough." I sunk in the water, suddenly so bone tired, only the bottom of the tub stopped me from slipping under and passing out. "No one has a problem. Dominic, please, give us a minute. I need to talk to him too."

A beat passed.

"I'll be right outside if you need me."

"Dom, you should get some food and rest," I protested. "I'll find you after."

"I'll be outside."

I sighed as the door closed. Titana, save me from stubborn men.

Silence, then shuffling on the other side of the wall. I had a sense Velez was on the floor, leaning against it. His voice floated softly to my ears.

"I am happy, Ainsley. Happy to see you. Happy that you survived. I'm not happy that Sister Aven, Rosaleen, and—and our brothers and sisters are gone. I loved them just as much as you."

"But you left us." I tried to keep my tone even, and managed a choked rasp. "You left. You stopped writing, sending money, and visiting. We thought you were dead."

"There were reasons for that," he insisted. "I didn't want to disappear from your lives. It wasn't my choice."

"How was it not your choice?" I ducked my head under the water, letting four months of grime wash into the tub. "Stop giving me more questions and give me answers. Why did you leave, Velez!"

"Because I was ordered to!" Something hit the wall. "Fuck! Tenille's sake, Ains, I've been with you almost your whole life. You're my best friend. Don't you know I hated being apart?"

"Why would I know that? I never knew you at all."

Silence.

"Okay, I deserve that." I heard a deep intake of breath. "Here's the truth, Ains. Your mother didn't just drop you under a tree and leave. Back then, Sister Aven took the same path through the woods to the market every other day. Your mother purposely put you there, knowing the kind woman who ran the orphanage would find you.

"She couldn't stay with you, but she couldn't leave you on your own either. So I was sent to the orphanage to watch over you. Protect you."

"Sent to me?" My mind tried processing that and refused. "Like a bodyguard... or a spy?"

"Neither," he said firmly. "I was sent as a friend and companion. Besides, we both know that no one dare be your bodyguard. You court trouble for fun."

"I do not!" Though I almost smiled. It was true. If Velez was supposed to stop me from getting into trouble, he did a terrible job. Most of the time, he was right there rooting me on when I got into mischief. "But how could you just be sent to me like a lady's maid? Didn't your parents miss you?"

"Don't have parents. I'm an orphan too. Believe me, Ainsley, I told the truth way more than I lied."

"So keep telling the truth." I reached for the hair oils and scrubbing stone. "Why did you leave?"

"I was forced to leave by order of the Five. They got impatient," he said. "You were almost of age and you still hadn't come into your true power. They decided I was the problem. If hardship triggered your ability, I couldn't be around protecting you from it.

"I left for the *new job*, but I still wrote and sent ryus for you and the kids. When they found out, they put a stop to that too."

I nodded slow. "How did you end up stalking me around Golden City if they ordered you to stay away from me?"

"When you bonded with your first dragon, they thought that was the sign you were ready. I was sent to bring you home, but two minutes into watching you flail around uselessly on a field, running away from those dirt Druks, I knew you weren't."

I flushed remembering that first day of assessment with Lieutenant Colonel Phiala. Flail around uselessly was putting it nicely.

"I stuck around, and fell into the role of protecting you again. You looked happy, Ainsley." His voiced softened. "I wanted that to last as long as possible."

I was quiet running my fingers through my hair. I didn't know yet if any of this excused his lies, but the pain in his voice was real. At the very least, I believe he didn't want to hurt me.

"How much did you know?" I gazed into the depths of the water, eyes unfocused. "About Maili, Ormr, and Queen Kisandra? About the kind of *hardship* I had to experience to come into my full power?"

"If you're asking if I knew everyone we loved would have to die, then let me clear that up right fucking now. No. Of course not. No one knew. Prophesized goddesses aren't born every damn day. How was anyone supposed to know what it took to trigger your power?"

"But you did know about Maili and Ormr. You watched me get chummy with my sister and sibling, knowing they secretly hated my guts."

"I didn't know it was them," he cried. "Yes, your mother knew you had siblings, but they must've changed their names around the time they changed their entire legacy to appear as children from House Moros, not House Boreen. The names your mother knew were Valeria and Tamerlane. Pretty sure it goes without saying that your father didn't introduce his dragon slayer mistress to his twins, so she never knew their faces."

I scoffed. "You have an answer for everything."

"I thought you wanted answers. Make up your mind, Pain-in-the-Ains."

I made an obscene gesture at the wall. "Fine. You didn't know and there was nothing you could do to prevent what happened that day, but what happens now? What does everyone here want with me? What have they been waiting all this time for me to do?"

"Your mother will explain all of that. Before she does, there's one more thing I need to tell you. It's important."

"I'm listening."

"Can you come out first? I need to tell you face to face."

I frowned, but gave in. I was done anyway.

Standing up, I grabbed the towel off the hook, wrapped myself up, and padded out. Velez rose to face me. I couldn't place the expression on his face. I just knew it wasn't one I'd seen before.

"There are some—one more thing you don't know about me," he said to the wall.

I craned my neck, trying to meet his eyes. "What? Can't be worse than having my own personal stalker for almost two decades." I laughed but he didn't join in. "What is it, Velez?"

"My parents," he began. "I didn't lie about being an orphan. They died when I was two. I don't know much about them except they were born in Nevaeh."

"Nevaeh? Where's that? I've never heard of it."

"Because it's a land beyond this one, Ains. On the other side of the sea."

"Wow."

Naturally, the people of Adalinda suspected there could be other nations out there, but none of us could go and find out. The Dark Border surrounded the entire country, and if anyone made it through to explore new worlds, they never made it back to share the news.

"That's what you wanted to tell me? That you're Navaehan? If that's the right term."

"I'm not done yet."

I inclined my head for him to go on.

"The people of Nevaeh aren't like us. They worship different gods. Have different magics and abilities. And different struggles." He started pacing, bouncing my eyes back and forth in my head. "There's a curse that pops up in the bloodline. No one knows it's coming. You could have six children born perfectly fine, then the seventh comes out with the curse. There's no stopping or reversing it when it does.

"My brother and I—my twin—were born with this curse."

My eyes blew wide. "You have a brother?"

"Yes, and you know him."

"I know him? You have a twin brother and I know him?" I sounded like an idiot, repeating everything he was saying. "Who?"

Velez took a deep breath, holding up his hands. "The first thing you need to know is that he had orders too— He didn't want—" He tossed his head. "Let me start at the beginning. The curse is called the Gemini curse. What happens is—" Velez's eyes bugged. "Wait, no!"

I jumped at his shout.

"Don't do it, you shit—!" Velez winked out of existence.

One moment he was standing in front of me, the next a Druk was standing in his place. Six feet tall to the head, eight feet with moss-green wings stretching to the ceiling. He gazed at me and eyes the same dark, fathomless green as the patches of scales on his broad shoulders and thick arms, glittered back at me. He bared his teeth, and unnaturally long, sharp canines gleamed through the shadows.

He was terrifying... and familiar.

"You!"

He grinned. "Hello, Ainsley darling. Sorry about my brother. He can waffle on, can't he? But I thought it best to get to the point."

I screamed.

"Come now, there's no need for that." He moved toward me.

Shooting around the wall, I grabbed the bottles of hair oils. He came around, then jumped back when a bottle went whizzing through the spot his head was in.

"Ahhh!" I chased him out, throwing everything I could get my hands on.

He flicked them out of the air with quick snaps of his wings. His whole body relaxed and face riddled with amusement just like it was every time he attacked me, year after year. And year after year, he smiled just like that, laughing at the broken, terrified, magicless weakling.

I lunged at him, and went flying.

My foot slipped on the wet stone, and I fell hard at his feet. My towel didn't come with me.

"Ainsley!" Dominic burst in.

I gaped at him—naked and bleeding on the floor with a Druk standing over me.

The fireball came at him so fast, there wasn't time to shout.

He tossed me a wink, flashed away, and Velez claimed his space—standing in the path of oncoming death.

"Noooo!"

Chapter Nine

Stones flew from the wall, rushing to shield Velez. I knew even as they formed that they wouldn't be enough. My brother didn't have a chance.

Hellfire blew through the stone shield, and Velez snapped out of the way. He stood blinking behind Dominic as the wall went up in flames.

"Atlas."

I froze. I knew that voice. I heard it once, but I'd know it forever.

"I've told you about causing trouble and making your brother bail you out." Her wings came into the room first, opening the door for her like hands did for the rest of us. "You would've died right along with him if that strike connected."

"The asshole knows that," Velez gruffed from under her hold. "He's fine with getting us killed as long as he still looks pretty on his death day. I'm to be the burned-out corpse."

My mother chuckled. "He was always incorrigible."

Dominic quickly came over and covered me with the towel.

I pulled him in front of me, hiding behind him and not because I was half naked.

This isn't how I was supposed to meet her. A frazzled, bleeding, drowned rat in the middle of watching my fiancé murder my brother.

She smiled at me over Dominic's shoulder. "Gentlemen, leave us, please. I'd like time alone with my daughter."

"Of course."

Dominic walked off easily, breaking free of my death grip. A plea trapped in my throat. All too quickly we were alone.

The last and first time I met my mother, we were in the middle of a battle and she tried to crack my head open on the cobblestones. She was even more than I remembered in the light.

I saw in one look that most of me came from her. Her eyes, her mouth, her nose, and her hair. We only differed in the shape of our face, and my sticky-outty ears—not unlike the glimpse of my father from that vision. Even the way we dressed was similar. She wore loose, comfortable, black cotton pants; leather boots, and a breezy top that wasn't so tight it revealed the things you stuffed in there from pickpocketing.

There was also the fact she was a Druk with black, horn-tipped wings; patches of scales on her arms and neck; razor-tipped claws where nails should be; and gleaming fangs when she smiled. A smile so wide and genuine, it made my heart ache.

"Oh, my beautiful girl," she breathed. "How I've longed for this day."

I didn't move. My lips parted, and nothing came out.

Her smile turned down. "Ainsley? Is it—? Do I look repulsive to you?"

I started. "What? No," I cried. "That's not it. I just— I don't know what to say. Which is crazy because I've imagined what I'd say to you millions of times, but now I'm here and... I don't know what to say."

"You don't have to say anything. Why don't you get dressed?" She moved over to my bed and lifted her wings to sit down. They almost touched the opposite walls. "I'll be right here."

I took that chance to grab my clothes, run behind the partition, and breathe. Why was I so nervous? I said it myself. I waited years for this moment, and I was ruining it.

Dressing quickly, I padded back out. I headed for the bed, then stopped—keeping some distance. "Hi."

She smiled. "Hello, dear."

Silence spread like spilled milk.

"I was going to come to you," I spoke up. "I was hoping to be put together, and dressed, for our first meeting."

"You attacked me during our first meeting and I tried to kill you." Her tone fell flat. "As terrible first impressions go, we already got those out of the way."

I bit back a grin, chuckling. "Good point."

"Go on, my love. I know you have questions. Ask them. All of them." She held out a hand to me. "Don't be afraid to hurt my feelings."

What a thing to offer a kid raised as an orphan. All we were was questions.

"There's one very important question I want to ask," I rasped. "What's your name?"

"It's Meriall. Meriall Persis in my old life. Meriall Shadowslayer in my new one." She flicked to the window, looking out. "In our society, we all have the same last name. We're all the same clan."

I backed into the wall, sinking down to the floor. *The same clan.*

Like my clan. My dragons.

What they were feeling, I didn't know. Well, not exactly. I felt hungry, bloodlust, worry, protectiveness, and a myriad of other emotions. But no anger and disgust at where I was and who I was with. If dragons understood one thing, it's the love all creatures have for their mother.

"It's okay," she whispered. "Ask the question."

I squeezed my eyes shut, fists balling so tight my nails dug half-moons in my palms. "Why did you leave me? How could you just drop me in the dirt and walk away?"

"I didn't want t-to." Her voice cracked. "I wanted you, Ainsley. My sweet, perfect miracle baby, born from the man I loved. There was nothing in this world I wanted more than you."

"So why did you do it!"

She sighed, head falling back to the ceiling. "Because I had an impossible choice. Your father knew about the prophecy. He believed it was about Zalina... until my stomach started to swell. You know what became of her," she said. "She went mad, then was brutally defeated by her former lover. She's now the most reviled person in Adalindian history.

"We didn't want that for you, so we decided to run far away. Farther than slayer country to the lands beyond the sea." She swallowed visibly. "We didn't make it."

"You mean you didn't want this for me? To be the child of vengeance and fury?"

She shook her head. "I wanted you to be happy. To live a life of your choosing. Not a life forced on you by the ramblings of a drunken soothsayer in the back of a pub."

I took that in. "Then what changed?"

"Kisandra killed your father." Getting up, she came to my side, gently taking my hand. "I was so consumed with hate and anger, I summoned the goddess of vengeance by will alone. When she came, she told me it wasn't my destiny to avenge your father. It was yours.

"You were the child of the prophecy, and running from that was pointless. No matter how far I ran, your fate would follow you." My mother looked down at our clasped hands. "Then she went on to say more."

"What? What did she say?"

"She…" She took a breath and tried again. "She said there was only one way to unlock your power, and I now knew what it was. You had to experience loss, hardship, and powerlessness, for you couldn't be a weapon for vengeance without someone to avenge."

I made a harsh noise in my throat. "Sounds familiar."

Meriall nodded. "She couldn't say much more, but I understood. You had to live a hard and difficult life, and I couldn't do it. I'm your mother, Ainsley. I couldn't purposely make you miserable. I couldn't—wouldn't—stand by and let terrible things happen to you. But I also couldn't stop it. Fate always finds us in the end. At the time, the only action I could think to take was to give you up."

My face gave no reaction. "So you left me for Sister Aven to find."

"I'd been watching her for days. She was a good and kind person. I knew she would care for you," she said. "After, I sent Velez to be with you. Make sure you always had someone on your side. Your life wasn't perfect, but you seemed happy.

"The Four didn't like that."

"The Four?" I repeated. "Who is that? Are they like the people Velez was talking about? The Five?"

"They are who Velez was talking about. They were the Four before I joined." She stood up and tugged me toward the bed. We sat down, giving her wings room to spread again. "Before we were gifted the ability to control our instincts, representatives of the four great clans reluctantly came together four times a year to make decisions on protecting the slayer nation.

"When they found out about you, they overruled my wish to let you be, and ordered Atlas to begin his yearly tests to provoke your ability. When that didn't work, they ordered Velez to abandon you."

"Wait." I threw up my hands. "How did they find out about me?"

"A pregnant dragon slayer? There was no hiding that. Everyone knew about me and you," she said. "But they didn't know you were more until the slayers learned about the prophecy."

I opened my mouth to ask who told them, and stopped. Kai said it to me himself. Every person blessed with his mother's gift recites the prophecy at some point in their life. A thousand people could know the prophecy. That wasn't a secret that was ever going to be hidden.

I groaned, pushing up. Meriall watched me move to the window. "I don't understand any of this. I don't understand this place, or these people, or you. You've all made a home on the carcasses of innocent shadow dragons. How could you do it?" I felt Suoh's sorrow keenly. "How am I supposed to reconcile the loving, caring mother you claim to be, with the person who cut a dragon open for power?"

"That's fair. It is hard to understand." She joined me at the window, smiling at the scene I frowned at. "My father and brother raped me repeatedly. For years."

I went still.

"I was born with shadow magic, but it was weak. Useless. All I could do was detach my shadow, send it away, and see through its metaphorical eyes. Which I did the many times... during. But that power didn't stop it. It couldn't save me."

"Meriall..." I trailed off, falling quiet.

"I was from a poor village deeply affected by the ban on education. They didn't know what shadow magic was, so they thought I was a curse. People saw the bruises. They knew my father and brother were doing terrible things to me, but they believed I deserved it for being a demon child. No one helped me or would."

Bile burned my throat. I almost threw up.

"One day, my shadow found a shadow dragon." She tossed her head. "Or maybe the shadow dragon found it—sensing my magic. I don't know. But listen to me, I make no excuses, Ainsley. I do not and nor have I ever thought myself justified. I loved dragons and love them still. They are beautiful, magnificent creatures. I know I did a terrible thing."

"But," I softly prompted.

She sighed. "But it's the same for dragon slayers as it is for dragon riders. They can only bond with their own type. We can only consume the power of our own type. When my shadow discovered that dragon, I saw my only hope of escaping my hellish life... and I took it."

I didn't speak for a while. "Okay."

"Okay?" She grasped my chin, turning me to face her. "That's all?"

"I... I can't imagine going through what you did. People spit on me and called me a cursed child, but then I went home to a safe place with people who loved me. You didn't, so... maybe I... don't get to judge."

We lapsed into another silence.

"What was it like for you after?" I finally ventured. "Battling the instincts?"

"It was impossible. Dragons are vengeful creatures. They don't allow anyone who hurts them to steal another breath."

I knew this well.

"After I changed, I flew back to my village in an almost trance... and slaughtered everyone."

My eyes widened. "You what?"

"I couldn't stop myself." Filtered light danced on her golden locks. "Everyone who looked the other way. Everyone who dragged me screaming back to my father the times I ran away. I tore them to shreds—leaving my father and brother last. I wanted them to feel true and all-consuming fear, and know there was nothing they could do to stop it."

That sounded familiar to me too.

"I killed all but the children. Dragons value younglings above all else. Dragon slayers are the same," she said. "I fear many an overfilled orphanage is the result of a newly born dragon slayer losing control against all who've wronged them."

"But you're not that way anymore," I said. "You've changed. Evolved to work together and keep your minds. When did it happen?"

"It happened three years and two moons ago, and it was not because of evolution. We owe our change to a unique mage called Evron Soulslayer. We don't know how his magic works any more than any other unique mage, but he freed our minds from the grips of the dragon's last revenge. And not just that," she continued. "People with nightly screaming nightmares sleep like babes after seeing him. Jumpy, battle-worn soldiers find their peace. Because of Evron—"

"You've become powerful enough to defeat Ryuku squads."

She fixed out the window, tone cool. "Yes, there has been that result."

"This is where I once again lose understanding. You hated your father, brother, and that awful little village, and they gave you every reason. But did you hate Adalinda and the five kingdoms? Why become its enemy? Why attack Golden City, and fight alongside willing dragon killers, if you were never proud of hurting that shadow dragon?"

"Ainsley." She backed away, pinching the bridge of her nose. "These are complicated questions."

"Questions you said you'd answer."

"I don't know that any of my answers will satisfy you," she cried. Her wings twitched agitatedly. "It wasn't my intent in the beginning to become an enemy to the kingdom, but that's what every dragon slayer is. After I slaughtered the village, the Riders hunted me down like a rabid animal. There was nowhere for me to go except across the border.

"It was only when I did that I learned everything I was told about dragon slayers, about *Druks*, was wrong."

I ran around her to keep eye contact. "Like what? Did someone give you the same speech about pets? I'm sure Velez practiced that, because he delivered it with just the right amount of self-righteousness."

She chuckled. "You will get quite a few passionate speeches when asked about the anger against Adalinda, but I assure you, that anger is justified. My dear, you look outside and see a city of cold, unfeeling monsters. But what you are actually looking at is a community of refugees."

"Refugees?"

"All either fleeing their own brand of horrors, or searching for new hope," she said, gesturing with her left arm and wing. "Velez and Atlas's parents looking far and wide for any magic that can help their sons. Women fleeing abusive husbands. Parents fleeing tyrants that won't let their children go to school, or have any future that isn't tumbling or scrubbing a noble's latrines.

"Our population *swelled* during Kisandra's reign." She spat the name. "That mad, evil woman closed the borders after inheriting the throne, and hunted down all the mixed couples and *mongrels* that didn't belong in her Adalinda. People ran away to survive. They became dragon slayers to fight back against the kill squads she'd send after innocent families causing no one any harm.

"There are nearly as many unchanged humans here as there are dragon slayers, my sweet one, and that's because this is the place you go, when you're lost."

I folded my arms, jaw tight. "I can believe that some made a terrible choice during a desperate situation, but you want me to believe all, or even most of the *dragon slayers* did not want to be exactly what they are? This is about power. It's always about power." I jabbed out of the window. "And they think I'm going to give them that power, don't they? That the prophecy means I'm going to free them?"

"Yes, but it's not that simple—"

"It's as simple as this. My destiny is not to help your people conquer Adalinda and slaughter the dragons. If that's what everyone has been waiting for, let me rid them of that fantasy now."

"By the veil, Ainsley, it is your fantasies that need to be corrected. No one is interested in conquering Adalinda, or slaughtering the dragons." She scoffed, shaking her head. "But I'm sure the pets have you all thinking otherwise. They have everyone convinced we're your greatest enemy, when the truth is, all we want is to live in peace, but we can't, because Adalinda is broke."

A buzzing sounded in my ears, rattling my thoughts. "Excuse me?"

"Broke. Destitute. In ruin."

The words slingshot from her lips, striking me down on the bed. "Destitute? That—that can't be true."

"It is true," she stated. "The downfall of the five kingdoms started over a century ago. When Queen Kisandra closed the borders, she shut down trade. Naturally, she ignored every single one of her advisors who said it would negatively impact the economy. Adalinda didn't need the *inferior* goods coming in from the other countries.

"She was quickly proved wrong. Eventually, she gave in and allowed trade under strict terms, but the other rulers taxed their goods heavily for the insult. Nehebkan steel went from two silvers a gram, to thirty gold ryus."

My eyes bugged. "No one could afford that."

"Exactly. The palace coffers were dangerously low by the time Zalina overthrew her," Meriall said. "Zalina united the kingdoms, but she wasn't kind about it. Untold damage was done all over the nations.

"When the general took over, he was forced to pour millions of ryus into rebuilding Golden City and the other capitals. Then the awful man went on a campaign, forcing all those queens and princesses to marry him so that he'd have rights to their coffers by law, throne, marriage, and bloodline."

Understanding punched me in the gut. "And he raised taxes and outlawed education for commoners to keep us out of the workforce. The less qualified people there are, the less demanding more and equal wages." My lips twisted. "He has most of the population so desperate, we'll take whatever few coins are thrown our way and be thankful for it."

"Yes," she said, tinged with relief. I saw the truth.

"I knew it didn't make sense. He's not flying Adalinda into the dirt because he hates peasants. He's doing it because the money's gone."

"And he's gotten more and more desperate to get it back. You're a generation away from famine, rations, riots, and violent uprisings," Meriall said. "But his methods of bailing the country out have only contributed to the problem."

"How?"

She held out her hands. "The Dark Border. He can't safely cross it to trade or borrow money from the lands beyond the sea, so that leaves only us and our land to plunder.

"Most of his raiding parties were successful—slaughtering peaceful colonies and plundering their wealth—until Evron returned our minds, and we were able to fight together. Even so, we were being attacked and killed by Ryuku squads almost every day until the queen returned and unseated him. But we're not stupid enough to believe it's over."

"Hold on. Raiding parties? What are they raiding for? Gold?"

"You're looking at it, my dear." She gestured with her chin, turning my gaze to the shining city under the dome. "Pure black jadeite. The foundation and bricks of our city. It's ten times stronger than Nehebkan steel, and beautiful. Oh so very beautiful.

"A princess from beyond the sea would pay a hundred thousand gold ryus to wear a string of those stones on her neck, and she has. One brick would feed the five kingdoms for a month."

I wondered if I looked silly with my mouth hanging open. My mother was in the best position to know.

"And you just use the stuff to build your latrines!" My mind blew realizing I just bathed in a tub worth more than my life. "I saw kids throwing them at each other in the street."

She shrugged. "Why not? There's always more where that came from." She trailed a hand down her arm. "It's made from our scales." Meriall popped one off like it was nothing. "They shed, and we melt them down to make jewelry, weapons, and more."

"And the general wants it."

"He wants it all," she corrected. "Dragon slayers have amassed incredible resources and wealth due to our very nature. Earth dragon slayers don't have to dig and mine for diamonds and gold. They sense them in the earth. Plant dragon slayers grow food that'll feed an entire village with a snap of their fingers.

"Fire dragon slayers create incredible fire-blown glass that we trade across the seas. We are not broke and struggling." She laughed, making me sheepish. "We have no interest in destitute little Adalinda. It is very much the other way around."

I shook my head. "Except there is a resource that we have and you don't. Dragons."

"We don't want to harm the dragons."

"You just said you owe your peace and prosperity to the power you stole from them."

"Ainsley, people become dragon slayers by luck. Because they cornered one who was alone, ill, or unsuspecting. Even then, eight out of ten are killed in the attempt. After we change, we claim the spoils of our victory by capturing dragons we defeat in battle. But we do not, nor have we ever wanted a war against all of dragonkin. It's suicide. We'd be wiped out in a week."

"Why?"

She barked a laugh. "Let me count the ways. We just learned how to fight together. Dragons overcame that limitation centuries ago when they formed the hive mind. They breathe fire. Dragon slayers don't. We have the advantage in wielding precise and different magics, but once they overcome that, they have bigger claws, wings, fangs, and boundless bloodlust on their side. They can go weeks without sleep, and their magical ability lasts longer than ours. We do not want a war with the dragons, my child. It's a war we'd lose."

"But you want me for something. You want a weapon of vengeance." I gave her a hard look. "Against who?"

"All of that will be explained." She made for the door. "The rest of the Five are waiting. Let us—"

"No," I sliced in. "I don't want to hear from the people who sent a big, scary Druk after a small child to terrorize the power out of her. I want to hear from the mother who was told I had to grow up in hardship, and still made sure I was found by a kind woman, and gave me a brother. You tell me what they want." My eyes sharpened. "And then tell me what they *really* want."

Meriall stilled—from her pacing feet to her softly flapping wings. Sliding off my face, she flicked to the window.

"There's only one thing that they want," she said. "For you to protect the dragon slayer nation from pets and invaders." Meriall took my hands in hers. "You were born with the power of a goddess. You're stronger than any force General Roark or Queen Kisandra could throw at us. Now that you're home, we'll have peace."

"Oh." I rocked back. "I guess that's—"

Meriall tugged me forward, snapping her wings around us. I penned in a cry when her face stuck in mine.

"War," she hissed. "They want war, and you're the only one who can stop it. The only one the dragon slayers will listen to."

I sputtered. "What? Me—?"

"Listen." She grasped my cheeks, bringing me close. "Ryuku squads have attacked us again and again. Killing so many. Causing untold damage and havoc. Destroying the safe, happy places we built for ourselves after those tyrants drove us out. What you see around you is the only city that's survived unscathed. The dome protects us, but now that Kisandra has an army of unique mages. Who knows what power she has in her arsenal.

"Our home, our wealth... and me," she whispered. "She will see it all gone. It's not a matter of if, but when, and the Four will not let that happen."

"How do they mean to stop it?"

It was the look in her eyes. It quieted my soul before she spoke.

"Evron Soulslayer. His power to separate and free a mind." Her gaze pinned me through. "It works on dragons too."

Six dragons came to attention. I couldn't say how I knew but I did. They were listening close.

"What does that mean?"

"Over the last two years, they've been secretly capturing dragons and removing their minds from the hive. It's perfect because other dragons assume they're dead. No one comes looking for them."

"Comes looking? Where are they?"

"Hidden." She rose on tiptoe, straining to see over her wings. "I don't know where. They refuse to tell me and there's not much I can do to make them. My position is honorary. Given to me as mother of the savior. The other four constantly outvote me—as they did with this plan."

"What plan?" I almost screamed. My dragons' impatience fed into me. "Tell me."

"The plan to give the child of vengeance the army she needs to conquer all of Adalinda," she rasped. "The clock started ticking the moment you walked through the gates. In three days' time, ten thousand dragons will be slaughtered, ten thousand dragon slayers will be born, and Ainsley of House Titana leads us to war."

Rage exploded in my head, doubling me over. "Are you insane!"

"Shh!" She dropped down. Grasping my shoulders, she cocooned us tighter within her wings. "You never know to whose ears the wind will carry your words."

I shivered under such a chilling sentence. "But you said they didn't want Adalinda," I cried, dropping my voice. "You said they'd never provoke a war with the dragons. Was all of that bullshit?"

"It wasn't bullshit. They removed the dragons from the hive mind *be-cause* they fear the dragonkin. You were never supposed to know about this. No one on the other side of the border has an accurate count of our popula-tion. If ten thousand new dragon slayers arrived to meet you, you wouldn't know the difference."

"But Adalinda—"

"Adalinda isn't for them. *It's for you.*" Huge, probing eyes captured me. "They believe it's your destiny to rule over the *six* kingdoms as a child of our world, their world, and the world beyond. When you're queen, you'll unite us all, recognize us as equal citizens, and put an end to it. The fighting, the raids, the attacks, the impending doom of famine and ruin to Adalinda. You will bring true peace... and they're willing to kill everyone you tell them to in order to make that happen."

I choked, jaw working. "I don't want that. I never asked for this!"

She shook me. "You cannot escape it. Kisandra is back on the throne. I promise you on all I hold dear, she has terrible plans for all of us. She will do whatever it takes to return the nation to the *pure,* perfect world she en-visions, but she has no reason to undo the gift Zalina and Roark gave her by conquering the other nations.

"Hyelong, Nehebkau, Edjer, and Ghidorah are hers now. The native populations she reviles so much... are under her rule. Do I need to tell you what's in store for them? Do I need to tell you what's in store for us? The disgusting abominations that bewitched and ruined her only child."

Neck stiff, I shook my head.

"War is coming, my love. It is not a matter of if, but when," she said. "And it's a war we mean to win... for you. The prophecy is told. Fate will be fulfilled, and the Four will see to it."

My throat was a desert. I couldn't breathe. I couldn't croak a whisper. "What—what am I supposed to do? I want the high bitch and her pet gen-eral in the ground as much as anyone, but ten thousand dragons will *not* die to make it happen."

"We don't have the strength or numbers to take on the entire force of the five kingdoms as we are. You have to find a way to make us war-ready, and you must do it in three days."

"I have to do it?" My voice shot up a dozen octaves. "Why me? Why can't we all sit down and come up with a sane plan together?"

"Because they're convinced this is the only plan and will not have any suggestions for you. *I* don't have any alternatives for you," she said. "I've tried, but I can think of no other way for us to become strong enough to defeat Kisandra's forces. But I am not you."

Cupping my cheek, her eyes softened. "This is your birthright, my sweet girl. It's your destiny. You will know the right thing to do, and they will listen when they hear it. Trust yourself."

I internally screamed, and not just because my dragons were raging in my head. Rebuilding the walls in my mind didn't keep out their emotions, and those emotions were exploding right then.

Trust myself? Trust myself to devise a war plan in three days!

"But why would they wait three days? What's to stop them doing it now? How do you know they haven't already begun?"

"I know because I do have an accurate count of our population, and ten thousand dragon slayers have not been born," she said. "Three days. We worship Mother Zaeah too. They will spend those three days in seclusion, begging Mother Zaeah for forgiveness, then they'll proceed."

"But what if—?"

A sharp rap sounded on the door. My mother was upright and helping me to my feet as four towering figures entered the room.

I didn't have to ask if they were her counterparts. Mottled green wings of an earth dragon. Aquamarine wings of a sky dragon. Brilliant, flaming scales of a fire dragon. And dark, shimmering blue scales of a sea dragon.

The Four.

"Princess Ainsley." Snapping their left hands over their hearts, they tipped their heads to the ceiling. "Forgive our intrusion. We know this is your first meeting with your mother, but we've been most anxious to meet you. It is an honor."

I don't know what I expected of them. Being a dragon slayer slowed the appearance of age and extended their lives just like dragon riders. These three men and woman looked to be in their fifties, but they could be one hundred and fifty, and their faces wouldn't give them away.

I prayed nothing shown on my own as I flicked between them and my mother. There was a reason I was supposed to be brought to the five of them, instead of meeting with my mother alone. They had their own ideas for how to win a war against High Queen Kisandra, and planned to ask my forgiveness, not my permission.

Chosen by a goddess or not, I was a young girl of twenty while they had decades on me and experience leading a community. They didn't trust me to have a plan.

And they're right. I don't.

"Princess, I am Nerilla," said the fire Druk woman. "It is my privilege to introduce Sanjiro, Ramses, and Zenebe." She gestured to the earth slayer, sky slayer, then water slayer. "If you're ready, let us adjourn to the tower—"

"No. I'm leaving."

"Excuse me? Leaving?" All four looked straight at my mother. I didn't like the frowns forming. "Why?"

"I told this to Velez on the way in," I replied. "I can't stay here because my dragons won't stay here. My friends, my guests, and I will make camp near the Gaia Curves."

"That won't be possible," Zenebe, the sea dragon slayer, said. He had shockingly white, long hair, and eyes so black, they looked blue. "As we speak, the pets are searching along the Ossian border, hunting for you. Eventually they'll conclude that you've crossed. When that happens, Queen Kisandra will send her forces after you."

"We know you're ready for battle," said Sanjiro. He smiled and dimples appeared in his smooth, unlined cheek. "Our spies relayed tales of the amazing things you've done over the last few months. You truly are a being unlike anything anyone has ever seen."

My chest tightened. Now was not a good time to tell them I was that being no more. The bonds that made me invincible were closed.

"But our people need to see it," he said. "We have people waiting to take you to every colony and city. You have to walk among them, reassure them, show them that the savior is here to end the war, and grant us equal rights and protections as citizens of Adalinda. The six kingdoms"—he dropped to his knees, bowing—"and you our queen."

My mind spun. All that time being ferried around this unknown nation, conducting a feel-good, vanity parade, would give them the space they needed to carry out their own plans.

"I absolutely agree," I announced. "The people do need to know that I'm here to stop the fighting and violence, but a lot of empty promises won't do that.

"I'm going to the Gaia Curves, and I'm not going alone. You're sending me off with maps, supply lists, population counts, and documents stating our weapons, resources, weaknesses, strengths, magical abilities, everything.

"After I've studied all the information, I'll return on Firesday with a battle plan that'll end the war, and see General Roark and Queen Kisandra in the ground." I met their frozen smiles with a smile of my own. "That'll reassure the people more than touching me and kissing my feet would ever do."

They once again looked to Meriall—who was grinning wide.

"We will of course let you review all of those things," Nerilla began slowly. "In the tower. Leaving the city with those documents is out of the question. This kind of information cannot get out."

"It won't get out." My voice was hard. "Who do you think I'm going to tell?"

A pregnant silence beat on the back of our necks.

"With respect." Ramses stepped forward. Salted dark locks and a pointed nose, he towered even higher than the others. "You travel with the general's sp—son. Along with many nobles. Our only advantage is that Adalinda doesn't know what's coming. We can't risk losing it."

"There's no risk. No one other than those I trust completely will see the documents or know the plan." I stepped to the side. "Meriall will get everything I need, and bring it to me on that cliff outside the dome."

"Of course, Ainsley." Meriall made to leave.

Ramses's wing snapped up, blocking her way. "Princess," he forced through gritted teeth. "I really must advise against this. At the very least, allow one of us to go with you. Sanjiro, Nerilla, Zenebe, or I. All the information you need is in our heads. We'll help you come up with this battle plan."

I shook my head. "My dragons won't come if there are dragon slayers around. It's them I need most of all if I'm to decide our next move."

"Princess—"

"You either trust me to lead you, or you don't." I met each of their eyes in turn. "Which is it?"

The pregnant silence birthed five litters of silences in the space of time we stared at each other.

"We trust you, Princess." Nerilla spoke to me but looked at Ramses, Zenebe, and Sanjiro. "You're the prophesied child come to save us. Fate is guiding you."

"Yes," Ramses replied. "It's not a question of if we trust you. Only that we want to help and support you in every way. How about this? One of our unchanged Itzalans will accompany you and the documents. They'll provide context, answer your questions, and make sure they don't fall into the wrong hands. Will that satisfy?"

I glanced at my mother who nodded. I did too.

"Excellent." He turned on the others. "You all help Meriall gather everything the princess needs. I'll remain here with her."

"Wait," I called. Meriall paused with her hand on the knob. "When will we have a chance to talk about... everything?"

Her smile was soft. "Firesday. When you return. I promise."

"Okay. Firesday."

***

Druks lifted my litter into the sky, carrying me away from the waving, hovering figure that was my mother.

I held my knees to my chest in the full litter, squeezed among Velez, Dominic, and Egan, the earth mage carrying and protecting the documents.

Ramses tried to get more people to go with me at the last minute, but I refused. No matter what he said, the man didn't trust me. I could feel him thinking it when he looked at me with my friends and fiancé.

Pet.

It was a quiet journey to the Gaia Curves. Actually, it was a noisy one—preventing us from talking.

When we arrived, the Druks set us down and immediately set about emptying the supply litter and building dirt huts.

I climbed out, squinting at the blast of sun.

"Incredible."

I don't know what I imagined this place to be, but I was wrong all the same.

Lush, verdant grass tickled my ankles, welcoming me home. Patches of delicate purple flowers burst out of the earth, spreading a lovely, sweet scent. Little furry creatures with long ears flitted among the flowers, so cute Mira and the children went chasing after them—squealing with glee.

All around me, volcanoes pierced the sky and rumbled the earth, making me vibrate where I stood.

No wonder this place was named for the bountiful curves of the world. I couldn't imagine a more beautiful place than this.

"Do you see, my beauties? There are no Druks here. Please come. We only have three days."

"Ainsley."

I dropped my chin, coming eye to eye with Velez.

"Can we talk?"

"Princess." One of the Druks waved to me. "Yours is ready."

Nodding at him, I said to Velez, "No."

I brushed past him, grasped Dominic's hand, and tugged him after me.

Together we stepped inside. It was a modest space with a chair, table, water basin, and a square of raised earth covered with a bedroll.

I closed the sliding wooden slab that served as a door.

"Dom, we have a problem," I cried, whirling on him. "A huge, fucking problem."

"What's wrong?" Dominic shrugged off his coat and tugged his tunic over his head. He rolled his shoulders, and every muscle rippled with the effort. "Sorry. Those Druk clothes are itchy as hell. What's it made out of?" He reclined on the bed. "Okay. What's the problem? What do you need me to do?"

"I..." Heat prickled the back of my neck. "I need—"

I jumped him.

It was only his quick and strong reflexes that caught me as I hurtled toward him like a boulder. I knocked his arms away and dropped, falling on that hard and muscled chest I'd been trying not to eye since we were freed. Grabbing his head, I crushed our lips together, releasing a groan of frustration that had been building in me for four months.

Dominic responded instantly. He grasped my hips and flipped me. I squealed as I went flying.

"Finally."

The growl was a straight shot to my heart, quickening it to a worrying pace. I was a swirl of heat, emotions, and arousal, and all of it crowded out the quieting voice that we shouldn't be doing this.

In a breath, Dominic was on top of me—kissing my lips, nipping my chin, tearing off my clothes, and pinning my arms to the bedroll.

Squeezing my knees between us, I placed my feet on his hips, and kicked him off.

"Oophf." Dominic dropped back and found me on top of him, scrabbling at his pants. "Ooooh. We're doing this today."

My speech was pants. "If by this you mean a deliciously good and rough fuck, then yes." I ripped his pants tearing it off. "We're doing that until I can't move."

"By the gods, you're the only woman for me."

His cock sprung free, hard and ready, from the confines of his underclothes. I pushed him down, lips parted and closing around—

We tumbled and I found myself on my back, blinking up at him. Dominic's palms rolled down from my shoulders—stroking my breasts, tweaking them to hard, wanton pebbles, and continuing on with an angry cry on my lips.

"Don't stop!"

"Don't stop what?" A wicked, wolfish grin danced on his lips. "This?"

He closed his mouth over my nipple, sucking hard. My back arched off the roll when he bit the poor, helpless thing—a deep groan riding off my lips on equal parts pain and pleasure.

"Or this?"

Two fingers spread my folds and plunged in. My eyes rolled up on my head as he dipped in and out—slow at first, then picking up the pace with my rising moans encouraging him.

I was a squirming, noisy mess tossing my head and fisting the sheets while he tortured my nipples and pussy, commanding their obedience like his mere presence naturally did to my body. The man said I wouldn't last ten seconds alone with him, and he was so wrong, it was laughable.

I didn't last five.

"Yes, Dom." I spread my legs, opening myself to all of him. "Gods, that's amazing."

A third finger slipped inside, and I swore I was transported beyond the veil to Elora Meadows—the paradise for the saintly.

"Do it," I rasped. "Do the—the thing. The thing you do."

"Hmm." He flicked my nipple with his tongue. "What thing?"

"You know the thing!" I smacked the wall. "The third thing you do when you're doing this."

His smirk could only be described as evil. It clung even as he dropped nipping kisses on and through the valley of my breasts. "I'm sure I don't know the thing to which you're referring. Describe it."

My face caught fire. He damn well knew what I wanted him to do. He just wanted me to say it.

"I'm going to kill you."

Dominic hummed. "If you do, then I can't do the thing."

Never had anyone made a better plea for their life.

"Damn it, Dom! Stick your finger in my ass!"

"Ahhhh. *That* thing." A teasing thumb stroked my puckered entrance. "Beg."

I almost wept. My core was coiled like a spring, desperate for him to release the pressure. "Gods, you're the worst. The most evil man I know."

A swat landed on my backside, shooting electric shocks spiraling up my body, and choking me on a moan. "That doesn't sound like begging."

Mother Zaeah, why was Dominic Roark so darkly sexy? I swear as we walked through Itzala, there were just as many people staring at him as they were at me. He wore sex, power, and control like a cloak around his broad shoulders. You wanted to give him everything you were in the mere hope he looked your way.

"Please, Dom." I bit my lip hard. "I need you, please. Need you inside me. Stick your finger in my ass, please, baby."

"You only had to say, my love."

My reply was lost as he dipped into my hole.

Was the human body meant to handle four fingers inside of them? Dominic didn't ask such questions when we were in bed. He explored my body like a lost world—discovering new things, claiming everything he found.

His fingers played me—*in, out, in, out*—while he sucked hard on my nipple.

My moans ratcheted higher and higher. My lower belly was tighter than a drum. One right move and I'd—

Dominic struck that special spot inside me, the spot none of my other forgettable lovers ever found, and I exploded.

"Ah! Yes, Dom!"

Bright spots danced above my eyes, blinding me while my orgasm turned me inside out. My heels dug into the bed, lifting me off my back. I flopped, spasmed, and nearly fell off as crashing waves of delight lit my every nerve ending on fire.

Collapsing in a limbless, happy pile, my grin slowly turned down. "What is...?"

White and bright things were dancing over my head, but my orgasm wasn't only to blame.

Feathers floated in the air, and burned with a flash as they met hellfire—dropping sooty cinders on his glistening chin.

"It's been a while since you lost control of your magic during sex."

"Not me." Dominic was staring at something. And it wasn't what I was looking at. "It's you."

I flicked down, and my eyes widened. Fisting the ruined bedroll were scaled hands tipped with red claws. "Reyna," I breathed. "I channeled her magic. How?"

"I thought the bonds were closed." He lifted me onto his lap, wrapping my legs around his waist. Dom's touch was featherlight skimming over my fingers. "Beautiful."

I blushed stupidly. Dominic saw everything common, unique, weird, and frightening about me as beautiful. It was heady stuff being perfect in someone's eyes.

"They are closed, but Kai told me we can still wield power as one. I just had to find a new way."

He kissed the corner of my mouth, turning it up into a smile. "What were you thinking about when it happened?"

I bit my lip to stop me saying. It tumbled out anyway. "That I felt light, bright, and on fire. That I never have nor will be... this happy again."

Dominic kissed me hard—tongues tangling, moans mingling. Then he was gone.

I blinked rapidly at the empty air as he dropped, wiggling under my open legs. "Hold on to that thought, Princess."

I didn't know what he meant until his tongue swiped my pussy, collecting my naughty juices, then coming back for more.

"Oh, gods." My body rocked when he spanked me again, making me drive his seeking tongue deeper. "Ugh, more, please."

He grasped my hips, rocking that tight bundle of nerves over his tongue. Warmth spread through my body, filling the darkest corners of my soul, and the hellfire balls grew bigger and brighter—joined by ones I instinctively knew weren't mine.

The temperature rose in our little hut—popping beads of sweat on our skin, and slicking our bodies. Leaning forward, I anchored on the bed and rode his face like a madwoman. Grinding, arching, snapping my hips, drowning him in my arousal. Control vanished.

Dominic's hand was already there when I reached. He was lifting me just as I fell back. He was kissing me before the thought that I was desperate to taste myself on his lips crossed my mind.

Our bodies. Our moans. Our minds. Our magic. All entwined as one.

I broke away, gasping as he entered me. Four long moons I'd been without my love and mate inside me. Four moons we'd been apart, and him holding me then, it felt like no time had passed.

Dominic groaned low in his chest, his fingers digging into my thighs when my walls pushed back—embracing his cock to strangle. "Fuck's sake, Ainsley, you're incredible."

I giggled. "I'm always incredible when you're inside me."

"You're incredible when I'm outside you too." He pulled a face. "Wait, that doesn't make any sense. Fuck! See what you're doing to my head, woman?" Dominic reared up, pinning me between the bedroll and his mountain of a body. "Can't think straight when you're near me. Let me return the favor."

That was all the warning I got before he started pumping. *Hard.*

Dominic pounded my pussy until it wept. I clung to him like the curious, long-limbed furry creature I stumbled on in the Royal Wood one day, screaming loud and unintelligible pleas for more, harder, and deeper.

"Yes, Dom! Gods, yes!"

Heat rose within my skin, filling me to bursting. A floating ember touched the bedroll, and it went up in flames.

A searing hot inferno, and us lost in our own world. Moaning, kissing, writhing, and holding on to him for dear life, I saw nothing but Dominic and hellfire—both deadly. Both all-consuming. Both mine until the world burned down around me, and after.

Dominic struck that spot and I came hard, screaming his name. Cursing foully, Dominic was a beat behind me—seed spilling into my open and willing body.

We collapsed in a heap, fire licking at our skin and encasing us in our own world.

"Wow," Dominic breathed. He rolled hellfire over his fingertips like playing with a toy. "That was worth waiting four moons for."

I might've replied if I wasn't still catching my breath.

"Princess, lift your hand for me, please."

Brows furrowing, I raised my right hand.

He hissed.

"What?" I looked at my hand for something wrong. "What is it?"

"Looks like you can still move." His frown morphed into a smirk. "Means we're not nearly done."

"I— Ah!"

He jumped on me, capturing my shriek with a kiss.

Chapter Ten

We lay there—chests heaving, sweat cooling on our skin, limbs tangled—as smoke climbed the air, drifting off dying embers.

"Be honest," I gasped. "Your clothes weren't really itchy, were they?"

Dominic burst out laughing, bouncing my head on his chest. "They were and I'll swear to it if need be. Not even torture will make me say otherwise."

I rolled my eyes, though I couldn't restrain a small smile. Curse this man for knowing me so well. He did say it himself. Of all the things my heart desired, it was him I wanted in that dreamworld.

"Oh, Dom..." My smile melted away. "I'm sorry. It wasn't you. It was me. I can't even explain how I lost control, I—"

"Ainsley, why are you apologizing? Did I somehow give you the impression over the last several hours that I didn't want to do exactly what we were doing?"

"I know you wanted to do it," I cried, pushing up. "I wanted to do it too, but I said we can't have sex, and I meant it. We can't make these rules, then break them whenever we want. What's the point?"

"I don't know!" he burst out. "What is the point!"

"You know what the point is! We're broken up. We can't be together right now." I stormed off and stopped. I didn't have anywhere to go. I didn't even have something to hide behind. Everything in the small hut was ash. It amazed me we kept the shred of control needed to stop the hut from crumbling down around us. "We have to focus on taking down the queen and your father. We have to avenge my family!"

"We can do that and be together!"

"No, we can't!" I screamed.

"Why!"

"Because I only have three days to save ten thousand dragons from slaughter, and I just spent half of one rolling around in bed with you! We knock each other off course, Dominic. We always have."

"That's not true."

"You've died twice since you met me," I shot back. "How much farther off course can you get?"

He stood, facing me. "Ainsley, no offense, but who fucking cares? I died protecting you, and I'd die a thousand more times to keep you safe. Stop bringing up inconsequential shit. I don't have a life if it's not with you."

"Why do you have to say things like that when I'm trying to be pissed at you!"

"Because I love you, you madwoman!"

We glared at each other, chests heaving for a different reason.

Dominic ground his teeth, vein throbbing in his forehead. His eyes kept flicking on and off my face. "Fuck's sake," he shouted, blowing my brows up. "It's impossible to be mad at you when you're naked!"

I clapped my hands over my bits, reddening deeper than hellfire.

Sighing, Dominic headed for the door. "I'll be right back."

"Where—?"

A ring of fire was the only thing covering his bits as he walked out bold as ever, and naked as the day he was born.

"Ahh, everything okay in there, Dom?" I heard Poet say. "We saw smoke..."

Their conversation, if they were having one, faded when the door closed.

Dominic soon returned with clothes for both of us. "Here. I borrowed this off Keely."

We didn't speak while we dressed. I tugged on a colorful, tight shift—unlike the loose and drab thief clothes I was used to wearing.

Dominic was leaning against the wall, watching me when I finished. "Shall we start again?"

I nodded.

"What's the problem? I assume it has to do with those ten thousand dragons you mentioned?"

"Yes." The raised platform that was my bed survived our passionate encounter. I sat down heavily on it. "The Five— I think they're like the High Command. Well, the Five have spent the last two years kidnapping dragons in preparation for me coming into my full power and crossing the Dark Border to take up my destiny. In three days, they're going to kill ten thousand dragons to give me the Druk army I need to take on the might of Adalinda."

He stared at me. I couldn't place the look on his face, but I'm pretty sure I made the same one when my mother told me. "You're not serious."

"I've never been more serious."

"Ainsley, that—that's insane!"

"Same thing I said." I dropped back, looking up to the ceiling.

"They can't kill all those dragons. Do they want the dragonkin to raze this land to the ground?" he said. "What are we doing here? You have to go back and tell them not to do this."

I shook my head. "My mother made it clear that won't do any good. Besides, you heard Velez's speech. Something tells me they don't take kindly to royalty blowing in and ordering them around.

"The fact is, they don't have the strength or numbers to take on Royal Riders, Watchers, guards and everyone else the queen will throw at them."

He came into my line of vision, frowning down at me. "Why are they assuming anyone is coming after them?"

"Because they've been doing it unchecked for years."

I told Dominic all that my mother told me.

"Broke? Adalinda is broke." He dropped down next to me, disbelief etched into his pores. "I can't believe this."

"You didn't know?"

"No, and that's why I don't believe it." He lay back and met my eye. "My father was grooming me to take over. Leaving out that the nation is broke, and we're surviving by raiding and attacking Druks like we're... Druks," he finished. "Why wouldn't he tell me this?"

"The place where we escaped from. Did you know he had some grand estate hidden deep in the Ossian Forest, so close to the Dark Border?"

His brows crumpled. "No," he said. "I guess I didn't."

"I've felt for a while that there was more to your father than meets the eye. He seems like such a cold, logical man, but then he does things only an ignorant madman would do. More and more I've been thinking there is an underlying plan to his every action," I said. "My mother telling me the kingdom is broke only confirmed it.

"He did have a reason for outlawing education for commoners, and marrying every royal daughter in the five kingdoms. He must have a reason for keeping everything he's done from you."

"What reason?" He brushed my hair from my eyes. The casual, affectionate touch of a lover, and guilt clenched my jaw. Dominic couldn't step out of the roles we'd fallen into. Truthfully, neither could I. "It's not like anyone would condemn him for stealing from the Druks. Literally no one would defend the rights of dragon murderers. He has no reason to hide it or send Ryuku squads on secret missions."

He took my hand, sitting us both up. "Ainsley, I hate to say this, but are you sure Meriall's telling the truth? She may be your mother but... you don't know her."

His words didn't sting—much. "Why would she lie to me? She didn't even want to tell me. I had to drag it out of her."

"She could've lied to get you to do exactly what you're doing now. Devising a plan to help the Druks conquer Adalinda. As long as they can hold the threat of killing dragons over your head, you'll lend your power to protect the dragonkin"—his gaze stuck me through—"and it's your power they want."

"I..." I trailed off. Everything Dominic said made a horrifying amount of sense.

"But what if she's telling the truth about the raids, the money, the dragons, all of it? Can I really gamble everything on the chance it's a lie?"

"Honestly... yes." He lifted his shoulders. "You're not here for them. The Druks don't know that they've got it wrong. The prophecy is about you freeing the gods, not creating the *six kingdoms*. You owe them nothing."

I looked away, considering. As sure as I was that we couldn't be together while I focused on the task of murdering his monstrous father and rending everything he loved from his hands, I knew I couldn't be without Dominic. He was my voice of reason and calm, helping me see through the fog.

"You're right," I said softly. "You are."

Anger, irritation, and a host of negative emotions flooded me.

"He is right," I said, and not to Dominic. "But it changes nothing. If there is even a chance they're telling the truth about the dragons, I have to save them. Free them from wherever they are and return them home."

Dominic came around to look me in my eyes. "Ainsley, I admit there's much we don't know. This place... Itzala..." He tossed his head. "I thought the land beyond the Dark Border was a brutal wasteland, and instead we find a thriving city, happy people, and beauty like I've never seen.

"But I also saw hundreds of unchanged women and children—waiting until they're of age or finished having kids," he said. "We save those dragons in three days, only for their hearts to be cut out over the next several moons and years when new Druks are ready to be born. My father and the queen are our enemies, yes. But the Druks are our enemies too.

"You said it yourself. They don't take kindly to being pets, blindly following the orders of tyrants, so why would they willingly join their free kingdom with Adalinda and submit to your rule?"

"They wouldn't," I whispered.

"They're using you, baby." He kissed my fingertips. "Maybe your mother isn't, but those other four, I don't trust a fucking word out of their mouths."

"I know that you're right, Dominic, but if it's true that your father knew the whole time what was beyond the Dark Border, and has been pillaging this land to his heart's content, that means he's not afraid to send Ryuku squads after me.

"He's coming after me, and I'm coming after him. The battle between us is inevitable, but he's got an entire army behind him." Getting up, I paced a hole in the floor. "The bonds are closed, Dom. I don't know how I channeled that hellfire while we were together, because nothing is coming to me now.

"When he attacks, he'll kill me, and I won't come back from the veil this time. Calthoon will make sure of it." I threw out my hands. "I need an army behind me too, and the Druks are giving me that. Maybe my fate isn't to create the six kingdoms, but I do believe I was meant to be here. I was meant to use them just as much as they mean to use me. I can't free the gods if my heart is cut out of my chest, and Ladon Roark is reborn with Titana's power."

"I would never let that happen," he growled, lips peeled back from his teeth.

"We can't stop him alone."

He dropped his head on my head, letting out a long breath. He was right, but he knew I was too. "Okay. Okay, I hear you." He stood to face me, equal parts resignation and determination on his face. "We have three days to figure out how to make the Druks strong enough to face the Adalindian forces without harming a single dragon."

My dragons battered my head with their urgency before I said yes.

I reclaimed my seat. "Okay, so what do we do?"

He looked around. "You're asking me?"

"Course I'm asking you," I cried. "You're the general's son. Raised to take over the kingdom. Even if he didn't tell you the truth about plundering this land, you know more about the military, and how he thinks, than anyone. How would you defeat him?"

His brows were nearly lost in his hairline. "Princess, you knew my plan to defeat him. Play the loyal son, get him to hand me the throne, and make his power mine. I have no idea how to defeat the full might of Adalinda. I wasn't planning to be her enemy."

"I—"

Booms shook the ground, snapping my head around. I was up and out the door without another word.

The meadow had been transformed during my interlude with Dominic. A collection of earth huts encircled the green. Directly across from mine was a large, open-air space with a long table, and people already beginning to put food on it.

The children chased each other across the grass, tossing around balls, or playing with the toys Velez brought.

A group of Druks stood by the fire pit, handing out clothes, shoes, and other essentials. They quickly took off and abandoned the crates as snaps and growls cut the air.

Tizor, Mireu, Cadmus, Kenna, Suoh, and Reyna towered over the trees, as mighty as the volcanoes.

"You came." I threw out my hands as Sarcany, Scartha, and Ur clambered off their sire's back—bouncing and chirping. "My beauties, I'm so happy to see you."

"Ainsley, look out," Keely shouted.

The baby death dragons tackled me, climbing and clambering all over me.

Keely ground to a halt, threads falling short, watching me laugh and giggle with the babies—very much alive.

"You can touch them?"

"You can too," I said from the ground. Ur snuggled into my neck. "They can control their death power. They usually don't, but they do with people they trust."

She stopped with her hand out. "How do I know if they trust me?"

"That's the question."

Keely backed away. "Best not to tempt fate. I'll leave you guys to it, but I just wanted to say, I'm sorry, Ainsley. I'm so sorry about your friend, and your borrowed family."

My smile melted away.

"I never thought General Roark was a good man, but after what he did..." Her expression hardened. "There's no man worse."

"I agree completely." Tears choked my voice.

I looked at Keely and my dragons. "Can I ask you something?"

"Anything." She dropped down on the grass with me, though she kept a healthy distance.

"You're from Ghidorah. Do you ever wish things were like before? Not the closed-borders bullshit, but the days when Ghidorah was a sovereign nation."

"I wasn't around for those days." She smiled mirthlessly, passing her hand over the trembling earth. "But my grandfather was. He speaks like it was paradise, where we were all at peace and happy under Dominic's grandmother's rule. How could I not want to live in the kingdom he described? But I know it won't happen." She cocked her head. "Why do you ask?"

"I've been given this power that everyone says is meant to change Adalinda as we know it, but what does that mean? How can I know what's best for five kingdoms when I know so little about them? And who says it should be up to me to decide? Power or not."

She studied me. "I don't know anything about Adalinda, but I do know this. The first time I met you, you spat in the face of everyone who called my magic useless and promised to create a kingdom where people like me were valued and celebrated for what we could do, not thrown into fodder battalions.

"You didn't have some life-altering power then, and still you promised to change the kingdom for a girl you just met. You know more about what's best for the five kingdoms and the people in it than anyone I know. Certainly more than High Queen fucking Kisandra and her pet general. Don't start doubting yourself now."

I sat there long after she left, a still ship weathering the tide of my dragons' emotions, and Dominic's wisdom.

The Four were using me. They had to be. But didn't I already know what I needed to do?

"Not one dragon will be sacrificed to create an army for me, or to fulfill a prophecy that they have wrong. Not one." I met each of their eyes in turn. "That I promise you."

***

I mumbled to myself, rubbing my nose as I shuffled the mess of papers around.

I tapped a page. "What's this word?"

"Census, Princess Ainsley," Egan said. He hovered on the edge of my vision, stepping when I stepped, breathing when I breathed.

"I told you to call me Ainsley."

"Yes, Princess."

I let it go. It was important to know when you were fighting a losing battle, and if I understood the documents, I was looking at one. "Is this saying what I think it does? There are about three hundred thousand citizens in the free kingdom of the dragon slayers?"

"Yes, ma'am." We were making progress on the princess thing. "More than half are dragon slayers. The rest are unchanged."

"So there's around one hundred and fifty thousand dragon slayers who can fight—assuming they're all willing to," I said. "What about your spies in the kingdom? How big do they estimate Adalinda's forces are?"

"There are three million people in the five kingdoms." Egan tugged out another map, and laid it over the three maps I was looking at. "There are four hundred thousand dragon riders—that includes the elite Ryuku squads. But if we include the Royal Watchers and the Royal Renders, the number goes up to six hundred thousand," he said. "We have to include them because they can all be conscripted to fight if there's a war."

I goggled at him. "You're telling me there are more dragon riders, just dragon riders, than there are people in this entire kingdom."

He inclined his head.

"How in the name of Titana could ten thousand extra dragon slayers make a difference? We are vastly outnumbered."

"Ten thousand extra dragon slayers?" Egan's brows crumpled. "I'm not sure what you mean."

Of course he didn't. The Four weren't going to leave me alone with another person who knew their terrible plan. "Hypothetically," I corrected. "If ten thousand newly born dragon slayers joined our ranks. Would it make a difference?"

"It would make a huge difference, ma'am," he replied, surprising me. "To be frank, the Renders and Watchers are nothing. Most of them have high magical ability, but they aren't bonded. Dragon slayers won't have much of a fight on their hands if they were only facing them."

"How was General Roark and his raiding parties able to do so much damage if two hundred thousand Renders and Watchers are laughable to you?"

"Because he was smart."

Egan waved a hand over the map. It was unlike one I'd ever seen, because it included Adalinda and the massive Druk kingdom that surrounded it on all sides.

"Back when the dragon slayers were still ruled by their instincts, the colonies were separate." He pointed to a section of land outside Ghidorah. "The fire slayers lived here. The sea slayers claimed this entire stretch of land along the coast." His finger left Ghidorah and continued down to Nehebkau. "The ice slayers lived here outside of Edjer. The earth slayers lived here west of Nehebkau and the part of Ossian Forest that's on our side of the border.

"Then, there are the smaller colonies. Shadow slayers, bone slayers, blood slayers, and so on," he said. "General Roark didn't need to send four hundred thousand dragon riders after us. He just had to be smart. Send his strongest ice bondeds to the fire colony, knowing cold is their weakness. Send the fire bondeds to the ice colony and... you get the idea."

I nodded along. Egan was right. General Roark didn't need strength when he was wise. Cold was a fire Druk's weakness. Send the right dragon rider pairs to a colony with only fire Druks, and they'd do a lot of damage before the Druks ran them out.

"But all of that changed when they got their minds back and the colonies intermingled," I mumbled to myself. "You slaughtered the last two Ryuku squads that attacked you because they weren't expecting to find you all together. They didn't have the right mix of bondeds to fight back."

"Exactly." Pride laced his voice. "Now that we are one, we cover each other's weaknesses."

We were in Egan's hut. Similar to mine, he had a bed and few furniture, but his limited space was largely taken up by the large table that held the documents. And no windows. No one was chancing the odd, covert peek, or the wind carrying our words to the wrong ears.

"But we're still outnumbered more than two to one," I said.

For some reason, he shook his head. "Dragon riders don't fight like that, ma'am. Sure, if two bonded pairs came across one dragon slayer in a field, they'd destroy him. But battles don't happen in such convenient places.

"The first rule of the Royal Riders is no collateral damage. Dragons are massive, bulky creatures without precise control of their magic. Their flames rage out of control. Their ice freezes all in their path. When there are cities and towns underneath them, dragons are forced to hold back the full strength of their power while their rider fights.

"Only half the pair is fighting at full strength," he said. "Half a dragon rider force cuts that four hundred thousand army in half. With ten thousand more dragon slayers... and you... we can't lose."

"Me? You believe I'm worth forty thousand dragon riders?"

"Oh, Princess," he breathed, eyes shining. "How could you not be worth more? You steal the magic of anyone who attacks you, you can't die, you break bonds and make them your own, and you're gifted the power of the goddess. With you on our side, the dragon slayer nation will be victorious."

Lips pressed tight, I turned away from him, gazing down at the maps. I traced a section of land near the Hyelong border. "The summer palace. With Golden City and her castle gone, Queen Kisandra has taken residence in the summer palace in Aurelias. The second-largest city of Old Adalinda.

"The Four aren't going to wait for the queen to bring the fight to us. They plan for the entire slayer army to attack the summer palace. Queen Kisandra won't let her throne and kingdom be taken away from her a second time. She'll call on the entire might of the five kingdoms to protect her.

"But with dragon riders needing to both fight and protect the city folk, they won't let their dragons use their full power just as you said. Over one hundred fifty thousand dragon slayers against a force that's holding back…" I bobbed my head. "The odds of winning start closing in. Who knows if another ten thousand dragon slayers give a big enough edge, but dragon slayers are smart too. If the Four believe they're enough to close the gap, they likely are."

"Aurelias?" Egan's voice snapped me out of my thoughts. "That's your plan. We attack Aurelias. Genius, Princess, just tell me when and I'll send word to the—"

"No one is sending word to anybody," I cut in. "Aurelias is not the plan. We're going nowhere near it." I made for the door. "When I decide what we're doing, I'll tell the Five myself."

I stepped outside and turned my face to the setting sun.

Reyna was a speck in the distance, flying and diving above a volcano's mouth. Kenna chased her. Or maybe Reyna was doing the chasing. Either way, I felt their warmth and contentment like it was my own.

Suoh slept in the nearest cave. Cadmus found a swampy mud patch and made his camp there. Tizor tended to the babies, and Mireu lay open and relaxed around the fire, enduring the children crawling over her, and shooting flames at the pit when the logs burned low.

My dragons were relaxed because they trusted me to find a solution. All night and all day I locked myself in the hut with Egan, going over every page four times, and I had nothing.

"—can't believe you ate the last one."

Poet reclined in our eating space, munching on a mango, and facing down an irate Keely with her hands on her hips. "I didn't eat the last one. I picked this myself."

"There is no picking food for ourselves. The Druks can't come back to bring us more food or supplies. Everything we forage we have to pool together and ration among everyone."

Poet took a lazy bite. "And a single mango tips us all off the edge of starvation."

"That's not the point!"

"No, the point is I told you, me fine royal lady, to stay behind at that shadow Druk mansion." He wandered off. "You're not cut out for living rough."

"Excuse me?" No one knew outrage like she did right then. "What does me being a royal have to do with anything? Last I checked, you're a noble and— Don't walk away from me!"

Heaving a sigh, I left them to it. Poet and Keely had been snipping and sniping at each other every chance they got. Apparently, they had history as kids. Poet used to pick on her for being a unique mage, then when they wound up at rider training together, he opted to ignore her. But during those two months they were locked up, Poet took extra punishments to spare Keely, and flat-out refused to eat to make her take his meager portion of food.

I looked to Dominic—making faces at the kids while he chased them around Mireu. The smile was on my lips before I could stop it.

I'd leave Keely and Poet to it. I knew better than anyone how confusing it was when your greatest enemy is also your greatest protector.

I headed for Dominic. I didn't care what Egan or the Four said. I ranked second in scholarship because of the guy who ranked first. If anyone could look at those maps, lists, and documents and come up with a battle plan in less than a day, it was Dominic Roark.

"Ainsley." Quick footfalls sounded on my heels.

I didn't even turn my head. "Not now, Velez."

"You can't avoid me forever." He ran out in front of me, pulling me up short. "Please. I can explain everything. We can."

"There's nothing more that *either of you* can say." I tried sidestepping him. He moved with me. "You were under orders to lie, terrify, and stalk me, so you did it. Never even crossed your mind to tell me the truth, or reveal you've known who my mother is the whole time." I stepped to the left, so did he. "You've got some balls calling other people pets. You were more than happy to not do the right thing if the Four said so."

He winced. "I deserve that, but if you'd just listen, I'll tell you the whole story."

Over his shoulder, Dominic waved goodbye to the kids and headed into the forest. Irritated, I gave up on following him. I tried the night before too and lost him in the trees. When Dominic wanted space, he got it.

I turned the full force of my frown on him. "Why bother, Velez? I've accepted it. I never really knew you at all."

"We bother because it's just us left."

I halted in my tracks.

"Only me and you left to remember Rosaleen, Sister Aven, Ilemka, Colm, Ari, and all of our brothers and sisters." A gentle hand rested on my shoulder. "If I lose you too... then nothing really will matter."

My fists clenched and unclenched. I didn't have time to argue with him. I had ten thousand dragons to save, and a war to win, but—

"You have until they ring the supper bell."

"That's all I need," he said. "Thank you."

Stiffly, I followed Velez to my hut. We went inside and closed the door. Taking a seat on my bed, I waited.

"Where to start?" he said, pacing.

"The beginning is usually a good place."

The corner of his mouth quirked up. Leaning against the door, he slid down to the floor. "In the beginning, there's a curse."

"A curse that makes you turn into a Druk." I gripped my arms tight. "How could you do that to me, Velez? The first time, you chased me into a cave. I was so scared, I stayed there for hours after you left, shaking in my own pee. You did that to me!"

"It wasn't me," he cried. "It was my brother."

"What the fuck is that supposed to mean? You. Him. You're the same person."

"No." He surged forward, rising up on his knees. "That's what I'm trying to tell you. We're not the same person, Ainsley. He is my twin brother—exactly like I said. His own mind. His own body. His own man. A shared soul."

My anger cracked the slightest bit, letting confusion through. "How is that possible?"

"It's called the Gemini curse. Two babies in the womb become one." His eyes glazed. "Three days after I was born, my parents walked into the nursery and found an old man wheezing on the broken remains of my cot. My brother, Atlas."

My anger broke again, letting more through, and getting pushed back. "An old man?"

"Yes. It's called a curse for a reason, Ains. Twins," he said. "It was our destiny to live our lives side by side. Myself reflected in him and him in me. But because of the curse, we're opposites.

"I was born young, healthy, and strong. Atlas was born an old man—sick and already dying from half a dozen old man's illnesses."

I sank onto the floor next to him, eyes huge. "You're not serious."

"I wish I wasn't." He shook his head. "I age in the right order, but Atlas ages in reverse. My parents nursed him, trying to keep him strong enough to last the years he needed to get younger and healthy, but he wasn't going to make it. Desperate, they sailed across the ocean to a land of dragons—where eating one's heart can make you young, strong, and filled with power."

"Your parents killed a dragon to save your brother?" I asked softly.

"To save us both. If Atlas dies, I die." Turning around, he sat next to me—shoulder leaning against mine. I let him. "They killed the earth dragon, but didn't see his mate coming behind. My father was killed," he dropped, tone dead. "Mother was able to give Atlas the heart, then she died two days later from her injuries."

I almost asked how he knew all of this. *Atlas was a grown man, not a helpless toddler. He was probably right there with her when their mother passed.*

"Atlas was himself most during those days. He took me to the orphanage so I could be me, but when he was him, he wandered around and got into trouble."

My mind spun keeping up with the way he talked about *him* and *me*, and being *him* and *me*.

"He was fucking around with a couple Itzalan girls, sleeping with all three of them, then they found out. They went after him to kick his ass when—"

"He switched places with cute, sweet, helpless baby you."

Velez gave me a cocked-brow look. I nailed that spot on.

"The girls didn't know what to do with me. We were far from the earth dragon slayer colony, and they didn't mix in those days. So they took me to your mother."

"My mother? Why her?"

"She was a midwife back then," he explained. "They assumed she knew what to do with a child."

I nodded slow. "She sent you to be with me."

"Not right away. I lived with her for a few years, and she was good to me. Atlas too. She treated us like her own sons. We love her," he confessed. "When she asked us to watch over her daughter, it was like she was asking us to take care of our little sister. Of course we said yes."

I didn't reply for a minute, letting that sink in. "But then Atlas agreed to put me through yearly torture. Why? Why didn't he say no?"

Velez hesitated. "Ainsley, when I said we're opposites, I meant it. We're two people cursed to share one soul, and there isn't enough for both of us."

"Enough of a soul?" I asked, heavy on disbelief.

His nod blew it away. "Yes."

"Oh. Okay. What does that mean?"

"It means if I'm kind, he's mean. If I'm generous, he's selfish. If I'm weak..." Stones flew to him, spinning over his outstretched palm. One shot away and hit my thigh. I don't think it was meant to. "He's strong.

"If I would do anything for the people I love, he'll do anything for the *person* he loves—himself."

I sensed him hesitating again. "What? Tell me."

"Okay," he sighed, blowing out a breath. "Atlas agreed to try scaring the magic out of you because the Four told him there was boundless, incredible power hidden within you. They said if he brought it forward, you'd use your power to break our curse, and we'd finally be able to live our own lives."

My jaw hung open. "Excuse me?"

"I know."

"What the fuck!" I shot up. Anger swelled up in me hot and fast.

"I know," Velez said.

"Where in the hell do they get off making promises like that! They don't even know if it's true that I can break a curse I've never heard of," I raged, "and even if I could, the only one who decides what to do with my power is me. Scheming fucks have a lot of nerve bargaining my abilities."

"Ains, I agree with everything you're saying," he said. "But I was a little kid at the time, and Atlas has never let anything I say stop him from doing exactly what he—"

"Enough." Velez vanished. A full-sized Druk winked at me. "I'll take over from here."

I scrambled back so far and fast, I crashed into the wall.

Atlas rose to his full height, dominating the small space in all his dark, menacing glory.

"Get out."

He pouted. Lips turned down, nose wrinkled, eyes huge and everything. "But why? You said you'd give us a chance to explain. Don't I have the right to speak for myself?"

"You have the right to get the fuck out of here!"

Atlas slowly tipped his head. His mock pout morphed into a frown. "You're still afraid of me."

My nails dug into the wall. "I'm not—"

"Don't lie!" he hissed. "Your heart rattles its cage trying to get out. Your palms smell of sweat. The ground beneath you trembles with your shakes. The little princess, she stinks of fear. Ooooh," Atlas moaned. "Does the mwean Druk make you afraid? Gonna go running to Mommy now?"

I rocked back like he slapped me. He was mocking me? Velez would never—

His own mind. His own body. His own man.

This is not Velez.

I peeled off the wall, looking him in the eye. "I'm not afraid of you, bitch. Little pussy Druks who can't close the deal don't scare me."

Inexplicably, he grinned. "Good. That's better. Then let's skip all the pointless yammering about the past, and deals that may or may not have been made. Time you and I started over. Move forward. Can't have a mate who trembles in her boots over a few games of hide-and-seek. I need the warrior you are."

I almost snapped at him calling what he did to me a child's game, then one lone word penetrated. "Wait a moment. Did you say mate?"

"I did indeed." Atlas flapped his wings, wafting a soft breeze over me. "As my brother told you, I age in reverse. Every year I get younger, and soon, I'll be too old for the girls who look my age, and look too young for the women who are my age. Right now I'm in the sweet spot for mating and fatherhood. And I choose you."

Pressure beat on my ears, popping my drums. That was the only explanation for why I thought I was hearing what I was not hearing.

"Choose... me...?"

"How could I choose anyone else?" Atlas dropped to one knee. "You are exquisite. One of a kind. The impossible child. The goddess's vessel. Heir to the throne of Adalinda. The wielder of all magics and none. Our children will be legends." He grabbed my hand and kissed it before I could stop him. "You are skeptical, I know. Normally I would take my time wooing you, but time is what we don't have. Especially with war on the horizon."

"Get out."

"We are meant to be." He kissed me again before I snatched my hand away. "I will make you see that, my love and light."

"Now."

He backed out of the hut, still flapping his wings. It irritated me to know this was a dragon mating act. They bathed their potential mate in their scent to attract them.

"Until later." Atlas blew me a kiss on the wind of one last waft.

I stared at the door after he left, wondering what the hell just happened.

***

A sliver of sunlight rushed through the door, falling over me. I turned my head away, hand flying up.

"Ainsley, are you okay?" Dominic pushed inside. "You've been in here all night."

"I have? What time is it?"

"After breakfast." It was then I noticed he was carrying a plate. "You've got to eat something. Some sleep wouldn't hurt either."

I clutched my head, standing up. At some point in the night I fell into a corner surrounded by papers. "I can't do either of those things, Dom," I croaked. "Tomorrow is Firesday and I have nothing. The Druks have interesting, and scary, ideas for how to win battles against dragon riders even when they're outnumbered, but this time they believe all they need to win is ten thousand more dragon slayers, and me."

I hurriedly pulled him in and closed the door. Dominic wisely timed his visit during Egan's bath. We wouldn't have much time.

"I can hardly tell them that my power is gone and I don't know when it's coming back. That will do the opposite of convincing them we don't need more dragon slayers."

Dominic moved to the table, and the map. His expression froze seeing the true and accurate map of the kingdom penning us in on all sides. "They're everywhere," he whispered. "So many."

"Yes."

"How could my father know and keep it to himself?" He slammed his fist on the map. "He's kept us all clueless about information that could've saved lives. Why?"

"I don't know." I ached to touch him. "That's one of the many things I don't know. I can't think of a single reason he'd hide his plunder of the Druk colonies. It's like you said. No one would've condemned him."

Shoving away the map, he shook himself. "Enough about my bastard of a father. This is about you, Ainsley. If it's a matter of needing to learn how to wield magic again, I can train you. We all can train you," he said. "You don't need to tell them you don't have your power, because you soon will again."

"But I do need to tell them how we can stop the general and the queen without more dragon slayers," I said. "The worst part is I can see a path to defeating Queen Kisandra and the general. No doubt the same one the Four see. But it's one that is littered with the bodies of innocent riders, giving their lives to protect the two people in the world who don't deserve it."

I leaned—fell—on the table. If I closed my eyes, I'd sleep for a year. So I wouldn't close my eyes.

"Ainsley, will you come with me for a moment?" Dominic laced his fingers through mine. "There's something I want to show you."

"Dom, I have to focus on—"

"Please. It won't take long." He smiled—so sweet and disarming, I forgot my protests.

I let him lead me outside, past the fire pit and playing children, and through the trees.

Wind whispered through the trees and tickled his hair, trying to hold on as they breezed past, carrying the sweet scent of his handmade lavender and honey soap.

I felt my temperature rise a hundred degrees. We'd never had sex outside before. All our courting was done in a freezing, barren wasteland, then we returned to Golden City and everything went wrong.

We can't do this, a voice shouted at the rising tide of my arousal. *There's no such thing as casual tumbling with the love of your life. Say no. You have to say—*

"Ainsley, I—"

"Yes."

He tossed me a curious look. "Yes what?"

I shook myself, grabbing hold of my need and wrestling it down. "Nothing. What were you going to say?"

"I was thinking about you and your family." He stopped us beside a pine tree. "They were good to you. They loved you. Because of Rosaleen, we found each other."

I tensed with every word. Lingering traces of arousal vanished. "Yes. Why are you saying this now?"

"Because they were good people. The best. They weren't honored in life, but they deserve dignity and respect in death."

I didn't know what he was talking about as we rounded the tree.

I froze.

A clearing spread out before me—kissed by sun and sprinkled with those beautiful purple flowers—and everywhere—rows and rows... were headstones.

Dominic was still talking. His voice washed away under the roaring in my ears.

Cyrus, Bodhi, Pema, Aven, Rosaleen, their names plastered on the dead's final parting gift—a bit of stone stuck in the dirt.

My lungs seized, snatching the air back before it left my body. Their last moments tumbled through my head. The children crying and struggling in the grip of Kisandra's living magic. Vines gagging Rosaleen as she begged for my forgiveness. Sister Aven pleading to take her life and spare us. And in a moment, all of them dust. Nothing left of them to sprinkle on these empty graves.

I ran.

"Ainsley? Ainsley!"

I didn't know where I was going. I didn't turn back to find him. I didn't look to see. My eyes swam—bending and warping my vision to block out everything but my family and best friend's final, terrifying moments.

There was nothing left. I sobbed, a scream trapped behind my clenched teeth. It hit me right then, and kept hitting me—knocking down all the walls I erected to keep the pain at bay. They'd never have the dignity of proper Adalindian funeral rights.

A three-day feast and gathering of remembering. The preparing and anointing of the body, dressing them in their best clothes to travel beyond the veil. And the statue made in their likeness and placed on their final resting spot so that they'd never be forgotten.

My borrowed family and best friend never had dignity in life, and because of my selfishness, I stole their chance of having it in death.

They hate me. They look down on me now, and wonder how I became this useless, pathetic person. An entire army stands willing to fight for me, and I still can't avenge their deaths.

Kai rose ahead of me—so clear. So disappointed. "You chose wrong! I am no weapon of vengeance! I can't save anyone. I never could—"

I rammed into a tree and spun, twisting off my feet. I swiped blindly for a low-hanging branch—

—and fell.

"Ahhh!"

A blast of heat and wind blew my tears away, opening my eyes to the crevice below—cut through by a free-flowing river of lava.

"Reyna!" I dipped deep into my mind, ramming against our bond and finding nothing. Feeling nothing. "Reyna!" Heat singed my skin, hastening to consume me, begging for its treat.

"*Death will come for you.*"

"Help!"

A hard force slammed into my body, snatching me inches from the flaming river. Hard pants wracked my chest, making me bump against the binds around my middle.

No. Not binds. *Arms.*

Twisting my neck, I met Atlas's smirk.

"You..."

"Before you say it, you're welcome." Atlas flew over the ravine's edge and set me down. "It's a full-time job keeping you alive, Boreen. Pissing off a death dragon? Setting the building you're standing in aflame? Falling into a lake of lava?" He snorted. "Consider seeing a shaman. Those bastards in Ossian weren't mocking you, they were warning you. You're cursed."

I blinked at him, mind lost in the fog of grief and near-death. I kneeled on the grass, gazing around as though nothing I saw made sense to me. "What?"

"Almost. The words you're looking for are *thank you.*"

"You... saved me." My voice was a thin rasp.

"You were about to die." Atlas hovered off the ground, his bare toes tickled blades of grass. His shirt was nowhere to be found, and a loop was jumped by his pants' belt, as if he was in the middle of dressing when interrupted. "That tends to be when one needs saving."

"Where did you come from?"

"Over there." Atlas pointed through the trees. "I had to make camp away from your dragons, but it hasn't stopped them hunting me whenever they catch wind of my scent. Feel free to tell them to stop."

Anger and disgust welled inside of me—not my own. They were not going to stop.

I was still shaking. "You got to me so fast."

"I'm used to being on hand for every time you throw yourself into danger." He finally touched down. "Besides... I saw that little project the general's spawn was working on."

My jaw clenched.

"I was anticipating having to pull you out," he said, sitting next to me. His wing draped over my head, shading me from the sun. "Gods, he really doesn't know you at all, does he?"

"He does," I cried. "Dominic was just trying to be kind. He didn't know—"

"Anyone with a lick of sense in their head would know there's nothing nice about a mass grave. Especially an empty one."

Defense for him stuck behind my teeth. Sinking down, I cried.

"Hey, hey. None of that now." A warm hand fell on the back of my hand. "You know they'd hate to see you like this. Weeping, wailing, and throwing yourself into ravines." He chuckled. "Colm, for sure. He'd go running the other way when people cried. The boy didn't do wet shoulders."

"How would you—!" I cut off the snap at his knowing look.

Of course he knew my brother. He knew us all. He'd always been there, though we didn't know it.

"And Pema," he continued. "Remember that day we watched the funeral procession go through the square? All those sad, somber faces. Pema said no way. When she crosses the veil, she wanted feasts, parties, and celebrations sending her off. Not a bucket of tears and snot."

I laughed—a tiny sound that went away quick. Pushing up, I sat back on my haunches, remembering that day. "She even told us the food to serve, the songs to sing, and what to wear."

"That was Pema. A commander to the last."

I laughed again. "That's what we called her. Commander Pema. It was a free-for-all until she came to the orphanage. She organized bath and shower schedules. She followed me to the market even when I tried to sneak away and leave her behind, just to tell me what to get with our meager coin."

"You talk like she was more of a tyrant than Kamala."

"No one was more of a tyrant than Kamala," we belted at the same time, cracking up.

The laugh freed something in my chest, pushing back on the crushing weight that slammed me when I saw those headstones.

"How does it work with you two?" I asked. "Do you see through each other's eyes?"

"Something like that." His left wing bent and scratched his cheek. It took getting used to—being around Druks and seeing how their stolen wings became extensions of themselves. "It's not true seeing. It's more knowing. Kind of like you know my wing is behind you without needing to see it. You feel its presence. You bask in its shadow.

"When he is him, I wait in the light and warm, seeing the shadows of his life play out and know that he is happy with the brothers and sisters whose hands he can shake and faces he can see." He half smiled. "It's actually quite peaceful for a life-ruining curse."

"But in Nevaeh, this curse is common?"

He nodded.

"Why? How?"

"If they knew how, they'd know how to break it," he said. "But the why is easy. Centuries ago, the very first twins struck with the Gemini curse... pissed off the wrong woman."

I snorted, giggles bursting out of me. I clapped my hands over my mouth. "You're funny, and you saved my life," I said. "If only I got to see this side of you growing up, and not the evil, smirking bastard who terrorized me."

His grin widened. "You have seen this side of me, Boreen. I couldn't show my face to you guys, naturally. Even if you accepted me, if the town found out the orphanage was harboring a Druk..."

I shivered. He didn't have to finish that sentence. They would've stormed our little peaceful plot of land with torches and pitchforks.

"But even though you couldn't know me, I helped you all where I could," he said. "Gannon fell off the roof, then wound up confused and unharmed ten feet away. A group of men followed Raziah one night." He tapped his ear. "I overheard their whispers of what they were going to do to her. They disappeared before they turned down that alley, and they'll never be found.

"I even tried looting noble houses and leaving the goods in the donation box, but Sister Aven thought thieves were using it as a hiding place and would soon come back, so she quickly turned it in to the magistrate. After that, I left the thieving to you and Velez."

He nudged my shoulder, tugging a smile on my lips. "You may not have seen me, but I saw all of you. You gave my brother a home and a family. He refused to be him for a whole month after they died—hiding from his grief in the light and warm.

"And I..." An expression I knew well twisted his face. "I vowed to kill General Roark by a thousand cuts." He cracked his clawed fingers. "The slowest, most agonizing death is still too good for him, so I hope that all-powerful magic can bring people back from the veil, because I plan to kill him over and over again until the seas overflow with his blood."

"I take back what I said about people making plans for my power without my permission," I gritted. "That is the best use for my ability that I'll ever hear."

"I'm sorry, Ainsley." He put his arm around me. I didn't stop him. "I couldn't be more sorry that you lost them. I loved our little, crowded family," he admitted, smiling. "Some say there's not enough love for both me and Velez. But there was enough for them. More than."

I turned my face to him—crying, but smiling. "Thank you, Atlas."

He bobbed his head. Closing his eyes, Atlas leaned over—mouth open and tongue out.

I clapped my hand on his face and shoved him away. "What the fuck are you doing!"

Howling, he rolled and quickly found his footing. "What? You can't blame me for taking my shot. We were having a moment."

"No, we weren't!"

"You—" Atlas stiffened, grin vanishing. He took off with a blast of wind that blew my hair back.

Reyna's roar cut through the valley. I fell over when her boom rattled the ground.

"It's okay, my beauty." I hurried over to my growling dragon. She snarled and snapped the air where she smelled his scent. "That idiot is gone," I said, kissing her snout. "Impeccable timing as always."

A flood of feeling washed down the bond. Anger, annoyance, sympathy, and one or two I couldn't place. I wanted to say the months that we freely communicated through the bond helped me translate these feelings into words, but they didn't. She was mad about Atlas, of course, but if she sympathized because the fool tried to kiss me, or because I almost died, or because my family's death weighed heavily on my mind, I didn't know.

It was like my best friend moved away and could only send letters, but every letter was in a language I couldn't read. How could we get back where we were when we no longer understood each other?

"We have to train." I hugged her tight. "Figure out how to open the bonds again. Do you know where to start?"

She shook me. I took that as a no.

"We never learned how to do this the right way. I died, then ripped open our bond to save myself. I can't do that again." I looked into her beautiful, intelligent eyes. "If it takes anger and a desire for vengeance to open and control the bonds, do I have to accept that I can't open the bonds? I just have to wait for another horrible thing to happen and then my power will take over?"

Reyna dropped to the side, lying out. I burrowed between her chest and jaw, curling up like I did the many nights we slept under the stars.

"I wish I understood how this all works," I muttered. "Kai told me so much, but couldn't tell me that. Why is it Titana gives Gaius Daoud the siphoner's blade, and he has no problem wielding it to victory? But the power she gives me has the added, and serious, side effect of stealing my grip on reality, and hiding away unless I literally die.

"Am I cursed to struggle with her power because I didn't sacrifice my own child to get it? Definitely not worth the—"

I bolted upright, making Reyna snort in surprise. "Oh my gods, that's it," I breathed. "That's it! Reyna, I have to go."

I took off running, riding the wave of Reyna's pleasure. She heard the thought as soon as my mind voiced it. She clearly thought it was a good idea, or I wouldn't feel her satisfaction. That was all the approval I needed for my plan.

It took longer than I wanted to find a path around the ravine. Eventually, Suoh took pity on me, shadow-traveled to me, then took me the same way back to camp. Dominic ran up to me as I slid off his back.

"Ainsley, there you are." He breathed hard. "I'm sorry. I'm so sorry. That was a stupid idea. I promise, I got rid of all the headstones. You won't—"

"Dom, stop." I grabbed his shoulders. "You were trying to be kind, I know that. Besides, I was just with someone who did all the right things with bad intentions. I'll take your good intentions any day."

"Ah." I could tell he didn't understand. "Okay, but I am sorry."

"Let's put it behind us. What matters now is that I have a plan."

His brow smoothed out. "A plan to defeat my father and the queen?"

"To defeat them, avenge my family, save the dragons, unite the kingdoms, *and* free the gods! We can do it all, Dom." I was jumping up and down. I couldn't stay still. "We really can."

"That's amazing," he cried, grabbing my shoulders right back. "What do we have to do?"

"We only need two things." I scanned the camp until I fell on them. "Actually, I should say two *people*."

Chapter Eleven

"This is ludicrous." Ramses slammed his fist on the table. "You said you would go away and come back with a plan to defeat our enemies, and instead you return with fairy stories? We assumed you'd take this seriously!"

"I've never been more serious."

The six of us were standing in the chamber of the Five, high above the city of Itzala. A grand room, it boasted a large circular table with five chairs, resting under a glass dome. I stood on a small platform before them like a convict before a tribunal.

"You wanted a plan and you have one," I said. "Forbidden magic."

"Preposterous!" It was almost refreshing in a way that Ramses had stopped pretending to tolerate me. "How can you suggest this nonsense with a straight face?"

"Because it works." I held up the sheaf of notes I brought. "The only reason this magic is forbidden is because it's considered an affront to Tenille to ask for more magic than he deigns to give us."

"And because it demands horrible sacrifices," Nerilla added. "Most often murder."

"I—" I blew out a breath. "Yes, that too. But no one will die in this case, as I've explained. Tenille, Mother Zaeah, Father Parthelan, and Calthoon trapped the other gods in an eternal prison so that they could rule over us unchecked."

"Blasphemy," Ramses said.

"But they are not completely gone from this world. Their names can be invoked and their power gifted to those who demand it, which is what happened for Gaius Daoud—"

"No proof of this."

"—and my mother," I gritted. "There are over two hundred thousand adult-age citizens of the dragon slayer kingdom. If two hundred thousand people invoke the name of the old gods, and sacrifice to receive their power, it'll give them the strength to break from their prison. In return, they'll give us the strength to fight back against General Roark and Queen Kisandra."

Blank and skeptical faces stared back at me.

"How can this be a discussion?" I asked. "The power of a god is infinitely stronger than the power of a dragon rider. Am I not proof of that?"

Sanjiro rose from his seat. "We're not questioning the power of forbidden magic. It's merely that what you're suggesting we do to get the power of these gods we've never heard of is—"

"Impossible," Ramses finished.

"It's not impossible." I shuffled through the papers, looking for— "Here. This was written in the very books General Roark keeps on forbidden magic. I asked Osman the details with Junia standing next to him, so he could only tell me the truth.

"To beseech a god's favor, we have to bring down the walls between our realm and the eternal nothingness. Naturally, this takes items of great power, and Junia and Osman already did the research to discover what those items are." I stepped off the platform and handed the page to my mother. "Water from the Well of Sorrows—"

"Myth," Ramses stated.

"Fire from the Everlasting Flame—"

"Suicide."

"A claw from a celestial dragon—"

"Went extinct over two thousand years ago."

I was having a hard time keeping my voice even. "Bark from the Infinity Tree."

"Never heard of such a thing." Ramses reached over and snatched the page from Meriall. It ended up crumpled and tossed over his shoulder. "Are we done entertaining these games? We have important matters to discuss. The spies reported just this morning that General Roark has figured out Princess Ainsley has crossed the Dark Border."

"This is not a game," I said. "That news is exactly why you need to listen to me. One of these things wouldn't bring down the wall, but there is power in four. Four elements. For main magics. Four gods holding the chains.

"All four together will give us the power to reach across realms and call on countless gods, who *will* respond. They want to be free. They want their names spoken, their temples resurrected, and worship for saving them from tyrants to sing out with thousands of voices. We cannot fail."

Ramses scoffed. "Only failure awaits. You ask us to keep our wings tucked while you flounce off on a journey to collect the impossible, all so we can spit in the face of Mother Zaeah, and demand power she doesn't deem fit for us to have."

"And you think slaughtering ten thousand dragons doesn't spit in her face!"

Ramses reeled like I slapped him. "How—? You!" He whirled on my mother. "How dare you? What is discussed within this chamber is never to be shared outside this room!"

Meriall cast him a disinterested glance, and flicked off. "She had a right to know. I will not apologize."

I never respected anyone more.

Zenebe held a hand up to both of them. Cutting through the argument, he addressed me. "Since you clearly know, let us speak plainly. Mother Zaeah will forgive us for the terrible thing we must do, because we do it for survival, not slaughter. But if everything you're saying is to be believed, you're asking us to call upon her enemies and free them from the prison she saw fit to throw them in. You're asking us to forsake our god."

"I understand," I replied. "But she will forgive this too, because we're righting a wrong. We're fulfilling what the prophecy truly speaks of, and returning the gods—all the gods—to harmony. It's because we've been out of harmony that we're here now. Unique mages hunted and enslaved because we don't remember the gods who gave them their magic. Fighting, war, hatred, and separation because we're all missing something, and we don't know what it is.

"This is what Father Past and Mother Future want. I know it because I'm standing before you now—against all the odds." I took a deep breath. "Mother Zaeah will also forgive you because...

"Because this magic calls for a sacrifice too, and in return for their power, you will give back the souls of her children. You'll give up being dragon slayers."

If I expected jumping, shouting, and carrying on, I didn't get it.

"Excuse me?" Sanjiro said.

"You have to sacrifice something you love. Most people assume that's a person, but I realized it when General Roark was willing to maim himself and give up his position as general. We love many things," I said. "People, money, status, and power."

I nodded at my mother. "I see you all and what you've built. You love being dragon slayers. You went from lives I can only imagine you hated, to soaring through the skies, and wielding power that makes mere humans tremble just to think of you. What could be a more worthy sacrifice to a god than to give all of it up?"

"No." The tone of finality in Ramses's voice chilled me.

"Your answer cannot be no. I've spent three days coming to the same conclusion you all did. We don't have the numbers to fight back. When three boys twice your size corner you in an alley, you don't lie down and cry. You fight dirty. You attack their soft parts, and you make sure they can't see your next move coming."

"This isn't some back-alley street brawl!"

"That's exactly what it is!"

Sanjiro said something about calming down, but I barely heard him amidst my locked glare with Ramses.

"The general so desires the power of unique mages that he's plotted for decades to bind them to his will. Can you imagine what he'll do if he flies into an entire country of them?" I spun, addressing all of them. "Time mages, thread mages, body mages, nightmare mages, portal mages, love mages, and thief mages like me. They will have no defense. Their training, formations, and ordered fighting will break down in the chaos. This is our only way."

"You—!"

"Enough," Zenebe rang out, silencing us. "Princess, we hear you. The goddess gifted you power no one has ever seen. Power destined to change the world. If we all had that power, no one could stand against us. Your thinking is sound... but your plan is not.

"It hinges on the collection of mythical and impossible things. Since that's the case, the argument ends here," he stated. "It can't be done. Let's move on."

"It can be done. At the very least, you can let me try." I stood up tall. "One month. Give me one month to get what we need. If I fail, we discuss other options then, but during that month, you don't *touch* those dragons."

I turned my hard gaze on Ramses. "Actually, you spend that time freeing them and returning their minds to the dragonkin."

"Preposterous," he dismissed. "You'd have us give away our only hope of winning this war while you go off to chase legends? No."

"Junia and Osman researched all of these things in hope of finding a way to give the general my power without killing me. We have possibilities. All we need is time to track down what's true."

"We?" Meriall asked.

"Dominic, Poet, Keely, Velez, Akasha, and Junia have volunteered to go with me. Junia is certain we can do this. I am certain. Trust me."

"Trust you?"

Ramses's scoffing tone was starting to grate on my nerves.

"If this Junia was so certain, why didn't she bring her theories to the general?"

"Because the items themselves have power. In the end, they couldn't know if it would steal my power, or I'd steal theirs and become deadlier." I tipped my head. "I'm sure becoming more powerful isn't a worry for all of you."

Somehow, that comment made Ramses angrier. "I won't debate this any longer. My answer is no. We gave the princess an opportunity to lead, and this is the best she can come up with. Now we return to seasoned experience and sane minds."

Expression blank, I turned to the others. "Is that how you all feel? Are you so certain you know everything about this realm and the next, that you won't even let me try?"

They exchanged looks—none so heated and probing as the look Ramses gave his companions as their silence stretched on.

Meriall stood up. "I believe we can all agree there is no harm in letting her try. If she doesn't succeed, we're in the same position that we were before. If she does succeed, then her logic can't be faulted. The power of a dragon can't compare to the power of a god."

"She asks too much of us," Ramses argued.

"She asks for two weeks. We can give her that." Meriall turned to me. "Two weeks. That's all you have. In return, no dragons will be harmed while you're away. You have our word."

She said that, but I looked at Ramses. His expression wasn't encouraging.

"Are we agreed?" Meriall pressed.

"No," Ramses replied. "We don't have two weeks to waste. General Roark knows she crossed the border. He's mobilizing his forces as we speak."

I broke in. "Then I'll make sure the same spies know that I crossed back into Adalinda. My dragons are coming with me. A sighting of me in Ghidorah. Days later Reyna is spotted over Hyelong. The general will spend two weeks chasing rumors, and ignore Itzala." I flashed him a mirthless smile. "Is that all? Any more protests?"

"Watch how you speak to me, girl—"

"Ah, there it is," I snapped. "Finally you've dropped the phony deference and reveal how you truly see me. Just another silly girl. Well, this silly little girl is going to do everything she can to stop Queen Kisandra and General Roark, because no matter what you think, I wouldn't hang the hope of avenging my family and friend on fairy stories. I will find what we need because *I have to*! So go ahead and keep doubting me." I snatched up my things and stormed off. "You're not the first man I've proved wrong."

I stomped to the edge, towering over the gaping hole in the wall that threatened to drop me on the city. I waved down the pair of hovering Druks waiting to carry me back down to Dominic and our party.

"All right, Princess."

I stopped moving when Ramses's voice reached me.

"Prove me wrong." I couldn't be certain, but had respect crept into his voice? "Two weeks. They're yours."

I tipped my chin. "Two weeks."

***

Dominic, Keely, Poet, Junia, Akasha, and Velez waited at the bottom of the tower—each with varying degrees of concern on their faces.

"Did they go for it?" Velez asked. "Will they let us try?"

I nodded. "We have two weeks."

The blowback was immediate.

"Two weeks?"

"That's not enough time."

"Go back and ask for more."

"Two weeks or two months," Poet muttered. "Why not two years? What we're doing is impossible anyway."

"Stop being so negative," Keely snapped at him. "If Ainsley says we can do this. We can."

Junia pushed through them, face pale. "I really feel like I need to say *again* that I don't have proof three of these things even exist. And the fourth thing we can't get to at all!" She flicked up to the top of the tower. "You didn't make any guarantees, did you?"

"They wouldn't have said yes without some guarantee," I replied.

She groaned, looking ill. "Ainsley, the Well of Sorrows and Infinity Tree are myths. More than myths, they're legends. And celestial dragons died out thousands of years ago."

"None of that means we don't have a chance. Legends come from somewhere. We'll follow them back to the source," I said. "The Everlasting Flame. We know exactly where it is. It's just a matter of getting to it. As for celestial dragons, dragons don't vanish into vapor when they die. All we need is a claw. It's possible if we find the burial place of a celestial dragon, we'll have hope of recovering its claw." I tapped my forehead. "My dragons can lead us to such a place.

"We're not without hope until we're without hope."

"Why are we doing this again?" Akasha asked. "You're the most powerful unique mage I've come across. Surely you don't need more power."

I shared a look with Dominic. We knew this question was coming, and already prepared a lie for it. "Because if we don't, the Druks are going to slaughter ten thousand dragons to build their army and make them strong enough to meet the might of Adalinda," I blurted. Eyes bugging, I realized my mistake immediately, but couldn't stop. The rest came tumbling out. "I made a deal with the Five to find an alternate way to make the Druks strong enough to beat the general and Queen Kisandra. Forbidden magic is the only way.

"It's my vow to you and all the unique mages to fix what I've broken, and make Adalinda a safe place for you all to live in peace once again," I said to their astonished faces. "I will do so in two weeks. In two weeks, we will face General Roark and Queen Kisandra in a battle they won't walk away from. In two weeks, Adalinda will be the first step closer to the end of tyranny. Will you help me?"

They all stared at me.

"An army?" Junia repeated. "You're giving the Druks the power of forbidden magic to stop them slaughtering dragons?"

"Ten thousand dragons," Poet clarified, looking sick. "Are they insane?"

"They're desperate," I said. "But they will follow my lead and trade the power of dragons for the power of the gods who gave you your unique magics."

Akasha blinked. "A god gave me my magic?"

I nodded. "There's nothing strange or impossible about you. Any of you. A god gave you your power just like Tenille gave Poet his," I said. "We've been killing and hurting each other over ignorance and lies, and it stops now— Actually, it will stop in two weeks." I met their eyes in turn. "If you help me."

"Yes," Akasha said before I finished the sentence. "I will help you. My power is yours to command."

"We'll all help you," Poet agreed.

Dominic hummed. "Course we will, but wouldn't you say there's too many of us?"

"Too many of us?" I repeated.

"It's hard to be stealthy with a party of seven on top of six dragons." He slid a sideways glance to the right. "I'm sure Velez has no problem staying behind."

Ah. There it is.

"It's what's best for your success," Dominic finished to my flat look.

"What's best for her success is not being weighed down by the general's spawn," Velez broke in just as smoothly. "All you've done since you've entered her life is fuck it up."

"She was stealing to feed herself before I entered her life. So I guess that fuckup is on you."

"When are you going to do us all a favor and walk into the sea?"

"Right after I burn your worthless ass into a crisp."

"Enough," I cried, throwing up my hands. "We're *all* going. Dominic, your scattershot makes you an army all by yourself. Keely, your threads get past every lock and closed door. Akasha, your power to make people see and hear whatever you want is all the stealth we need. Poet, we won't even be able to look upon the Everlasting Flame without you.

"Junia, your truth magic will cut through all the lies and bullshit, and make sure we're always looking in the right place. Velez, you know who our allies are on both sides of the Dark Border, and Atlas is a powerful stone mage. I need every single one of you if we're to succeed, and we will succeed."

My speech did nothing to stop the glares Dominic and Velez were throwing at each other.

Keely edged to my side. "Give up on making the two of them friends. In their eyes, the other failed you. That can never be forgiven."

I couldn't voice the discomfort that made me feel. I wasn't used to being loved so wholly.

"You all head back to the Gaia Curves," I said instead. "Tell the dragons we leave at first light."

"Why are we telling them?" Poet asked. "You're not coming with us?"

"There's something I have to do first."

"I'll stay with you," Dominic and Velez said at the same time.

"You're not staying anywhere," Dominic barked at him. "Fuck off."

"I have to do this alone," I said over their rising voices. "Please. I'll see you in the morning."

Naturally, they did not go as easily as that. After much arguing and fussing back and forth, I finally waved off the litter carrying them away. When it was a speck in the distance, I ventured back through the gates and passed the waving city folk, heading for the home they built just for me.

"Hello?" I shut the door behind. The thud echoed through the cavernous space. "Are you here?"

"Of course I'm here, my sweet girl." Meriall stepped out of the hallway. "Hello, Ainsley."

I swallowed hard. I was a little girl again, searching for a face that looked like mine in every passing woman I met. Except this time, I finally found her. "Hi, Mother."

"Come." She held her arms to me. "I have all the ingredients. We'll cook your favorite foods tonight, and talk. Just talk."

I took a step, then I was running. Throwing myself in her arms, I said, "I'd like that more than anything."

"Oh, my baby." A soft kiss pressed against my forehead. "You're finally home."

***

My party milled around the fire when I arrived—checking and re-checking their packs. Counting the remains of our money and food. Getting ready for an impossible mission.

Keely ran over when she saw me. "Morning, Ainsley." We hugged. "We're ready to go here. The only thing is, are you sure your dragons will let us ride them?"

"All but Tizor, who is staying behind to watch over the younglings—his and mine. The others know that what we do is important, and we don't have a lot of time to do it. The fastest way to get around is by dragon-back."

"Ghidorah is our first stop."

I turned around at Dominic's voice. He stepped forward as if expecting a hug too.

My arms stayed by my side.

A tic in his jaw was the only sign he noticed. "My mother used to read us stories every night," he continued. "One night, she told us the tale of the Well of Sorrows. It made my sister cry, so she never told it again, but it was about a Ghidorian princess. If all legends are based in truth, then Ghidorah is where we begin."

"Ghidorah it is." I went up to Reyna and kissed her snout. "Ready, my beauties?"

She knocked me around. I was beginning to understand that as yes.

"Dominic, you ride Reyna. Lead the way."

While Dominic, Keely, and Poet were captives, they treated the son of the general marginally better, so they didn't take his clothes and boots like they did Poet and Keely.

Dominic hopped on Reyna with his stick boots. They took off like happy lovers reunited.

Mireu left with Keely. Poet and Junia hopped on Cadmus. Kenna carried Akasha. Velez placed his hand on Suoh, who whipped around and snapped at him, making Velez fall flat on his ass.

Annoyance rippled through Suoh's bond. I stifled a giggle. Suoh wasn't even mad about Atlas, he was just grumpy about being touched. My Suoh had the soul of a wet cat.

I quickly ran off to hug the hatchlings and kiss Tizor goodbye, then I coaxed Velez back to Suoh's side.

"Come on. You and I are arriving ahead of everyone," I said. "Suoh is going to shadow-travel us to Calixto. Edjer's capital. We'll pop in, get spotted by dozens of people, and the general will take his eyes off the Dark Border and send riders there to search for me."

"Atlas can just fly there," he said. "With Akasha on our side, she can make him look like a pigeon."

"She said her magic doesn't work on dragons. If Atlas flies near them, they'll waste too much time trying to kill him."

He tipped his head. "Good point."

I put his hand on Suoh, then rubbed my scaly boy when he started growling. "Ready?" I asked them both.

"Read—"

Darkness swamped us—swallowing light, sound, air, and life. It pressed in like four collapsing walls, crushing to squeeze everything out of me until there was nothing left.

Just when it became unbearable, a wave of sound and cold bowled us over. It was like a bubble popped and it all came in—people, sun, buildings, and screams.

Suoh brought us right into the middle of Calixto's square. We must've interrupted prayers because we swept out over a crowd of people on their knees, who shot up screaming when the dragon thief appeared in their midst.

Water, fire, and stone flew through the air.

I touched Suoh and we were gone.

"Ugh!" Velez stumbled away from the dragon, and dropped hard on the grass. "Do you ever get used to that? Feels like being squeezed through a one-inch tube."

Suoh left us immediately. He had more than his fill of sun and people for the week.

"Where are we?"

"Ghidorah." I left the shade of the trees, gazing up at the towering spires, painted windows, and crumbling facade. "Dominic's home."

****

Velez and I walked the lonely hallways. No portraits greeted. No rugs dampened our echoing steps.

There were only cobwebs, and silence.

"This is the ancestral home of the Altairas, Dominic's mother's family name. The royal family lived here for twenty generations. It even survived through Zalina's siege."

We turned a corner and found ourselves in an empty ballroom. Ghosts of happy, dancing people and parties past played before my eyes.

"Did you know Ghidorah was the last kingdom to fall? A hundred days and a hundred nights, Zalina and her dragons attacked the castle but couldn't get in."

"How is that possible?"

I don't know why we whispered. Maybe we both knew this place deserved reverence.

"Domain magic. It can happen when so many people of the same bloodline live and grow in one place." The knowledge I gleaned from my time in the hive mind poured out of me.

"A part of themselves, their magic, is left behind to protect their loved ones after. Their home protected them from Zalina until she gave up and started burning down the outer towns and villages.

"Dominic's grandmother couldn't let her people suffer to hold on to a throne, so she surrendered."

Velez whistled. "I know you said Zalina lost her mind toward the end, and this all started because Kisandra murdered her family, but it's hard to think of her as the victim when you hear the tales of what she did to the people of this land."

I nodded. "I lost myself in the dragonkin, and still it never occurred to me to cut down every innocent person in my path. Zalina didn't get that from the dragons. That was all her."

"I guess that's the reality of life. To some we're their victim. To others, we're their nightmare."

I thought of the people of Calixto, screaming and attacking on sight of me. I didn't have to ask what I was to them.

"Why is it empty if this is the spawn's home?"

"You can call him Dominic, you know."

"I had it right the first time."

I rolled my eyes. "General Roark hated it here. The domain magic knew he wasn't wanted, and it made his life hell. Doorknobs heating up and burning when he touched them. Rooms locking him in. Freezing cold baths.

"But the marriage contract stated that Celandine, Dominic's mother, would remain in her home for as long as she wished. When Celandine... fell ill... Roark finally had the excuse to move her out. With their mother gone, Roark took Dominic with him and sent his sisters to live with relatives. No one can be here if the royal family isn't, so now it just sits here." I placed my hand on the wall. "The only one strong enough to survive the fall of the kingdoms, and it wastes away. Alone."

I looked to Velez. He had a thoughtful look on his face, gazing up at the painted scenes on the ceiling. A happy, smiling family. Now crumbling away.

Going over, I patted his shoulder. "Have you found some sympathy for the general's spawn?"

Velez blinked away. Atlas whipped around and grabbed my hand. I squawked when he kissed it.

"Is that what holds you two together? Pity?" He scoffed. "Pathetic. Leave him, my love and light. He's been letting his daddy push him around his whole life. But me? I'll protect you and our children from all threats."

"You can't even protect yourself from the beating I'll give you if you slobber on me again!"

Atlas flew back, easily dodging my coming smack.

"And we're not held together by pity. We're held together by respect, support, love, and blisteringly hot sex. Thank you very much."

Atlas cocked his head. "Is that why you flinch when he touches you? Your bluster reeks of lies, darling." He tapped his nose. "Give your false speech to someone who can't sniff them out."

I flinched then. Atlas had been watching how Dominic and I interacted the last few days? Was everyone watching and wondering what was going on with us?

Awful. I didn't want the world seeing us and thinking I didn't love Dominic Roark in every way. But there couldn't be an us when there were fifty-nine people on the other side of the veil who I failed to protect. I couldn't fail to avenge them too.

"Don't," I rasped. "Don't talk about things you don't understand."

"I understand very well." It was his tone, not his words that stopped me turning away. An uncharacteristic seriousness etched into his face. "I understand you better than everyone, Ainsley Shadowslayer. You can deny it, but it'll always be true."

"You—!"

Velez stood in his place. It was truly frightening how quickly they could do that. No wonder I never found Velez all those times we played hide-and-seek. Atlas simply took over and flew them away.

"Sorry," Velez said, shrugging with that lopsided grin. "Atlas likes to have the last word."

"If I punch him, does it hurt both of you?"

He laughed. "No, thank the gods. Beat him up all you want."

"Your permission is all I need," I replied, making him laugh louder. A smile tugged on my lips too. Velez's laugh reminded me of summer days, and chasing my siblings through the forest. "Can I ask you something?"

"You might as well get them all out." He moved to the window. "People have nothing but questions about the curse."

Guilt stung me. It *was* a question about the curse. "Sorry. I don't want to make you feel like an oddity."

"I am an oddity. Especially here," he said, sweeping over the forest. "No one in or around Adalinda has come across the likes of us."

"What would you do to be free of the curse?" I blurted. "Would you do forbidden magic? Because if there is something in those texts that can help you, I'll storm the general's estate and find it."

"You would, wouldn't you?" Smiling, Velez bumped my shoulder. "But no. Atlas had the same thought, but decided it was too risky in the end. Those texts are based on your magics and your gods. We're Nevaehan. This is a Nevaehan curse. No predicting what would happen."

My brows crumpled. "But you have the same magic as us. Stone magic."

He shook his head. "We stole it, Ainsley. From the dragon."

When their parents cut out its heart and fed it to Atlas.

"Oh." I was quiet for a beat. "But my mother said people can only take the power of a dragon of their own type. Why did it work for you?"

"I can only guess, but I think it's because Nevaehans are more similar to dragons than they are to Adalindians."

"Because you can... fly? Breathe fire? Make the world your privy?"

He cracked up. "No, dummy, but thank you for the laugh. You know the hive mind the dragonkin has? We have that too.

"Not in the same way," he quickly added at my hanging jaw. "But our magic connects us in this way that... can't be explained. We just know and understand each other. In Nevaeh, there are no wars. No murders. No crime. Same way that the dragons would never go to war with each other.

"The fighting and conflict you have on this side of the sea." Velez shook his head. "We can't understand it."

"Hmm." I looked out as my dragons and the others arrived, touching down behind the castle as Dominic instructed. "I should like to visit your homeland one day. You brought me to my home." I smiled. "I want you to bring me to yours."

Atlas smiled back at me. "I shall take you anywhere you wish, my blossom."

Rolling my eyes, I walked away. "Idiot."

I weaved through the corridors and stepped out the back door. The others waited for me, along with four sky dragons in disguise. They flew in packs all over the kingdom. No one would look up, spot them, and look any closer. Akasha's power was truly marvelous. I wondered at the god who gave it to her... and what an army of sensory mages could do.

Velez returned to join us on the grass. Our eyes all flew to Dominic—who stood there staring at his home. For so many years he was happy here... then his father came to stay.

"Follow me," he said simply, taking off.

We rushed to follow behind as Dominic began his story.

"The Well of Sorrows comes from the story of Inaya Altaira." He turned a corner and climbed the stairs. His voice bounced off the stone, floating back down to us. "Her father, the king, loved her more than anything. All he cared for was her happiness, so he rejected all the suitors offering money, land, and jewels for her hand in marriage.

"He decreed that Inaya would decide her fate, and marry whoever she loved and chose," he said. "Men came from all over, and like fools, they simply offered her the money, land, jewels directly—believing they could buy her.

"Every night, she'd stay up late in the stables with the stable boy. He lived at the palace all his life, and all that time they'd been friends," he said. "They'd laugh over whatever ridiculous, pompous thing the men had done. All those nights together, they fell in love."

Topping the staircase, we spilled out into a long hallway. Different-colored double doors lined the walls up and down, the only spot of brightness in a sea of gray stone.

"When the time came to make her decision, the stable boy made his offer. *I have no money, land, or jewels, but for as long as you live, I will fill your life with laughter, love, and happiness.*

"She said yes."

"Aww." Akasha clapped. "But this is such a sweet story. What does it have to do with sorrow?"

"Because on their wedding night, they left in a carriage for their honeymoon. The stable boy slit her throat the minute they were alone, then threw her body in a well."

I stopped dead, gaping at him as wide as Poet, Velez, and Akasha. We knew of the legend of the Well of Sorrows, but we didn't know all the details.

"He slit her throat?" I cried. "Her childhood friend? The one she chose over land and riches? Why?"

"Because he never loved her. He loved her younger brother, who couldn't inherit the throne with his older sister in the way, so they hatched a plan the minute the king announced Princess Inaya would choose her husband." Dominic halted in front of the door at the end of the hallway, and pushed inside. We followed him into a small room with walls covered in red poppy flowers. The only spot of cheer amidst this lonely place. "The stable boy came back from the honeymoon, claiming she changed her mind and ran away with one of the other suitors.

"A suitor did go missing—thanks to the brother—so people believed it," Dominic said. "The younger brother inherited the throne, and lived happy with the stable boy for the rest of their days."

You could hear a bird flap its wings a mile away, it was so quiet.

"Wow," Poet breathed. "And your mother told you this as a bedtime story? Remind me never to cross her."

Dominic chuckled. "All Ghidorian children are told this story. It's not the story that scared my sister," he said, crossing to the window. "She was scared... because the Well of Sorrows is right there."

We rushed to the window. Looking over the trees, a small clearing made itself known, and resting among overgrown grass and a grazing deer... was a small well.

"My goodness," I said softly. "What does this mean? Did someone eventually find her body down there and figure out what happened to her?"

"They didn't need to." Junia came to my side. "Princess Inaya told them herself."

"She did what?" Poet stuck his head between us. "I assume we're missing the rest of the story."

"You'd hear it if you'd shut up a minute," Keely snapped. "Basically, Princess Inaya was dying, not dead, when the stable boy threw her in. They say her tears filled the well, and called out to the magic of her ancestors. They kept her soul from crossing the veil and preserved it down there.

"Ever since, people who've been betrayed by love visit the well, and beg for the power to get revenge. If she comes to you and gives you her tears, it's all you need to curse your betrayer."

I nodded slow, gazing out at the solitary pile of stones. "What if... it wasn't Princess Inaya's ancestors," I whispered. "I mean, what if it wasn't just them. What if that moment as she sank to the bottom of the well, her soul cried out and summoned power no one knew or understood. The god pitied her, so along with the land's natural domain magic, they were able to preserve Inaya's soul in her final resting place, and give her the power to bestow misery on all who lie and betray those who love them."

"If that's true," Dominic said. "It means we're not just here for some rancid old well water. We're here for water that's been blessed by a god."

"That's exactly what we need." Junia yelped when I shook her. "Junia, you're a genius."

"But I haven't done anything," she sputtered.

"So how do we do it?" I plowed on. "It shouldn't be hard, right? I mean, no one gets through love unscathed. Cheated on, lied to, abandoned for someone else. Most of us have been betrayed by a lover, yes?"

Keely, Poet, and Junia nodded while Velez and Akasha shook their heads. Dominic nodded too.

I halted. "Wait, Dom, you have?"

"Yes."

"Who? You told me you didn't truly love anyone before me."

He flicked over my shoulder to the others. "Can we talk about this later?"

"So there is something to talk about?" Jealousy reared up in me hot and fierce. I had my mind back to know these were dragon emotions, and I didn't give a shit. "I don't understand. We talked about past lovers, and you told me it wasn't serious with any of them. Now come to find you were so in love, their leaving you was a betrayal? Why didn't you tell me?"

Dominic held my gaze for a long, blank pause. "Because, Ainsley. It hadn't happened yet."

"What? What is that supposed to—?" I snapped my mouth shut. A sick, twisting feeling churned my stomach.

"Ahem. Just to clarify." Atlas's voice grated on my ears. "He means you, darling."

Dominic whipped a fireball over my head. A blast of air and raucous laughter, and Atlas was out the window, brimming such glee—the whole of the world couldn't contain it.

"Too slow, General Sp—"

Roars cut through the air.

"Shit!"

Atlas took off. The castle rumbled as four dragons launched off the ground, chasing after him.

I almost hoped they killed him. If only the parasite wasn't attached to my brother's soul.

I stared at the ground, face burning. "Dominic... I haven't betrayed you."

"I'll remember that the next time you flinch at my touch."

Keely loudly cleared her throat. "Come on, guys. We're going to check out the well. Now."

They all quickly left, leaving us in that terrible silence.

"Dom, I'm sorry." My voice was low and pained. "I'm not doing this to hurt you. Betrayed is the last thing I want you to feel."

He cupped my cheek, lifting me to meet his soft, sad smile. "I hear your words, Ainsley, but this is what I know. I know the look in someone's eyes when they're looking at me... but seeing him." Dominic's hand shook. "It's the real reason why you want distance between us. Because you look into your lover's face, and see the eyes, nose, and mouth of your family's murderer, and it disgusts you."

Tears spilled down my cheek. "Dominic—"

"Tell me I'm wrong," he rasped. "Tell me and I'll believe you."

"I— You and me— I just—" Tears clogged my throat. I choked on the words—desperate to tell him all the things I was feeling at once. "You know I... I..."

"I love you too, Ainsley."

He said that but he dropped his hand, and backed away.

"We should go get them," he announced. "Keely dragged them out there to give us space, but she knows the legend says Inaya only appears on a full moon night. We came here first because the full moon is tomorrow. Tonight we'll bed down in an inn not far from here." He rattled off plans, not giving space for me to get a word in. "With Akasha's power, no one will know who we are, but even if she slips, I know the owner. He won't betray us."

"Dominic."

I stopped him with his hand on the knob. "Is there anything more to say, Ainsley?"

Our eyes met. After a beat, I shook my head.

He swept out without another word. It was for the best. I didn't want him to watch me cry.

Chapter Twelve

We made our way through the city, walking close and closer together.

Rain thickened the air, and darkened the clouds—weighing down their bellies. That's what it felt like. A thick, sludgy weight in the pit of my stomach weighing me down with every narrow-eyed glance and behind-the-hand whisper that came our way.

As it was, I barely glanced at the steeply sloping roofs with their gold-dipped, upturned edges; the open-air lush gardens placed between buildings and shops, or wonder of a city I'd never been in before—different in every way to Ossian, Golden City, and Itzala.

My eyes couldn't linger too long on Laykan, Ghidorah's beautiful capital city, because all eyes were on us.

"Akasha," I whispered. "Are you sure they can't see our real faces?"

"I'm sure. I changed everything about us. Hair color, eye color, clothes, height, weight. We even sound like we're speaking Old Nehebkan. They're staring at us because—"

"We're strangers," Poet finished. "We look like we don't belong."

"Have we become this already?" Keely whispered. "Looking at others like they don't belong?"

"They're scared," Junia spoke up, voice flat. "Watchers walk around in plain clothes these days, searching for a whiff of unique magic, offering rewards to those willing to whiff it out for them, and punishing anyone who conceals a unique mage from them.

"That's how I was found." She drew her shawl tighter around her, warding off a chill that wasn't in the warm air. "I was manning the dress shop for my mother one day, when a Watcher in disguise came in and tried acting friendly with me—asking questions about our customers. She was trying to hide her intentions, but couldn't. She tackled me two seconds after blurting that she was sleeping with her married commander. Just like that, my life was over."

Junia's eyes shone. "So yes, this is where we are now. No one trusts anyone anymore."

Akasha laid her hand on her shoulder. They shared a look a magicless girl like me knew well.

"Let's just get inside," Junia said. "I'll feel better when we're behind closed doors. Roark, are we close?"

"Very close." He veered off and climbed the short steps of a pretty, red-brick building with a golden, steepled roof. The hanging sign above the door read Grand Laykan Inn.

We piled inside—thankful to be free of the stares... for all of a millisecond.

We burst into the dining room, stopping a host of spoons and mugs halfway to people's lips.

"Grab that booth in the back." Dominic gestured to the corner booth off the bar. "I'll order and tell Adan we need six rooms."

The five of us passed tracking eyes and hushed whispers, walking over the red and gold marble floor to the bright blue upholstered booth in the back. Nothing about the golden utensils, ceramic plates, fancy mugs, or crystal chandeliers screamed nondescript place to lie low out of sight.

Dominic said the owner would never betray us, and I believed him, but what about all these coin-heavy nobles looking at us like we walked into the wrong place?

We all slid into the booth, barring Atlas who made his appearance as we stepped into the inn. Breaking off, he plucked a chair up just as a guy in traditional, red Ghidorian robes made to sit down.

He crashed to the floor, shouting like he'd been murdered. "What the—?"

Atlas walked off.

"Hey—! How dare—!" The man scrambled up and chased hot on Atlas's heels, the slight hitch in his step barely slowing him down. "Come back here! Do you have any idea who I am? I should—"

"You should back off is what you should do," Atlas growled, whirling on him. I didn't know what face Akasha's magic gave him, but it couldn't be anything like the dragon-pupiled, gleaming-fanged snarl that I was seeing. If it was, the man would be wetting his robes. "We're here on important business for General Roark and High Queen Kisandra. What is your name? Write it down. I want to make sure I have it right when I tell the high queen who got in our way."

Paling, the man sputtered. His robes were certainly wet now. "No! No, no, no, forgive me, sir. I had no intention of—" He backed away, nearly tripping on another chair. "I apologize. I didn't mean—" He stuttered and apologized his way out the door.

Atlas sat down next to the booth, spreading his wings wide. He beamed at our open-mouthed gaping. "You're welcome. No one's going to be staring or talking about us now."

I fumed, though it pained me to see he was right. All of a sudden, everyone was looking anywhere other than our side of the room.

"Do you see, queen of my heart?" he said to me.

"Excuse me? See what?"

"How I clear all annoyances from your path. You merely need to think it, and I make your wish come true. That will be your life after we marry."

Keely's brows shot up her forehead. "Marry?"

The look I gave Atlas could've peeled paint. "Do you know what I'm thinking right now?" I forced through clenched teeth.

His brows shot up, riding the impish mirth on his grin. "Really? In front of everyone? If you insist." Atlas leaned in, mouth open and tongue ready for a sloppy kiss.

I shoved a bread roll in the fool's mouth. He howled through the stale treat, woefully undeterred.

Dominic returned with two tenders in tow. They held five plates while he held one. He placed it in front of me.

"Akina guram," he explained. "Traditional Ghidorian food. You said you wanted to try it."

"I did," I said, surprised. Dominic hadn't spoken to me since we left the abandoned palace. "I do. Thank you."

The tenders passed out everyone else's food. I noticed it was different than mine. Poet did too.

I had a fragrant, mouthwatering dish of food I'd never seen before. Junia, Akasha, and Keely were given hearty bowls of beef barley, buttered bread, and cookies, while Atlas and Poet had—

"Rice, peas, and under-seasoned chicken?" He lifted the plate like there might be something tastier underneath. "Why didn't you order us some of that akina stuff too?"

"Why didn't you order it yourself with your own damn money?" Dominic smoothly replied. "I wasn't given my allowance while locked up in the cell next to yours, and we've got to make the coin the Druks gave us stretch for two weeks."

"Right, so let me get this straight. While you've got the coin purse, Ainsley gets all the good, fancy food, and we get whatever they find half-rotten in the back of the larder."

"Exactly. Glad you understand."

"No," I cried, face flaming. "Everything will be equal."

"No, it won't," Dominic lofted. "I made sure they gave you the best room too. Ladies, you're on the first floor, but you've got private bathrooms. Poet just got downgraded to the shed outside for complaining."

Poet tossed his head. "All those beatings, and they just couldn't ass-kick the bastard out of you."

"Nah." My love grinned roguishly. "That's here to stay."

I opened my mouth to stop them, then paused. It'd been a while since I'd been around the abuse guys called banter that I didn't notice. Sometime during their hellish experience, Poet and Dominic became friends.

"You're being a bastard, Poet," Keely said. "At least Dominic is enough of a gentleman to make sure the women around him are comfortable."

"You make yourself comfortable everywhere you go, milady." Poet bowed exaggeratedly in his seat. "Forgive me for not realizing it's all about you. Please, let me chew your food for you. Carry you to your room. Stay up and fan you through the night. Would that be gentlemanly enough?"

She sniffed, turning her nose up. "Good place to start."

"We'll put the room keys in a pile and pick at random," I sliced in. Once they got going, they wouldn't stop until someone stopped them. "No special treatment for me."

Dominic reached for my plate. "Then you'll be giving this back, I assume."

"What? No! This is mine!" I snatched it back, fork flying up and ready to strike.

Dominic cracked up. "That's my girl. Some things never change."

A giggle escaped me. Gods, it felt so good to laugh with him after such an emotionally shredding day. Made me believe that... we'd be okay.

"Nothing wrong with a little special treatment for you, my treasure." Atlas drove a carriage through our pleasant moment. "You should take the big room, because it'll come with a big bed. I need space for my wings."

That stopped them.

Poet, Keely, Junia, and Akasha froze. Only their eyes moved, flicking between Atlas and Dominic.

Dominic slowly raised his head, expression blank. "What are you trying to say?"

Atlas was an idiot, so he met Dominic's blazing eyes head-on instead of running. "You don't know? Huh. I never figured you for a virgin, Roark."

Dominic nodded slow, jutting out his chin. "I see. You meant she needed space over the headboard for when I cut off those fucking wings and mount them on the wall... under your severed head."

Akasha shrank away from Dominic, eyes huge. "This turned violent very fast."

"My doing," Junia squeaked. "I think I should take my food to my room—"

"What's wrong, Roark? Surely you knew this was coming," Atlas said, grinning away. "You were never good enough for Ainsley. She was going to leave you anyway—"

I choked.

"—what difference does it make if I steal her away?"

A matching grin stretched across Dominic's face. Alarm bells rang like thunder in my head. "Try it, Stoneslayer. You won't get far."

"Why would she want you?" Leaning in, Atlas dropped his voice. "You look just like your daddy."

They jumped at the same time, fists flying up. I shot between them, veering their hits wide.

"Enough. We don't have time for this," I snapped. "We have two weeks to collect four impossible items. The only thing we're talking about now is how to get the first.

"You." I jabbed Atlas's chest. "Bring back my brother. Now."

Atlas tipped his head. "As you wish, my sunflower. We'll continue this tonight whilst in the throes of passion."

"We're not—!"

Velez lifted his head. A sheepish grin was all he had to say for his brother. I had a feeling the guy spent most of his life apologizing for him.

"Don't worry about him. Atlas will leave us be while we're planning for tomorrow," Velez said. "He didn't join us to help anyway."

"He didn't?" Keely said. "So he's only here because—uh— Because you're here?"

"Nah, Atlas takes off if he doesn't want to be somewhere. He's flown me out of baths and off the privy when he's felt like it. My brother is sticking around because..." Velez glanced at me, then quickly looked away.

"Anyway," I said firmly. "We have one shot at reaching Inaya tomorrow night. We need a plan."

"Do we?" Poet asked as Dominic, Velez, and I finally settled and took our seats. "All we need is water from the Well of Sorrows. Let's tie a rope to a bucket and be done with it."

"Can't," Dominic said. "The well is dry. Has been for decades."

"Are you kidding me?"

"He's not." Keely wiped out her butter bowl, filled it with soup, and passed it to Poet. Half her bread went to him too. "That's why the legend's survived. Because somehow, on every full moon's night, the dry well fills with water."

Akasha shivered. "Has to be a water mage pulling pranks. We don't really believe a god we've never heard of, trapped some poor dying girl's soul at the bottom of a well, do we? Calthoon would never let a soul be treated so terribly."

"Some part of it needs to be true," I said. "We have to sacrifice things of power because cutting out our own hearts isn't an option."

"She's right," Junia agreed. "Actually, our hearts wouldn't work. Bringing down the walls between realms is impossible. You need the impossible to do it."

"So what does the legend say we're supposed to do?" Poet asked. "Do I lean over a dark hole, pour my heart out, then wait for a long-ago princess to give me her tears?"

We looked at Keely, Junia, and Dominic. They shrugged.

"I don't know," Keely said. "You go out on a full moon night, and ask her help against your betrayer. A few of my friends would goof around and try it, but nothing came of it. If they were doing something wrong, I don't know what it was. We'll just have to go out there tomorrow night, and try."

"Is that good enough?" Poet asked. "We've got one chance at this. We have to get it right."

Velez nodded. "If this isn't all a hoax, then Inaya's soul is trapped in the well, and she does appear before people who need her. That means the people she ignored did do something wrong." Velez leaned back in his chair, chewing his lip like he did when wrestling with a problem. "She must be able to read intent. She won't waste her time on someone who's goofing off."

I leaned in, jumping on his train of thought. "You're right. It's called the Well of Sorrows. She has to sense true, deep sorrow within you."

Velez's face darkened. "Then she won't have trouble finding that in us."

My fist balled under the table. "No," I croaked, "but an ex-lover isn't responsible for that sorrow. What if she can tell that too?"

"We're really doing this," Akasha said. "We're taking this impossible story as fact?"

"At this point, we're assuming everything we've ever heard is real," I told her. "We—"

"Wait," Poet cried, throwing his hands over the table.

"Don't interrupt her," Keely said.

"No, listen!" Poet fixed on me, more intense than I'd ever seen him. "He said they did something wrong. What if nearly *everyone* has been doing it wrong because the legend has been twisted and retold so many times, they don't understand it?"

Dominic frowned. "Don't understand it? It's the story of my ancestor. I got nothing twisted."

"But we did," he hissed. "We all did. All of us heard the story of Inaya being betrayed by the one she loved, and we naturally assumed it was the stable boy, but that story isn't just about them. Someone else she loved betrayed her too."

My eyes bugged. "Her brother," Poet and I said at the same time.

"Of course the brother!" Half a dozen people glanced at me, then quickly looked away. I lowered my voice. "Of course it's the brother. I said it before, plenty of people are cheated on, or left by a lover. A terrible betrayal, but too common to summon a god and create an entire legend around them.

"But Inaya..." I shook my head. "The brother that she loved and protected since he was born, had her murdered, then stole her kingdom out from under her. To not only have your own family do that to you, but for the act to be committed in a rare and special place infused with the magic of your ancestors. All of those things coming together could create something... impossible."

"I... I think they're right," Junia whispered. "I've learned enough about forbidden magic to dirty my soul, and if Inaya was able to tap into her ancestors' magic as she cried out with her last breath, trading her soul in the name of vengeance, she might've gotten what she asked for."

Poet jumped in. We were on a roll and couldn't be stopped. "That means if she'll only appear to people who've experienced the same betrayal—weeping and wailing over your ex will do nothing. It's got to be your family. The people you're supposed to trust above all."

"If it has to be someone betrayed by family..." Velez trailed off as he glanced to his right.

He was looking at the same person we all were—at Dominic's unreadable face.

"It has to be you, Dom," Poet said. "Your own father locked you in a dungeon, and had you tortured to find out your fiancée's location, so he could kill her."

"Oh, did he?" Dominic gritted. "I almost forgot."

"You're also an Altaira," I said gently. "If her soul is a part of the domain magic, she's been protecting you as long as you've lived there. She'll come to you now."

"I've spent many a full moon night cursing my father and training for the strength to defeat him. I'm to believe she didn't appear before me any of those times, because I didn't do it while weeping over a hole in the ground?"

Keely shrugged. "You weren't asking for her help then. We are doing all of this to stop your father and the queen, and take our country back. If she wasn't hearing you before, she'll hear you now."

"What do you think, Dom?" I asked.

His nostrils flared. The only clue to what was going on behind those stormy amber eyes. "I think all we have are guesses and theories. Junia came with us so we could cut through the bullshit and get the truth, so that's what we'll do." He rose from his seat. "There are retired, bonded royals in Laykan who are one hundred years old and older. If Princess Inaya has appeared and helped people punish traitorous family members, they've been around long enough to know about it.

"Tomorrow, Junia, Akasha, and I will question them. Poet, you and Keely go to the blacksmith's. He won't question why your faces are covered. He's used to customers who desire discretion.

"Ainsley, you sleep in and get some rest tomorrow." Dominic gestured in Velez's general direction. "You and your bastard brother do whatever it is you fucking do. Preferably far away from here." He walked off. "I'll grab our room keys."

They looked to me after he was gone.

"He's right," I said. "It wouldn't hurt to get facts, not theories. People thought they knew everything about my power, and they were wrong. We can't be wrong about this.

"Plus, Poet, you were saying we needed something to hold the Everlasting Flame. Might as well get it now." I nudged Velez. "Obviously, you're staying, but you might want to keep Atlas in. Dominic will kill him the next time he sees him."

I wasn't exaggerating.

"I can't keep Atlas in. He is him when he wants to be him. I am me when I want to be me. No twin has more control over the other."

Keely blinked. "That sounds simple, but when you think about it, that's the most complicated situation I've ever heard."

"Yes, it is."

Dominic returned with our room keys. As promised, I put them in a pile and we picked at random. It didn't escape me that Dominic asked for six rooms, meaning we weren't sharing a bed.

That's for the best. He's respecting your wishes for distance.

But the thought did nothing to loosen the knot in my stomach.

Finally, we settled in and ate, drank, talked, and laughed. The akina guram burned its way into my gut. It was the spiciest food I ever swallowed. That didn't stop me devouring the whole thing. I never tasted anything so good. Plus there was something impressive about food that fought back.

"I'm going to head up," Junia said, dropping her spoon. "Roark, I'll be down early tomorrow morning. We can leave whenever."

"I'm going up too," Akasha said.

That started the trickle of good nights and goodbyes. Everyone headed to their rooms, leaving me and Dominic alone... with the twins.

"Velez," I asked, "would you mind giving us a minute alone?"

"He doesn't need to." Dominic rose up and held out his hand. "I'll walk you to your room."

I ended up with a room on the third floor. We fell into silence climbing the stairs. Dominic was right next to me, shoulder brushing mine, but he had never been further away.

"I don't look at you and see your father," I whispered. "I never have, Dom. I never will."

He said nothing.

"Do you believe me?"

"I hear you."

"But do you believe me?" I cried, surging in front of him. I pulled Dominic up short. "This is important, Dom. That piece of dragon shit has ruined everything in my life. He doesn't get to ruin us too. He's not the reason we can't be together right now."

"Then what is the reason? Because it's not because you think we knock each other off course, or because you really believe the wonderful people you described to me would think you heartless or selfless for finding some semblance of happiness with the man you love." His gaze pierced me through. "Tell me the real reason, and I'll believe you."

I held his gaze, lips pressed tight.

I looked away.

"Good night, Ainsley." A soft kiss pressed to my forehead. "I love you."

Slumping on the steps, I let him go, feeling my heart break into pieces. Irritation came down strong from Reyna's bond. I didn't need to hear her thoughts to guess them. I was being stupid, driving my mate away, and needed to bang my genitals against his until he forgave me.

"It's not as simple for humans as it is for dragons." I trudged upstairs. "And it's more difficult for us. Other couples will never go through what we're going through."

The number on my key led me to the door at the end of the hall. The rooms up here were meant for the guys, and didn't have privies or bathtubs.

Didn't bother me. The only thing I wanted to do was hit my bed running. We spent most of the afternoon walking the grounds of the palace, waiting until dusk filled the streets with people coming and going to hide the pack of strangers who suddenly came to town.

That plan didn't work, but all those hours I spent trying to keep it together, holding back tears at the distance between me and Dominic, wore me down.

I finally had privacy to break down in peace.

I stuck my key in the lock and pushed inside.

A blast of air blew my hair back, and watered my eyes.

Blinking my sight back, my vision cleared.

"What the—?"

"Hello, my sun and stars."

Atlas winked across the pillows and comforter, wings gently flapping.

The half-man reclined against the headboard, naked as the day he was born.

Although on that day, I'm sure the wrinkly, dying sack of ridiculousness didn't cover himself with a pepper grinder.

Why on earth does he have that? Does he think he's going to put that—?

My brows shot up my head. That was *not* a pepper grinder between his legs.

"Come, my precious. Let us make love."

"How did you get in here?" I shrieked. "I went up before you. I have the key."

Another waft of his scent made me sneeze.

"Love finds a way."

"Atlas." I forced the curse that was his name through my lips. "My repeated threats and rejections weren't clear enough for you, so let me be plain—"

"Ainsley, wait." Rapid footfalls, then Dominic topped the stairs, running to me. "I'm sorry. I don't blame you for—"

He ground to a halt, coming eye to eye with the naked Druk in my bed. There was no defining the look on his face.

"Go away, General Spawn." Atlas waved his hand and a stone flower appeared in the air. It floated over to me—so beautiful, intricate, and delicate in its design, I'd have thought it a true, gray rose. "We're busy."

"No, we are not!" I slapped the rock out of the air. "Dom, I swear this is nothing! He was here when I got here. I didn't invite him—!"

"Yes, she did," Atlas breezed.

"No, I didn't!"

"Did it with your eyes, darling." More roses lit in the air. "They said save me from this dreadful, boring pet with his cheese breath and tiny dick." Atlas shook his monstrosity. "How did you describe your sex with him today, as we held each other in the ruins of his palace—another symbol of his failure." He snapped his fingers at my dumbfounded, open-mouthed shock. "Ah, yes. I believe the words you used were blandly horrible."

"I said blisteringly hot, you asshole!"

"Ooh, want to see?" Atlas flipped over and flashed his ass, shaking it in my face.

I shot between him and the too-still Dominic. "Dom, he's clearly insane, so whatever you're thinking of doing, don't—"

Dominic erupted in hellfire. Flames consumed him. The room bleached in the blinding light of a thousand suns, blotting out my vision.

Screaming, I blindly swung around—swiping at him. Trying to stop him.

Dominic punched the air, and a torrent of fire unleased on Atlas.

Atlas looked right at me, winked, then Velez sat in his place. Very naked, and very surprised.

My brother bellowed as Calthoon's veil rose up to swallow him.

He was dead.

"Noo!" I jumped on Dominic's back, screeching unintelligibly. Heat from a thousand suns engulfed me.

"Ainsley!" Dominic extinguished his flames as we dropped, but it was too late.

I hit the floor, burning all over. Screaming, I slapped my chest, thighs, and face—knowing it was too late. Nothing stopped hellfire when it found its victim.

"Ainsley? Ainsley, stop," Dominic cried. "You're... not burning."

Shooting up, I peeled my eyes open, blinking down at myself. Dominic was right. There wasn't a spark of embers on me. My clothes weren't even scorched.

"Oh my gosh." I collapsed against him. "Thank Titana you stopped your magic in time. I thought Calthoon had me."

"Ainsley." A strange emotion crumpled his brow. "I didn't stop my magic in time. I didn't stop my magic at all. It was taken from me. You," he said slowly, "took it from me."

"I..." Plain Adalindian, and I didn't understand a word he said. "What are you talking about?"

"You stole my magic, baby. You had to because I was going to kill that winged piece of shit no matter how many souls the pus-filled sac was growing on.

"Ainsley, you took my magic without dying, or drawing from the dragons." He grasped my shoulders, blowing my eyes wide. "Quick, what were you feeling when you did it? What were you thinking?"

"I—I wasn't thinking. I had to save Velez. That's all I knew."

Behind his back, said brother scrambled to cover himself with blankets.

"Do you still have it?" Excitement lit Dominic's voice. I drained him like a river, and all he cared about was what that meant for me. "Is my fire still in you?"

I took a second, but I nodded. "I think so. My skin feels warmer than usual. Like yours," I admitted. "You always feel like curling up next to a warm fire."

"Okay, don't use it. When you do, it's gone. Just hold on to it until you need it, and I'll teach you to use only as much as you want. Can you do that?"

Could I hold on to his magic instead of dribbling it all back out like a baby who hadn't gotten her milk teeth? I wasn't sure.

I felt fine. The hellfire surging within me seemed willing to stay there forever. It wasn't hurting me. Wasn't bursting from my pores. Could I actually keep it this time, and use it how I chose?

"I'll try." I shook my head. "No, I can. I can do it."

"Okay, good. Now see if you can do it again."

A blast of hellfire roared toward Velez, who was almost out the door.

Bellowing, he summoned a wall of stone that Dominic blew through like paper. I tackled my love, screaming my head off. The fire went out in the same breath that it filled me up.

"Stop that!" Velez and I shouted over Dominic's laughter.

"I'm not a fucking target, asshole!"

Dominic's laugh abruptly cut off. I scrabbled at him, trying to stop him shoving up and storming toward Velez.

"No, what you are is collateral damage," he growled. "If I ever see that flying piece of shit again, I'll burn his wings off, then shove the crispy fuckers down his throat. You dying too is just a bonus. You're not good enough to call yourself Ainsley's brother."

"Dominic," I cried.

"Get this through both your fucking heads. *She. Is. Mine.*"

With that, Dominic opened the door and threw him out.

"What was that for? Atlas did it, not him." I ran to help him. "I have to see if he's okay—"

The world spun.

I flew through the air, bouncing down on the mattress. I blinked up at the ceiling, questioning how I got here.

"It's funny that I ran back up here to apologize." Dominic popped the top button of his tunic. "Say that I understand you're going through a hard time right now, and if you need to push me away to get through it, then that's fine, because in the end, we're meant to be together. And that will always be true.

"You're mine, Ainsley Boreen, and nothing—even breaking up—can change that." My eyes were huge watching him peel off his shirt. "But those are just words."

A flash of heat, and his body caught fire. Replies trapped in my throat as his pants and underclothes became burning cinders at his feet.

"I'd rather show you."

"Show... me?"

"That's right. There's no future that doesn't end with us together. If I die before we've done what we must, I'll simply wait for you beyond the veil, and we'll be together there. You and I are fate." He stalked toward me—body tight and coiled like a panther. "But, as we both know, you get weird ideas in your head when you're left in your thoughts too long."

"I do?" I croaked.

"Mmm," he hummed. "You saw me talk to Nuala, and convinced yourself that I don't love you in every single way. You read part of our marriage contract and assumed you stopped being my reason for living. And now you think that just because we're broken up, that I've stopped being yours and you mine."

"I think that?" My voice was barely higher than a squeak.

The bed dipped with his weight. My breath trapped in my lungs as his hands came down on either side of the pillow, encasing me in a haze of citrus, and a scent that was just Dominic.

"Yes. Complete nonsense, of course." Hooking through my collar, his fingertip lit with hellfire, and carved its path down—splitting my top in half.

Dizziness labored my heaving chest while the rest of my clothes were slowly and deliberately burned off. I meant to say something, but couldn't. I thought to get up, but didn't move. This wasn't dragon influence, or mating heat.

This was purely Dominic Roark, and his control over me had always been absolute.

A god didn't need to rescue my sanity from the dragons. Dominic only had to smile, and I'd have fetched my mind and heart, and given it to him where it belonged.

The remains of my last boot banged against the door, and Dom reclaimed my ankle. Skimming up my leg, he popped goose bumps on my thigh that spelled my need for him in every known and unknown language.

He brushed the gold band resting on my belly button. A gift given by Ghidorian lovers. A gift for his. Broken up or not, I would never take it off.

"On your knees."

I swallowed hard, shivering. Three words and my nipples hardened into glass cutters. Something about when he used that commanding, dominating tone in bed made me lose all sense, which he knew all too well.

"Dom," I rasped. "Let's just take a minute and breathe. I know it must've pissed you off to walk in and find that naked idiot in my bed, but—"

"Now."

I was flat on my stomach and pushing up on hands and knees before I knew what was happening. I'd been under the control of a mage who needed only words to turn women into their puppets. The magic of Dominic's husky, sultry voice was remarkably similar.

My fist curled into the pillow. I was trembling and didn't know why. "Are— Are you going to spank me?"

A lazy finger traveled up my inner thigh. "Do you want me to spank you?"

I bit my lip, stopping something foolish coming out. The last thing I should be telling my ex-fiancé to do is spank my naked ass. It was wrong to keep leading him on like this. Keep giving in to every need and want that arose in me. I meant it when I said there couldn't be a we while this battle remained unwaged.

But it's not me doing the leading right now.

"Well?" Dominic stopped short of my middle, then carved his path back down. "Do you?"

If I thought I was shaking with need before. The man had barely done anything to me, and sweat was pricking at the nape of my neck. I had always found his complete control of every situation all too sexy, but this was the first time he had control over me. And I wasn't handling it cooly at all.

"I should say no," I whispered.

"Should you?" He sounded merely curious.

I curled my toes when that finger caressed a path back up, going closer but not close enough to my pussy. "I should say..." I squeezed my eyes shut. "What you want me to say."

"And what do I want you to say, Ainsley?" Soft kisses followed his hands' burning trail.

"Something that I can't say."

"Hmm." His shadow fell over me. I squeaked when his palms came down on the headboard. "Then my only option is to fuck you so hard, I pound through that stubbornness, and the words I want to hear fall out."

If there was a reply for that, I didn't know it.

You should stop this, said my voice of reason. It was getting quieter and quieter. *You know how important it is that you and Dom be apart. Don't risk everything for a tumble.*

But he said he had no other option. My back arched of its own accord, readying for my spanking. *What am I to do if there are no choices left?*

"Spread your legs."

I slid those bitches as wide as they'd go. My voice of reason was still going. Thankfully, my need had gotten loud enough to draw it out.

"Say it, Ainsley."

I faced the pillow, shaking my head. I didn't know what would happen if I tried to look him in the eyes.

That trailing finger dipped between my folds, catching my breath. A second followed and sank in deep. I groaned when he spread them apart, gently stretching me. I didn't know what was hotter, his punishing me, or his delaying my punishment with this slow and lazy teasing.

"Do you have any idea how beautiful you are?"

I blinked at the floral pattern on my sheets. I wasn't expecting that question.

"You walk into a room, and the air goes out of it. People stop breathing. They fucking forget how at the sight of you." Grasping my hips, he rocked me back on his fingers, driving deeper still. I was like a tumbler's toy—under his mercy for my pleasure. "I could try a thousand times, and I have, to capture your likeness, and my talent will never be enough."

"Dom..."

"There's no paint"—he tipped my chin, bringing my face up to his—"that matches the fiery crimson of your plump, sweet lips." Warm breath ghosted my ear as he painted my lips with my own juices.

I almost came on the spot.

"Although I say sweet," he whispered. "There's nothing sweeter than the warm honey nectar of your pussy." He parted my lips. "I can tell you don't believe me. Let me prove it."

I think I tried to say something, but it would've been unintelligible even if he wasn't finger-fucking my mouth, coating my tongue in my own arousal. My stomach contracted so tightly I jerked against him, bumping his insanely hard cock.

This was new. *Very new.*

"And the perfect curve of your hips," he gruffed, other hand rolling down my side while the left held me firm, working my mouth. "My palm made to fit right *here,* and you were made to fit right there—" Dominic's hips snapped forward, pushing his cock past my folds in a single thrust.

"Ah," I moaned, nails piercing his leg.

"Say it."

I just shook my head, sucking harder on his fingers to stop something stupid slipping out.

"I think about you every second of every day." He continued like I hadn't denied him. Resting my head on his shoulder, he nipped along my chin but didn't start pumping. His firm grasp on my hip kept me just as still. "The way you wrinkle your nose when you're lying, and bite your tongue when you're laughing. The way you narrow your eyes before you start yelling at me, and blush when I tell you I love you.

"And gods, help me, do I love you," he gruffed. "For twenty long, pointless years, I believed my destiny was to be king general, save Adalinda from my father, and restore balance to the five kingdoms. Then I met you and knew in an instant that was all bullshit.

"I was born to love you."

My eyes were huge and filling beholding him.

"Say it."

I choked holding the words back. I was ready and eager to be spanked. I expected him to be hard, domineering, and sexy. I anticipated him denying orgasm after orgasm until I was a quivering mess, willing to give him any and everything he wanted.

But I wasn't ready for this.

Dominic Roark wasn't one to lose a battle, and this time was no different. He chose to do the worst thing he possibly could.

Make me fall in love with him all over again.

"When we're married, we'll have a little house in the woods." His slick fingers slid from my mouth and marked a trail down to my breasts. I wound tighter than a bowstring when he traced a circle around my nipple, then the other one. Taking his time hardening them into wanton pebbles desperate for his touch.

"I'll cook for you all the foods my mother taught me, and draw you under the trees in the fading evening's light. You'll teach our children to climb trees, pick out poisonous plants and flowers, and tell them our adventures as bedtimes stories—their favorite of all, the story of Mama and Papa falling in love while trying to destroy each other."

I laughed softly, eyes filling. The picture formed so clearly, my chest ached. Beautiful little babies with my sunburnt hair and Dominic's amber eyes. Our son running around with his mischievous smirk. Our daughter with his confidence and authority. They'd rule our little patch of land until they went off to rule the world.

"Every morning, you'll wake up to freshly made breakfast and my head between your legs. Every night, I'll make love to you until you fall asleep."

Giggles escaped my tear-painted lips. I had no trouble believing he'd keep this promise. He did so every night we huddled together in that cabin. Despair couldn't find me there with Dominic's arms around me.

"And every day, you'll say those words, because there'll be nothing to fear." He palmed my breasts, rolling my sensitive nubs over his calluses. Electric shocks surged straight to my core, tightening me around his cock. "I'll make our home a safe place for you, Ainsley. One where there're no prophecies, no wars, no battles, no destinies other than me and you, loving each other until the end of everything."

His sweet words were so at odds with the firm and sure tweaks on my nipples, tugging desperate, breathy sounds from me. He wasn't moving. Why wasn't he moving?! Gods, some punishments don't come in the form of hard, delicious smacks to the bottom.

"Wha—?"

My head was spinning. Mouth dry. Was the man playing the harp? He lazily plucked my nubs like dancing over strings. The effect was having a devastating on my sanity. I had to jump Dom the first time we had sex, because he was way too comfortable taking his time. Something told me I wasn't getting anywhere near on top that night. Dom was dominating me, body and soul. If I was lucky, he'd let me come before my screaming pleas woke everyone in the inn.

I tried again to speak. "What about... ruling the six kingdoms? Hard to do that from our little cabin in the woods?"

"No one said anything about a little cabin." Bending over my shoulder, he closed his mouth over my nipple, sucking hard. I moaned sudden and loud. "It will be a grand estate in the woods where we'll make our home. There have been plenty of times in history where the High Council had to step in to rule.

"We'll let them make all the big decisions, then when the children are grown, the six kingdoms will be their problem."

I laughed even as I bucked in his hold, causing delicious friction between our middles. It was a wonder he could always do that. No matter where we were, what I was going through, or what he was currently doing to me, Dominic Roark could always make me laugh. "Oooh, he's thought of everything."

"Giving you an amazing life is all I think about. Every minute of every day." He nipped my sensitive flesh, making me squeak. "That's when I'm not thinking of some new and shamefully sinful thing to do to your body next."

I ground against his lap, ripping groans from both of us. "I can think of a few new things you can do right now."

He smiled into my eyes. "Nothing would give me more pleasure, my love. Say it."

"Dom," I cried, biting my lip. "Please."

"Of course, Princess." That smile curled quick. "You only had to ask."

I didn't know what that meant until he hooked me under the knees, spreading me wide. Pulling out to the tip, Dominic thrust in *hard*.

Pleasure crashed through my body, resounding all the way up till it blew my eyeballs up in my head. I think I screamed "yes" or "finally" or a mix of the two. I wasn't sure. I was so damn loud, I didn't even hear myself.

Dominic didn't give me a second to recover. He drew me up and dropped me down, using my whole body to wax his pole, and make sure he wasn't missing a millimeter.

I may as well have been a sack of feathers. Not even a grunt of effort as he pumped me up, down, around, and a little to the left to hit that spot he knew reduced me to a dribbling moron.

My moans were screams. I clung to the headboard, its carved design digging permanent grooves in my palms.

Warmth filled me like hellfire, setting alight my inhibitions and unleashing something primal and feral within me. To think I used to see sex as something of a chore. An act to get through with a passably attractive man who respected me just enough to care if I orgasmed too.

It was only because of Dominic that I learned it could be this. Wild, hot, sweaty, loud, and *good*.

"Yes, yes, yes," I breathed. I pitched forward, dropping my face on the pillow. My feet were drumming the mattress, I was alive with so much sexual energy for him. "Do the thing."

"Say the thing."

I groaned, back bending as I held back my orgasm by magic because it couldn't be anything else. "Dom, please."

"That's not it."

"You know why I can't," I blurted. "It's not fair to you, and I can't hurt you anymore."

He stroked down my spine, popping shivers up my neck. "You can hurt me all you like," he growled.

I groaned, control nearly snapping. Only Father Parthelan knew if he made Dominic to love me, but one thing was for certain, he was definitely made to scramble my head and keep me off-balance.

"It won't change anything," I cried.

He was still teasing the bumps of my spine. "Hmm. It'll change your odds of being able to walk straight tomorrow morning."

Titana, give me strength.

"Dom—"

He started pumping—slow to start, then hard, quick snaps of his hips within the space of a breath. Dominic clearly wanted to fuck my protests back down my throat, and it worked. I forgot the rest of my sentence when his thumb probed my puckered entrance.

"I love you, Ainsley."

"Ah, ah," I moaned. I couldn't lift my head from the pillow before the force of his thrusts pushed me back down.

"So much, the hellfire in my soul set it ablaze, and burned away everything I used to be."

"I've seen into his heart. You've taken it over, Ainsley of House Boreen. Even the parts of him once rotted and corroded by hatred of his father, now beats for you."

"I'm yours, Princess. Soon you'll be my queen. One day you'll be my wife." He struck that spot one last time, tipping me over the edge. "Always you're my everything."

I clung to the sheets—falling in every way that mattered. Sunspots danced behind my eyelids, beautiful tiny explosions like the ones bursting all over my body.

"I love you. I'm yours."

I said it. As if there was any doubt that I would.

Dominic got me to say many more things as the night wore on. He pounded me in every position known and unknown to man. I didn't channel Reyna's hellfire, and still we destroyed the room. Broken lamp, knocked-over nightstand, ripped pillows, and torn blankets.

If he thought to drive Atlas out of my head and firmly implant himself in it, he needn't have gone through the trouble. Atlas never had a space in there. Even so, I didn't stop him trying.

All night we worshipped each other's bodies. It wasn't what former lovers did. It wasn't what friends do. But I was his and he was mine.

For one night, I wanted to indulge the love I was sacrificing everything for.

Everything. Even him.

***

I woke up in the ruins of our sheets, covered in feathers and pleasantly sore all over.

Dominic was nowhere to be found, but I expected that. He had to get a head start on questioning the royals. The full moon was that night. There was no time to waste.

Slipping off the mattress, I instantly regretted my commitment to fairness. Dominic requested a room with a bath for me and I gave it away. Now I had to hunt down the public baths, and wash my collection of love bites and marks before peeking eyes.

I got dressed and went downstairs. The innkeeper kindly gave me a towel and bath items, then pointed me in the right direction.

Keely waved at me when I walked in.

I'd never been in a Ghidorian bath. I wasn't expecting the dozen open stalls with stools and buckets. In the middle of the room, water fell like rain from the ceiling, and drained through a hole in the floor.

Keely washed the sudsy bubbles from her hair, not bothered about her nakedness.

"Morning, Ainsley."

"Morning." I ducked into the stall, grabbed the bucket, and used the rainfall to fill it up.

Back bucket and I went into the stall to scrub up.

Keely grabbed a stool of her own, and placed it across from me.

I shot glances at her, confusion rising at her steady stare and rising grin.

"Um, everything okay, Keely?"

"Everything's great. I just wanted to mention that I have the room next to yours."

I stopped scrubbing.

"Didn't get much sleep last night." Her smirk was huge. "Sounded like you didn't either."

I forced a laugh. "Oh, what? No. No, no, no. I bet that sounded kind of weird, but we were just training. I'm getting better control of my magic, and Dominic was showing me how to—"

"He fucked the shit out of you, didn't he."

"Yes," I said, dropping the lie immediately. "The ever-loving shit. He left to research the well and I don't know why. I swear we brought down the wall between realms last night, all by ourselves. The man did things to me beyond the understanding of gods and magic."

She laughed. "Don't know about that, but you certainly screamed every mortal wall down. I wouldn't have figured you for a screamer. All those times Reyna broke your bones during training, you didn't utter a peep. Turns out all it takes is a good, hard—"

"Keely!" I clapped my hands over my flaming cheeks. "If you're trying to make me blush, it's working."

"I'm not trying to embarrass you. I'm trying to find out if Dominic has any decent brothers you want to set me up with."

I snorted, dipping my scrubber back in the bucket. "He gave me a list, as it happens. It's yours, but are you really looking for someone?"

She tipped her head. "Why wouldn't I be? Because the last sack of shit I wasted my time with was Awnan?"

My teeth clenched at the name. "No. It's because... Well, what about you and Poet?"

"Me and Poet? Ha!"

I jumped.

"That's ridiculous, Ainsley. Where did you get that from?"

"I don't know. Just the way you guys are with each other."

"You mean the mutual disdain?" She sniffed, flipping her hair back. It cut the air like a scythe. "We're not like you and Dom—hiding an ocean of sexual tension beneath a rivalry. I can't stand him. He can't stand me."

"Okay."

"And I know what you're thinking," she blared, blowing me back. "That I'm in denial? I'm not."

"I believe you."

"Ugh, he's just so annoying."

I was pretty sure she wasn't listening to a word I was saying.

"He acts like I'm a stuck-up royal, when he was the one who wouldn't talk to me because I'm a unique mage." Keely plucked me up and tugged me over to the rainfall. I didn't know what she was doing until she spun me around, and rubbed soaps and oils into my hair. In a moment I was transported to the days I bathed and laughed with my sisters in the river, while we talked about crushes.

The corner of my mouth quirked up. *Is that what Keely and I are? Sisters.*

It's what you and Maili are, another voice said. *How is that working out?* My smile disappeared.

"—when he got to training, he pretended like I didn't exist," she raged. "Who but an actual stuck-up asshole would do that?"

"Want to trade assholes?" I asked. "I'll take Poet, and you take Atlas."

She snorted. "No, that Druk is all yours. Besides, you're benefiting from his attention. Don't tell me last night with Dominic wasn't a result of Atlas's constant flirting. What is it with guys needing to prove their dominance with their dicks?" She sighed. "Not that I'm complaining. Jealous sex is the best sex."

I reached behind and poked her, making her giggle. "I'm getting the sense it's been a long time."

She groaned. "You have no idea. The last person I was with was *him.*" *Awnan.*

"And it wasn't even that good," she continued. "He was just someone to be with. A unique mage like me." Her voice fell. "Then he turned out to be nothing like me, and exactly like every manipulative, evil, garbage guy who looks at women and only sees what they can take. I *hate* that he was the last person to touch me."

"Keely…" Facing her, I took her hands. "I'm so sorry. I hate it for you. I wish he hadn't gotten away."

"He didn't get away, Ainsley." Her voice was hard. "He only delayed his punishment."

It occurred to me then… that Keely wasn't someone to mess with.

She shook herself. "Oh no, I'm holding you up, aren't I? You've got a million things on your plate. You don't have time to help me figure out why I can't find a decent lover."

"First, I always have time for you," I said, squeezing her hands. "Second, the only thing on my plate today is training. You're the one who has to go. Isn't Poet waiting for you to go to the blacksmith's?"

She hummed. "He is, but I've got a better idea. Why don't we send Velez and Poet to the blacksmith, and I train with you? I don't know why I didn't think of this before. Me training with you makes the most sense."

I agreed because why wouldn't I?

Soon, we finished our baths, headed upstairs to dress, then told the guys we were switching up our Dom-given assignments.

Poet made a crack about Keely being too prim and proper to spend the day in a dirty, smoky blacksmith's shop, and she told him to kiss her ass. I don't know if there was sexual tension there, but there was definitely tension. Eventually, it was going to explode. I just hoped I had cover when it did.

Keely and I found heavy cowls and slipped out into the city, hanging our heads low and whispering across an inch of distance.

"I spent twice as many years learning to control my magic," Keely was saying. "I didn't have instructors who knew what thread magic was, let alone had it themselves. Everything about what I could do I had to learn on my own."

"I never thought of it like that before," I admitted. "Growing up, everyone around me used their magic like a third arm. Always seemed to come so naturally to them."

"Of course, they had so many people to show them. But me—" She laughed. "My parents thought I was magicless until I was five. One morning, I woke up covered in threads. I mean enough to sew an entire winter wardrobe.

"I was kicking and crying trying to get the strange stuff off me but, which I found out later, I make more threads when I'm upset, so they kept coming and coming. My threads were strangling me by the time my parents rushed in."

"Oh my gods," I breathed. "You must've been terrified."

"I was." Keely ducked slyly to avoid a glance that came her way, making like she was scratching an itchy elbow. "I was bawling my eyes out while my parents jumped around, kissing me all over. They were so relieved I wasn't magicless, they didn't care at all that I was a unique mage."

"Hmm."

She winced under her hood. "Yeah, doesn't sound too good, does it? I swear they're great parents, and wouldn't have loved me less. They were just worried about what I would go through if I was magicless. I don't have to tell you it's not an easy life."

I tipped my head, and my cowl nearly slipped. I quickly righted it, and moved even closer to Keely. We were having a very dangerous conversation.

"After all that, you had to teach yourself to master this impossible new power that nearly killed you on the first day?"

She bumped my shoulder. "Just like you."

"True," I muttered. "How did you do it?"

"Wasn't easy. My threads don't only shoot out of my fingers. I can make them from any part of my body." She lifted her head, gifting me a look at the thick, thready mustache growing over her lip.

I snorted, clapping my hand on my mouth to cover the laugh.

"It requires extreme focus. I have to control each individual thread, and they get harder to control the longer they are," she said. "I was watching when Commandant Drake was putting you through his idea of training. He kept shouting at you to pay attention to what you feel when your magic takes over. Made me think you really are like us unique mages, but I wasn't sure because your magic is so... impossible."

I latched on to part of her speech. "I'm like unique mages? What does that mean? Are they different in another way?"

"Absolutely." We rounded a golden building, taking a cobblestone path that led to the abandoned palace. "For most mages, the source of their magic is Tenille and their connection to the elements. They draw on that connection to use their power. It wells up inside of them like they're drawing from—"

"—a bond," I whispered.

"Exactly. It's not like that for us. We don't draw on anything. We don't feel anything." She shrugged. "Our magic is like—like—" Keely screwed up her face. "Like chickens."

"What?" I snorted. "Chickens?"

"Chickens," she said firmly. "Imagine if all you had to do was picture a chicken in your mind, and it appeared before you. As simple as drawing from what's in here and here." Keely pointed to her head and heart. "But for a unique mage, if you want to summon a chicken, you've got to find the chicken coop in your soul, and chase after the scampering, squawking little bastards till you catch one, then you've got to haul it all the way back to the surface and outside.

"Someone who has only ever had to think and make it happen, couldn't teach someone who can't."

I nodded slow. "I think I get it. It's the difference between turning a tap and water pouring out, or having to fetch a bucket, climb the hill, and get water from the well. Unique magic doesn't just come to us. You've got to bring it forth the hard way, and learn to control it all on our own."

I let that thought stew for a minute, thinking it over. "But the chickens can get out on their own, can't they?"

"Oh yes. The first year after my magic came was spent trying to make it *stop* coming."

"Thief magic," I began. "Sometimes it takes things that I need, but other times it steals for fun." I thought of my tumble with Dominic, when hellfire appeared all around us—out of my control. "A little quick-fingered troublemaker flitting through the marketplace, taking whatever it can get its hands on. How do I get control of something like that? How did you?"

"Wasn't easy. Every day, I take the threads and knot them, weave them, entwine them into a ball." She tapped her chest. "When I use my magic, I only unravel as much as I need.

"Your magic isn't like mine, but we know killing you over and over again doesn't teach you control. Can't hurt to try something else."

The palace loomed above, drawing us in with no guards or mages to turn us away. There was nothing here but memories and echoes of a once happy family. Not even a thief like me could steal that.

"I kind of controlled my power last night," I said. "I needed to save my brother. No hesitation. No gruesome death. I had to take Dominic's magic, and I did."

"You're close to Dominic. As close as your dragons. You know him, know his magic, and you trust him," she said. "No part of you needed to hesitate." Pausing, Keely studied me. "Maybe that's part of it. You call it thief magic, as if it's not yours. You're stealing it from someone else."

"I am."

"You're borrowing," she said, winking. "And making it your own. Common mages don't steal from Tenille. Akasha isn't robbing the senses, and Junia doesn't steal truth. This magic, as special as it is, is yours. Don't think of your magic as something you stole or shouldn't have. It's a part of who you are, and as long as you're not hurting people, you have the same right to use *your* magic as anyone else."

"Huh. I... never thought of it like that."

"Think of it like that now." She clapped my shoulders, giving me a little shake. "This is your magic. You use it when you want. You're in control."

"I'm in control."

I repeated the sentence, but didn't believe a word coming out of my mouth. Yes, all magic came from the gods, but this particular magic was the gift of a fearsome goddess of vengeance and fury who expected me to use it to fight against the most powerful beings in all the realms. She herself said I didn't have magic, I had *power*. Nothing about that screamed tameable by a little human woman of twenty.

"You look skeptical."

"No," I cried, caught. "I just don't know what else to do besides saying the words."

"That's why we're going to practice."

Keely set off, leaving the cobblestone path behind for overgrown grass and stooped trees. Reyna lounged behind the castle, sunning her scales. She made a rumbling noise in her chest when I hugged her snout.

"I have some of Dominic's in me still," I told Keely. "But it's not safe to throw around hellfire. We shouldn't practice without him here."

"I would've said that anyway. You know what to do with the magic when you've got it," she replied. "It's borrowing it at will that you need to work on."

"Agreed."

I looked to Reyna. She had wandered away to rub against the rough stone walls, scouring away dirt I couldn't see.

I had accidentally taken her magic, but only hers. I had yet to tap into the other bonds since Kai closed them. Was it a trust thing like Keely said? I thought of Reyna as my beauty, while Mireu, Suoh, Cadmus, Tizor, and Kenna felt stolen.

When I thought I was a dragon, we were all as one. They were mine and I was their dragon mother. I didn't ask permission, but I also didn't see it as theft. We were one.

Dragonkin.

"Keely, you said every day you take the threads and knot them. The farmer putting the chicken back in the coop," I said slowly, "you imagine you have control, and that makes it so."

"In the simplest terms, yes."

I gazed at Reyna. "I have to be like I was. Completely open and trusting of the dragons, the bonds, the magic—*my magic*—while also protecting my mind from being taken over."

"*You can't stop the tide. You can only put obstacles in its way.*"

"Keely." I spun around. "Attack me."

"Excuse me?"

"I was thinking of this all wrong. I thought I had to be in some extreme life-or-death situation for my magic to take over, but it was only when I was in those situations that I subconsciously gave myself permission to use my magic.

"I can't be a weapon of vengeance without someone to avenge. Well, I've got plenty of people to avenge now. My magic is at my fingertips, I need to stop asking for permission to use it, and just use it." I threw out my hands. "Attack me. Give me everything you got. Don't hold back."

"Are you sure?"

"I'm sure." I raised my chin. "This will work."

***

It didn't work.

I lay flat on the grass, chest heaving and sweat cooling on my skin. Reyna stretched out next to me, laughing her horns off.

"*Grr, grr, grr, grr,*" she huffed, body shaking. Amusement rolled heavy and deep through the bond, and had been the whole time I kicked and flailed at Keely's threads, uselessly shouting commands at my unresponsive magic, and all around making a fool of myself. In the end, despite what I said, I lost my temper and burned the threads with every drop of borrowed hellfire. Reyna truly lost it then.

"I didn't know you knew how to laugh," I snapped at her. "You decide today of all days to learn!"

"*Grr, grr, grr.*"

I swore she laughed harder.

"It's okay, Ainsley." Keely patted my shin. "It's my fault for getting your hopes up. I thought I could help you, but I'm no better than Commandant Drake—pretending I have your magic all figured out."

"You're ten thousand times better than Commandant Drake." I sat up and draped my arms over my knees. "What you said really did help me, Keely. I can't sit around waiting for my magic to act. I have to take charge of it, and I have to do it the right way. No shortcuts."

"Any ideas where to start?"

I blew out a breath, flopping back down. "Not a one."

The ground thudded with heavy footfalls. I twisted my neck to watch Junia, Akasha, and Dominic arrive.

Dom crossed to Reyna and headbutted her. "What's so funny, my beauty?"

I was many and all things to Dominic, but only Reyna was his beauty. I couldn't explain it, but I loved the way he was with her. The sweetest mix of love, tenderness, and loyalty that made me see the kind of father he'd be.

He'd be the perfect father to our hatchlings. If only all these people weren't around, I'd take him into the forest and—

I cut the thought off and dragged my gaze off his ass. My body wanted a repeat of the night before. My mind had to hold on to all the reasons it couldn't happen.

"She's laughing at me," I spoke up. "She finds my failure hilarious."

Dominic chuckled. "Then she'll be laughing at me next. We failed too," he said. "We talked to every royal that we conned into letting us through the door. They all said they knew nothing about the Well of Sorrows other than what the legend states."

Junia nodded. "It's true. My magic can't be fooled. Legends, stories, and guesses are all we have."

"We've got one shot at this," Akasha said, "and we're going in blind."

"It's okay," I said. "We're dealing with legends, gods, and whispers of a whisper. It was never going to be easy."

"The sun is setting." Dominic turned his face to the sky. "There's nothing for us to wait for. Let's do this now."

"Wait. What about Poet and Velez?" Keely asked.

"Poet isn't finished at the blacksmith's." Dominic set off, expecting us to follow his lead as everyone else did in his life. "He's had the man redo it five times, claiming the holder isn't strong enough to hold the Everlasting Flame. They'll be at this all night at this rate. No point in us waiting."

I jogged to catch up with him. Glancing behind at the others, I dropped my voice. "Are you okay with this? We got so excited last night about figuring out the legend, I didn't take a minute to think about how shitty this is for you. Having to drag up all the horrible things your father has done to you in the place where... Roderick died."

Dominic's neck muscles bulged stark and thick, he was clenching his jaw so hard. "It's not about me or Roderick right now. Besides, if this gives us the means to take down my father and the high queen, it's worth it."

I let him be.

Falling quiet, I heard the rustle of my dragons in the forest. It gave me courage having them nearby. For four months, we survived the worst life had to throw at us because we trusted each other. We would get through this.

The Well of Sorrows shone in the fading sun—a truly unimpressive pile of stones laid around a hole in the ground. We fanned out, approaching it in a circle.

Wind whipped through the trees and rushed down into the well, singing a lonely, whistling tune that drew me closer. Down and down I gazed as a vision shrouded me. I was there that night.

The night a sneaking, duplicitous snake destroyed a young woman's belief in truth and love. I passed under the trees that concealed his betrayal. I felt the nails ripped from her fingers as she clawed at the wall, desperately seeking salvation from this cold, unforgiving pit.

I floated in the water beside her, swearing with my last breath, my brother would know my pain if it took an eternity.

"Ainsley? Ainsley."

I snapped back, shaking my head. "Huh? What is it?"

They all stared at me.

"Are you okay?" Akasha asked. "You had a strange look on your face."

"Ye—" I cleared my throat. "Yes, I'm fine. The sun's set. There's no reason for us to wait. Let's do this and move on to the Everlasting Flame."

"Ummm." Keely looked around. "Do what exactly? Is Princess Inaya just supposed to appear? Is Dominic supposed to say something?"

"Couldn't hurt if you did," I said to Dominic's impassive expression. "Tell Inaya we need her help. If she was watching when you all lived in the palace, she'll know why."

"Inaya," he dropped. "We need your help."

I gave him the same flat look he was giving me. "Maybe try a little harder than that, Dom. Try not to make it sound like you're asking her for a knife in the gut."

He bowed low. "As you wish," he mocked, making Junia, Akasha, and Keely drop their eyes in discomfort. "Oh great and terrible Princess Inaya," Dom shouted, waving his hands over the well. "I, your humble descendant, beseech ye! Lend us your ire. Gift us the waters of the Well of Sorrows that we may destroy my father, and avenge a century of murder, conquest, and pain."

Dominic dropped his hands, giving me a look. "Happy?"

"Yes," I forced through gritted teeth. "Thank you."

We stood in a silence growing more and more awkward by the minute.

"Is that it?" Keely popped it like a bubble. "Is she supposed to appear to us? Did the legend have that right?"

"Don't know." Junia rose on tiptoe, straining to see down the deep, dark hole. "We couldn't confirm anything about the legend as true or false. Everyone just repeated the same story we've all heard."

"Well... there's one way we can know for sure." All eyes flew to Akasha, who flinched. "I, uh— You guys said the well is dry. One thing we did learn while out today is that it hasn't rained in weeks. If we drop a bucket down there and it comes up filled with water—"

"—then we know it's Inaya," I finished. "She's right. Water in a dry well. It has to be what we came for. Does anyone have something we can drop down there?"

"Here." Keely waved one hand above her palm. Before our eyes, a thread weaved a fine, interlocking web on her hand that grew, twisted, writhed, formed until a bucket so delicate and incredible sat on her hand.

Cautiously, I poked it but it pushed back—solid and unbreakable. "Amazing."

"We haven't seen amazing yet." Moving slow, Keely held the bucket over the well and let it go, carefully lowering it down by a wispy, spider-silk rope.

I don't know if the others were holding their breath while Keely worked, but I definitely was. This was it. It was the chance to prove my plan had a hope of working, saving the dragons, freeing the gods, destroying General Roark, overthrowing the high queen, and restoring Adalinda to the prosperous kingdom it once was.

One bucket of water would either do all of that, or it'd prove me a failure flailing around in the dirt while my dragon laughed at me.

A faint sound echoed up the well, blowing our brows up.

"Was that—?"

"Water!"

We flew to the edge of the well, leaning over as Keey hurriedly pulled the thread back up.

Shadows peeled back, allowing me the barest glimpse that grew brighter and clearer in the moonlight. There was no question. The proof glistened and sloshed over the swinging bucket.

"We did it," I breathed. "Water from the Well of Sorrows. We've got it."

"B-b-b-but how can it be that simple?" Junia cried. "Roark yells down a hole and water comes up? The legend says water from the Well of Sorrows will curse your betrayer with a fate worse than death. And that's all we had to do to retrieve it? It's too simple."

"Who says it has to be hard?" Keely took the vial Akasha gave her and carefully poured the water. "The same people who said the legend was about Inaya and the stable boy instead of Inaya and her brother? The same people who believe it's a tale about an angry, bitter woman when it's actually about a grieving sister who'll protect her descendants from meeting her fate?

"If I've learned one thing from Ainsley," she said, snapping my head up. "It's that we should never be so confidently clueless to believe we have everything and everyone figured out. Inaya knows the kind of monster General Roark is, and she wants to help Dominic stop him. Why would she make it hard for him?"

"I guess you're right," Junia said, though she didn't sound sure. "No one said it had to be hard."

"Let's go." I tucked the vial in my pocket. "We'll see if Velez and Poet are finished with the blacksmith, then we'll clear out of the inn and leave right away. There's not a minute to waste. One thing we know for certain is that retrieving fire from the Everlasting Flame will *not* be simple."

No one argued because there was no reason to. We left the moon-soaked well behind.

The others pulled ahead while I fell back with Dominic. He wore a neutral expression, which would not have worried anyone else, but me.

"What's wrong?" I made to grab his hand and stopped. My arm fell back at my side. "We've got the water. We did it. Why don't you look happy?"

The mask cracked for the barest second, letting out a scoff. "Happy? What should I be happy about, Ainsley? That was the most embarrassing fucking thing I've ever gone through."

I gaped at him. "Embarrassing? Why? Because you put on that ridiculous show? No one told you to behave like an ass."

He snorted. "Nothing like the sweet, loving support of my fiancée—Oh wait, you're not my fiancée. We're broken up while you seek vengeance against my father, because it's always about my father."

Heat bloomed under my collar. "We've talked about this," I hissed, straining to keep my voice down. "We've talked about it again and again. I just can't be with you right now, but when this is over, we can. What more do you want me to say?"

"It's not what you're saying, Ainsley!" He rounded on me, glaring into my wide eyes. "It's that you have to say it at all!

"Want to know why I'm pissed?" Dominic jabbed a finger toward the well. "Because it was easy. Getting the means to destroy my father was as simple as shouting down a well. A well that was right outside my fucking window my whole life!"

"Oh, Dom," I whispered. Understanding cracked my chest open. "Don't do this. Don't let your mind go down that path."

"I could've ended this years ago." Dominic slumped. My sweet puppet, his strings had all been cut. "Your family, my siblings, Roderick, my mother, my life..." His eyes drifted to the lonely palace. "I could've saved us all if only I believed the legend. What's a little fucking water? Tip it into his glass, and my father never would've known the difference.

"All of my watching, waiting, training, lying, and k-killing." His voice cracked. "All I had to do was figure out what you did in one night, Ainsley, so... yes... I'm embarrassed. I'm humiliated. I'm a joke.

"No wonder you want nothing to do with me."

"Dominic," I cried. "That's not—"

He walked away from me.

I stood there. Everything in me screamed to run after him, but my feet stayed.

What could I say that would make him feel better? I could tell him over and over again that I loved and didn't blame him, but deep down, he knew those things. He just needed to be angry, upset, guilt-ridden, and feel it all until he didn't anymore.

We didn't talk on the walk back to the inn. Akasha suggested we not walk in a group to avoid attracting attention again. Dominic took to that suggestion too easily, and blew ahead of us without a word.

I was the last one to cross the threshold. Velez, Poet, Keely, and Akasha were already seated at our booth in the back.

"Junia had a headache," Keely explained when I sat down. "Dominic went to order dinner."

"I should do that." I rose to my feet again. "Dom needs space right now."

"Before you go, you need to hear this." She tipped her head at Poet.

He winced. "I'm sorry, Ainsley, but the blacksmith couldn't make us anything that would work. We don't have a holder for the Everlasting Flame."

"What?" I plopped back down. "The best iron mage in Ghidorah couldn't craft a holder strong enough for the Flame? Are you sure?"

"We're sure," Velez replied. "Poet tested each one under his hottest flames. They didn't survive his magic. They won't survive the Flame."

"I don't believe this." I fell back against the seat, mind whirling. "What do we do? We've got to think of something. We can't take the whole thing with us."

"We—"

"Here." Dominic arrived loaded down with a tray. "Dinner."

I blinked at the bowl of orange mush in front of me. A pungent smell wafted from it, wrinkling my nose. "Dom, what is this?"

"Fuck's sake, Ainsley. Not you too," he snapped. "I told you if you're going to complain about the cheap eats, you should've asked the Druks for more money."

Three pairs of eyes flew to us.

"Keep your voice down," I gritted. "I wasn't complaining. I was just asking a question."

"A pointless question, because it doesn't matter what it is." He slammed the rest of the bowls down. The bread tray and knife received the same rough treatment. "You either eat it, or go hungry."

He dropped down next to me. I didn't know it was possible to rage-eat soup, but Dominic found a way.

"Anyway." Poet firmly pushed his soup away. "None of the holders worked. It's possible there isn't an iron mage anywhere that could create a holder strong enough to withstand the Flame. We might need to consider giving up on this one."

"We can't," I said.

Poet leaned around Keely. "Would it really be so bad if we only have three? I know, I know. There's power in four, and even more power in bringing all of the elements together. They're the foundation of our magic world. But we can't get near the Flame, and we couldn't do anything with it even if we did. We tried, Ainsley." He shrugged. "Let's just move on to the next impossible thing."

Keely half smiled, half grimaced. "Ainsley, I'm sorry, but he's right."

"What are you two saying?" Disbelief made me drop my spoon harder in the bowl than needed. "One iron mage fails and that's it? You're ready to quit? Well, I'm not. Ten thousand dragons are relying on me, and that's just to start.

"There're also the unique mages currently being hunted down and enslaved, and an entire nation that doesn't know war is coming. We have the knowledge to stop it, all we need is the power. Power that will come from the strongest representations of water, fire, earth, and air." I slapped the table. "We can do this, guys. Dominic, tell them."

"We do this—"

"See? Dominic believes in us—"

"—because we've got everything we need in Ainsley's pocket." Dominic took a long slurp of his soup. "We need to kill my father and the high queen, and stop the war with the Druks before it starts? We use the water from the Well of Sorrows. Simple."

I spun on him. He didn't bother lifting his head to face me.

"It's not simple." It was a strain to keep my voice even. "You know that. My goal is much bigger than stopping a war. You're the one who reminded me of that, Dom."

He lifted his shoulders, still slurping away. "That was then, this is now. We're dicking around for two weeks, chasing after legends and stories when we just discovered this legend is true. In our hands is the means to kill my father, and I'm not making the same mistake again. I'm putting him down now before he takes someone else from me. Before he takes you."

I inhaled a deep breath, and let it out slow. *He's worried about you. He's still reeling from the shock of discovering Inaya could've helped him years ago, and he hasn't faced that yet. He doesn't know what he's saying.*

"Dom, that's sweet." I squeezed his shoulder. "I know you're only thinking of me, but it's not about me right now. So many people are relying on me, and I'm not going to let them down." I nodded firm. "We're going to Hyelong for the Everlasting Flame. I'm sure if we put our heads together, we'll come up with a way to—"

"No."

My lips pulled a fraction lower. "Excuse me?"

"No," Dominic said, looking me straight in the eye. "We're not going to Hyelong. What's going to happen is you'll put that vial in my hands, and I'll take care of the rest. This pointless quest ends today."

"Dom—"

He punched the table. "This isn't a discussion, Ainsley. My ancestor gave that water to me, not you. I'll decide what we do with it, and the decision is made. Give it to me."

My eyes narrowed to slits. I felt the gaze of my friends and half the patrons beating down on my neck. "Who are you?"

Scoffing, Dominic rolled his eyes. "Don't be so dramatic. It's not that big of a deal. I've still got friends in the Riders. More importantly, my father has enemies. They'll help me get close to him and the queen. So give it to me."

I didn't move.

"Ainsley, give it to me!"

He lunged, and I struck.

Snatching up the bread knife, I plunged it in his neck.

"I'm serious." I kicked him out of the booth. "Who are you?"

"Ahh!"

Screams erupted in the dining room. Bowls smashing, chairs tipping, tables knocked over—patrons fled toward the door, shouting murder.

"Ainsley, what did you do!" Poet bellowed.

Keely burst into tears.

I paid none of it any mind as I stood over Dominic.

"Ain— Ain—" He clutched his bloody neck, gasping and choking on the knife sticking out of it. "H-help... me... Hel—?"

I rolled my eyes. "Save it. The show's over. The curtains are up. You—whoever the hell you are—are not my Dominic."

His feet drummed the floor. Desperately he clawed at the booth, trying to pull himself up. "Pl— Please... I l-l-l-love you—"

"Shut the hell up and reveal yourself already. Dominic's not afraid to challenge me, but he'd never treat me like this. You're not him, and I'll keep stabbing until you quit the act."

"Aaahh—" Dominic cut off mid-wail. The pain and betrayal melted off his face. "Okay. Act over."

Before my eyes, he yanked out the knife. It clanged on the floor as he rose—calm and healthy like a freshly birthed calf.

All around me, everything changed.

Keely and Poet ceased their bellowing and faded into mist. The patrons disappeared. The booth vanished. And Dominic...

Short hair grew long—growing and curling to the tip of his knees. Amber eyes lightened. Sun-kissed skin darkened. A flat, muscled chest grew out, and across her neck, a bloodless seam split her skin.

"Princess Inaya."

She inclined her head.

Looking at her, there wasn't a single resemblance to Dominic. She was small and slight. Almost delicate. She looked like a fragile little bird. The kind you wanted to bring inside, because the real world was surely too big for them. If anything, she more resembled me.

Inaya wore the silky blue robes of her wedding dress. Forever marking the moment that was supposed to be the happiest of her life... as the day she lost everything.

Inaya wore sorrow in her wide, shining eyes; deep frown; and the stooped, slumped shoulders as if there was no point to holding herself up. There was no point to anything.

"What's going on?" I rasped. "Why this game? Why impersonate Dominic to steal back the water you gave him?"

"I gave him nothing." Dominic's stolen voice was gone—replaced by a light, musical tenor. "You have not moved, Ainsley Boreen. The four of you still stand around my well, begging your favors. I only bothered to respond because I sensed one of my own blood.

"The other three are also being tested," she said. "This was one of your tests."

"My test?"

"To discover what you want of my cursed waters, and what you'd do if you received it."

I crossed my arms, holding tight to myself. It wasn't every day I stood before a child's bedtime story. "You only had to ask."

"And you only had to lie." She circled me. "If you were to tell anyone your true intentions, it was your beloved."

I spun to follow her. "Why do my intentions matter? Dominic was why you came out. Dominic is making the request—"

"—on your behalf," she finished. "Yes, I know this. Yes, I've seen into his heart.

"You've taken it over, Ainsley of House Boreen. Even the parts of him once rotted and corroded by hatred of his father, now beats for you." Her voice was whispers on the wind, washing over, around, and through me. "I had to meet the woman who healed a pain so many have never and will never overcome.

"Who so rid him of bitterness that he would take the means to kill his hated father... and then give it to you."

Stiffening, I raised my chin. "How do I compare?"

"We will find out." She snapped her fingers, and it all faded.

The inn, the lights, the color. Laykan.

My feet plunged through cold, icy water to reach the earth. I gasped, twisting this way and that to nothing.

Nothing greeted me except a cavern of stone walls, and water so dark, I couldn't see my legs.

"Don't tell me..." I tipped my head. The moon peeked through the tiniest sliver of a hole. Somehow it seemed even more miles away than it always was. "We're in the Well of Sorrows."

"That is the name it has been dubbed, yes."

Inaya floated on the water. A swan gliding effortlessly through her home.

"Why am I here?"

The question seemed to shatter her. Inaya's frown deepened, bringing damp to her eyes. "You've all been tested. The waters are for you, but I see no reason I should give it to you. You do not seek revenge against blood."

"But I do," I cried, advancing on her. Inaya floated away, maintaining her distance. "My sister, my sibling, my grandmother. They all betrayed me."

"And you do not care," she returned. "Their relation doesn't matter to you in the slightest. You hate them only because they murdered your true family."

I paused for a beat. "Okay, yes. I don't consider them my family and never will. No matter what blood says. But what does that mean? Did you bring me here to refuse to help me because I want revenge against the wrong people?"

She floated along the edge of my sight. "I brought you here because you have a question for me. Ask it."

My lips parted, and I stopped. Taking a deep breath, I pushed down my first reply, and asked the question.

"I need water from the Well of Sorrows for a forbidden ritual that will bring down the walls between realms, flood this world with the power of the forgotten gods, and help me win two wars—both seen and unseen.

"Will you help me?"

Inaya looked me in the eyes. "No."

"What? Why?"

"How can I?" she hissed, lips trembling. "One does not shout down a well and beg the water to come to them. If they want it, they must be resourceful enough to claim it.

"So you shall be as well, Ainsley Boreen. You desire my cursed waters..." She waved a hand. Four figures appeared behind her.

Dominic, Junia, Keely, and Akasha were still as statues. Their eyes closed and faces frozen in the serenity of sleep.

"Guys!" I ran to them, splashing and kicking up water that tasted bitter and stale on my lips. They came no closer.

"You have four chances to take it."

"Four chances?" A lodestone sank in my gut, dropping me to my knees. "What does that mean?"

Inaya shook her head, eyes swimming. "You know."

I clambered to my feet, and an unseen weight pushed me back down. I wasn't getting to them. I wasn't getting out of here. The Well of Sorrows had us all.

"What do you want!"

My scream did not move her. "It is very simple, Ainsley Boreen. All you have to do is answer correctly. Do so, and you may leave this place with your friends and my cursed waters."

"But I—"

"*I am the secret carried on the wind. I am the shadow of the sun. I appear in the light but cannot be seen. I disappear in the dark but cannot be hidden. I am love's lie, but truth's desire.*

"*What am I?*"

"So it's a riddle?"

"Wrong."

Akasha yanked out of the air. She plunged into the water and disappeared.

"No! Bring her—!"

"Wrong."

The waters seized Junia, carrying her away.

I clapped my hand over my mouth, screaming through my fingers.

They were gone. Just like that, Junia and Akasha were gone.

I looked at weeping, solemn Inaya in horror. Dominic was right. Of course he was right because when was my love ever wrong? We had no business walking into this legend when we knew nothing about it... or her.

Calm down. Calm down, Ainsley. My heart beat out of my chest. My hands trembled on my mouth. *It's a simple riddle. Answer it, and you can get out of here. We* all *will get out of here.*

The words of the riddle tumbled through my mind. I couldn't be sure I recalled all of it, or even most of it correctly, but I dare not ask her to repeat herself.

Secret carried on the wind. Sun's shadow. Love's lie. Cannot be seen.

"Is it..." My voice shook. "Darkness?"

"Wrong."

I screamed when Keely flung away, sinking into the depths. Only Dominic remained. My last chance to save everyone. To save him.

No, no, no! Think, Ainsley. You cannot get this wrong. You will not get this wrong!

I didn't know how much time passed while I knelt there, repeating the riddle over and over again in my head. I was silent, but Inaya was not.

"What is your answer, Ainsley Boreen?

"Surely you've figured it out now.

"Why do you hesitate? You know the answer, speak it."

She moved closer and closer with every taunt until she bore over me—a shrinking mortal in her shadow. "You seek to save the beings on both sides of the realm, and yet you fall down at the first hurdle. Oh, the arrogance. You blunder into situations of which you have no understanding, and it is those you love who pay the price."

My jaw clenched. That taunt struck a soft, wounded part of me.

"What?" she asked softly. "Do you think if you remain silent, you can delay the inevitable? Failure awaits. Welcome it on your feet, instead of cowering on your knees."

I pressed my lips tighter, pressure blooming in my chest. Dominic hung there waiting for me. Trusting me.

"Answer my riddle, Ainsley Boreen." A shrillness leaked into her voice. "Answer me!"

I couldn't hold it back. I exploded.

"Nothing!" My scream bounced off the stone, echoing through the well. "The answer is nothing because that riddle is nonsense! Sun's shadow? Love's lie? It's a bunch of bullshit that—" I halted, eyes widening.

"It's bullshit," I whispered. "All of this. Everything. It's just another show. It's wasted time and mental torture without any fucking point to it because... because..." I pushed myself up... and away from her. "Because you're not Princess Inaya."

Large, solemn, tear-filled eyes drooped in confusion. "What nonsense do you speak?"

"It's not nonsense," I snapped. "It's a truth I was too slow to see. How can there be such a well-known, detailed legend of a princess in a well, perfectly crafted to draw people in, and yet no one can confirm any of it is real?

"Why didn't Dominic know all he had to do was come to this well, and his ancestor would help him get rid of his monstrous father—? No, forget Dominic. Why didn't his mother know? Or her mother? Or hers? Or the generation of Altairas living right here on the land who passed down the story without knowing it was real?

"Because it's not," I flung. "Dominic's sister heard the tale and instinctively felt fear. She knew the Well of Sorrows was no good, because the true familial magics dwelling within this land were protecting her from the trap. From you!

"You're not Princess Inaya." The same fear gripped me, even as anger battled it. "You're the thing that ate her."

"How dare you?" she shrieked. "You come here begging for favor, and presume to insult me?"

Narrowed eyes beheld her. "If I'm wrong... why haven't you taken Dominic yet?"

She flicked to my love.

"I'll tell you that too. It's because I answered correctly. And the answer is, that riddle is a bunch of bullshit crafted by a trickster. A trap. A lie."

Her eyes watered, lips trembled, and shoulders shook. Doubling over, she burst into guffaws.

"Good," she shrieked. "Very good. Oh my gods, I could barely get through that with a straight face, but you"—she shot up, startling me—"you were magnificent!

"No wonder Titana is always going on about you. *Blah, blah, my daughter will save us. Blah, blah, my child is like nothing no one has ever seen.*

"I hope you forgive my little show." She snapped her fingers and Keely, Junia, and Akasha reappeared. Unharmed. "I had to test you, and naturally, punish you if you failed. Those four—" She drew a line across her ruined throat. "I would've drowned them, and you, without a care if you didn't see all this for what it was.

"The prophesized child going off to face the most powerful beings in the universe, but she can't even fight her way out of a grotty old well?" She howled. "I would've laughed that story right in Titana's face.

"But I can't..." She slowly sobered. "Because you didn't."

I swallowed through needles. I couldn't help it. That fear clung to me like a spiderweb—sticking and clinging to me though I desperately tried to peel it off. I was in the presence of something old, terrifying, and *wrong*. My soul knew it like a child knew how to suckle at their mother's breast. Instinct is gods given.

"Who are you?" My voice was a thin rasp.

"Don't you know?"

Stiffly, I nodded. "You're a god. One of the trapped gods that forced their way through a crack in the realms when Inaya's soul cried out for help."

She beamed. "Cried out to your mother for help, as it happens."

She wasn't talking about Meriall.

"Ugh. Everyone begs and moans for Titana to help them, save them, avenge them." She rolled her eyes. "You mortals. Can't fight your own battles, so you always beg a god to do it for you. Too bad for little Inaya, the manner and location of her death left an opening not just for Titana, but for me." Her grin was terrible. "And I got here first."

The pieces fell into place. "Ever since, you've used her and her tragedy to keep the legend of the Well of Sorrows alive, because a god feeds on belief. Even so, when people come here and you do whatever it is you truly do to help, they leave remembering nothing but the story of a betrayed princess.

"That's if they leave at all."

"Don't look so angry, dear," she said, waving my accusations away. "It's not called the Well of Glee. One carries tragedy to this place, and tragedy is what they find. But not the Altairas." She drew closer, standing my hairs on end. "You are correct that the domain magic in this land protected them as it has for generations. Filled them with an irrational fear of my home that kept them all away. Dominic Altaira felt that same fear," she murmured in my ear. "Even though the domain magic fades from this place, he sensed something was wrong. And yet he came... for you."

Damp fingers pinched my chin. I internally screamed as they turned me to face her. "He loves you."

"I know," I rasped.

"You love him."

I looked into her eyes. "With all my heart."

"Then why is it all I feel from you... is sorrow."

I didn't speak for a long stretch, and neither did she. We were both waiting for something. I had a feeling my patience was not as boundless as hers.

"God of the well." I infused strength I didn't feel into my voice. "I request the safe return of me and my friends to the surface, and the gift of your cursed waters."

Her eyes shone. "Why would I do that?"

"Because there's a reason the story of the Well hasn't traveled. You're just as stuck down here as you are in the cage beyond the veil. You're forced to rely on whispers and stories to bring your victims to you, instead of hunting them down yourself.

"But if you let us go and give me your power, I can defeat your brothers and sister and—and—"

"Yes..." Her grin curled into her cheeks. "Say it."

"I can free you."

She laughed wild and high-pitched. "Free, free, FREE! I will be freed to haunt, and stalk, and devour this world. I will become so strong, no one dare put me in a cage again. And you—" She giggled. "You, child of Titana, will help me. Save me. Free *me*. Isn't it funny?" She certainly thought so.

"Now the gods need a mortal for their battle." She winked, stepping back. "Want to know what's funnier? You're strong enough to win this war, Ainsley Boreen. But if you do..."

Black crept into the edges of my vision. This horrible world faded around me, melting through my consciousness like a nightmare. Slipping through... like water.

"...you'll regret it for the rest of a short, miserable life."

Chapter Thirteen

"Ainsley? Ainsley."

I blinked. My vision cleared on Junia, Akasha, Keely, and Dominic's concerned expressions.

"Are you okay?" Akasha asked. "You had a strange look on your face."

I shot back, whipping my head around. She—whoever she was—was gone.

No Princess Inaya. No god living in her image. No dark cavern. No tepid water soaking my fears. No crushing fear that made me want to stick my head under the water and never come up.

We were freed, and going by the looks on my friends' faces, they didn't know we were ever caught.

"I... uh..." A weight settled in my pocket, drawing my attention down.

I dug inside and pulled out a tiny crystal tear-shaped vial. Holding it up to the moonlight, the cursed waters of the well glistened inside.

"I have what we came here for," I finished. "We can go."

***

I was deluded if I thought it would be that simple.

Dominic and the others pelted me with a million questions on the way to the inn. I couldn't answer one before another came at me. Thanks to Junia, I couldn't hold a thing back.

"If it's not Inaya down there, who the fuck is it?" Keely cried.

"A god." I shivered under memory of that smile. "I don't know of what, or their name. I can only say that they could not have been a god with many temples, worshippers, or praise. That being does not like humans, and humans do not like them."

"Goodness," Keely breathed. "What does that mean? Why did she just let us go?"

"And how do we know she gave us what we need?" Dominic asked, pulling ahead of me. "You described her as an insane, cackling trickster.

How much would she laugh when we find out in the middle of the ritual that she gave us plain water?"

"No." Certainty settled into my bones. "She gave us what we need. I know she did for the same reason she let us go. She wants us to succeed, because then we'll free her from her prison. Allowing her to roam the realms again—feasting."

Junia stopped dead. "Excuse me? Are you telling me that if we go through with the ritual, we'll free that—that *thing*! We can't do that!"

"She's right, Ainsley," Keely said. "We can't set that creature loose on the world, even if they are a god. We have to come up with another plan."

"There is no other plan."

"But don't you understand now?" Junia shot in front of me too. "You didn't get the full story. Tenille, Mother Zaeah, Calthoon, and Father Parthelan didn't lock them away because they were power-hungry. They did it because they're dangerous!

"Our true gods were good and just in their actions. We can't betray them by unleashing the very beings they were protecting us from. We have to stop—"

"That's not how things are! It's how you're choosing to see them because you're scared!"

Junia lurched back, brows blown.

"Ainsley..." Keely whispered.

"Ugh, I'm sorry." I clutched my head. "I didn't mean to say it like that. Look, guys, I'm scared too. We've always seen our gods as good, just, and working for our benefit, but Titana told me the truth. She said they each gave us a bit of them to make humans who they are. And who we are is complicated.

"We're capable of great kindness, bravery, love... but we're also capable of great evil. It follows that the gods are too."

Junia straightened. "Sure, it does. But what do we do when we cross paths with a human committing great evil? Put them in a cage."

We locked stares—fists balled and neither backing down.

"I admit it," I blurted. "I didn't think this all through. Never in a billion years did I consider freeing the gods would mean letting beings like the god of the well loose on the world, but there are consequences to not completing the ritual too."

"Like what?"

"Like you! You went to work one day and never came home because we forgot the god that gave you your power. Unique mages are murdered, experimented on, enslaved, and believed to be cursed. Why aren't the good and just Mother Zaeah and Father Parthelan protecting us from that?"

"That's blasphemy!"

"Our world is wrong, Junia. We're broken, and we have been for a long time." I threw out my hand. "Velez speaks of a land beyond the sea where there is no war. No fighting, no poverty, no hatred. His people live in peace.

"Why don't we? Why haven't we for ten thousand years?" I shook my head. "We've lost balance. We're missing the parts of us that make us who we are, so we're filling those holes with greed, power, and fear. This is our chance to put things right."

Her gaze pierced me through. "That's not how things are. That's how you want them to be because you're scared."

She stomped off, leaving the four of us standing at the end of the cobblestone lane.

Keely and Akasha were looking everywhere but at me. Only Dominic looked me in the eye.

"You're uncharacteristically quiet, Dom. What do you think?"

He smiled slightly. "I don't know about uncharacteristic, but I do know we can't let some creature lurking at the bottom of a hole stop us from saving the dragons and preventing a war that will rip Adalinda apart. We go on. Because we have to."

Nodding, I looked to Keely and Akasha. "Are you guys still with me?"

Keely blew out a breath. "I won't pretend I understand all of this, but we've got water from the Well of Sorrows. Yesterday, it was a myth. Today, it's in your pocket. I've seen you do a lot of impossible things, Ainsley. If you say you can save Adalinda and all of us, I believe you."

Akasha squeezed my hand. "Keely said what I was going to. She just said it better."

"Thanks, guys."

They walked on, leaving me and Dominic to linger under shadow of the palace.

"I'm glad you're okay," I whispered. "I can't believe I was so stupid that I didn't see something was wrong earlier. It was all too easy. Predators don't make a trap too hard to spring."

"Ainsley." Dominic cupped my cheek. His rough and calloused thumb stroked the sensitive skin, popping goose bumps down my back. Moonlight danced in his amber eyes, making them shine like Inaya's fake tears. But unlike her twisted deception, Dominic shone with love... for me. "You weren't stupid. You figured it out, got us out of there, and achieved what we came here for. You're amazing, baby. When are you going to stop talking shit about the woman I love and realize that already?"

A tiny snort escaped me. "Okay, fine, but I'm allowed to be hard on myself right now. I was so naïve. It never crossed my mind to think—really think—about what it meant to not only free all those gods, but to give the Druks magics like the god of the well.

"I'm telling myself that I'm saving Adalinda and putting things right but..."

"You're strong enough to win this war, Ainsley Boreen, but if you do. You'll regret it for the rest of a short, miserable life."

"But I don't know what's going to happen."

"Hey." Dominic tipped my chin. "No one does. All we know is that the prophecy is real, and this is your destiny. You can run from it, or you can make it your own." He smiled. "We both know what you're going to pick."

I rested my hand on his, stroking his knuckles. "Thank you."

Grinning that grin, he leaned in.

I quickly dropped my head.

He didn't say anything as he stepped back, though I felt his disappointment like the irritation coming through all six bonds.

"I know, guys. I know."

"We should go," Dominic said.

"All right."

We didn't say anything to each other on the way back.

***

"All that for this?" Poet shook the vial. "How do we know it does... whatever it's supposed to do? If the legend of Inaya isn't real, then we don't know what this is."

I shoved spare clothes in my pack, then placed my wrapped lunch on top. It was hard to believe our adventure at the well only happened the night before. We woke up that morning, ate a quick breakfast, and set to leave for Hyelong. There was no time to waste.

"It's water cursed by a terrifying god," I replied. "It has to be enough."

He hummed. "I hope so, because we won't get another chance."

"Speaking of the crushing deadline over our heads, did the blacksmith create a holder we can use?"

"He gave us the best and strongest his magic could create." Poet raised his shoulders. "We'll have to hope that's enough."

"Hope?" I dropped my pack. "We can't complete the ritual with hope. We need to know it'll hold up. Ooh!" I snapped my fingers. "We'll have my dragons test it."

Poet shook his head. "It could hold up to their flames and still melt under the heat of the Everlasting Flame."

"Goodness. How hot does this fire burn?"

"Hot."

Then how can we possibly get close to it?

I pushed the thought away. We'd get close and steal it because we had to. There was no other way.

A knock sounded at my door.

"Come in."

Velez stuck his head inside. "Ready to go?"

"We're ready."

Slinging my pack over my shoulder, Poet, Velez, and I headed downstairs to join the others. Junia stopped me at the foot of the stairs.

"Hey, Ainsley."

I paused, letting the others go ahead. Junia tried to hold my gaze, but flicked down to my shoes.

"Ainsley, I wanted to apologize," she said. "I'm sorry for how I reacted last night. What you're doing is important, and I know better than anyone that you have good intentions. You're trying to save Adalinda from war. Why am I giving you a hard time about it when I should be helping you?"

"Junia." I took her hands. "You are helping me. We couldn't do any of this without you. Besides, I want you to be honest with me. Yell at me. Let me have it." I winked. "Thanks to you, I know how good it feels."

She laughed. "Pretty sure you're the first person ever to say something nice about my magic." Junia sobered. "Thank you."

"Ainsley. Junia."

Something in Dominic's voice made me turn. He and Keely stood at the window. He jerked his head for me to come over.

"Something's going on outside."

"What?" I rushed over.

That early in the morning, there was no one in the dining room barring one tired owner, polishing glasses behind the bar. It was so early—

"—that all of these people shouldn't be in the street."

A crowd of people rushed past the window—calling across and pointing to the top of the street as they went. I counted twenty—twenty-five—thirty before I stopped.

"What's going on?" I shrank back when a dark-haired woman glanced toward me. "Something has all these people excited."

"They're running right past the inn," Akasha said. "They're not looking for us."

"Or they don't know this is where we are," Poet dropped.

Keely visibly swallowed. "What do we do?"

"You relax." Atlas's shadow cast over me. "This isn't a problem for us—"

Growling, Dominic spun on him, fist covered in hellfire.

"—because it's a gift for Ainsley," he finished. "And if you kill me before she sees it, you'll nail the coffin on this dead relationship."

It was my jumping between them that stopped his death more than what he said. I held Dominic back. "A gift for me? What are you talking about?"

Atlas shrugged his shoulders and wings. "Well, gift isn't exactly the right word, but it's something you need." He held out his hand. "Come. I'll show you."

"We don't have time for whatever bullshit you pulled," Dominic snapped.

"Believe me." Atlas was more serious than I'd ever seen him. "We have time for this."

Eyes narrowed, I studied him, but his expression didn't break.

"Fine. I'll see whatever it is, but then we have to leave."

Atlas reached for my hand and Dominic knocked his away. "After you."

"No."

I suddenly found myself blinking behind Dominic's back. "No, after you," he gritted. "If anyone's springing the trap, it's you."

A smirk was his only reply. Setting off, our group followed behind Atlas, who stepped out into the morning sun without a care.

I don't know what Akasha made him look like to everyone else, but they all streamed around the towering, deadly Druk without paying him any mind.

"Did you see it?"

"Where did it come from?"

"Is it an attack?"

Two women knocked into me rushing past.

"Who would attack like this?" one hissed. "Hardly sneaking around."

"What does it mean, then?"

"I'm sure someone's gone to fetch the regent," she replied. "She'll take care of..."

Distance carried their conversation away. It didn't take my rising tension with it.

Atlas had done something bad enough to bring the regent down on our heads. What was wrong with him? I kept calling the half-man insane, and it sounded like I was right.

"Gods, help me," I hissed at Atlas's back. "If you risked us over some bizarre seduction attempt, I'll—"

"Take a look before you finish that threat." He stopped at the top of the cross street and gestured down the way. "If you're seduced by it, that's all on you."

Confused, I jogged up to see—matching the speed of the hurrying crowd. Breaking free of the buildings, I froze on the cobblestone—shoes glued where I stood.

"Atlas..." Words failed me. Sight failed me.

I couldn't be seeing what I thought I was, but no matter how many times I blinked, the vision didn't disappear.

"Gannon."

It was impossible. Absolutely impossible. But my brother stood before me.

Wild curls, impish smile, even the freckles on his nose and chin, the statue captured every bit of his likeness. So real, I swear I heard his laughing, "Sister Ainsley!" carry on the wind.

I slowly approached, jostled by half a dozen people crowding the very thing they whispered about in worried tones.

Gannon wasn't alone. Standing at his shoulders were Pema and Ilemka.

My feet carried me around them, taking in the smiling and laughing faces of Niahm, Colm, Belig, and Fabia. The statues stood as high as the building—towering above even a rearing Reyna.

"What nonsense is this?" a shrill voice drew me to the foot of Ilemka's statue. "Blasphemy? A joke? A prank? What's the point?"

I shoved through to see, ignoring her outraged cry.

Gannon. God of little inventors and big minds.

I gasped—half a cry, half a laugh. Racing around, I read all the inscriptions on the plaques beneath their feet.

Ilemka. Goddess of beloved daughters.

Niahm. Goddess of justice. I giggled. Niahm was fervently focused on all things being fair, and took on many a shopkeeper who dared to raise their prices at the sight of us.

Colm. God of mischief.

Belig. God of fireside stories. That was so perfect for him. Almost every night Belig, the strongest fire mage in our bunch, lit a fire in the pit behind the orphanage where we spent many a night telling stories until we fell asleep under the stars.

A soft voice reached me. "I know it's not enough," Atlas said. "We can't do the anointing or the three-day feast, but the statues..." His heavy hand settled on my crown. "I made them the biggest statues I could—forged by dragon slayer stone magic. They'll stand for a thousand years, Ainsley. No one will forget our family."

I didn't know I was crying until Pema's inscription blurred.

"I realize that you're now overcome with affection for me. Please give in to that feeling and—"

Spinning on my heels, I threw my arms around him. I was crying so hard, he probably couldn't tell that I was happy.

"Thank y-you." I smiled into his neck. "It's perfect. It's just so... perfect."

Atlas was stiff like he hadn't expected his little joke to come true. After a beat, his hands slid around me. He held me tight. "You're welcome, Ainsley. Anything for you."

I can't say what it was. All of a sudden, I lifted my head and latched on to Dominic.

He stood a distance away, watching me through the crowd. Watching us. Nothing in his expression gave his thoughts away.

The crowd shifted. People jostling, arguing, and blocking my view. By the time they moved out of the way, he was gone.

***

A soft, tinkling laugh floated through the steam.

I stayed low in the water, trying not to look or see anything. Keely's muttering kept interrupting, making it harder to imagine I was somewhere else.

"How many fucking times is she going to touch his arm!"

I mumbled something in return, and drifted closer to Dominic. He lay at the rim of the pool—one hand under his head and the other holding his book. My love stretched out in nothing but his loincloth, and though it tried gallantly, it did nothing to conceal the long and wonderfully thick cock it was my privilege to ride. If I didn't know this, all the open stares coming his way would give a clue.

Two naked women suddenly left the cool pool and approached.

Very cold water it seems, I thought, lips peeling back.

The taller one cleared her throat. "Hey, Book Boy. We were wondering if you wanted to—?"

"Back the fuck off or you'll lose those nipples!"

They beat it so fast, the talker slipped on the slick floor and splashed face-first into the cool pool.

Dominic howled. "You are single-handedly changing the rules against clothes in the bathhouse."

I snapped—*snapped*—at a wading bather who looked his way. He swam off quick. "Put your pants back on!" I ordered Dom.

Dominic chuckled like his life wasn't in danger. "That's the first time you've said that to me."

"You make jokes at the expense of their lives."

Flipping over, he popped a kiss on my squawking mouth. Over as quick as it started, he left a tingle on my mouth that spread down my spine.

"It's all right, baby. Poet's got this. We'll be out of here soon."

Despite myself, his reply—and his kiss—soothed me.

Thanks to the dragons, we left Ghidorah that morning and arrived in Hyelong that afternoon. That's when our trouble started.

The area around the Everlasting Flame was all flatland patrolled by the Watchers. We couldn't risk being under their noses, and we wouldn't be able to hide if we tried.

We needed somewhere to stay, but the only place to find accommodations was in the nearest town ten miles away. Thus, we said goodbye to the dragons and made the trek through muggy swampland to the town of Luzon.

By the time we got there, we were sweaty, sticky, and covered in mud. The only place to go was the bathhouse.

As Dominic explained, in Hyelong, bathhouses were a part of their culture of hospitality. Travelers only had to walk in with their road-weary troubles, and they were given a cheap meal and a free bath. The catch—the baths were co-ed.

I flicked to Poet.

He was the only one of us who spoke Old Hyelongan. That went a long way in small Hyelong towns—also according to Dominic—and he was currently in the process of scoping out a discreet place for us to stay.

I thought it many times before, but I couldn't have done this without them. With every day that passed I knew our little group would succeed. What I didn't know—

Is if Dom and I will be okay. I eyed him out of the corner of my vision.

Dominic didn't say anything about the statues, or my hugging Atlas. I couldn't tell what he was thinking about me reacting so badly to his tribute to my family, while thanking Atlas for his. I couldn't stand for him to believe it was a test that he failed.

But he seems okay now. He's laughing and joking with me as usual. Does he understand? Would it cause a fight if I accused him of being petty and jealous when he never said he was? Do I just leave it alone and let us move on?

I plunged my head under the water and screamed. I hated this! Everything was so simple in the cabin. Sure, we were trapped in a barren wasteland, but it was just us. No general. No high queen. No treacherous siblings. No gods. No wars. No destiny. Nothing but two people who loved each other.

I could've stayed in that cabin with Dominic forever. At least there, I never wondered if we would make it.

Sticking my head up, I met half a dozen raised-brow looks.

Keely heaved a sigh. "Fine. I'll stop complaining about that asshole, but I still say he's over there arranging how to get his dick wet, and not looking for a place for us. It doesn't require that much giggling and touching to say 'can me and my friends sleep in your barn?'" Keely heaved out of the bathing pool. "I'll ask around myself."

"Gods, they're so obvious." Akasha leaned against the rim—naked and loving it. Only Junia and I kept our breastbands and underclothes on in defiance of the no-clothes-allowed rule. "When will they stop this pointless, bickering foreplay and get on with it?"

"Seriously," Dominic replied.

"Agreed," Junia chimed in, floating over.

"Gods willing," said Velez. He stood across from me, washing his long golden locks. He was also naked and didn't care.

I smothered a laugh. It was too funny that literally everyone could see what those two couldn't.

"They'll have to figure this one out on their own," I said. "Pointing it out will only make them more stubborn."

"Hmm. Like when you insisted you didn't have a crush on the magistrate's son." Velez's smile widened as mine disappeared. "Even though you made such sweet songs for him—"

"Shut it, Stoneslayer!"

"Whoa, don't shut it," Dominic said, dropping the book. "Let's hear some of these sweet songs."

"Evan, Evan, you smell like heaven," Velez belted—loud and off-key.

Heat erupted in my face.

"How much do I love you? Not a ten, but an eleven."

"Ahh!" I jumped on him, shoving his head under the water. Dom and my friends fell over themselves laughing. "I'll have you know I was nine years old, and this stalker only heard the song because he'd followed me out to the forest when I thought I was alone."

"And now you're going to kill him for it?' Junia cracked up at the currently drowning Velez.

"Yes."

Velez popped up, throwing me off. "Evan, Evan, I have a confession. I love you. You're my obsession!"

It was me who needed to be drowned. "I'm warning you," I shrieked, mortified. "You don't need balls to live."

"Hey, I'm mad too," Dominic said, shoulders shaking. "I just found out Evan gets all these sweet love songs, and I got nothing."

I flashed him an obscene gesture. "You get this. Just for you, baby."

They were dying. Everyone was looking at us, they were laughing so loud.

Despite myself, I couldn't help but giggle too. I knew in my heart that it'd been a long time since any of us laughed so hard we couldn't breathe. But here we were, a ragtag bunch of rebels, traitors, Druk-lovers, deserters, and aberrants, finding joy in a stolen moment in a random bathhouse in a small Hyelong town. Even Dominic and Velez were laughing with each other.

If only it wasn't at my expense.

"What's the joke?" Poet jumped in, splashing me in the face. "What'd I miss?"

"Keely's ranting about you trying to hook up instead of getting us a place for the night," Junia supplied.

"I wasn't trying to hook up." Poet spun around, tossing an outraged look in Keely's direction. "I'll have you know, I did find us a place. Bonet's parents have a guesthouse on their property. It's small, only two bedrooms, but it's got a kitchen, privy, and ten miles between it and the Watcher patrols."

"It's perfect," Dominic said. "How much does she want?"

"Three silvers a day."

"It's a deal as long as we can see it first."

"Told her the same."

The two of them climbed up and left to make the deal. Our fun moment was over. Back to business.

"Come on." Akasha climbed out too. "Let's get some food. Dinner is only a copper, and you can eat anything off the buffet. I love this place. Why aren't bathhouses a thing everywhere?"

Junia went with her, leaving me and Velez alone.

He bumped me, grinning. "As much as you're cursing me out in your head right now, I got you to smile."

"Next time," I deadpanned, "just tickle me."

He laughed. "Seriously though, I love you, Ains. I want to see you smile. That's all I've ever wanted."

I ducked my head. When had all the men in my life become so sincere and sweet? How was a girl supposed to handle it? "I know, brother." I bumped him back. "Thank you."

"Come on. Let's get some food in your belly."

"Yes, please."

We finally left the room of steamed and boiled naked people behind, got dressed, and moved our party to the dining hall. An hour later, Poet and Dominic returned to tell us to grab our stuff.

"It's a nice place," Dominic remarked. "Two bedrooms like she said, but there's a loft space large enough for our bedrolls. And the beds are big enough for the ladies to be comfortable to share."

Keely harrumphed, glaring at Poet. "Guess that means you've got to tell your new girlfriend there's no room for you two to fuck."

"Nah." Poet plucked a spiced roll off her plate. "We can always fuck outside. Lay out a couple blankets and candles, and women swoon over the romance. But of course, that's not good enough for you, milady." He bowed deep. "A speck of dirt or a blade of grass could touch milady's fine, delicate skin. Perish the thought."

"Fuck you," she snapped. We all exchanged humorous looks behind their back. "It'd burn your eyebrows off if you knew all the wild and dirty places I've had sex."

"Yeah, in your head—where all the virgins play out their fantasies." He walked off. "No one's impressed by your daydreams, Keels."

"I am not a virgin!" No one would know outrage like her. "And I told you to stop calling me Keels!" Naturally, she chased after him. Keely never let Poet have the last word.

Their argument got loud fast.

"It's a good thing we're leaving," Akasha said, shaking her head at them. "Because they're going to get us kicked out."

Dominic moved behind me. Grasping my shoulders, he kneaded them without hesitation.

"Oooh," I breathed, eyes growing heavy. Between him and the hot bath, my tension knots melted like butter in the sun.

"Poet will show you guys the way," he said. "I'm going to hit the marketplace and stock up on food before the stalls break down."

"Who do I go with?" Akasha asked. "I have to be near someone to shield them with my magic."

"Go with them to the guesthouse. We don't want to be spotted, but we definitely don't want whoever spots us to see where we're staying. The Watchers would strike while we're asleep." Strong, probing fingers traveled down my back. Our clothes were on but I felt even more exposed than I did in the bath.

His hands felt too good on me. His presence too soothing. His scent too spicy sweet. I felt the need rising like a physical being beneath my skin, getting ready to grab, throw him down on the table, and have its way with him if I wasn't going to do it myself.

"I'll keep my hood low and my coin pouch jingling. Merchants will only be looking at that."

I shook my head, pulling myself out of the fantasy where Dominic and I were alone, and he was rubbing me down with honey and melted chocolate. Like Poet said, there was no time for my daydreams.

"I'll go with you," I told Dominic. "You'll need another pair of hands. Plus, one lone random guy with his face covered attracts more attention than a couple."

"It's true," Velez said. "Ainsley and I stole more together than I ever did scoping out the market alone."

Dominic hummed. "Like I'd say no to your company."

His finger glided up my spine, tangled in my hair, and tugged. I moaned loud and sudden, drawing huge eyes from Junia and Akasha.

Dominic strolled off chuckling while I sat there red-faced and stuttering. It was that asshole who always got the last word.

Soon, we left the bathhouse and split ways on the road. Poet took the others to the guesthouse. Their conversation comparing who had sex in the dirtiest place faded down the street. It was just me and Dominic.

I cleared my throat. "Which way to the market?"

"That way."

"Okay."

"Okay."

We lapsed into silence.

My first ever visit to Hyelong, and I couldn't take note of the beautiful buildings, unique burlap clothes, or the Old Hyelongan on everyone's tongue. The only thing holding my attention was the back of Dominic's head, and wishing I could pierce through that steel trap and figure out what he was thinking.

Every now and then he glanced back to check on me, but otherwise didn't comment.

We passed by a group of women loitering under a wooden awning.

"Whoa, whoa, whoa." They slinked out of the doorway and surrounded him in seconds. "Where you going so fast, Ghidorian?"

They were wearing burlap clothes too, but theirs were strategically cut to show every bit of their bodies. It was more accurate to say they were wearing burlap strings.

"No, thank you." Dominic peeled half a dozen hands off. "I'm busy."

"Busy? No one's ever too busy for a good tumble."

"Yeah. Don't run off before you get a taste of Hyelong." The lady giggled, running her hands as freely over him as her friends. "Trust me, we know your type loves foreign food."

"Ahhh, ladies." He flicked to me. "This is a very bad idea."

"What are you talking about?" A woman with long, white hair, bee-stung lips, and big golden eyes plastered herself against Dominic. "We haven't even started behaving badly."

Her friend next to her frowned. "Perla, wait. Doesn't he look famil-iar—?"

Perla grabbed his cock.

I moved so fast, I didn't know what I was doing before my fist connected with her jaw, exploding pain in my knuckles.

Her head snapped around. Spinning on her heels, she collapsed into the woman staring at Dominic intently, and took them both down.

"Remember this as the day you learned no means no." I snarled at the screeching, fleeing tumblers. "Stay away from my mate!"

"Help! Help!" Perla ran away with a bleeding lip. "That crazy bitch hit me!"

Men poured out of the brothel, summoned by their bellowing. Each one was bigger than the last.

"Time to go." Snatching me up, Dominic took off running down a side alley.

I didn't help our getaway. Too busy shouting abuse the whole way.

Shouts, clomping heels, and heavy boots gave chase.

Dom whipped around a corner and hit a short brick wall, connecting two pubs—if the heavenly smells coming from them were anything to go by. Heaving me up, he vaulted me over the side.

I landed on my feet, then spun away in time for him to come over too. He clapped a hand over my mouth and tugged me down. I did the same, muffling his pants as our pursuers burst into the alley.

"Where the fuck did they go!"

"It was the general's son. I swear it was, Niclan. He was with some crazy, ugly girl. I bet it was the dragon thief."

We both tensed.

"How could you let them get away?" *Slap!* A voice cried out. "The reward for their capture is two hundred thousand gold ryus each. Worth a hundred times more than your ass will ever be."

"We'll find them." Her voice was thick with unshed tears. "My blood magic can sense a heartbeat from a mile away. Theirs will be beating faster from running. I just need a minute to focus."

"You have ten seconds." Another cry, then a body hit the ground. "Do it."

Dominic and I shared a look. His thumb stroked my cheek. For the first time that day, I didn't wonder what he was thinking.

He wasn't letting them take me.

"Okay... Wait, I hear something."

"What?" that harsh voice demanded. "Have you found them or not?"

"Yes, but— This can't be right," she cried. "My magic senses they're right next to—"

Dominic rose to his feet—his air calm and relaxed. The firm hand keeping me down was the only tense part of him. "I'm right here, fellas. What seems to be the problem?"

"Well, well. Look at this. It is the general's son." A low whistle cut through the air. "And the girl? The dragon thief. I'm guessing she's cowering next to you."

"I'm guessing you never planned on living a long life."

Laughter.

"You're going to make us so much money, Roark."

"Actually, I'm going to burn you where you stand. Not even Mommy will be able to pick out your crispy corpse among your friends."

That set off another bout of howling.

"What do they teach you in those noble schools, because it's not how to count? There are more of us than there are of you."

"It's cute you think ten is enough."

"*Tsk, tsk, tsk.* Another thing they didn't teach you in that fancy school." Niclan didn't sound in the least bit intimidated. "Ten water mages against one fire mage is more than enough."

Dominic's grin was terrible. "We'll find out, won't we."

"Yes," I said, "we will."

I used the hand holding me down to pull myself up. Standing tall, I faced down ten smirking men and a woman crouched on the ground.

The guys moved around her, forming a line from wall to wall. If we were planning to run that way, it was blocked.

"There you are, dragon thief." The voice revealed Niclan. Unfortunate for him, his voice was nicer than his face.

Beady eyes set under a pronounced brow ridge. Acne scars riddled his cheeks, and a lumpy nose cast a long shadow over his thin slash of a mouth. "Our payday just doubled."

"If you know who I am, you know what I can do." I matched their smiles. "Came by the thief title dishonestly. If you use any magic on us, I'll just steal it. So why don't you run along. Every Rider, Watcher, and guard chased me for four months, then they lost me again.

"You're not taking us in, and you know it." I mock-pouted. "Weak, pathetic little man like you who gets off smacking women around, isn't strong enough to go up against one who isn't afraid of you."

He wasn't smirking anymore. "We'll see who's strong enough when I put you on your knees, bitch—"

Hellfire blasted him off his feet. Niclan was dead before he hit the ground.

"That's the future queen of Adalinda and my wife you're speaking to," Dominic growled. "Disrespect is a death sentence."

"Enough of this," one shouted. "Now!"

They linked arms. Closing the gap seconds after the woman shot through and escaped the alley.

Hellfire appeared all around us, raising the temperature a hundred degrees. They shot through the air—

—and stopped.

"What the hell?"

They were gone. Our attackers were gone.

All nine, and one body, disappeared and only two people remained in the spot where they stood.

Us.

"I don't—" I gaped at me. "How is this possible?"

The imposter spoke in time with me, sharing my open-mouthed shock.

"A reflection?" Dominic waved. His mirrored image waved back. "Reflective magic. I've never met a water mage who could—"

Water shot out of nowhere and blasted him in the face.

"Dominic!"

He dropped flat on his back, clawing his skin. I fell on him and another blast shot through the spot I was in. I barely noticed. Horror gripped me as water rushed into his nose, mouth, and sank into his pores—drowning him.

"Dom, no!"

"What was that about us being no match for him?"

I whipped my head around. The disembodied voice came from everywhere and nowhere.

"Guess the rumors about the general's favorite son weren't true. He's just another puffed-up royal who let a good bit of pussy make him weak."

"Dom? Dom! Stay with me."

He choked. Eyes bulged, he slapped and grabbed at his neck.

I clutched his throat, willing my magic to do something. *Anything!*

A force knocked me over the head, sending me toppling over Dominic. I didn't get out a cry before the water rushed into my nose and mouth.

"Ahhh!"

Thud!

Something struck the ground beside me. Through my darkening vision, I met shocked, unseeing eyes.

Thud!

Suddenly, the water stopped its perilous journey to my lungs. I flipped over, retching and hacking the horrid stuff up.

Thud!

Dominic bolted up, doing the same. We were freed. Why?

A blur out of the corner of my eye snapped my head up.

Atlas took to the skies—wings flapping, borrowed scales glinting, and mouth snarling a growl more fearsome than Suoh's on his best day. He lifted two struggling, shouting water mages into the air... and let go.

I hissed when their skulls cracked the ground. Whatever impressive power they had, it wasn't magic that made stone softer.

Their reflection broke apart. Four remaining attackers fled in every direction.

"Druk! Help, there's a Druk! He— Ahhhh!" His shout abruptly cut with a long fall and sudden stop.

The last three ran left, right, and back the way we came. Atlas sliced the air, and three fist-sized pieces of stone ripped from the earth and went sailing after them. I looked away as they struck. Three bodies hitting the ground told me he hit his target.

Atlas touched down and brushed himself off. There wasn't a scratch on him. Didn't look like he even broke a sweat. "Hello, my jewel."

"Shut up." I clutched Dominic to me, pressing my ear to his heart. It beat strong and steady at my command. "And thank you. I... I didn't think we were going to make it out of that one."

"Of course you despaired. You were in trouble, and Roark was lying around on his ass as usual."

Dominic was too busy wheezing to kill him.

"You were following us?"

He tipped his head. "The others have the sensory mage watching them. You needed me."

I wasn't in a position to deny that.

"A Druk!" Shouts sounded down the alley. "I swear I saw it somewhere over there. Summon the Watchers. Quick!"

"Get out of here," Atlas hissed. "They won't question the bodies if they find me standing over them. They will if you're standing alive next to me."

"But are you going to be okay?"

"Oh, no. He's dead!" someone shouted. Rapid footfalls followed, and they were headed in our direction.

"Go, Ainsley! I can't leave until you do!"

I didn't have a chance to fight him. Dominic scooped me up and ran.

"Dom, wait." I strained to see over his shoulder. We rounded the corner just as the first person happened into the gruesome scene and found Atlas. "We have to help him. He's a Druk. They'll try to kill him on sight."

"Hopefully they succeed."

"Dom!" I bumped and jostled in his hold. "How can you say that right now? He saved your life."

"He saved *your* life. That's the only reason he gets a stay of execution from me." He held me closer. "Bastard did the first thing right in his life, and protected you."

"Dom..." I cupped his cheek. "Dom, slow down. No one's following us, and you need a minute to rest."

"I'm fine," he said, but he did slow to a stop.

We made it far enough through the maze of alleys and side streets to leave the shouting and fighting behind. In our nondescript corner of brick, stone, and mortar, there was only silence.

Dominic sank against the wall, carrying me down with him. I traced the lines of his face as he tipped toward the setting sun, soaking in the rays of orange and gold.

"Princess," he gasped, catching his breath. "Maybe it's because we did most of our courting in a frozen wasteland, but I don't remember you being this violently possessive."

I flushed. "That stings, but it's fair." Sighing, I dropped my head on his shoulder. "It's not you or me. It's ninety percent that bitch grabbing what's mine."

Amusement laced his voice. "What's the other ten?"

"The dragons." Offense came down the bond as if they didn't know it was true. "Both Kenna and Mireu are in heat. Dragons don't mate for life which is why they get— What was the phrase you used? Oh yeah, violently possessive. They know the male has plenty of options, and they refuse to let their eggs go unfertilized when their time comes, so they—"

"Violently fight off the competition." Oh yes, he was holding back a laugh. "You're telling me you're guarding my seed to keep them all for your eggs?"

"I hate you right now."

"You know you don't have to go through all that trouble." He brushed a stray lock of hair behind my ear. "I do mate for life. My seed is yours."

"Are you sure?" My tone took all the joking out of the moment. "Look at what just happened, Dom. Even mental walls erected by a god aren't enough to keep the dragon instincts out entirely. I almost got us both captured because I couldn't control myself.

"It's possible I'll always be like this. Snapping, growling, possessive, and trying to jump you every five seconds."

He cocked his head. "I'm sorry. I was waiting for you to get to the problem."

"Dom," I cried, climbing off his lap. "I'm serious. Want to know how messed up I am? Because their influence is so strong on me, everything in me is screaming to have—to have eggs!

"I've been trying to get pregnant, even though I know this is the absolute *worst* time for that. And I can't get pregnant right now anyway! I forget that every time I look at you. You'll be dealing with that for the rest of our lives—living with a woman who has to remind herself she's not a dragon."

If I was waiting for shock, horror, or disgust, none of it shone in his eyes. "What does it feel like?"

"It..." It amazed me I could still blush about sex after all the things we'd gotten up to in bed. "It feels like wanting you. Like falling asleep beside the fireplace in your arms. Like waking up to you dropping kisses on my neck, and nights where we'd just hide from the world under the covers—talking about everything and nothing.

"It feels like the memory of how perfect and wonderful those moments were, have their own voices that are constantly calling out to me, saying it's a crime against every deity known and unknown to do anything but make you mine."

He pressed his forehead to mine. I felt his smile on my lips. "Why would any of that freak me out, Ainsley? It's exactly how I feel about you."

"Dom..." Stupidly, tears filled my eyes. No matter how many times he said it. No matter how much I knew it. My heart broke and reknit a million broken pieces back together again every time that unconditional love danced in his eyes. "I love you too."

Dominic squeezed his eyes shut, holding me tight. "I know you do." His voice was ragged. "That's why I don't get this."

I drew back. "Dom, please—"

"I love you. You love me. We want to be together," he burst out. "Why are we pretending otherwise? Who are we putting this show on for!"

"We're not putting on a show. I need space right now. Why is that so hard to understand?"

"Because there's something you're not telling me." He tried turning my chin to look him in the eyes, but I dodged him—untangling myself, getting to my feet. "I know you, Ains. I know when you're holding something back."

"If this is about Atlas, then let me clear it up, his advances are not in any way wanted. No one is competition against you—"

"Are you kidding me?" He shoved up. "I'm trying to have a serious conversation with you, and you're making it about jealousy? Of course I'm not worried about that flying piece of shit."

I turned away. "Then what are we talking about, Dom? We're going in circles with this conversation. There's no point to it."

His hand on my arm stopped me walking away. "Ainsley," he said softly. "You can keep me at arm's length if you need to. Tenille knows, I'm not going anywhere. I'll wait as long as it takes. But please stop lying to me. Tell me the reason—the real reason—that we can't be together, and I'll accept it.

"I just need you to be honest with me." Again he tried moving to look me in the eye, but I faced the wall. "It's driving me crazy that the woman I love pulls away when I reach for her, and she won't tell me why."

"I have told you."

No, I haven't.

"There isn't some big, mysterious reason."

Yes, there is.

"Your refusal to let this go is making it harder on both of us. I need to focus on avenging my family, freeing the gods, and saving Adalinda. That's it. That's all."

No, it isn't.

I broke free of him, continuing on. "Let it go already."

"Okay, Ainsley." The resignation in his voice crushed my heart into pieces, and that time they didn't knit themselves back together. "If that's what you want."

This is not what I want. I'm sorry, Dom. I'm so sorry.

"I love you."

I was far enough away he could assume I didn't hear him. I was also far enough away that he couldn't tell I was crying.

***

It was a long, quiet walk back to the guesthouse.

We left the town behind, and embraced the open air and tall, tickling grass. Cicadas buzzed in the trees, chiming their tune loud enough to drown out our awkward silence.

Dominic drew ahead as a modest, two-story brick building came into view. He walked the stone-laid path leading to the door and held it open for me. Considerate of me even when I was being a major ass.

The act only made me feel guiltier.

"Thank you," I muttered.

Poet looked up from his hand. He and Keely were playing a card game at the table. You wouldn't have known a couple hours ago, they were shouting about privy sex in the street.

"Hey, guys. What happened to the food and supplies?"

I moved to the fireplace, letting him share the story while I peeled off my coat and boots and sat before the flames. There wasn't much to say for a space that clearly wasn't used often. There was a small kitchen, dining table with two chairs, and a couch next to the fireplace. Barring a single painting of a landscape beside the front door, there was no decorations to speak of. Even so, it was warm, and safe, and filled with people I could talk to, allowing it to not be so obvious that I wasn't talking to Dominic.

"We couldn't get it," Dominic replied. "Word spread of a Druk sighting. The market cleared out before we got there."

"Druk sighting?" Keely said. "Are you talking about Atlas and Velez?"

"That bastard and that winged piece of shit didn't have a choice." Dominic used his new names for them without inflection or irony. "Ainsley and I were recognized. That flying piece of shit had to kill our attackers to let us get away."

"What?"

Akasha and Junia jumped up from the couch.

"Oh no. I knew I should've gone with you," Akasha cried. "What does this mean? Were they captured? Are we safe? Should we leave?"

Velez blew inside, answering half her questions.

"Velez, thank the gods." Akasha ran over and hugged him, drawing my brow up. "Are you okay?"

"I'm fine, but I'm sure Ainsley told you what happened." He kicked off his boots and joined me by the fire. "Not only is the town on high alert now because of Atlas, but word is spreading about the arrival of Dominic Roark and the dragon thief."

"What do we do?" Keely asked. "We can't leave. We still need fire from the Everlasting Flame."

"Actually." Dominic scratched his chin, nodding. "This might've helped us. The nearest Watchers are those guarding the Everlasting Flame. They're not going to ignore a Druk sighting along with the potential to make a quick four hundred thousand ryus.

"No doubt tomorrow morning's rotation is going to be pretty light in favor of half their force swarming the town, looking for us."

"He's got a point," Poet said, exchanging looks with the others. "This might've helped us. No Watcher was going to sit by while I skipped over to the Everlasting Flame and took a bit for myself. Having less eyes on the Flame is going to make this impossible mission slightly less hopeless."

"But our next stop is Edjer to research the last known nesting spot of the celestial dragon," Junia said. "Trying to fly unprotected to Edjer on dragon-back is suicide. We're going to need boots, coats, mittens, and every piece of covering we can find, or our frozen bodies will rain from the sky."

Keely winced. "Horrifying, but true."

"I think you all should go to the Flame while I stay back and get what we need. I won't need Akasha's power to protect me. No one will be looking for a lowly truth mage when the general's son and the dragon thief are nearby."

"Are you sure?" Keely asked. "Splitting up is exactly what got us in trouble."

"I'm sure. I didn't want to say this, but in a lot of ways, I'm in more danger than the rest of you are." Junia hugged herself. "I have no control over my magic. It influences everyone around me, and Akasha's magic can't stop it. What happens if a Watcher gets too close to me and questions why they can't stop spilling their secrets? No, it's better that I'm nowhere near the Flame."

Poet leaned back in his seat, shaking his head. "I was about to suggest it be the other way around. You won't be allowed past the gate, so why risk coming with me? You all stay and get what we need. I'll go alone."

"No." That came from me and Keely.

"You're known as a friend of the dragon thief," I said. "The same dragon thief who killed most of the people who came to see your public execution, and whisked you away. We can bet there's a bounty on your and Keely's heads too."

"Then what do you say?"

All eyes turned to me. Another thing I had to constantly remind myself of—I was in charge.

I straightened. "Okay. None of us are splitting off. You're right, Junia, it won't be good if your magic makes the Watcher notice something is off, but it would be worse if a stall owner notices the same and brings them down on your head with none of us around to help.

"We'll stick together but we'll be smart. Only Poet needs to enter, so only Poet faces scrutiny. We'll stay close by so Akasha can protect him, but she'll hide us with her magic so they don't know we're there. Neither the Watchers nor anyone will look our way.

"Afterward, we'll leave Luzon, do our shopping in another town that's not swarming with Watchers and water mages who combine their magic in ways I didn't know was possible, and then we leave for Edjer. Deal?"

Nods and murmurs of agreement went around.

"You should all get some sleep. Poet said it's busiest around sunrise. We want lots of people around to disguise what we're doing," I said, making for the door. "There's something I need to do. I'll be back later."

I escaped outside before anyone could stop me, and didn't stop running until the tall reeds welcomed me, hiding the guesthouse from view.

Dropping to my knees, I held my breath—fighting to push away the memory of the look on Dominic's face.

I hated this! I hated doing this to him. *If only I could tell him the truth.*

You can't, another voice sharply cut in. *He'd say all the wonderful, loving things he always says that'll make you doubt yourself. You'll believe for a second that the danger has passed, and in that second, you'll lose him.*

He doesn't understand now, but when it's all over, he will. And because he's a wonderful man that you don't deserve... he'll forgive you for everything.

I don't know how long I stayed out there ruminating, but eventually my aching knees and chilled skin forced me on my feet. I wasn't ready to go inside, so I turned my thoughts to practicing.

"Kai said I have to build up my own walls that will take in what I need, and keep out what I don't," I told the air and my dragons. "Keely said she pictures her magic as one big ball of thread in her mind, and having power over it gives her power over her abilities.

"What if I need to imagine the walls between us as just that. I need to learn how to build them up before I can take them down. Like Keely winds and unwinds the ball."

Curiosity, agreement, encouragement, boredom, and an arousal filtered back through the bond. The last belonging to Kenna. Seemed she found a mate for the night.

"One of us should relieve our tension," I mumbled. "Have fun."

Sighing, I walked a little bit aways, went back, caught sight of a tree and made for it, then stopped again. Where the hell was I going and how did I start?

The night I stole Calthoon's and Tenille's power to save Dominic, I flat-out demanded it. I screamed at the sky and, through sheer will, made their power mine. Every time I died, I used Calthoon's power to return me to the right side of the veil. But with my dragons, their power was gifted to me in the form of bonds that made us both stronger.

There was never truly any stealing between me and the dragons. Reyna chose to bond with me that fateful day. She could just as easily dump me and return to Dominic if she wasn't interested in me making use of her hell-fire.

Where does the answer lie within all of this? Ever since the day those nobles attacked me in the woods, I've used my magic more times than I could count. Trouble was, the only connection between the events was I was avenging someone or myself.

Did that mean I'll only ever be able to tap into the strength to bring the walls up and down when an enemy hurts me or someone I care about? Do I have to live within a shadow of grief and rage like the creature who wandered the five kingdom for four months, or is there a path to using my magic on my terms—no matter what I'm feeling?

You did it once.

My skin warmed, beating back the chill when I remembered the day Dominic and I almost burned the hut down around us.

What did it mean that I was able to tap into Reyna's hellfire then? I wasn't thinking about her, gods, vengeance, high queens, murderous gener-als, or any of the things that kept me up until the wee hours of the night.

It was simply me and Dominic, and I was relaxed in a way that—

I froze. I'd been pacing and barely noticed it.

What if that was it? Keely's magic didn't appear during a bout of beg-ging and praying to Tenille to not be magicless. She simply woke up one day and was covered in threads.

Her magic appeared during a relaxed and vulnerable moment. Sleep. I didn't need anger and hate to channel my magic. I just need to let go, and let it come to me. Only when it does can I learn to control it.

"Okay, okay." I shook out my hands and rolled my neck, channeling calm.

I used to watch Sister Aven sometimes in the chapel. She'd sit in silence before the altar, sometimes for hours, looking completely calm and at peace as she communed with Tenille. Didn't matter if us children were screaming, shouting, or jumping off the walls. Nothing fazed her.

I asked her once how she did it, and she told me she learned how to shut the world out by turning off her mind, focusing on her breathing, and brushing away every thought that wasn't about Tenille.

I can do that.

Dropping on the ground, I crossed my legs and turned my face to the starry night—filling my vision with nothing but the endless beauty of the glittering, diamond-painted universe.

"Relax," I whispered. "Breathe. Brush away all thoughts."

My breaths slowed. My mind calmed. I sank deep within myself, floating in an inky blank sea of starlight like the one above me. In a blink, my Reyna was there. She flew past followed by Mireu, Tizor, Cadmus, Kenna, and Suoh.

My dragons. Our bonds. There were no walls between us. No memory of pain. No feeble thrashing against barriers. No torrent of sweeping, consuming dragon thoughts and instincts.

It was just us, and all I had to do was relax, not think, and my ability would come to be.

My knee itched.

I scratched it, then refocused.

A few minutes passed. A bug flew on my cheek and I freaked out. Flinging away, I slapped my cheek and the air, screeching at the disgusting thing and all its friends who thought to take their shot.

I sat back down to waves of amusement coming through the bonds, and of course, Kenna's purring, grumbling satisfaction as she mated.

"Come on, guys, this is serious." I tried to get comfortable again as I refocused on the stars. "No laughing." But from then on, I twitched and jumped at the slightest tickle against my skin, fearing the dead bug's family was looking for revenge.

"Enough." I ran out of the tall, tickling reeds, and claimed a spot on the grass. I crossed my legs, took a deep breath, tipped to the sky, and tried again. "I'm calm. I'm open. I brush away all thoughts. There is nothing but me and my drag—"

"What the hell are you doing?"

Velez approached from the other side of the field. It looked like he was coming from town, even though he should've been inside with the others.

"I'm trying and failing to meditate like Sister Aven. What are you doing?"

"That house isn't built for Druks," he offered, claiming the spot next to me. "Atlas went for a fly to stretch his wings."

"Why would he do that? The town is on high alert searching for the Druk that killed ten men."

"He did it because they're on high alert. We need the Watchers guarding the Flame to flood the town. No reason to if they think the menace Druk has left the area."

"Oh. Okay, that makes sense."

Velez dropped flat on his back, folding his arms under his head. He looked like he did the many nights we lay under the stars, talking until one, then both of us passed out. "So why are you trying to meditate?"

"I thought it might help me connect with my bonds." There was no need to lie. "Help me open and close them. Learn control."

"Hmm." He tugged on my shirt till I lay down too. Wiggling on the tickling grass, comfort and familiarity spread through my bones. "Why does it have to be you? The dragons put those bonds in your mind. Can't they control them? Open them when you ask them to. Close them when you need."

I blew out a breath. "It'd be so simple if that was true. But no. My dragons can't do this for me. It's my mind. Not having control over it resulted in me going four months without a bath."

He chuckled. "Fair enough. Can I help?"

"I'm not sure actually. Keely says our magic is different from other mages. We don't draw upon our connection with Tenille, but I guess, neither do you. What does it feel like when you wield your stone magic?"

"It's..." Velez gazed at his hand. "It's like climbing a tree."

"Climbing a tree?"

"Yes," he said, nodding to himself. "Climbing a tree. You stretch and heave and sweat—the whole time fearing the next branch won't hold your weight. The bark cuts your palms. The branches scratch your cheeks. Irate mama birds screech and attack you for disturbing their babies, but then..." A smile settled on his lips. "Then you reach the top, and the whole of the world spreads before you. Beautiful. Vast. Waiting for anyone strong enough to make the climb."

He dropped his hand, shaking himself. "That's what it's like for me anyway, but you know I'm a weak magic user. No stronger than the average commoner. I'm not the one to ask."

I nudged his arm. "Yes, you are. Talking to different people is teaching me that there's no one way to connect with magic. I just need to find my way."

"Can I give you a meditation tip? Sister Aven meditated in the chapel because that was her safe place. Yes, you're a forest child, but outside was never your safe place. It's just the place you ran to to escape your troubles. There's a difference."

"What difference? If this isn't my safe place, what is?"

His smile remained. "The orphanage, Ains."

My lips pressed tight. I felt my breaths coming short.

"The place where you were loved. Where no one would hurt, reject, or scare you. It was home." His hand found mine across the scant distance. "Can't say I know much about these things, but seems to me if you're trying to achieve a state of perfect calm and openness, your best shot is to do it in a place where you feel all of those things anyway."

"Guess there's some truth in there," I rasped. "But I don't have a place like that anymore, Velez. So why bring it up?"

"Who says that place can only be four walls and a roof? I have a safe place too. I feel calm, relaxed, and open whenever they're near... and I can't tell you how it's been to be apart from her all these years."

I blinked. "Wait— Me?"

"Yeah, you, dummy." He laughed. "Who else would I be talking about? You're my sister, best friend, partner-in-crime. I'm always relaxed with you because I know whatever happens, you've got my back. Who's that person for you, Ains?"

Dominic appeared in my mind's eye—crisp, clear, and immediate. It was never going to be anyone else.

"Hmm. Let me get this straight. All I have to do is close my eyes and sit on him, and I'll have this meditation thing kicked?"

"Couldn't hurt, right?"

We cracked up.

I threw up my hands. "I've tried everything else, so why not."

We lapsed into companionable silence—only broken by the occasional chuckle.

"Can I ask you something?"

"You will anyway," he replied.

"Was it your idea to make those statues of our siblings? Did Atlas take the credit because he had to be the one to do it?"

He shook his head. "As impossible as it is to believe, that was all Atlas from idea to execution. It's amazing, to be honest. He's never done anything like that."

"What do you mean?"

"Did something for someone without there being a direct benefit for himself." He shrugged. "I didn't know he had it in him to be so... nice. You bring out something new in him, Ains."

Discomfort I couldn't describe climbed my spine. "But he didn't do it for me. They were his siblings too. And yours."

Velez snorted. "That guy's never done a kind thing for me in his life. He wasn't going to start now. And Atlas has dealt with his grief. He didn't erect fifty-foot statues of our siblings because he wanted them to be remembered. He did it because you do."

"Oh." I shook myself. "That aside, I've got a real question for you."

"Yeah?"

"All that stuff about me being your safe place and wasting away without me all these years?" My brows were in my hairline. "How long have you been in love with me, Stoneslayer?"

"Shut up."

"You love me! Admit it." I tickled his sides. Velez yelped and tried to get away. "Admit it. Say it. Say you love me."

"I take it back!" He held my shoulders back. "I only said it because all these years made me forget how annoying you are!"

"Liar." I smooched the air, coming in fast for his face. "You love me. I'm your best friend in the whole world, and you can't be without—"

Lips reared up and devoured by mouth.

I lurched back. Clapping my hand over my mouth, I screamed through my fingers.

"Ah, that was beautiful." Atlas grinned that wicked fucking grin. "I love you."

"You little—!"

"Big, darling." He winked. "You know better than anyone there's nothing little about me. Lucky for you, because I heard you're on the hunt to have a few *eggs*."

How?!

"My seed is yours for the taking, my rain-kissed rose." He leaned in, lips puckered.

My fist went flying.

***

"What happened to your eye?" Keely asked.

We were gathered outside the guesthouse, indulging the final dusting of stars and night's cool air before we set off.

"It had an unfortunate run-in with a fist." Atlas blew me a kiss over her shoulder. "I forgive you, my delicate dewdrop."

"Fuck you!"

The only good thing that came out of the night before was that, deep down, I finally forgave Velez for abandoning us for all those years. And I killed any lingering notion that there was good in Atlas.

He was an insufferable ass through and through.

Velez returned when Dominic and Akasha crested the hill.

"Poet was right," Dominic said by way of good morning. "The town is swarming with Watchers. That flying piece of shit should make another appearance, get them really riled up, then we'll head to the Flame."

"The names are Atlas and Velez, General Spawn. I would've thought the education only you were legally allowed to get would've—"

Dominic walked inside and shut the door like he wasn't speaking.

Velez slammed inside after him.

I didn't bother to intervene. I grew up with more brothers than anyone. Nothing I said or did would make them stop being idiots.

Eventually, Dominic came out again in his leather vest and thick, spiked-sole boots. He was ready to go. He asked if we were too.

I swept over Keely, Junia, Akasha, and lastly, Poet.

"It's you who is taking all the risk. Are you ready?"

He nodded. "This is my birthplace, Ainsley. It's where I belong. Of course I'm ready."

Velez set off first to walk Atlas into the middle of town, then we left.

Poet spoke on the way.

"No one knows exactly when the Everlasting Flame began—"

"Ten thousand years," I blurted.

All eyes turned to me.

"Sorry." I pulled a face. "Before I was booted out of the hive mind, I learned it was started by one of the first colonies of fire dragons as an offering to Mother Zaeah."

"Exactly," Poet continued. "All dragons are her children and offer their blessings to her in their own way, but the fire dragons have the Flame."

"It's truly existed for ten thousand years?" Keely asked. "All that time and it's never gone out?"

"Never." Poet's eyes shone. I'd never seen him so animated when talking about something. Not even back during training when he'd excuse himself to go hook up with Maili in the barracks.

That's what I want for you, Poet. A woman who makes you light up whenever you talk about her. I hid a secret smile at Keely. *Even if you're lighting up because you're shouting at each other.*

"All fire dragons and fire mages feed the Flame," he continued. "And when a fire dragon dies, their colony carries their body to the Flame, so they're returned to the ash that birthed them—continuing the cycle.

"It's a sacred, but well-known place. That became a problem when humans noticed fire dragons weren't just giving their bodies as offerings. They were also sacrificing diamonds, jewels, rare fruit trees, and anything of value to Mother Zaeah.

"More than a few people got ideas, and those that weren't burned to a crisp for daring to steal from Mother Zaeah, were igniting a war by attacking dragons to take their offerings."

Keely nodded along. "That's why they employed Watchers to guard it."

"And why only fire mages are allowed near it," he added. "As much as people believe our magic comes from Tenille. It's Mother Zaeah who gifts the flame. It's her gift to every single dragon... and us. A fire mage would never dare desecrate the Flame, and going back to Great Mage Windlass's times, the dragons began allowing us to make offerings too."

"But how do we know it's enough for the ritual?" Akasha asked. "It sounds special and amazing, but it's not god-cursed water or the remains of the most powerful dragon in existence. Are we sure it can help bring down the wall between realms?"

I tipped my head. "I guess there's no true way for us to be sure until we do the ritual, but like Poet explained, this isn't just any fire. Fire dragons have kept it burning for ten thousand years, feeding it with their faith and love for Mother Zaeah. We need the strongest representation of the fire element, and I can't think of anything stronger."

"Are you sure you're okay with this, Poet?" Junia put in. "You just said it's so sacred a place, it has to be protected around the clock, and the rest of us aren't allowed near it. Now we're asking you to break the trust the dragons put in fire mages, and desecrate the Everlasting Flame.

"We can't force you into blasphemy," she said. "There are other famous representations of fire. Other legends we can plumb. Akasha's right. We should think of another way."

Akasha blinked. "Uhh, I was just curious. I didn't mean to suggest he shouldn't do it, but of course, it's up to Poet."

"Of course it is," I agreed. "Poet?"

He waved our concerns away. "Guys, I'm fine. It's not as serious as that. I'm not stealing offerings or trying to put out the Flame. The dragons won't care if I take a little for myself." He patted the holder. "But the Watchers will, so they're our only problem. Besides, it's for a good cause. The dragons should know that, right?" He looked to me. "Your dragons are connected to your mind. Everything we're doing, the hive mind knows. If the fire dragons had a problem with it, we'd be lumps of burning flesh right now."

I pushed up my lips. "Actually, in case you guys were secretly worried about this, our dragon bondeds don't share what's in our minds with the others. We'd have to be connected completely for that to happen anyway, but more than that, they respect our privacy. What is shared between rider and bonded, stays between them.

"But this isn't just about us," I said slowly, examining the many emotions coming through my bonds. "We're doing all of this to save the ten thousand dragons that were stolen from them. My beauties would share that with the fire dragons, especially if it meant easing our way. They have to know our plan. They must want us to succeed."

"They do." Dominic's fingertips skated over the back of my hand, popping goose bumps up my arm. "And we will."

On the way, we talked about the hive mind, history of the Everlasting Flame, and how Poet would get the holder up to the Flame and trot away with it without being stopped.

Akasha's magic concealed us, but it didn't make our bodies air. With the danger of people walking into us and shouting about invisible people, we stuck to walking the outskirts of the town. Velez joined us halfway there.

"Atlas put on a big show. Threw some boulders around. Sent people running away screaming. Got into a little fight with a few Watchers. By the end, they were shouting for more backup," he dropped. "Then, I became me, blended into the fleeing crowd, and drove them even madder searching for him. We're good to go."

That put extra speed and a bounce in our steps. We hurried the rest of the way—assured our plan would succeed. How could it not with the fire dragons on our side? They wanted us to save the dragons. They wanted us to save Adalinda.

We rode on a high I couldn't describe... then we arrived.

"What...?" The holder slipped through Poet's fingers. "What the fuck is this?"

The Everlasting Flame was everything and nothing like I expected.

Grand, white stone stairs led to an incredible circular iron fire pit the width of Altaira Palace. It dominated the horizon, beckoning everyone far and wide to come and be humbled before this temple to Mother Zaeah.

Fire dragons swooped and dove overhead, sparking crimson under burning sunlight glinting off their scales, and roaring flames at the pit. The entire hillside was like stepping into an inferno. Three miles away, I peeled off my coat. Two miles in, I loosened my top buttons. As we climbed the steps, Dominic shed his shirt, and Keely ripped the sleeves off her top. It was *hot*.

Atop the hill stood a small contingent of guards. I couldn't say how many usually were on duty, but I had to guess more than four. They stood at the east, west, north, and southern points—watchful gaze sweeping everything around, behind, and above them.

Our play act worked. We forced the Watchers to send most of their people to Luzon, chasing a Druk that was no longer there. It was the only thing right about that morning.

"What happened here?" Poet trudged across the uneven stones, barely noticing when he tripped.

A few people among the crowd gathered around the Flame glanced at the fallen newcomer, then returned to the sight everyone was staring silently at.

The ten-foot-tall metal fence around the entire area. As thick and impenetrable as the cage over the Flame.

"I don't understand," Akasha said. "I don't remember you mentioning a fence or cage. Is it supposed to be like this?"

"Supposed to be like this?" Poet clutched his chest. He looked seconds away from being violently ill. "No, it's not supposed to be like this! Where the fuck did this fence come from!"

A Hyelongan woman peeled off the fence and ran up to him. I jumped out of her way.

"Shh," she hissed. Throwing her arm around him, she led him away from the northern-stationed Watcher who glanced his way. We hurried to stay with them.

"—careful. Don't let them hear."

"What is this?" he asked, dropping his voice. "Who put this fence up?"

"Who do you think?" Her lips twisted. "High Queen Kisandra."

It was a second before I realized I bore the same disgusted scowl. Seemed the high queen naturally brought that out of people.

"My name's Livia," she said. "What's yours, brother?"

The familiarity was expected. Akasha made him look Hyelongan so he'd blend in, but her caution wasn't needed. None of the people clinging to the fence would've noticed if an elephant marched through here.

"Poet," he whispered, forgetting the fake name he chose. He held his hands out to the fence—to the Flame—as if he couldn't help it. "Why?"

"She—" Her lips trembled. "That woman has decreed the Everlasting Flame will be put out."

Poet rocked back like she slapped him. The looks on our invisible faces were no less shocked.

"She tried having it moved," Livia continued, "but the dragons attacked. Brutally. They slaughtered the entire Ryuku squad, and the squad's dragons didn't stop them."

My eyes bugged.

"That's never happened before."

Damn right, that's never happened before! A bonded licking their scales in the sun while their rider is slaughtered? They just didn't do that.

The mere fact that their riders dared carry out Kisandra's orders must've so offended and enraged them, they broke the bond in all but act.

"She got the hint not to touch it," Livia said. "If only she gave up."

"But—but—but why!" Poet clutched his head. If he had longer hair, he'd be pulling it out by the root. "Why would she move it? Why is she doing anything to it?"

Livia gazed blankly at the roaring fire. "It has been Hyelong's honor and privilege to be home to the Everlasting Flame for thousands of blessed years. The high queen has decided that honor is too good for us. It belongs on the land that used to be Old Adalinda." She shook her head. "She's already erected a new fire pit on the remains of Golden City. She believes once the Everlasting Flame dies out, they'll be forced to move there."

I exchanged wide-eyed looks with everyone, except Dominic. Nose flaring, he balled his fists—clenching his teeth like it was only a devastating head injury that stopped him from charging the fence.

"Dom?" My brows furrowed. "Why do you look angry, but not surprised?"

"Because I'm not, Ains. This is worse. Far, far worse than she knows," he said, jerking a chin at Livia.

"What does that mean?" Akasha asked.

"My—" He struggled getting the word out. "*Father* had an idea," he gritted. "All those precious, rare, expensive offerings the dragons throw in the Flame? What if there was a way to retrieve them without the dragons knowing? They'd be happy, and the coin would be put to use for the kingdom instead of melting away to nothing.

"That idea never got past my ear, because even he knew the High Council would never allow it. Not to mention the piercing, eye-watering headache he got seconds after the words came out of his mouth."

"Tizor told him what the fuck he thought of that evil plan," I spat, clutching my head. "Just like he's telling me. How can they do this!"

"But how do we know that's their plan?" Keely asked. "If the High Council wouldn't approve it for your father. They wouldn't do it for her."

"We have no reason to believe they told the High Council the full truth, but this—" He waved at the crushing scene of dragons trying and failing to take off the grate.

"This has my father written all over it. He must've played on Kisandra's prejudices. Convinced her that Hyelong was bestowed an honor they didn't deserve, then he snuck in a suggestion to fill her coffers with riches fitting for a high queen.

"He had a vague idea to move it somewhere out of reach of mages, so there was no chance of anyone finding out." Dominic gestured to the bystanders. "Kisandra is making that plan reality. Those two together are the worst thing that's ever happened to this kingdom. With my father by her side, playing on her prejudices and vanity, every horrible thing politics prevented him from doing, will come to be."

Keely looked as sick as I felt. "What kind of a rotted soul could do something like this? You can't just—just—take a being's offering to their god. Poet said a fire dragon will search for years until they find the right one to give to Mother Zaeah.

"They've kept this flame alive for ten thousand years! Generation after generation, and human greed is what puts it out?" Keely flung around, almost quick enough to hide the tear staining her cheek. "I can't believe I once thought us superior to Druks. We're no better to the dragons. We just find other ways to steal from them."

"That'll be true—"

Our heads snapped up. Poet looked directly at us, bearing an expression I rarely saw on my joking, happy friend's face.

Rage.

"—if we don't stop this. Now."

"Stop this?" I repeated.

Livia stared at Poet. *Who are you talking to?* etched in the confused woman's wide eyes.

"We have to free the Flame," he said. "Today. Now."

"We—"

"We can't," Livia hissed. She peered over her shoulder. "Most of the Watchers ran off to deal with some trouble in a nearby town, but they left their strongest behind. Death mages.

"All of them." Livia raised a trembling finger. "That one has miasma magic. Poisons the air you breathe. That one shoots death arrows that always hit their target. That woman turns living things to stone, and that man who keeps looking our way, wields hellfire."

Dominic stilled.

"You're not the first person to suggest freeing the Flame, but it's no use. Even if we brought down the fence, removed the grate, and defeated those death mages, our victory would last only as long as the high queen sent another Royal Rider squad to punish us and do it all over again."

"She has a point, Poet," Junia said. "Our victory would last a day."

"No." Poet agitatedly ripped off his vest and tunic. "Not if we free it from the base, and the dragons carry it away from here. Dominic's father had one thing right. It needs to be taken somewhere humans can't reach.

"They trusted us to be guardians of the Flame. That trust is broken. The Flame must be taken from us until we earn it back."

"Free it from the base?" Keely eyed said twenty-foot-wide concrete base. "But how can we? You said the dragons killed the last group of people who tried moving the Flame."

Poet tore strips off his tunic and tied them around his hands and forehead. If the hellfire mage was only glancing at him before, he was staring at him now.

"That won't happen to us thanks to Ainsley." I looked around like he could be talking about someone else. "She'll tell her dragons, then her dragons will tell them that we're here to help.

"This is what we do. Dominic, you take out the death mages. Keely, you can weave your threads together to create things stronger than steel. I need you to bring down this fence."

He was talking too fast for any of us to get a word in.

"Akasha, you cover them. Velez, tell your brother to create stone pillars under the pit and keep growing them until they pry it off the base. Junia, hang back and stay safe." He struck his chest. "I'll get the grate off the Flame."

"Wait—!"

"Hold on—!"

"Let's talk this through first," Keely cried. "You can't just—!"

"Oh, Keels. One more thing." Poet spun back. Tangling in her hair, he tugged her forward and crushed his lips on hers, cutting her off mid-rant. Poet kissed her so thoroughly and passionately, I looked away—sensing my dragon-heightened instincts stirring.

A man didn't kiss a woman like that unless he was testing if it was possible to give her an orgasm through kiss alone. Judging by Keely's face when they broke apart, he aced the test.

She gaped at his back when he took off, jaw working and unsteady knees nearly toppling her over. Our collective shock slowed our tongues. Poet took his chance, unleashed a flaming rope of fire, and whipped it over the top of the fence.

The hellfire mage let out a shout when he went flying, soaring over the gate. He took off after him—summoning hellfire on his palms, as deadly and unstoppable as I knew it to be.

"Poet!" Keely screeched. "Fuck's sake! What do we do!"

Dominic and I twisted on each other. A clear message went through our wide eyes.

"We do what he said to do," I shouted.

Dominic was already running.

"Atlas, the fire pit. Keely, bring down the gate." I clutched my head, mentally shouting down the bonds. "Akasha, make Poet invisible."

Poet hit the ground and ran for the Everlasting Flame. Ropes of fire not unlike Keely's threads burst from his palms, latching on the grate. Behind him, hellfire shot at his back.

"Make him invisible now!"

Poet disappeared from view.

"What the—" The Watcher whipped around, his fire disappearing. "Attack! We're under attack! Enemy invisible and number unknown!" he shouted all too quickly.

They didn't just leave their strongest Watchers behind. They also left their smartest.

We sprang into action.

Threads whipped and soared through the air—knotting, twining, twisting, and growing. Her ropes soared to the gate and lashed around. Screaming, she yanked with all her might.

Reyna! I shouted down the bond. *Fuck privacy! Tell the fire dragons that we're here to help.*

"Ainsley." Velez was suddenly in front of me, grabbing my shoulders. "Are you sure the dragons will listen to you?"

Creaking, groaning metal pierced my ears. The metal began bowing and bending, drawing the hellfire Watcher's attention. He threw fireballs wildly—sending the crowd running and screaming in every direction. Unable to see Keely, they stampeded right toward her.

"Yes!" I bellowed at Velez, running around him to help Keely. "They'll listen. Just do it!"

"We're under attack—"

Dominic punched the death mage in the jaw, sending him spinning off his feet. He hit the ground and burst into an inferno—so bright and burning, Dominic clapped his hands over his eyes, stumbling back.

"Dominic!" I couldn't run to him when I was already racing to Keely. "Keely, look out!"

ARRGGHH!

My eardrums blew out.

The circling dragons roared. Winging around, they dive-bombed the crowd, coming straight at me.

"Ainsley!" A gust of wind blew my hair in my open mouth. Atlas flew off as fast as his wings could carry them. "Make them stop!"

"Dragons," I rasped—jerking and running in three different directions. "Akasha's magic doesn't work on dragons!"

How could I forget that!

Atlas tucked wing and dropped out of the path of a snapping jaw. The dragon collided with his brethren—all five of them snapping, snarling, and furiously fighting to kill the abomination. "Ainsley, do something!"

"Stop," I screamed. "Tizor, tell them to stop!"

They unleashed their flame, sweeping and igniting the sky in fire. I couldn't see Atlas anymore. I couldn't see anything through the bursting balls of yellow light stealing my vision.

Where was Keely? Where was Dominic? Where was Poet, Akasha, and Junia?

"Stop!"

A billion emotions came through the bonds. I knew in an indescribable way that my dragons were trying to help me. Their desperation and fear roared as loud as mine, but instincts were instincts. Dragons never let a be-ing that hurt them draw breath. It didn't matter that he was trying to help them.

Atlas had to die.

I blinked the spots away as Atlas zipped over the fence. The dragons crashed through it, ripping it and Keely off the ground.

"Ahhh!"

"No! Keely!"

The fencing crashed over the Everlasting Flame. I didn't see where Keely went. I couldn't see her at all.

Dominic threw himself on the flaming mound that was the death mage. Getting hands on him, he hauled him up and punched him once, twice, three times in the face fighting to put him down. For the first time, his god-like deadly magic wouldn't end the battle before it started. All he had were his fists.

A fiery punch swung from the left side, and struck Dominic's jaw. Blood spurted from his mouth. The Watcher was fighting an invisible en-emy and still holding his own. Dominic had met his match in power and strength.

Flames sprayed the heavens, sweeping the skies to ignite Atlas into a smoldering pile of revenge. He dove to escape two dragons on his heels, and they let loose—setting alight the Flame and all around it. Livia tripped run-ning away. She didn't get out a scream before the flames consumed her.

"Stop this! Listen to me," I shouted into the wind. "Stop attacking!"

Fangs snapped over Atlas's left wing. His bellow echoed through the countryside. Narrowing in on their kill, the dragons winged fast to him—their jaws open wide.

"STOP!"

Throwing my hands up, I fisted the air and *pulllled*, tapping into something as natural as breathing.

Fire ignited in my soul—all-consuming and unstoppable, I exploded into a ball of flame. The dragons faltered. Wings curling, they veered off course and collided into each other. They roared as they dropped from the sky.

I drew their fire within me. Wings bursting from my back, I took to the skies.

"*Dragon mother,*" countless voices chimed as one—so many more than six.

Wings of fire cut the air—deadly and fierce in their beauty. Claws tipped my fingertips. Scales rippled down my arms.

"STAND DOWN."

The dragons dropped their heads, wings prostrate in supplication.

Atlas struggled to stay airborne. His mangled, bleeding wing pumped desperately to stop from dropping him on the fire dragons' heads.

I hit him with a blast of magic that blew him through the air. Crying out, he stopped his tumbling and righted himself. Wide eyes beheld his perfectly healed wing.

Power hummed through me, filling every corner of my soul. Not just fire magic, but Reyna's hellfire, Mireu's healing, Suoh's shadows, Tizor's strength, and the fury of a goddess. All magic was mine for the taking.

No one could stand before me.

I screeched at Atlas—flames exploding off me in a blast of power.

He snapped to without more prompting. Dropping his fists, he raised them up and the earth rumbled.

Six columns shot out of the base and clanged against the fire pit. His face purpled as he strained.

"Yes, Atlas!"

My gaze dropped, falling on Poet, and the alive-and-well Keely who he carried in his arms.

He rushed her to the part of the fence still standing, set her down, and ran back. "Just like that. Don't stop!" Fire ropes like tendrils sprang from his back and latched on to the grate.

They were okay, and so was Dominic.

He ducked, weaved, and spun around every wildly thrown punch and kick.

"*Umpfh,*" the Watcher grunted as Dominic buried his fist in his gut. His lip wept blood. Both eyes were beginning to swell. It was stubbornness alone keeping the man on his feet.

"Who's doing that!"

Two Watchers got as close to the Flame as the heat would let them. One shot arrow after arrow at the columns. "Yul, do something!"

Yul did something.

Turning on the frenzied crowd, she swept her hand in an arc over her head, and turned everyone before her into stone.

I didn't think.

I swooped down and grabbed her under the shoulders.

"What the— Get off! Let me go!"

She thrashed and flailed in my grip. I sprang into the air before shock wore off and sense returned. Ten, fifteen, thirty feet off the ground, the hands groping for her captor stopped. She could turn me to stone... then we'd both fall and die.

"Put me down! By order of High Queen Kisandra, you are under arrest—"

I flew higher.

Movement dragged my attention to the horizon. The death mage slipped through my slackened grip.

"Ahhh!"

Wind mages.

Fire mages. Earth mages. Water mages.

They flew through the air. Rode the rumbling, shifting ground. Propelled themselves with geysers, and headed straight for us.

The entire cohort of Watchers. They were done chasing after fake Druk sightings, and were now heading straight for the real one.

No, they can't have assigned this many Watchers to guard the Flame.

I counted two dozen before losing track. Did they call for backup? How did they get here so quickly?

A Dominic Roark and dragon thief sighting must be the reason, another voice said. *They're not just here for Atlas.*

"They're coming," I called to Atlas and Poet. "The Watchers are coming."

"It's t-too much!" Atlas dropped to the ground. He heaved his arms above his head, sweat pouring down his back, and his stone pillars groaning as loud as the ones leaking through his clenched teeth. "It's not coming off!"

I didn't need to ask how Poet was doing. He strained against the grate—heels dug in and head thrown back. At some point, Keely joined his side and lent her threads to the task. They burned up within feet of the ferocious Flame.

We were no closer to freeing it, and the Watchers were on their way.

Somewhere in all this chaos, Akasha is here protecting us. I turned on our oncoming problem. *As long as we have her, we'll be okay.*

"There! It's right there!"

"What is it?"

"The dragon thief!"

Dozens of fingers pointed up... at me.

They can see me? How—?

An arrow pierced the air, heading straight for me. It shot through my wing and burned up. I barely registered it before three more came at me in rapid succession.

I snapped my wing, catching and burning two. The third impossibly changed course and buried in my back.

Screaming, I fell out of the air. Pain like I'd never known resounded through my body—burning away every nerve ending, setting my muscles alight, boiling my blood. Scrabbling at my back, I ripped the thing out a few feet from the ground. My head cleared enough to slow, not stop, my descent.

I hit the ground hard.

"Oh ho. I should've known it was you, Dominic Roark." A smug, if labored, voice hit my ear. "I've waited a long time to face you, hellfire mage." Out of the corner of my eye, the burning Watcher extinguished his flame. He stood before the world naked. "Today we find out who is strongest... before you die."

He can see him too? What about—?

"Druk?! It's a Druk!"

"What's it doing to the Everlasting Flame?"

"Kill it! Kill it now!"

"How?" I croaked, struggling to push myself up. My wings and scales were gone.

The realization barely went through my head before the fire dragons cracked the concrete shooting into the sky. I drained their magic to weaken them, and their recognition that the fiery, flying impossibility could only be dragon mother demanded their obedience.

I was back to looking like another weak, fleshy human. I had no sway over them anymore.

The death arrow mage leaped out of the way when they fell on Atlas like a pack of ravenous wolves.

Wings tangling, heads knocking, claws raking the stone—distressed, sharp barking growls sounded the air. Through their confused sniffing and shuffling, Velez stood stiller than the stone pillars no longer freeing the Flame.

"I don't understand." I clutched my aching arm, trying to stand. "Where's Akasha?"

"She's right here, bitch."

Junia materialized in front of me. Struggling and whimpering against the knife at her throat, was Akasha.

"Junia? What the fuck are you doing!"

"What's it look like I'm doing?" she snapped. "Over here!" She flagged them down. "The dragon thief is over here. She was using this traitor to conceal their attack on the Everlasting Flame."

Her blade arched through the air, slicing Akasha's throat in one smooth move. A scream of horror trapped behind my teeth as my friend dropped next to me—dead.

"They can't hide from you now," she told the Watchers—all the Watchers—who converged on us. Their black uniforms shone as starkly as the arrowhead narrowed between my eyes. "Just like I told you."

"How did it do that?" the death arrow mage hissed. "It had wings of fire. It looked like a Druk but now it's human."

I didn't even look at him. "Why?" I whispered. "We're your friends. Akasha was your friend! What is wrong with you!"

Anger flashed in her eyes. "Wrong with me? You're asking what's wrong with me? You're the crazy, revenge-mad lunatic who thinks she's on some mission from the gods to destroy Adalinda!

"I was never your *friend*. I only came along because I knew you would never succeed... then you got the water from the well." She tossed her head. "I realized then that you were more dangerous than I thought."

"I'm dangerous?" The Watchers were shouting and clamoring at me to drop my head and surrender. "You're fighting for the people who enslaved you!"

"I'm not fighting for them! I fight for my country. I fight for the true gods. General Roark and Queen Kisandra shouldn't be in charge." Hate-filled eyes pierced my heart. "But I'll take them over you any day."

"That's enough."

A brown and fast-moving glob flew through the air and smacked into Junia. She cried out, kicking and punching as the thing covered her in seconds, encasing her to the ground in—

I stiffened.

"Mud?"

"Hello again, fiancée."

Of all the horrid pieces of shit to ever curse this earth, the most filthy and vile pushed through the Watchers, standing before me in full uniform.

"You're looking terrible," Awnan said, smirking away. "To think, you could've been safe and comfortable in my ancestral home—wanting for nothing while I ran the country."

"You?" I croaked. "After all you've done, they made you a Watcher?"

He shrugged. "The Royal Renders tracked me down and brought me before the high queen. I thought I'd be executed, but it turned out she was impressed that out of everyone, I saw you as the threat to the kingdom you are, and got the jump on you.

"Look at this"—he held out his hands, grinning—"I've done it again."

"You didn't get the jump on anyone, you muddy shit stain."

I observed my friends and love out of the corner of my eye. All the Watchers were so focused on the dragon thief, they weren't looking at Keely and Poet... yet.

Velez was surrounded by growling, snapping dragons who couldn't understand why they smelled Druk, but saw a human. Wild as it was, he was safer than the rest of us right then. And my Dominic—

He traded blows in a fight that was quickly becoming five on one. Four Watchers broke off to run to their naked, bleeding comrade.

"Junia betrayed us." I spoke to give my mind time to work something out. "I should've noticed something was wrong yesterday, when she kept coming up with phony reasons to separate from us. I'm guessing she finally did it this morning when we were all asleep."

"She did—"

"Enough of this, Elsher!" The death archer kicked me, knocking me flat on my back. "Our orders are to bring this traitor before the high queen, not have a chat over tea and biscuits."

"Stop," Awnan barked. "Your orders are to follow my lead, and I order you to calm the fuck down! She's no ordinary unique mage. Somewhere close by she's got six dragons waiting to do her bidding. They'll do it that much quicker if she's hurt, so *fall back*."

Clenching his teeth, the archer obeyed.

"Of course," he continued, "she doesn't know there are no less than twelve bone mages with us, willing to break those dragons' wings if they do attack. We'll have to do it anyway to get them back to their true riders, but we won't be half as gentle about it if they try to protect her."

I swallowed hard. *He's smart, my Reyna.* My dragons' anger, and readiness, flowed through the bonds. *He always was too smart.*

Awnan cleared his throat, smile wide. "As I was saying. Junia did pop over to let us know the dragon thief and her band of traitors were planning an attack on the Everlasting Flame, but that wasn't half as interesting as what else she had to tell us."

Oh no.

Awnan encircled me. Waves of smugness radiated off him. "Quite a fanciful tale about you being the child of a goddess prophesized to bring the return of forgotten gods, and to do so, you're collecting impossible, mythical items that'll bring down the walls of the realm, and imbibe your Druk army with power as amazing and unbeatable as yours."

I mentally screamed at Junia. *Stupid, stupid bitch!*

"Even more impossible," he continued, "you actually succeeded in retrieving water from the Well of Sorrows, and going by the shitshow we crashed, you were attempting to take the Flame too. That part of her story wasn't a lie, but the rest of it..." His eyes narrowed to slits. "How? How are you the child of a goddess? How is a nothing like you prophesized to end the reign of Tenille, Calthoon, Zaeah, and Parthelan, and bring about the rise of the six kingdoms?"

I didn't speak.

"Hmm. This pinched-face silence reminds me so much of the wonderful day we signed our marriage contract."

I ached to punch him in the face.

"Too bad the wedding never happened. You were so much more of a prize than I thought."

"Am I?" The Watchers threw their hands up, taking battle stances the moment I opened my mouth. "A minute ago, you said I was nothing."

"Look at you," he said, smirk melting away. "Crouching in the dirt before me. You look a lot like nothing to me."

"Well, you're not nothing, Awnan."

His brows drew together.

"You're a stinking, rotted carcass with a pile of squirming maggots for a heart"—I beamed, freaking the Watchers out even more—"but you're not nothing."

He chuckled. "Save the sweet talk for later, beautiful. General Roark is anxious to get his hands on you. So anxious in fact, he's on his way here with the obscenely high reward money I'll get for your capture. Your little traitorous, blasphemous mission is over.

"I'm bringing you in. *All* of you in."

My smile was sweet. "And how do you think you're going to do that?"

"Elsher!" the archer shouted, hands shaking on his bow. "We end this now!"

"I said calm the hell down," he snapped. "Did you not read the information on her? Any magic used against her will be stolen. Any dragon that attacks will become her bonded. Not even death stops her. The only proven way to control this little dragon thief"—he snapped his fingers—"is to control her friends."

"Hey!"

"Let me go!"

I twisted as Poet and Keely were dragged away from the Flame, trapped and struggling uselessly against Awnan's mud golems.

I was the one who told him his magic was worthy of more than the fodder battalion. Damn him for believing me.

"Awnan!" Keely's shout resounded through my chest. "Thank you for coming to me. You just wait, bitch, this is the last time anything to do with you, touches me."

Awnan rolled his eyes. "Shut up."

Mud trickled up her arm and into her mouth, gagging her. Poet got the same treatment.

"Stop," I shouted.

"You don't need to worry about them as long as you come along quietly— And Roark surrenders now!"

My love was far from surrendering. He traded blows with his counterpart. The other mages who tried to stand against him were burning on the ground.

Calmly I looked from him, to the captured Keely and Poet, to the trapped Velez, and finally, to my friend, Akasha.

Tears prickled behind my eyes. *She believed in me more than anyone. She put her trust in me, and I put mine in the wrong person.*

After all we've done to come this far, failing here today would hurt more than just me. Keely, Velez, and Poet would be executed. The Everlasting Flame would be stolen and exploited by humans. General Roark would try again to steal my power. My dragons would be taken, and Dominic... I couldn't begin to guess what Roark had in mind for his favorite son turned betrayer.

"No."

"Excuse me?"

"I said no," I repeated clearly. "Here's what's actually going to happen. You let my friends go, help us free the Everlasting Flame and return it to the fire dragons, and I'll come with you willingly."

The Watchers exchanged looks behind him.

Awnan laughed. "You think this is some kind of negotiation? I'm not asking you, Boreen. I'm telling you."

I gave him the same eye roll. "You're wasting my time is what you're doing. If you know everything about my ability, then you know what happened at the general's estate. High Bitch Kisandra killed Dominic, Keely, and Poet, and I brought them back from the veil."

Awnan's eyes blew. He did not know that.

"You should have also been told that the terrible burns covering Kisandra—burns no healer could touch—were healed by me," I said. "You're stupid, so let me spell this out for you. There's no torture you could put my friends through that I won't heal. There's no death I won't reverse.

"You can't use them to control me," I said. "Your only hope is my gracious and willing surrender, which you'll get, if you help us free the Flame."

His eyes were darting around in his head, flicking from us to the waiting Watchers. His smirk was nowhere to be seen. "Why in the fuck do you want to free the Flame? We're not aiding you in your deluded mission to free imaginary gods!"

"This isn't about the gods. It's about the fire dragons. The Everlasting Flame means everything to them, and I won't let Kisandra and General Roark kick off the war we'll deserve if they steal and use it for their own gain."

I swept out over the hateful, curled-lip guards. "You all joined the Watchers to protect this nation. Prove it. Help us make this right."

Awnan studied me—expression blank. "That's all you want? For us to let the dragons fly off with the Flame, then you'll come quietly?"

"Yes."

"Awnan, what are you doing?" hissed the archer.

He held up a hand, silencing him. His gaze fixed on me. "What guarantees do we have that you won't attack after you've gotten what you want?"

Reaching into my pocket, I withdrew the vial. Fingers trembling, I put it in his hands. "Water from the Well of Sorrows. Given to me by the god who inhabits it."

"Ainsley, no!" Velez cried.

"Since that traitor told you everything, you know how much I need this water," I pushed on. "Without it, I can't fulfill my destiny, free my godly mother, stop the war with the Druks, or save Adalinda. This should tell you that control of the water is much more valuable than control of my friends."

He flicked from me to the vial. That familiar shrewdness leached into his furrowed brow. "How do I know you're telling the truth? What proof is there that this is what you say it is?"

"Because I've been standing next to her this entire time, dumbass." I pointed to Junia. "I can only speak the truth."

"Hmm. Touche." His grin returned. "So you say here, before these Watchers and while under influence of her magic, that you'll willingly surrender to the authority of the high queen? All you ask is that we let these dragons fly off with the Everlasting Flame?"

"Yes."

Awnan shrugged. "Eh, sure. Why not?"

"What!"

Yelling, shouting, protests, and refusals went up around us, but I didn't pay it any mind. Thanks to Junia, Awnan couldn't lie either. We had a deal.

"First, call him off," I ordered, pointing to the man still fighting Dominic.

Awnan jerked his head, sending two Watchers off to stop the fight. Hopefully Dom didn't kill them too.

"Release Poet and Keely."

Another nod, and his golems let go. My friends fell against each other, holding the other up. They were both banged up and pouring sweat, but they were alive. I would not lose another friend that day.

Only when the Watchers were hauling the bellowing hellfire mage off did I turn back to Elsher.

"Ains, no! Don't do this." Hellfire balls appeared in the air, hovering over their designated victims. "You don't have to anymore."

"Kill him!"

"No, wait—"

Fire, water, mud, sand, rock, mist, arrows, and a strange, cloying black smoke blasted Dominic. He, and my scream, was lost in the onslaught.

"Stop it. Stop!" I tried to run to him. "Dominic!"

"Don't worry, baby."

My head snapped up. Dominic hung twenty feet above us, suspended by... was that thread?

"Too slow." He cut the air.

"Your mother!" Awnan shouted.

Dominic paused.

Awnan ran out from underneath the fireball, or he tried to. It followed his every step—getting closer with each shrieking cry for it to go away.

"What about my mother?"

Awnan spoke so fast, the words blended together. "Yourfathersaidifyousurrenderyou'llbetakentoyourmother.   Ifyoudon'tshe'llbeexecutedfortreason."

It took me a beat to piece it apart. My jaw dropped. "He'll take him to his mother if he surrenders, and execute her if he doesn't? That's insane!"

"The choice is yours, Roark!" He conjured golem after golem to shield him. "Stand down. Stand down now!"

"Dom, please," I cried, forgetting about the pathetic little mud man. "I don't want you to do this."

"I'm not letting them take you!"

He wouldn't. I knew it as surely as I knew cheese pastries and making love to me were his favorite things in the world. And as surely as I read the agony etched in his eyes. His father never bluffed. This choice would kill his mother...

...and break him forever.

He raised his hand.

"Don't," I screamed. "Dom, your father taught you to see everyone who stands against you as your enemy, but that's not who they are. They're just normal, frightened people under sway of true evil. But if we kill them, no one will know that.

"Your father will sing the tale of the vicious, insane dragon thief and the heir she corrupted into doing her bidding. No one will hear the truth behind dozens of murdered Watchers."

Dominic shook—face reddening. "They're not taking you!"

"He doesn't get to do that to you anymore!" Tears soaked my cheeks. "He's done convincing the world that you're a monster, all to hide what he truly is. Today is the day you free the Everlasting Flame and give the greatest kindness to the fire dragon clan that any human in history ever will. Today's the day you found out your mother is alive and waiting for you.

"It's the day you show the people you're destined to lead that you're merciful, and General Roark is a manipulative liar. This is a good day, Dom," I said softly. "I won't let him take one more from you."

Slowly, shakily, Dominic dropped his arm.

"Okay." His ragged voice echoed over the roar of the Flame. "You're right, baby. You're right. He doesn't get to use me anymore."

"Yes." I reached my arms out to him.

Behind us, they bleated and shouted for us to surrender.

"But he's not taking you either."

"What—?"

"Keely, now!"

Tiny, barely there binds lashed around my wrists and under my arms. Screaming, they ripped me off my feet and launched me into the air.

"Save her, you flying piece of shit!"

Velez shot past me. We cleared the fence—two human projectiles catapulted by thread magic—and dropped.

"Dommm!"

A blast of air hit my face, then Atlas had me.

"Arrgh!" Dragon roars ripped apart the sky. The earth boomed as they launched off the ground, chasing after us.

Atlas held me tight against his chest, wings pumping furiously carrying us into the air.

Anger and death chased our tails. Growling, deadly fangs, slicing claws, and will for nothing but revenge. The dragons smashed into each other, racing to tear Atlas apart, and behind them, my love and friends dropped to the ground… and were surrounded.

"No!" I thrashed against Atlas. "Take me back. I can't leave them again. I won't! Take me back now!"

"I didn't take you back the night Golden City burned down around them."

A band clamped around my throat.

"I won't do it now," he bellowed against the wind. "I'm here for you, Ainsley. I protect you.

"And he does too."

His last words were said so softly, the wind tried to snatch them away.

Rage ripped through my chest.

"I don't want your protection!" I grabbed his head and shook. "Take me back!"

Reyna, I need you! My dragons, come to us. Save Dominic, Keely, and Poet!

"Hey—! Are you crazy?" He ripped free of me. "Do you not see the five homicidal dragons chasing us! I can't go ba— *Ogh.*"

"I won't leave them."

Come to me, my beauties!

Nothing came through the bonds, not even their emotions. Understanding turned my stomach. They weren't going to save them. They agreed with Dominic's decision. My clan would be sacrificed… to protect me.

"Atlas, you have to—"

"Agh!" A shout tore from his throat. Wings crumpling, Atlas contorted, bellowing so loud I ceased my shouting. He snapped forward and we dropped out of the sky.

Plummeting, spinning, and the dragons still chasing him. I saw the glint of a death arrow coming. It struck his back, burying deep next to the first one.

"Atlas! Velez!" Wind rushed into my mouth and ate my cry.

"I—I know you understand me," Atlas shouted. "I'm d-dying. Don't let her die too."

What is he talking about! The ground rushed to meet us, opening the welcome arms of Calthoon.

"Save her!"

Something broke off the ground and flew at me. *A hand.* I couldn't get out a scream before it caught me. I smashed painfully against its grip, head ringing.

But alive.

It's not a hand. It's stone. The thought no sooner crossed my mine than real appendages closed around me.

"Wait!"

Dragon claws sealed me within razor-sharp bars. Incredibly, impossibly, they unfurled their wings—stopping their free fall dead... and not chasing after Atlas.

I screamed as he struck the ground, and didn't move. "No, brother!"

Atlas, whose only wish for a good death was to look just as handsome as he did in life, stayed himself to the very end to give the dragons time to catch me. My brothers. The last of my family.

"No, no, no!" I sobbed. Heartrending cries strangled my throat and stole the breath in my lungs. "Take me back."

Cuts opened on my skin everywhere I threw myself against the claws. "I can't leave him there like that. He could still be alive. Mireu's magic will heal him. Dom, Keely, and Poet, I can save them. Take me back. Take me back!"

My demands fell on uncaring ears.

"Listen to me. I am dragon mother. I demand you take me back to Atlas and the Everlasting Flame."

The dragons flew straight. There was no indication they heard a word I said.

Calm down, Ainsley. I sucked in heaving, shuddering breaths—face soaked. *The power to turn them around is in you. You did it before. You can do it again. Focus.*

Summon your magic. Summon your fury at Awnan, the general, and the queen. Channel this pain into vengeance!

Nothing.

No flaming wings erupted from my back. No scales rippled down my skin, nor claws from my fingertips.

Heartbroken I cried, as the dragons carried me away from everyone I loved.

Chapter Fourteen

Shadows fell over my vision, blotting out the sun and everything I remembered of light.

Through warping tears, I blinked through the claws. It was dark. Why was it dark? Where had they taken me? Where—?

The dragon opened their paw, dropping me.

"Ahh!"

I plummeted through the air. My back struck something both firm and soft, throwing me back up. What was happening? Where was I? Why couldn't I see?

A roar battered my eardrums. I knew it better than my own voice.

"Kenna?"

I struggled and huffed flipping over. Pushing up, brilliant aquamarine scales glittered beneath my shaking, bleeding hands.

She roared again, and I swore, even though our bond remained closed, I heard her voice crisp and clear.

We're here, Ainsley. We never left you.

"We?" I tipped my head to the covered sky, lips parting. Speech failed me in face of the most beautiful sight.

Ruby scales, ivory horns, jeweled eyes, magical fire playing on their wings, and dancing through their scales. *Fire dragons.*

Young, old, horned, ridged, fast fliers, and slow. Above, below, to my left, and to my right. So many fire dragons blanketed the sky, they blotted out the sun. And flying among them were my beauties, Reyna, Suoh, Cadmus, Mireu, and Kenna.

"You d-didn't abandon them," I whispered. "You went to get help. You went... and got them all."

Suoh vanished in one blink, and returned in the other. Lying on my grumpy boy's back, was Atlas. Bleeding, broken, unconscious, and in full form, none of the dragons paid him any mind. They had one focus only, and it crested the horizon, radiating heat that sweated the entire countryside.

The Everlasting Flame.

Kenna was a spear through the clouds. She flew so fast, she pulled ahead of the others, and brought the platform into sight. Quickly, I wiped my eyes and scanned the moving dots surrounding the Flame. Dozens of Watchers, but also the surviving onlookers too—unable to walk away from their temple to Mother Zaeah, even as fighting raged around them.

Where's Dominic? Where's—?

There.

Dominic and my friends stood back-to-back within a ring of hellfire. Poet lashed flames like whips above and through their shield, deflecting their magical attacks, while Keely's threads plucked and tossed aside Watchers like raisins from a muffin.

I barked a laugh—a feeling I couldn't describe filled my heart. I stood beside the strongest and truest warriors in all of Adalinda. They were never going to go down without a fight.

A bright, moving dot came at them fast. The hellfire mage burst through Dominic's shield, fists raised and ready to continue the battle he'd been waiting for.

I understood what they were doing with a single look. Dominic couldn't fight the Watchers with hellfire because he'd kill them. A death mage was exactly that. His magic had one purpose. To honor my wishes, my love was staying out of the fighting, and protecting Poet and Keely while they thinned out the force against them.

Once they defeated the Watchers, they'd continue our true purpose of freeing the Everlasting Flame.

"If that's what's keeping them here, we'll fix that right now." I swept my hand. Not a drop of magic, borrowed or otherwise, flowed through me. But I didn't hesitate. "Mireu, save my brothers, please. Cadmus, break apart the concrete around the base. Suoh, shadow-travel those Watchers wherever you think best, and everyone else, let's free the Flame!"

They roared as one, rumbling the world to its very core.

Watchers whipped around at the sound. Taking one look, half a dozen dropped their hands, turned tail, and ran off the platform. The rest proved idiocy in the face of certain death wasn't just Atlas's fatal flaw.

They turned their magic on the dragons.

Death arrows pierced the air, and embedded in the scales of the dragon next to me. Tucking her wings, she dropped next to the mangled fence, swung her haunches, and smashed her tail into the archer—catching him mid-draw.

He flew screaming over the side. I didn't bother to watch him fall.

Kenna swooped low over Dominic, Keely, and Poet. Dominic smiled up at me.

"Princess, you're ok—"

"I'm going to fucking kill you, you selfish asshole," I barked. "How dare you send me away like some helpless damsel! Don't you ever, ever do that again!"

His smile went nowhere. "If it means you'll always be around to call me a selfish asshole, you've got a deal."

"Ainsley!" Poet jumped up and down. "You're amazing."

"This wasn't me," I called down. "It was all you. Just tell us what to do."

"Keep the Watchers busy." He took off running. "I'll get that damn grate off."

Poet made it two feet and stumbled. Pitching forward, he clutched his head, shouting louder than the crackling Flame.

I would've helped him if he wasn't laughing too.

"Yes," he shouted. "Yes! Haha! You're back."

Valor growled his joy. Blowing past me and Kenna, he retrieved his rider.

"Together, old man." Poet hopped astride Valor's back. Sunlight skimmed through his coarse hair, glistening off the damp sheen clinging to his rippling back, and the bumps and dips going down his front. Ropes of fire burst from him and seized the grate—ten times stronger with Valor's power behind him.

Poet heaved, every muscle in his body straining, and looked nothing like the bespectacled coward who ran away from Keir that first day of training. He looked like a warrior. A dragon rider.

A hero.

Something told me Keely was amending her view of her annoying, childhood friend, and that something was her open-mouthed stare, and the dusky hue staining her cheeks.

Groaning metal cut through the fighting. It was coming off.

"Cadmus."

My cow-loving boy dropped beside the pit and smashed his tail on the concrete. It split like butter. Stomping, smashing, moving around the pit, my earth dragon was a hammer amongst these finely honed fire blades.

"May as well give him a hand." Atlas's wing brushed my cheek flying down. "And let everyone see the true hero of the Everlasting Flame achieved victory."

My heart sang joy, too happy to care about his regular nonsense. "Have at it, hero."

Pillars from the broken concrete struck the underside and heaved. Inch by inch, the fire pit began to rise.

"Stop them!" Awnan cowered behind an army of golems, a tiny shouting sliver through the mass of mud and limbs. "Leave the dragons, and take the traitors. They can have the fucking Flame. Don't let the dragon thief get away again!"

A blast of wind slammed into me like a carriage, nearly knocking me off Kenna's back. They heeded Awnan's order all too quickly.

"Kenna, set me down beside them. I'm a moving target like this." A moving magicless target.

I dropped into Keely's strangling hug.

"Oh, Ains, I'm sorry we tried to send you away. We made a pact before we left that we wouldn't let the general or high queen get their hands on you."

"And that's why you three aren't allowed to be alone together anymore."

She laughed. "Thanks for bringing every fire dragon in Adalinda. We didn't know how we were getting out of this one."

"We're not out of it yet," Dominic said, tugging me out of her arms and into his. "The bounties for us are too high. They'll risk a few burns if it means retiring with a regency."

A fire dragon flew down, scooped a clawful of Watchers, and dropped them over the side.

"They risk more than that," I said. "The dragons aren't holding back."

I suddenly saw what Egan, the Five, and all the Druks saw. No, I saw the foundation for bonds and the reason for the dragon riders. At their core, dragons weren't a violent species. They didn't want to hurt humans maliciously, or even accidentally. But if they threw around their full power, the death toll would include the innocent and the guilty.

My Kenna was a cyclone—laying waste to all in her path—but through me, her magic was a blade—honed, lethal, precise.

There were no blades in this battle. The fire dragons *all* knew now that the grate over the Flame wasn't just some human foolishness. The revelation of the entire plan to force the Flame to go out, and set up in a new location where their offerings would be for the taking, had broken the unwritten rule between man and dragon.

The full ferocious power of dragons lay before me, and I knew one thing as certain as I knew Dominic's love would always be mine. We did not want a war with the dragons because the very next day after war was declared, Adalinda would fall.

Dominic tackled Keely, throwing her out of the way. A swirling tower of fire cut through the spot they'd both been standing in. Heat boiled my skin, singed my hairs, and blinded me. I didn't know I was screaming until the reigning roars and rumbles calmed.

Blinking away white spots, my vision cleared on... nothing.

No bodies. No bones. No burned uniforms.

All that was left of the force foolish enough to stand against the might of the dragons, was scorch marks that used to be people, and a smoking mound of mud.

The fight was over. The battle for the Everlasting Flame was won... and it only took seven minutes.

Keely staggered over to me, clutching her arm. It was covered in burns simply from being near the flames. My arms were no better.

"Wow," she breathed.

Livia picked herself off the ground. Quickly, she tied the remains of her clothes around herself to cover as much as possible, then ran past us to the fire pit.

There wasn't a mark on her. Nor were there burns on the other fire mages who refused to leave. They encircled the pit like they encircled the fence.

I was dumbfounded watching them take hands and tip their chins to the sky.

Was it instinct? Was it secret Hyelongan magical art that a girl who'd never been anywhere, including school, never got a chance to know? Was it simply the blessing of Mother Zaeah? So many of her children gathered in this place, pledged to serve her no matter the cost, and she responded—filling them with the knowledge of exactly what to do.

"Beautiful," Keely whispered.

I was speechless.

Mage and dragon alike glowed— No, they burned with a calming, gentle radiance that began like the flicker of candlelight, and grew until they shone from the inside out. Their bodies simply holders for the fire within, and burning brightest of all, was Poet.

"They're giving him their magic," Dominic breathed. "Their strength. How?"

I recalled my first day at the Royal Rider Academy vividly. The day Keir Stryker threw Poet at my feet, laughing at the common fire mage bonded to the even more common fire dragon.

"Arrrgh!" Poet heaved, shouting to the sky as the grate bent, crumpled, buckled, then gave away.

Twisting on Valor's back, he whipped his fire ropes around and high—his muscles straining to heft metal a hundred times his weight, and his rage and borrowed strength making up the distance. He flung the disgusting thing away, bellowing his victory to the tune of a thousand roars.

I can't curse the day Maili and Ormr latched on to my life, because it's also the day I met Poet.

I defy anyone to call the man before me a coward.

Ten dragons moved as one, flying over the fire mages, and dropping down before the Flame. One set down beside Atlas and screeched in his face. Velez was standing there before he was done.

I shook my head, eyes rolling up. Atlas's fleeting moment of selflessness was over. His parting wish to die handsome and whole made irate dragons Velez's problem.

Hands flying up, the pillars around the pit melted into the earth, unable to be maintained by Velez. He slowly backed away, letting the dragon who scolded his brother claim his spot.

Velez fell in beside me—all of us open-mouthed and wondering watching the dragons press their heads against the underside of the fire, and push.

The pit gave way like a knife sliding out of butter. Inch by inch, they raised our last obstacle out of the ground.

"We did it!" I jumped up and down, shaking Velez. "The Everlasting Flame is free."

Dominic beamed. No one could do anything but, in face of this historic, incredible moment. "The dragons got it from here. They'll take the Flame to a safe place, and won't let humans near it again until they earned the right.

"Whatever my father and the high queen had planned is over. They'll have to exploit someone—"

A shadow moved at the corner of my eyes. I barely turned my head when a large, brown mass surged on Dominic. Sprouting hands, the golem grabbed my love and threw him as the scream left my lips.

"No!"

Keely's threads burst from her fingertips, chasing after Dominic. They lashed around his wrists, and snapped—burned away in the scorching heat.

"Ains—" Dominic fell into the fire pit, consumed by the flames.

My jaw cracked screaming. "Dom!"

A red streak dropped out of the air. Reyna dove straight into the Everlasting Flame, going after her boy. I ran to help when Keely cried out. Mud overtook her in seconds—devouring her. Suffocating her.

Laughter broke the air.

"So ends the invincible Dominic Roark and his all-powerful hellfire dragon." The mound I dismissed as a pile of mud shifted and moved, revealing the true pile of shit it protected. The mud formed under Awnan and lifted him into the air. Reclining back, he smirked at me from his throne. "Don't worry, there's a reward for killing him too, but not as high as the one you're still going to fetch me."

He shook the vial from the Well of Sorrows. "Remember our deal. They've got their precious fire, so send them away. You come with me now, or I kill Keely. If I have to ask again, I drop this and—"

Threads burst out of the mud and flew to Awnan. Wrapping around his arms, legs, neck, and every part of him, Keely tore free of her prison. Her eyes burned with a rage that chilled me. Keely was my sister, because surely she was a child of vengeance and fury too.

"I told you," she snarled, "you'll never touch me again."

Slapping her palms together, she ripped them apart.

There wasn't a chance to look away as the threads pulled Awnan in every direction, and tore him to pieces. His head dropped down between my feet—his wide-eyed cowardly fear still frozen on his face.

I turned my back on him, forgetting him in that instant. Good riddance to a terrible human being.

"Keely, we have to do something," I cried. Reyna's agony ricocheted through the bond. Her pain made me scream.

The Everlasting Flame wasn't just any fire. It was more than hot enough to burn a hellfire dragon... and a hellfire mage.

"We have to do something now!"

"We need Poet," she said, racing to the line of fire mages. "We need everyone. They can do something. They can—"

I didn't see it until it was already on her—a rolling, low-hanging black cloud passing over the line.

"Keely, look out!"

She ran straight through it. Keely choked, eyes bugging and hands flying to her throat. My friend pitched to the ground. Jerking and convulsing, I lost her in a wave of falling bodies—people wheezing, choking, and dying.

"Traitors!" A face appeared in the chaos, familiar even with hatred twisting his features. He was one of the death mage Watchers. At some point during the fighting, he must've shed his uniform and hid among the fire mages. "You align with usurpers and Druks. You aid that cursed monster who bewitched all these innocent dragons!"

Waves and waves of deathly miasma poured from him like a rushing waterfall. All too quickly, the Everlasting Flame and everyone around it was consumed.

Poet fell from Valor's back, the glow of gifted magic gone before he hit the ground.

"No," I screamed, rushing this way and that. I called upon every bond, every drop of magic around me. I shrieked for Kai himself... but nothing came.

"I execute you in the name of Adalinda, by order of High Queen Kisandra," he ranted, spittle flying from his frothing mouth. "Our nation is unclean. Our people corrupted. I will save our country, and you—" A gray streak shot out of the ground and impaled him through the chest.

"And I execute you in the name of getting you to shut the fuck up," Atlas drawled, clapping his hands.

A horde of dragons flew over the Flame and hooked the pit with their claws. They readied to carry it away, undaunted by the poisoned air.

"Atlas." I ran to him. "You have to do something before they take the Flame away. Reyna and Dominic are still in there. Help me, please."

"Of course, my w-wish—" He coughed. "Wishing star. I serve your e-e—" Atlas doubled over, coughing and hacking his lungs up. "Ahh," he said, voice calm even as he wheezed. "Seems that ranting fool... had the last word."

Atlas collapsed. I tried to catch him and we both went down, falling hard on the broken ground.

"Atlas? Atlas!"

A whoosh of flame erupted from the fire pit. Reyna reached for the sky, but was called to the earth.

Crumpled wings failed her. She plummeted, and grasped between her claws, was—

"Dom!"

Carefully, I set Atlas down and raced to them as Reyna struck the ground. The reverberation threw me off my feet, but I didn't stop—crawling to my love and my beauty.

I clamped my hand over my mouth—trapping a cry. I didn't recognize the burned, wounded beings before me. There was no telling where Reyna ended and Dominic began. They were both broken, disfigured, and dying.

My head whipped from my friends, my brothers, Dominic, and my dragon as the fire dragons carried the Flame away, leaving us behind.

My scream echoed across the countryside.

Chapter Fifteen

"Ainsley? Ainsley?"

A hand grasped my shoulder. I shook it off.

"Why don't you come inside?" he asked. "Have something to eat? Get some rest. There's nothing more you can do."

"I'm not going anywhere," I snapped. "So either join me or go away."

After a beat, he sat down next to me on the top step. Velez took my hand.

I shook that off too.

I didn't want to be comforted, reassured, forgiven, complimented, or anything of the like. I didn't deserve it.

Silence lapsed between us. A thick and somber mood for such a beautiful place.

I gazed over the sprawling garden. Roses, dahlias, daffodils, lilies, tulips, marigolds, and endless more flowers I couldn't name. The flower mage who lived on this colorful patch of Hyelong built a small, cozy cottage on acres and acres of land. Her preference for the outdoors was clear, and in our favor.

Three people and one dragon lay on the ground, crushing a patch of zinnias. I hated that I couldn't bring them inside where it was warm and dry, but Mireu needed space to heal.

The water dragon tapped her snout to Dominic's forehead, then Keely's, then Poet's, the same to Reyna's wing. She'd been doing that for the last five hours since we arrived at the cottage with no break in rhythm, and no way to answer the questions shouting in my head.

"There's been no change," I burst out. "Why aren't they healing? Why aren't they waking up? When I channeled Mireu's magic, everyone around me was healed in an instant."

"Ains, from what you told me, you channeled so much of it, you became a being of pure healing magic, with a little bit of goddess power thrown in. Dragons don't wield magic same as humans, or a god." He firmly laced his fingers through mine. "But they are healing. It is working. They're alive.

"Atlas didn't breathe in nearly as much poison as Keely and Poet, and it knocked him out. It's only his dragon slayer–boosted healing that saved us, and right now," he said softly, "Mireu is healing them. Trust her." He brought both our hands up, catching a tear from my cheek. "She'll save them."

"Trust." I made a harsh noise in my throat. "What do I know about trust? I trusted Maili. I trusted Ormr. I trusted Junia. Only yesterday, we laughed and joked in the bathhouse. Just a couple of... friends," I whispered. "Now Akasha's dead because the person I told her to trust slit her throat."

"That wasn't your fault." He tried turning my chin to face him.

I held firm, refusing to look away from Dominic and my friends.

"None of us saw the real Junia," Velez said. "She fooled everyone."

"Did she fool you?" I looked at him then—hard. "You knew we couldn't trust her, didn't you."

"What?" he cried, leaning back. "What are you talking about?"

I threw out my hands. "This place. The woman who lives here. She introduced herself to me when you went off to check the area. She said she's Colonel Kinryu's niece. Kinryu was an ally and spy for the Druks, and you knew she was too."

"Yeah, so?"

"So, this cottage is only an hour away from the Luzon guesthouse. We could've stayed here the entire time, but you didn't say anything, because you didn't want exactly what happened today to happen to Kinryu's niece. For her to be found out and given up to the Watchers."

"Ains—"

"Admit it! You knew she couldn't be trusted and you didn't say anything. Why didn't you say!"

"Whoa, Ains," he said, putting his hands up. "Slow down. It's not like that. I didn't protect Cassia because I didn't trust Junia. I did because I didn't trust *any of them*. Junia, Akasha, Poet, Keely, and Roark. The only one I ever trusted from the start was you..." He looked away. "Until today.

"Your friends and Roark were willing to sacrifice everything, even being locked up and tortured again, to protect you. They have my trust." He held his hand out to me. "I'm sorry I ever doubted them."

My lips trembled—anger bursting at the seams. But it wasn't at Velez. The person I was truly angry with was sitting next to him.

"No," I said, turning away from him and continuing my vigil. "You don't have to apologize. Your caution is why we have a safe place to stay tonight, and my idiocy is why we needed it. All the apologies come from me now."

"Ains, you can't—"

"You're going to say I can't blame myself," I sliced in. "You'll say some garbage about it all being Junia's fault that we're here, but who is the one who insisted we needed a truth mage on our team? Who told the treacherous bitch that they knew for all of a few weeks, everything about me, my power, the prophecy, and what we're planning?"

"Who ignored her strange behavior and her attempts to separate from us the minute we were close enough to some Watchers? Who was it, Velez?"

My gaze pinned him through. "Me.

"So don't tell me it's not my fault. I put everyone I love in danger because I couldn't see what was right in front of me... again."

"You're right."

I jerked when Atlas appeared before me. Healing sores and mottled boils covered his face. Atlas was on his feet before the others, but the poison hadn't left him unscathed.

Seeing him up close shot bile into my throat. I could barely tell Poet and Keely apart when I went mad, desperately searching for them among the fallen mages. It wasn't enough to steal their lives. That death Watcher had to steal their kind and brave faces too.

They say Calthoon doesn't punish souls beyond the veil. All are equal and all are given a second chance. If I was ever to beg him for anything, it was that he make an exception for that poison mage, and Awnan Elsher.

"What?"

"You're right, Ainsley."

I leaned slightly back. Atlas didn't call me Ainsley when a ridiculous pet name would do. He also didn't look upon me with that expression.

"It is your fault," he stated, voice flat. "We all put our trust in you, and you let us down. Where was your great, god-blessed power when poison filled the air? Where was it when your dragon burned herself alive to save the ex-fiancé you just can't walk away from? Why didn't the quick and clever thief notice that Junia was draining us of secrets while giving up none of her own?"

His face warped through the tears. "Atlas—"

"Don't," he hissed. "Don't cry, or plead, or pull that 'how could you say that to me?' bullshit! You want the truth, Ainsley, so here it is. You don't know what the fuck you're doing. You've been making this up as you went along, and relying on us to cover your weaknesses.

"You can't think of a plan to save the dragons? *That's okay. Junia's got one.* Your shitty power is useless and unreliable? *That's okay, you've got strong friends who'll do anything for you.* You don't know how to get us out of the trouble you got us into? *No problem, the dragons you forcibly bonded to you will save the day.*"

I shook, jaw clenched tight. I couldn't speak to let a word in. I couldn't breathe to try.

"You think you're better than Kisandra and the general, and fucking hell, I don't know why. You use people just like them. You let them die for you while you skip off without a scratch."

"That's not true," I cried, sobs making me unintelligible. "I didn't want this to happen. Any of it."

"No? Then why are Keely and Poet here? Being close to you ruined their lives, and yet you dragged them along on this fatal, impossible quest anyway. Why the fuck is Roark here?" he demanded. "You dumped him, didn't you? But still you let him follow you around like a puppy, hoping and waiting you'll take him back, when all you really want is his protection."

"That's not true!" My scream blew his wings back. "I'm not using him. I would never use him. He has to stay with me so I can protect *him*!"

"Yeah?" His eyes were hard. "How is that working out for him?"

Burying my head in my hands, I wailed. Horrible, wretched cries that echoed through the bonds and sent despair back to me. My dragons couldn't take my pain. It was too much for one person. Why would seven be able to handle it?

"I didn't mean for this to happen. I just wanted to save everyone. I just wanted to make it right." Over and over I repeated that, pleading to who?

Praying to who? Tenille, Zaeah, Calthoon, and Parthelan have abandoned me. Titana's given up on me. I spoke truth all those weeks ago.

All I do is get people killed.

"Enough, Ainsley." A warm hand settled on my head. "You know what you need to do now, and crying in the dirt isn't it."

I heard the clang and clink of him setting something in front of me. I blinked to see the water from the Well and the holder—burning with the gift of the Everlasting Flame.

Even while my friends fought for their lives and legacy, Keely and Poet made sure to get and keep these things safe for me. The vial rolled out of Keely's grip when I put her on Cadmus's back. The holder was already on Valor's back, placed there for safekeeping. For me.

I lifted my head, shuddering breaths shaking my shoulders. "Awnan said he passed everything Junia told him to the general. He knows the prophecy is truly about me. He knows my power was given by a goddess to free that goddess. He knows where we're going next."

"Yep," he drawled. "Your borrowed plan's gone to shit. So what are you going to do about it, thief? Is it finally time for you to stop stealing every-one else's ideas and magic, and finally come up with your own?"

I flinched, shrinking back. His words were spears through my chest.

"Stop, you've said enough," Velez barked, taking over. "Back off her, At-las. This isn't her fault."

"She doesn't need coddling anymore," Atlas replied, back in a blink. "When are you going to wake up and see she's not a little girl anymore? The Four had one thing right. All your hand-holding and fawning only got in the way of her becoming who she needed to be. A true warrior doesn't sit around, refusing even now after all that's happened, to do what's right."

Please.

"You already know what you need to do, Ainsley."

Don't say it.

"Akasha's gone. She can't hide us anymore, and you can't walk around with the most well-known face in Adalinda."

There has to be another way.

"There's no other way," he said, echoing my thoughts. "You can't keep asking people to follow you when you can't protect them."

Please, gods, I can't.

"You have to return to Itzala, tell them you've failed, and that the birth of ten thousand new dragon slayers shall proceed."

Another way. Any other way.

"You have to tell your god to burn down the walls he erected in your mind, so that the fierce and all-powerful being who roamed the kingdoms undefeated can return."

Stop, Atlas. Don't say it.

"Then, you say goodbye to your friends because you know they only signed up for a war against General Roark and the high queen. Not one against their homes, their families, their friends, and the kingdom they love."

Don't. Don't!

"You say goodbye to Dominic Roark," he whispered, "because when he wakes up, you'll be his enemy."

I sat there long after Atlas left, staring unseeingly at the fire and water—two pieces of a plan that already failed.

Slowly, I wiped my face, stood up, and turned my back on Keely, Dominic, Poet, and my dragons.

My tearful vigil was over. Atlas said it in the way someone with no compassion would say it, but that didn't mean it wasn't true. There was no point to me sitting around, weeping and wailing.

I already knew what I had to do.

Heading inside, I found a quill and paper. It didn't take me long to write the letter. I knew for a long time what it had to say. I simply couldn't bear to say it.

The sun crested over the horizon when I returned to Dominic.

He looked leagues better than he did just an hour before. New, pink skin covered his arms and face, giving me a glimpse of my strong and handsome love. Taking his hand, I closed his fingers around the letter.

"I'm sorry," I whispered, holding his hand to my forehead. "I love you."

"Ains... ley..."

I placed his hand back as he stirred, quickly rising and leaving the garden.

"Atlas."

He stepped out of the shadows. He'd never really gone anywhere.

"Ainsley?" Dominic rasped. "Ainsley, where... are you?"

I walked to Atlas, steeling my heart. "Time to go."

"Yes, my queen." He bowed low. "I exist to serve you."

"Ains, please." Dominic's voice was barely a croak. "Wha... What's in my hand?"

"You exist to serve." I raised my chin. The fearsome, brutal godling is what the kingdom needed. That is who I would be. "We'll see if that's true."

I left the garden. The wind eventually stole Dominic's voice away.

***

We huddled in the alleyway, concealed behind stacked crates of fish—if the smell was anything to go by.

"You know, when you walked off all tough and determined, I thought it was for more than show," Atlas drawled, leaning against his wings.

It was dangerous for him to be out—crates of fish or no—but he ignored my repeated demands to switch with Velez. So much for an obedient servant.

"What are we doing here? You know we don't have a chance."

I pulled my hood low, shivering in my coat. Of course I didn't want to be here. No one wanted to be in the ice bucket called Edjer except for the heat-hating weirdos who lived here, but we didn't have a choice. Two thousand years ago, Edjerians built their capital on the spot of the last known nesting spot of the celestial dragon. Calixto was where they once lived, so Calixto was where we needed to be.

"We're not giving up," I gritted for what felt like the hundredth time. "If we do, it means everything Poet, Keely, and Dominic sacrificed was for nothing. We have the water and the fire. We're not stopping now."

"This is about General Spawn, Thread Girl, and Fire Boy?" he scoffed. "Sentiment. What happened to putting all that nonsense aside and thinking like a warrior. A queen."

I controlled my tongue with difficulty. "Shut the fuck up."

Yes, that was me in control.

Atlas chuckled. "Okay, if plain-speak won't work, let me try logic. I don't know if they ever got to this in the school you never went to, but celestial dragons were revered, even worshipped, because..." He looked up at the darkening sky. "They were stars.

"Beings made of pure and true starlight, they'd fall to the earth in an explosion of magic, and nest where they landed," he said. "Celestial dragons cannot give birth in the heavens, as such, they had no choice but to rear their offspring here."

"I know this," I cut in. "Sister Aven told us the tale. Dragons made of starlight. They were beautiful, rare, and possessed magic the world had never seen. One of those things is worth a lot of money to a collector. All three made them the most coveted target of every egg thief, dragon slayer, and bounty hunter.

"Like you said, they arrived on land in an explosion that told everyone within a hundred miles where to go," I said, nails piercing my palm imagining the dragon's pain and fear. "They attacked, killed, stripped, and mercilessly hunted mother and nestlings. Until two thousand years ago when the last celestial fell on this spot. She was killed and another never came again."

Atlas shook his head. "Maybe they believed every star is a dragon. Millions upon billions in the sky, they didn't know they were bringing about their extinction."

"Doesn't matter what they thought. Their greed and cruelty slaughtered thousands of innocent dragons."

Atlas simply inclined his head. It was hard to talk dragon cruelty with a dragon slayer.

"Since you know all this," he continued, "you know that any celestial dragon that landed here was taken apart, and their pieces sold to the highest bidders. If there were any remains left, like say a claw—" He held out his hands. "They built an entire city on top of it.

"This is a fool's mission, my beauty of the heavens, and not just because of them..."

Atlas trailed off, gazing at the reason we were hiding behind boxes of rotting fish.

The alley provided us only a partial glimpse of the street and part of the main square, and that didn't stop us counting dozens of Riders, Watchers, and two Renders circling the square in a steady rotation.

Calixto was overrun by the high queen's forces, and they were all here for me.

"Did you hear what the dragon thief did in Hyelong?"

Three women in expensive coats and fur-lined caps came out of one of the shops that housed our alley, and paused to lace on their skates.

"She bewitched thousands of fire dragons and forced them to steal the Everlasting Flame for her. When the Watchers tried to stop her, she killed them and everyone there."

"My gods," gasped a short woman with dark hair poking through her hood. "Vicious beast. Why can't they stop her already?"

The third woman leaned in, making a show of looking around and lowering her voice. "I heard that she's the bastard creation of a Druk whore. The half-woman performed unholy forbidden magic on her womb to bring forth the dragon thief, and the babe was cursed and insane. They say she stole the Everlasting Flame to use in a terrible forbidden ritual. If she's successful, she'll unleash the same dark magics that cursed her, and make everyone in Adalinda just like her."

"What!"

"That's awful."

"I know." She nodded, leaking satisfaction over her juicy gossip. "Even worse, they say she's coming here next. She could already be here."

I pressed tighter to the wall.

"Here?" squeaked the short one in a pink coat. "Why would she come here?"

"The next thing she needs for the ritual is here. That's why everyone is on alert," she said. "If the dragon thief gets what she's after before the high queen's guard stops her, she'll do the same thing here that she did to mark her victory over the Everlasting Flame. Destroy Calixto and erect monuments to her victims on the rubble."

"They can't let that happen," Pink Coat cried.

"What about the aberrant army?" the third woman asked. "General Roark promised those freaks would be the key to protecting the kingdom. Said their strange powers could stop almost any threat."

"I don't know but—"

The three stopped their conversation and lowered their heads. I didn't know why until a tall, older man in heavy furs walked past. He didn't spare them part of a glance, but they still didn't speak until he was gone.

My teeth gritted. Dominic told me a little about Edjer's backward views toward women when we were trapped in the cabin. Something about deeply held religious traditions, and twisting them to suit their needs. Father Parthelan—man. Tenille, lord of the heavens and earth—man. Calthoon—lord of the veil—man. And Zaeah, mother of dragons.

That made three men and a dragon the most powerful beings in all the realms. No women. As it is for the gods, so it shall be in Edjer. Men are in charge. Dragons are revered. And women are nothing.

"Like I was saying, the aberrant army is useless against her, because she can steal any magic she wants. I'm telling you, that thing isn't human. It's a half-Druk monster sent by the gods to..."

Skates on, the women finally set off, taking their conversation with them. The look on Atlas's face almost made me tell him to shut the fuck up again.

He didn't need to say it. I already knew. Everything I told Dominic about the general twisting events to make us the monsters came to pass. Didn't matter that we only acted in self-defense, or that I didn't steal the Everlasting Flame at all. I didn't even know where the dragons took it.

The poison mage's final, horrific act killed every witness other than my friends and me, and they weren't in a position to set the record straight. General Roark took that chance to do exactly what pieces of garbage like him did, but I never thought he'd find a way to take the beautiful statues Atlas built of my family, and ruin that too.

Before we left Hyelong behind, Atlas flew me over the monuments he erected up, down, on, and around the spot that was once honored by the Everlasting Flame. The statues dominated the skyline, standing to be seen for miles around. Looking upon Ivo's, Cyrus's, and Sabine's smiling faces healed a few pieces of my broken heart, especially when Atlas said they would forever watch over the souls who'd fallen there.

It took General Roark mere days to take that peaceful tribute, and turn it into another example of the dragon thief's violence and reign of terror.

What else would he do? It scared him when he learned the people in Awnan's old town didn't report me. Instead, they happily took the thousands of gold ryus I gave them, and moved on to greener, warmer places.

No matter what High Queen Kisandra screamed about, I was of Boreen blood. Her own cursed throne chose me to rule. If I gathered the people's love and loyalty, his shadow plots to remove Kisandra, Maili, and Ormr from the throne won't matter. They'll clamor for me to rule, and he wouldn't have the power to stop it. *My power.*

"But there's no chance of anyone choosing me now," I said. "General Roark is turning the five kingdoms against me, and I bet the high queen is sitting right by his side, convinced he's doing this all for her. When really, he's obsessed with getting back on the throne. How is it a snake can't recognize another snake?"

"Oh, I have a feeling she sees him exactly for what he is." There was a strange tone in Atlas's voice. "She has her own plans. Right now she's letting the general have free rein because those plans happen to align, but if he gets his hands on you, she'll swoop right in to take you for herself," he said. "That's why we have to leave, pillow lips."

Never thought I'd miss Pain-in-the-Ains.

"There are guards all over the place, everyone in the kingdom knows your face, and the general knows what you're after. We have to go back to Itzala and prepare for war—"

"Fuck's sake!" Velez burst on the scene. "I can't listen to this anymore. Ains, what are you doing?" he barked, blowing me back.

"What?" I flicked to the alley entrance. A passerby glanced our way, saw nothing, and moved on. "What are you talking about, and can you lower your voice?"

"Why are you listening to him? Why did you go off with him?" Velez closed the distance and grabbed my shoulders. "You talk about the high queen not seeing the snake. Why aren't you seeing the one in front of you? Atlas is manipulating you," he dropped. "He said all those horrible things to you the other night to get you away from Roark and the others. This—you and us alone together—is exactly what he wants—"

"That's not true," Atlas hissed.

"Yes, it is," Velez returned. "You're so selfish and full of yourself that you're convinced everything you want is what's best."

"And you're so soft, you're afraid the truth will break her."

My eyes crossed watching them rapid-fire switch bodies. "Stop," I gritted, grabbing on to whoever I got my hands on first. "What are you two doing? Are you trying to get us caught?"

"You have to listen to me, Ains," Velez rushed. "Atlas is—"

"I know exactly what Atlas is doing." It was the look in my eyes more than the heaviness in my tone that quieted him. "Despite what you *both* believe, I'm not that easily played. I knew Atlas wanted to separate me from the others. Just like I know you wanted the same thing."

"I— No— Okay, yes," he said, tossing his head. "I didn't trust Roark and the others. I thought they were pets who'd go running to their masters the first chance they got, but I see now that I was wrong about them." He flung out his hand. "I also see that we *need* them. There are dragon riders patrolling the city which means their dragons are waiting outside the city for their call.

"Atlas can't stand up to two dozen dragon riders, fifty Watchers, and ten Renders. He knows that, which is why he's pushing so hard for you to give up and go back to Itzala. He looks out for himself first. Always."

I pressed my palm to his chest, calming him. "It doesn't matter what he pushes for because I'm not going anywhere. I won't give up until we've got the claw. No matter what, I'll see this through to the end," I said. "Atlas is wrong to doubt me... but you're wrong too."

His brow crumpled. "I am? How?"

"I've no doubt you've witnessed your brother do some pretty selfish and messed-up things, but he isn't all bad any more than you're all good. Any more than anyone is all bad or all good. He's done kind and selfless things too, Velez," I whispered. "There's good in him. I've seen it."

Velez rolled his eyes. "Ains, give me a break. The guy throws up a few statues, and you think he's the god of goodwill. He did that to impress you, and get an up on Roark. Wake up. Men always have sweet words to sing when your pants are still on."

"Ugh." I shoved off him. "You're such an ass sometimes. I'm telling you Atlas is fine and I can handle myself. Now, stop talking down to me and bring him back. I have an idea."

Velez opened his mouth. Whatever he'd been about to say was snatched away with the appearance of Atlas. The dragon slayer's smirk was smugger than smug could be.

"Thank you, my jewel of the seas. I bask in your radiance and grow in your warmth."

"I don't even know what the hell that flowery shit means."

Laughing, he leaned in for a kiss. I threw his face away as usual.

"Enough of that," I said, turning back to watch the square. Two more Renders joined their friends on patrol. "I had an idea while those women were talking. General Roark has been on a campaign to turn the five kingdoms against me, but there's one thing people listen to louder than lies, common sense, or fear."

I told him what I had planned. His smirk widened.

"The queen of the six kingdoms rises."

I shook my head, hiding the faintest blush. "She hasn't risen anywhere yet. Are there any dragon slayer allies in Edjer? We need a place to work."

He nodded, setting off down the opposite end. "We're not far from two such allies. They'll protect you. I dare say, they'll do anything you ask."

***

I relaxed on the window seat, gazing out onto the street below.

I got a glimpse of Edjerian homes that fateful day Libelle flew me and Dominic back to Golden City. It was another thing entirely to be inside one.

Sitting in their home then was like falling asleep in a mother's embrace. Large, stone fireplaces dominated one wall in every room—spreading heat from the hypnotizing, crackling fire. The second story boasted bigger windows than the ground floor, and each lay claim to a cushioned window seat draped with blankets and pillows.

This home, like all the others on Cacklin Street, was made of light brown wood and metal sloping roofs. We walked into a living room covered with thick, fluffy rugs and were hurried straight into the kitchen where Madam Rabe set about stuffing me to bursting.

"Is there anything else you'd like, Princess?" Madam Rabe topped the stairs, peeking into the second-floor living room that sucked me in with its blankets and fire. "I can get you more tea."

Smiling, I lifted my full cup. "Still working on this one, but thank you, Madam Rabe."

"Tulsi, please," she corrected. "What about cookies? Or I also have biscuits fresh out of the oven?"

Madam Rabe was a tall, plump woman with freckles on her cheeks and gray patches in her hair. Yes, patches of gray in a sea of brown. I almost asked how hair could grow like that, but remembered my manners in time.

Velez told me before we knocked on the door that she earned the title when she graduated from the Edjerian University of Medicine and Healing. An immense honor for she was one of only two women to be admitted in one hundred years. For her to say I could set aside the title she worked so hard for and speak to her casually, showed how much this woman I just met respected me.

It's a big weight having so many rely on me. My grip tightened on the mug. *And all I've done up till now is let them down.*

"I'm fine, Tulsi, but thank you. I truly appreciate all you've done."

She flushed, bowing low. "It's my absolute honor, Princess. If I can't get you anything, then allow me to walk the streets and hear what people are saying. I won't be long."

"But—"

My protests were for no one. She was already down the stairs and slamming the front door.

Velez came up a minute after she left. He joined me at the window and got under my blankets. I yelped when he wiggled his cold toes against my leg.

"Hey, stop that."

"Make me."

"Quit it, or I'll spill my tea."

Only the threat of ruining Tulsi's nice things stopped him. I knew from experience he'd have happily kept teasing me. That was our normal. The argument in the alley the day before was already forgotten.

"How's it look out there?" he asked, pressing his forehead to the window.

"It looks bad for the queen's guards." I allowed myself the barest smirk. "Which is good for us."

"I don't know if your plan is genius or insane."

We took in a street very unlike the one we walked on the way to Tulsi's house. Those icy sidewalks had barely a crowd and not a speck of trash to be seen. The street we looked down on was filled with people all coming out of their homes to read the flyers that fell out of the sky that morning. It was clearly an interesting read because they kept passing them around, and running off to show more people.

"Offering one million gold ryus for the real and authentic claw of a celestial dragon?" He whistled. "Forget Calixto. This will spread through all of Adalinda by dawn."

"It's the only way," I replied between sips of tea. "The people in Elsher's old town feared me too until I started handing out bags of money. I was kind and generous to them while the Elshers were greedy and cruel. General Roark is doing such a great job turning everyone against me because they only know the insane, homicidal dragon thief that roamed the kingdoms for four months killing people.

"They don't know about the death of our family. They don't know the people I killed were murderers, rapists, and people sellers. They don't know anything, because I haven't told them. No more. I'm not standing by silently anymore. Let the general explain why the evil, insane dragon thief is willing to pay a fair price for the claw, instead of stealing and killing for it."

The corner of his mouth quirked up. "I mean, yeah, but that's not all you said on the flyers. You had me write that you're in search of the claw to break your curse, and return to normal so that everyone can live in peace again. How will it go over when people find out that's a lie?"

"Not one word of it is a lie," I replied. "Everyone will live in peace when the gods are freed and the high queen and general are removed from the throne. And I've been cursed since the day you met me, Velez. What worse curse is destiny?"

He was quiet for a spell. "Okay. I get it. Even if this doesn't change people's minds about you, it will make them question what the general is telling everyone. Is the dragon thief just looking for a way to end this? Does she want to do it peacefully? How come the children she rescued sing her praises? Why announce herself and offer a reward if she's an outlaw on the run? Why? Why? Why?

"The more people asking questions, the less blindly swallowing the bullshit General Roark and Queen Kisandra are spreading around the nation."

I tapped my nose. "Exactly."

Down below, Watchers swarmed the street—ripping up flyers and snatching them from every hand they walked past. I didn't need Tulsi to tell me what people were saying about the reward. If the queen's forces were this riled up, it was good news... for me.

"Changing public opinion aside," Velez continued. "Do you think there's really someone out there holding on to the preserved claw of a celestial dragon?"

I blew out a breath, dropping my head back on the wood. "That's the big question. Sister Aven told us collectors went after them. A dragon made of starlight—they had to have a piece. A scale. A horn. A claw. Something like that would've been passed down through a noble family."

"If it was, they didn't boast about it." Despite our conversation, Velez appeared content sitting there under the blankets with me, figuring things out as we always did. "Would they risk unearthing illegal dragon parts and bringing them to a secret meet with the most wanted woman in Adalinda?"

"Would you risk it for a million ryus?"

He snorted. "I'd risk it for three gold ryus. Don't let my devilish good looks and clean clothes fool you. I'm a very poor man."

I almost giggled. It was impossible to laugh when I was forced to leave Dominic, my friends, and my dragons behind, but Velez had a way of almost getting them out of me all the same.

Velez sobered quickly. "Ains, you know those flyers are as far as we'll ever get. It's impossible for us to go to a meet point. We'd never know if the person who shows up has the claw, or if they're a Render waiting to strike."

I held my hand out to him. He studied it, then took it.

"Brother, you have to trust me. I thought of that too. Someone who wants that money badly enough will find a way to get a message to me. They'll be discreet, clever, patient. None of that describes the members of the queen's forces."

Velez nodded slow. "Yes, of course. While the Watchers waste their time ripping up paper and yelling at innocent people in the street, the person we're after knows you're here in the city somewhere. They just have to send out a message that the Watchers will ignore, but you won't."

"Which is why we need to be on the lookout every minute of every day, waiting for that message."

"Yes, yes." He sat up straight, brows snapping together as he stared down the hapless people outside. "But..."

I sighed. "Were you always this much of a worrier? I feel like I would've remembered."

A sharp flick to the forehead made me yelp. "This is my last *but,* but it's a good one. Those guards may be idiots," he said, jerking his head at the window. "But the general is not. Elsher sent for him in Hyelong. He was on his way there to get you, and now the general knows you're here.

"I don't believe for a second that he left the unique mages behind. We'll be dealing with magics we've never seen before while waiting for a message that could just as easily be from the general."

My eyes narrowed. "This but isn't just a but."

"Ains." He leaned in. "When the message comes, I'll be the one to answer it. I'll go, and if this person has the claw, I'll pay them and leave. But if it's a trap, I'll spring it."

"No."

"This makes the most sense and you know it."

I snapped over, setting my cup down on the floor. Straightening, I looked him right in the eye. "It doesn't make any sense. You're not a faceless man moving unseen through the crowd anymore. Junia sold us all out. She told that fuckwit Elsher all about the borrowed brother sharing a soul with a stone dragon slayer.

"I left the others behind because I have to stop putting the people I love in danger. I'm not making an exception for you." I flicked his forehead right back. "Stop saying stupid things, dumbass."

"All right, all right." He chuckled. "I had to ask."

"We do everything together. As a team. Agreed?"

He shook the hand he was still holding. "Agreed."

***

I woke in the same spot the next morning, legs tangled with Velez.

My brother's head lolled off the edge of the seat. Snoring, his mouth hung open and arm dangled off the side. Blond strands masked half his face.

He never looked more ridiculous.

I almost smiled looking at him. I almost wanted to.

The moment passed quickly as my thoughts returned where they always went—to Dominic.

What was he doing right then? Had Mireu healed him? Had he read the letter? Was he standing in the most beautiful garden this side of the Valerian Seas, cursing the name Ainsley Boreen?

Velez grunted, pulling me out of my thoughts. He woke up and looked out the window, drawing my attention out there too.

"They've been busy," he remarked.

I nodded. All the flyers were gone. I didn't even see the pieces the Watchers ripped up sticking to the ice. "It's too late though. One million ryus? Everyone who doesn't know by now will in an hour. No one's going to keep quiet about this."

"I'll make sure of it." Madam Rabe came up the stairs, carrying a tray. She set it down in front of me, popping my brows up my forehead.

Roasted sweet potatoes, spiced eggs, spinach, toast, oatmeal, muffins, tea, and milk. There was enough for all three of us with plenty left over.

"I'm going down early to open the stall," she said. "I'll ask everyone who stops by if they've heard the news, and inform them if they haven't."

"Don't risk yourself," I said. "The guards aren't completely stupid. They've been dressing in plain clothes to spy and round up unique mages."

Her chestnut eyes filled. "I'm blessed that you would worry about me." She bowed low, and resisted my efforts to lift her back up. The lady was deceptively strong. "I'll be very careful."

Atlas helped himself to my muffin. It was only the fact jumping after it would've made me topple the entire tray that forced me to let him get away with it.

I waited until the door opened and shut, then carried the tray down to the kitchen. Atlas trailed behind, maneuvering his wings with difficulty. He snarled when they banged the rafters.

"Do you know why she's like that with me?" I asked. "It's like she'd jump off the roof if I asked."

"Hmm. Go on and ask," he drawled, shrugging. "I'm curious if she would."

I gave him a look. "Seriously. Why is she risking everything for me?"

"The same reason we all take risks. Because we want something in return."

I paused bringing the mug to my lips. "What does she want from me?"

"I leave listening to the boring sob stories to my brother." He reached for my oatmeal.

"You're taking a real big risk, Stoneslayer."

"Ahh." Atlas pouted. "So the widdle orphan never had enough to eat. Now she's so afwaid of going hungry, she won't share a pea—"

I casually ate my eggs. "That's not going to work."

"Fuck it." He dropped the mocking. "I had to try." Kicking the chair back, he sat down heavily—spreading his wings to cover the entire kitchen. "Real nice only cooking for you, but you would be her favorite. Going by the pieces of her story I heard while in the light and warm, she's got a dragon slayer lover across the Dark Border that she can't be with until you unite the six kingdoms." He eyed the food hanging out of my open mouth—hard. "Something like that anyway."

"She thinks I'm going to reunite her with her lover?" I blew back, head shaking. "Why me? Why can't she go across and be with him?"

His wings lifted with his shoulders. "Something about being the only female healer in town, and hundreds of women relying on her. Blah, blah, blah. Are you sure you're going to finish that? You don't even like sweet potatoes."

"Atlas, focus. You're telling me the Four have everyone this convinced that I'm going to turn all of Adalinda into Itzala's little sister? A place where dragons, humans, and dragon slayers all live together in peace?"

"You need to understand that's the story we've all grown up with. Ever since the Five learned of the prophecy, and that it was about you." He met my eyes. "You're our savior, Ainsley."

"But the prophecy isn't about the dragon slayers!"

Another shrug. "I know that now."

Frustration choked me, turning the delicious food to sawdust in my mouth. "Gods, this is too much. Dominic tried to warn me, but with ten thousand dragons prepped for slaughter, I didn't have time to be suspicious of the Four.

"Why are they hanging so much on a prophecy they don't even understand? Why are they pretending they're willing to give up their power and sovereignty to bow before a twenty-year-old woman?" I threw out my hands. "Not even regular people want to do that unless my rule gives them something in return. What do the Four want from me?"

Atlas cocked his head. "I know exactly what they want from you. We had a real long talk about it over breakfast and tea. Love to do the same with you."

"Fuck's sake, here."

The half-man chased down food more persistently than a beggar, and I'd know. I scraped half of everything onto plates and handed it over. Atlas was digging in before I pulled my hand back.

My fingers drummed the table, waiting impatiently for him to come up for air. It was past time I got some answers on what the Four were up to, as well as confirmation my mother wasn't up to it as well.

"Okay." Atlas pushed the empty plates away, leaning back. "Here it is... I lied. I have no idea what they want."

I snatched up my things and slammed out to his raucous laughter. "Ass!"

Heavy footfalls came after me. I turned on Velez's sheepish expression. "You fell pretty easily for that."

"Twin assholes," I snapped. "Never seen that before."

He laughed. "I'm sorry, Ains. Neither of us knows if the Four have another motive. But I do know that your mother is the kindest, most honest woman I've ever met. Right up on the pedestal next to Sister Aven. She's being straight with you, even if the others aren't."

"I..." I dropped down beside the fireplace. "I guess that does make me feel a bit better. Just feels like I've got the pieces of the puzzle, and I'm running out of time to put it together." My gaze blurred on the flames. "The thing about a savior... they're also the only person who gets blamed when everything goes wrong."

***

We spent the rest of Watersday trading theories about why the Four wanted the six kingdoms, in between Velez taking discreet walks outside to hear what people were saying about the dragon thief. The day ended with no signal or message of any kind.

The next day was Moonsday. I woke up early and went out myself. The terrible, bone-chilling cold gave me one advantage. No one looked twice at the walking mound of coats, jackets, mittens, and scarves. All anyone could see of me were my eyes, and despite Dominic's sweet whispers under the covers about them being the most beautiful emerald jewels in all the land, they weren't unique enough for people to pick the dragon thief out of the crowd.

No, people were looking at me for an entirely different reason.

I shuffled across the ice on my skates, hands windmilling and upper body wobbling like a top. "How do people live like this?" I snapped at no one. "Sliding around in an icebox strapped to torture devices!"

A chuckle drew my attention. A man stood under the butcher shop's awning, lacing up his skates. "It's not as bad as all that, but I can see why a newcomer wouldn't be a fan. Here. Let me help." He glided over and held out his elbow.

My first reaction was to say *no, thanks*, but who was I kidding? Continuing to flail and shout all over the place would bring the Watchers down on my head.

"Is this okay?" I asked, recalling all the women I passed who stopped walking and looked at their feet when men walked by. "Are you allowed to help me?"

He gave me a funny look. "Why wouldn't I be?"

I snorted. "Why, indeed." I grasped his arm. "Thank you."

"My name's Cormac. What's yours?"

"Taran." I said the first name that popped into my head.

"Where are you headed, Taran?"

"Nowhere in particular." He set off, easily taking me along for the ride. My skates slid behind with no effort from me. "First day in town. Wanted to see the sights a bit. Didn't know the sights don't want to be seen, and the weather does everything it can to force you back inside."

He laughed. Cormac's laugh was as pleasant as his smile. It dimpled his grizzled chin and caused little crinkles around his gray eyes. I put him at about thirty. "The cold takes some getting used to for sure. I moved here five years ago and I'm still not used to it myself. What brings you here?"

"Visiting family. My aunt." He glanced back at me, but I smoothly turned my head, pretending the clock tower captured my attention. "What brought you here?"

"Oooh, now that's a long and complicated question," Cormac replied, tipping his head to the sky. "I guess if I could sum it up, I'd say I came here looking for clarity. To peel back the layers of society's expectations, and discover truth within myself. Who am I? What do I want to be? What is my deepest wish?"

I blinked at the back of his head. "Wow. You came to this ice dragon's frostbitten backside of a place looking for all of that?"

Cormac howled. "Calixto's been called a lot of things. That just became my favorite. But to answer your question, yes. I did find what I was looking for." He looked to me again. "You can too, Taran."

"Me?"

"Have you ever heard of the Nyota Society?"

I shook my head.

"It's a community of like-minded individuals like us. We believe there's no point in living if we're not doing it honestly. If your deepest wish is wealth, chase wealth. Doesn't make you greedy or selfish. Just means you're being honest about your truth.

"If your deepest wish is have sex with every and any willing partner. Do it. Who cares what people call you? They're your legs. Open them as wide and often as you want."

I didn't know about my legs, but my eyes were open as wide as my gaping mouth. How did I end up hanging off this man's arm?

"If your deepest wish is knowledge, power, freedom—then it should be yours." Cormac expertly wove around two chatting friends coming out of a dress shop. "The only one getting in your way is you."

"The Nyota Society," I repeated. "So you're like hedonists?"

"Not at all," he replied, tone calm. "Hedonists chase pleasure. We pursue truth. Your deepest wish could be to give away all your money, move into a shack, and live a simple, modest life of poverty. That will not always be pleasurable, but that doesn't mean it's not right for you."

"Hmm." I nodded slow. "That makes sense. So you really moved here to join the Society? Do they not have other groups like that somewhere warm?"

Chuckle. "The Nyota Society was founded here. In this very town. It's the founder's wish we remain small and connected to this community."

"And you're all about respecting wishes," I finished. "Also makes sense. Very on form. I like it."

"You're funny, Taran. A few minutes in your presence, and I've smiled more than I have all morning." His smile was indeed wide and beaming on me. "I see the warm and comforting soul within you. If I can guess, your deepest wish is for everyone you know and love to be happy. And if I'm allowed another guess... you fulfill that wish, because you make them happy."

"Oh... I—I don't know about— Um..." I trailed off, blushing under my double scarves. If this was Edjerian flirting, it was both strange and effective.

"I was lost and searching for meaning when I arrived in this city five years ago. I didn't know I was looking for Nyota until they found me, and now I've found you," he said. "We have what you need, Taran."

Up ahead, the cathedral face of the clock tower came into view, signaling a chance for me to beg off and say goodbye to Cormac. He seemed like a nice guy who was nothing like the sexist windbags who expected me to bow as they passed, but I got a strong Brother of the True Fanatic Order whiff off him. I wasn't looking to be recruited into a cult, but you met all types when you travel.

"I do the shopping every Moonsday and Woodsday." We zipped around the corner at the top of the street. "When you're ready, meet me at—"

A hard body slammed into me, knocking me on my ass. Cold, vicious pain exploded up my tailbone.

"How dare you, stupid woman!"

Two pairs of leather boots and black trousers stood at my eye level.

"Do you have any idea who this is?" the man barked. "Why weren't you skating on the other side of the walk where the women belong?"

"Calm yourself, Badr."

The cold seized my spine, trapping me in place.

"Who I am is an ally and servant of the people. People like this young woman," said General Ladon Roark. "No harm done, ma'am. Let me help you up."

A hand appeared before my face.

I couldn't move. Couldn't breathe. After all his plotting and searching. All my running and hunting. We were right in front of each other. All it would take is one look in my hate-filled eyes, and he'd know it.

"Ma'am? Is something wrong?" His knees bent to drop down next to me... and look me in the eyes.

"Sadlefeen," I blurted.

"Excuse me?"

"Zvenir de daelema. Flueg kin attug redif bluef." I dipped and bobbed my head. "Xhos ma la. Xhos ma la."

Roark straightened, hand returning to his side. "I'm not familiar with that language. What is she saying, Badr?"

Badr started. "She... uh... She must be from one of the outer villages. Very remote and isolated. They have their own dialect. But I believe she's apologizing profusely, and asking to keep her head down out of respect."

I wasn't saying anything of the kind. Actual translation was *Jackass. Get that thing away from me. I wouldn't touch your hand with a shit-covered stick. Drop dead. Drop dead.*

I knew all that time Velez and I spent making up a fake language as children would come in handy one day.

"Let us continue on, sir," Badr said. "It's time to give your address."

"Very well."

The general brushed past me—his play-acting as a gentleman over.

"Taran, are you okay?" Cormac helped me up. "Wow. I can't believe General Roark is here."

I didn't get a chance to express my disbelief because coming out of the carriage behind the general were two faces I'd never expected to see. Two *small* faces.

Maili and Ormr exited their carriage, tugging at their clothes and adjusting their crowns like they didn't fit. From what I could see, their child-sized outfits fit fine, but everything's bound to feel off when it's on the wrong body.

I slowly moved back, melting into the gathering crowd. The miniature version of my sister and sibling stood right in front of me. Seemed they hadn't had any luck undoing the effects of Rickard's age magic. They wouldn't while he kicked back safe and sound in the Gaia Curves camp.

"General, wait for us," Maili snapped. "We told you to remain at our side at all times."

Roark slowly ground to a stop and turned back. The look in his eyes... There was the hatred. "Forgive me, my queen," he gritted. "I'm a military man. I'm used to marching double time. As it is, are you certain you wouldn't be more comfortable in the carriage?"

"No." She struggled with her cape, fighting to fix it comfortably around her coat's thick neck. "That bastard bitch is here, which means my Cadmus is here. I go where you go and do what you do until he's safely back with me."

"Same," Ormr agreed.

Maili tipped her chin. "Will that be an issue?"

It didn't matter how high she lifted her nose or how imperious she tried to sound. Between that squeaky voice and all four feet of her, Maili came off like a cranky child who needed to stop playing princess and take a nap.

Roark bowed low. "Of course not, Your Majesty. I live to serve."

"—get going." Cormac's voice broke in. "But remember what I said. Moonsday and Woodsday. Meet me there when you're ready to have all that you wish."

"Yeah, uh-huh." Fixed on Maili and Ormr, I waved goodbye in his general direction. "Thanks for your help."

Word spread through the streets, filling up the square. I was fairly certain this wasn't an announced visit, or Madam Rabe would've told me. The general abruptly changed course and came to Calixto because he knew I was here. Same for Maili and Ormr.

"Good evening, my good people," he called.

Roark stood on the steps of the cathedral, flanked by Maili and Ormr. I smothered a snort when two attendants rushed up carrying stools for them. Wouldn't do for the general to rise taller than them.

"You have questions and even more fears," Roark went on. "I tell you now, you are safe. The dragon thief will not take Calixto."

"She doesn't want Calixto," someone shouted. "She wants the remains of a celestial dragon to break her curse. She's offering one million ryus."

The floodgates opened.

"Is the reward real?"

"Will the claw really break the curse?"

"Why not just give it to her?"

"Maybe she doesn't want to hurt anyone. She wants this to be over just as much as we do."

"Everyone, please." Roark held up a hand. "I'm glad that you brought up this nonsense reward. Let me be frank: it is a trick and a lie."

If he wanted to set them off again, he did it. Roark had to call for calm again.

"This should not surprise you," said the general. "We are after all dealing with an insane, lying trickster. There is no reward. The dragon thief doesn't have one million grains of sand, let alone a million gold ryus. Those flyers were nothing more than a clever ruse to get you all to do her searching for her. If one of you had actually found a celestial dragon claw and arranged the trade, she'd have taken it and slit your throat for the trouble."

Gasps, shock, disbelief. The whole range of negative emotions rumbled through the crowd, but if feelings were for or against me, I couldn't say.

"But then why does she want the claw?" someone asked.

"The answer to that will horrify you. I didn't want to say this but—" Rubbing the bridge of his nose, he sighed, hanging his head. "No, no, it's best you know the truth. The ritual she's trying to complete is the most foul, forbidden magic known to mages. Necromancy."

I rolled my eyes as horrified cries rippled through the listeners.

"She stole the Everlasting Flame, vandalized an ancient resting place on my property, and now wants the claw of the celestial dragon, so she can bring the poor being back to life, forcibly bond with it, and siphon the magic of the most powerful dragon there ever was."

"That's awful!"

"The beast."

"Monster."

"Yes," Roark said. "This is why it's vital that anyone in possession of such a precious, ancient relic, or has knowledge of where one can be found, must come and surrender it to me personally. I will not allow her to defile this once-beautiful creature, or sacrifice all of your souls to complete the ritual."

I left. Nothing but lies was going to come out of his mouth, and I didn't need to stick around and listen to them.

But of all the stories he'd go with to explain away my want of the claw, that was clever. As clever as telling them there was no coin. All that awaited anyone looking for payment is death.

Roark's manipulations should bother me, but they didn't. I wanted people to know the truth. I also knew he wasn't going to let that happen while he drew breath. Everything I said would be twisted. Any truth I revealed corrupted. The only thing that made me feel better was that it was highly unlikely anyone loitering in the square, listening to his bullshit, had the ancient relic sitting in their pocket.

He didn't change the mind of anyone who could actually help me. Let's hope the person who could wanted one million ryus more than they wanted to swallow Roark's garbage.

I made it back to Madam Rabe's place with difficulty. Suddenly, I missed Cormac, member of the Holy Order of Oversharers. I stepped one foot inside, and flew.

"Ainsley? Ains!" Velez swept me off my feet, crushing me to his chest. "Do you have any idea how worried I was!" The guy managed to pepper my forehead with kisses and scold me at the same time. "Why did you take off like that without telling anyone? Do you have any idea who arrived in the city this morning?"

"General Roark," I cut in. "Along with everyone's favorite treacherous twins, Maili and Ormr."

He stepped back, brows high. "Wait, what? The first I knew. The last I didn't. The royal family came all the way up to find you?"

"To find my dragons. They want Cadmus and Kenna back, and they've wised up enough to know they shouldn't trust General Roark to do it."

Velez shared a look with Madam Rabe, who'd been in the middle of feeding the fire when I walked in.

"It's gotten too dangerous for you to leave the house," he said. "Is there any chance your stubborn ass will heed the warning and stay inside?"

I swatted his arm. "Only if your stubborn ass stays inside too. You know it's no safer for you or Atlas out there."

"You're really going to stay inside?" he pressed.

"There's no reason to go out there until I get a sign from the owner that he or she is willing to sell the claw. Otherwise, I'm tempting fate like I did today when I literally ran into the general."

"Excuse me?"

"Best not to give Mother Fate another reason to test me." I blew past, heading upstairs. "I need the hottest bath I can stand. When I come down, I'd like to make you lunch, Madam Tulsi. As a thank-you for all you've done for us."

"Me? Make me lunch?" She looked like she might faint. "Oh, how you honor me, Princess. I'm not worthy of such a gift, but of course, you would offer. You're kind and generous." She ran to the foot of the stairs, showering praise on me as I went up. "You're a blessing to the six kingdoms, and I despise that piece-of-shit, disgraced former king for daring to say an unkind thing about you.

"I pray dragons rip General Roark apart limb from limb, and shit him out into the belly of a volcano. Let that shit stain on the fabric of Adalinda be burned away. The pox-ridden, yellowbelly son of a toothless whore."

I goggled at her. "Nicely done, madam." That was the first I heard her curse, let alone let loose.

She blushed. "I'll make you a tray for your bath."

I let her go, knowing it was useless to stop her. I continued up—thoughts turning to where they always did whenever distraction couldn't take me.

Dominic.

***

The next day, the sun rose and fell on Firesday with nary a word or sign. The only change was the double patrols in the street. Seemed like every Watcher and Royal Rider in the queen's force had descended on Calixto.

A week passed, and we began to lose hope.

"Maybe they don't exist anymore," Velez said. The three of us sat before the fire, drinking mugs of cocoa. It was the preferred pastime in a place as cold as this. "Thousands of years ago, they were using celestial dragons for their magic, not encasing them behind glass. Maybe the answer is that there's nothing of them left."

"I don't believe that," I said. "I can't. Someone will have wanted a trophy. They got the better of a rare, powerful creature, and they'd want proof to lord over everyone. A claw is perfect. Someone at some time must've had one, and after they died, they passed it down."

"If that's the case," Velez said, lips quirked in a half smile. "Then their answer is no. They won't sell it to you. The general must've scared them out of it. Assuming they ever wanted to do it in the first place."

"Please, don't say that, Velez." Tulsi set aside her cup. "We can't lose hope. We're so close."

"Have you seen anything out of place?" I asked her. "Or heard anything strange from one of the women who visit your stall?"

She shook her head. "I'm so sorry, Princess Ainsley. I've asked. I've looked. But nothing. Calixto is the same as when this backwards place froze in the ice thousands of years ago and never changed."

Blowing out a breath, I slumped on the cushions. "If only I could go out and look too. Cover twice the ground. I've only been out once, and the only strange thing that happened is some random follower tried to recruit me for something called the Byota Society."

"Nyota, do you mean?" Tulsi laughed. "Did they say they were the key to truth and enlightenment? All you had to do was discover your deepest wish?"

"Said almost word for word."

She chuckled, getting to her feet. "What a funny coincidence."

"Coincidence?" Velez repeated. "What do you mean?"

"Oh, well, of course you know." Tulsi disappeared into the kitchen. "Because of celestial dragons."

"What about celestial dragons?"

"Why, that was their magic. It's where the phrase *wish upon a star* comes from." Her words floated back—calm and conversational. "They had power to grant almost any wish. Knowledge, wealth, love, good health."

Velez and I reflected twin slackened jaws and huge eyes.

"It's no wonder they were hunted down so mercilessly. No one could resist the lure of having all your dreams come true with one simple wish."

"By the gods!" Velez cried. We jumped to our feet at the same time. "That guy— Gormac. What did he say to you?"

"He said almost everything Tulsi just said." I paced the floor, clutching my head. "Knowledge, riches, lust. The guy said wish like eighty times, dropping the hint like a brick to the face. Oh my gods, I'm so stupid. He came right up to me. He—" A shiver climbed my spine. "He knew it was me."

"How could he know it was you?" Velez paced right alongside me. "You wear five coats to go from the living room to the bathroom. It's impossible."

I halted. "It's possible if he's the real thing. If he, or the Nyota Society have the remains of a celestial dragon, and those remains are still magical.

All he'd have to do is wish to find the dragon thief. Then, seemingly by chance, he crosses paths with her while doing the shopping."

Velez stilled too. "Ains, don't you know what that means?"

"Of course I do." A grin broke out on my lips. "We did it. We found it!"

"Ains..." His heavy, grave expression leeched away my smile.

"What? What is it?"

"If this Gormac guy found you with a simple wish to a pile of old bones, then the general can too. He can do so much more, and so much worse, to you if he gets his hands on them first, and that's exactly what he's trying to do."

I sat down hard. "Fucking hell, I'm so stupid. I didn't know what celestial magic was, but I bet the general does. He's even started offering a reward. I sat here for a whole damn week!" I punched the armrest. "What if Cormac gave up on me and went to him? We could already be too late."

"Whoa, whoa. We don't know that." Velez knelt in front of me. "The general is offering ten thousand gold ryus. Laughably less than a million. The Nyota Society obviously want the big reward.

"What else did this guy tell you? Where's the Society?"

"I—I don't know," I burst out. "I stopped listening. I think he said something about..." I wracked my brain, going back to the freezing cold day where I met a nice stranger. "Moonsday and Woodsday!" It slowly came back to me. "He said he does the shopping every Moonsday and Woodsday, and I only had to find him when I'm ready."

"Okay, find him where?"

"Um..."

Atlas rolled his eyes. "The queen of the six kingdoms strikes again."

My face heated. "Don't say that like an insult, you jerk. Just give me a minute. I'll remember." I shoved up and went to the fireplace. I cast back to the general's nonsense speech. Cormac had said something about where he does the shopping. What was it? What did he say?

Come on, Ains. You know this. He said a name right before he left—

"Pilchard's," I cried. "He said he does the shopping twice a week at Pilchard's market."

Atlas nodded. "Tulsi, my beautiful snow flower, where is Pilchard's market?"

A giggle floated out of the kitchen. "Oh, Atlas, behave. Pilchard's is Pilchard's courtyard on the other side of the cathedral. It's only open to merchants twice a week, so it makes sense that's when this man is there. Yesterday was Moonsday, meaning we missed him." She returned carrying a tray loaded down with more food. "Should I go on Woodsday? Make sure he's safe before you take the risk?"

I shook my head. "He knew who I was when he approached me, but he didn't reveal me to the general even when the man was standing right in front of him. That's a pretty good mark in his favor," I said. "We'll both go. I'll get the claw, pay him, then we'll leave without the general knowing we've gone. While he's wasting time searching for me here, we'll be in Nehebkau searching for the Infinity Tree."

"All right, but because no one has asked, and it feels like I should, how are you going to pay this guy?" Atlas asked. "Your beauty and intelligence are priceless. To be near you should cost one million ryus, but sadly, I doubt that will satisfy the debt."

Atlas received the flat look he deserved. "Believe it or not, I wasn't going to tell the man being in my presence was payment in full. I have the means to pay him. One million ryus as promised."

He arched a brow. "Elaborate."

"Can't."

"Why?"

I stifled a laugh. "Because Meriall told me not to. She said she learned not to keep anything expensive in the house after her prized shadow sword disappeared one night, and you showed up the next morning, hanging off the arms of five paid companions and so trashed on blackberry wine, you walked the entire length of the city with your pants on your wing." I giggled. "She said it was only the humiliation of all of Itzala seeing your bare backside that stopped her from tanning it."

"Hey, that was a coincidence! She can't prove I stole it."

"The guy you sold it to ratted you out."

"Martis lies," he cried. "Everyone knows that."

I beat it upstairs, laughing my ass off. Atlas chased hot on my tail. "I didn't steal any of those other things either. I'm a lot of things, but I'm not a thief."

"You're a liar," I sang.

"What I fucking am is a grown man. Have been since the day I was born. No one tans my backside!" He banged his wings on the rafters again and snarled. I'd never seen him this worked up, and it only made me laugh louder. "Meriall's got a lot of shitting nerve putting that on me. It's not my fault she'd lose her damn wings if they weren't attached to her back."

"She caught you red-handed sneaking her jadeite vase out under your wing."

"That was a misunderstanding! I was getting it polished for her. The woman never could graciously accept a present."

Tears ran down my cheeks. I skidded to a stop in front of my doorway and propped up against the wood. "You're not even a *good* liar."

I was learning a lot about dragon slayers thanks to Atlas. Top of which that their wings retracted when they were pissed. His were practically folded in on themselves.

He took a deep breath. "My precious love—"

"Not your precious love."

"—I assure you those incidents were misunderstandings." Atlas tried for a grin. "You can trust me. Your money—like your secrets and heart—is safe with me. Show me what you plan to give the man. You should have no fear that I'd try to take it from you."

"Hmm. Didn't you also try to steal a guy's shirt... while he was wearing it?" I cracked up at his reddening face. "Like, what were you even thinking there?"

"Fuck this!"

Atlas winked out, replaced by a howling Velez. He fell on me and we both went down, laughing till we cried.

"One thing he did right." Velez flicked my nose. "He made you laugh."

"No one could've kept a straight face," I wheezed. "Oh, Zaeah, I wish you could've seen his face. He was so mad."

"Yeah, he was. Call it the curse. Since I'm a good thief, he's a *terrible* one. He's been caught or failed every single time, and it pisses him off." Velez rolled on the floor. "He can't stand being bad at something."

"Now that you mention it, he did say he tried stealing for the orphanage, and Sister Aven just gave it all back." I couldn't breathe, I was laughing so hard. "He stole for the poorest people in Adalinda, and it still didn't go his way."

Our laughter filled the little, cozy warm house—light and free.

I laughed, and laughed, and laughed until the tears soaked my cheeks... and didn't stop.

My chest heaved, choking on a sob. Rolling over, I pressed the heel of my palms against my eyes as if trying to hold it back. That never worked before. Why would it work now?

"Ains, what's wrong?" A strong arm fell across my shoulder, pulling me in tight. "Where'd you go?"

"I'm s-sorry. I didn't mean to—to—" I struggled to catch a breath. "I was just thinking... how everyone else would laugh if they were here right now. Dominic would do that smirky chuckle. Poet would lose it, and Keely would roll her eyes at Poet while secretly watching him because she can't take her eyes off his smile. And Akasha would've covered her mouth and hidden her giggle." I sniffed. "Even with something like this, she wouldn't have wanted to hurt Atlas's feelings by laughing at him.

"That's how nice she was. The sweetest, kindest person I've ever met, and I didn't need to know her longer to say that."

"Ains..."

"She saved my life. She saved all our lives by shielding us with her magic, but when her life depended on me, I let her down. She was my friend," I whispered. "She needed me and I stood there—useless and no help to anybody. Again."

"Oh, Ainsley." His forehead pressed on my neck. A deep sigh warmed my ear. "I'm going to say this, and I really need you to hear it. You didn't fail Akasha. When she needed you, you saved her, and that day was when you freed her from chains and gave her her life back. It's when you gave her the power to make her own choices again, and she chose to come with us knowing the danger."

His words went in one ear, and out the other. Akasha didn't choose to be killed by someone she called a friend. She didn't choose to follow someone so dense, they couldn't see the truth mage for the lying, deceptive snake she was.

"I know what you're thinking," he said. "Akasha made a choice believing the danger was out there, not right next to her. But the danger did come from outside. It came from the thousands of years we've suffered in ignorance, and the hundreds of years her rulers put into turning this into a nation of pets—too afraid of defying their masters to set a foot out of line. She died because of General Roark, High Queen Kisandra, and everything they stand for," he stated, eyes glinting. "Let's the both of us stop grieving and regretting, and make the bastards who took our friends and family pay."

The truth of it sank into my bones. I was doing all the crying while the general and high queen did all the crowing. They were getting exactly what they wanted. Isolating me, taking away my allies, ruining my plans, boxing me into a corner. It was past time those monsters threw themselves on the ground—wailing and bawling because everything they loved was taken from them.

And just like that, my tears were over. For good.

I rose to my feet, wiping my face. "Thank you, brother. I needed to hear this."

"What are you going to do now?"

I slammed into my room. "Finish this."

Chapter Sixteen

Velez and I strolled through the marketplace, making bland conversation under our breath.

I wanted to split up to cover more ground, but that idea went out the window when I walked outside, put on my skates, and fell flat on my face.

"How are you so good at this?" I muttered. "We grew up in Ossian together. The only thing you skated on was the law."

"After I left, I spent some time traveling. I came to Edjer, met a girl, stuck around, learned to skate." He shrugged. "You know how it is."

"Wait, what girl?" I stopped us dead.

"You wouldn't know her."

"What happened between you two?"

"Same thing that always happens." Velez continued on, taking me for the ride. "She wanted to get serious, and I had to ask the question. Could I trust her with my biggest secret?"

I almost asked what that was. "Atlas," I said softly. "The Gemini curse."

He nodded. "Even someone who could accept that my twin brother is a Druk aging in reverse. It's hard to accept that we share the same soul. He sees everything, hears everything, and is a massive pain in the ass."

I smiled mirthlessly. "I'm guessing since this is the first you mentioned her, she didn't take it well."

"She didn't get the chance," he replied, sighing. "The very next day, you bonded with Reyna, and I was called back to watch over you. I couldn't tell her where I was going or why, so I ended it."

"Brother..." My heart cracked in two. "I'm so sorry. I had no idea. You've given up so much for me, and I... never even knew to thank you."

He flashed me a wry look, grinning away. "You've thanked me plenty, dummy, and don't go looking at me like I'm the portrait of tragedy. It's not conscription. No one forced me to stay by your side. It was always my choice, and I've always chosen you. I will always choose you."

"Not always," I mumbled, sinking low in my scarves.

I was thankful both my tattoos and the cold forced me to bundle up. I didn't need all the teasing I'd get for blushing.

"One day, you'll break the curse, and fall in love with someone who you can be with because you want to. Not because they can summon the deep and abiding patience needed to deal with Atlas."

He laughed. "That doesn't sound too bad."

A group of giggling children weaved around us, zipping in every direction. I didn't blame them for treating the place like a playground. It looked like one.

Glowing, multicolored balls of light hung over the marketplace, bathing the stalls in reds, golds, blues, purples, and greens. Cold weather brought cold-weather treats, and everywhere we looked, merchants sold mugs of hot cocoa, cider, Edjerian ginger rum, and flaky apple pastries I couldn't pronounce, but ate five of when Tulsi made them the day before.

The black courtyard slicked over with hard, pure white ice, and all around me, people laughed, flirted, bartered, and glided like swans on water. For the barest moment, I understood what brought people to this snow-covered land. There was magic in the very air, and it filled you with a feeling that anything was possible.

Then a man physically threw a woman who didn't see him coming up behind out of his way, and the feeling evaporated. This wasn't a winter paradise. It was just another troubled kingdom that took too many turns for the worst when despot after despot sat on the throne for centuries.

How will I change things? If the queen of the six kingdoms became a reality, what will I do to make the kingdoms into the home so many people want it to be?

"Ains? Ains?"

I tore out of my thoughts. "Yes?"

Velez gazed past me, eyes narrowing. "Is that who we're looking for?"

I twisted to see.

Standing beside a candy-apple cart, handing treats to jumping eager children, was Cormac. He beamed at the sight of my five scarves and green eyes. Passing out the last apple, he waved big and bold across the courtyard.

"Taran," he called. "Over here."

"Subtle, he is not," Velez gritted.

"At least he's here." I patted the pouch concealed within the folds of my coat. "Let's just find an out-of-the-way spot to make the trade, then we'll return to Tulsi's, say goodbye, and leave for Nehebkau at first light."

Cormac rushed up to us. He shook my hand warmly. "Taran, I'm so pleased you came. When you didn't come on Moonsday, I worried my message got lost with the arrival of the general."

I flicked around to make sure no one was looking our way. He was using my fake name, but it still wouldn't do to talk about the general in the open air. You never know where the wind will carry your words.

"I'm sorry I wasn't here sooner," I replied. "Why don't we talk about this somewhere private?"

"Somewhere private is exactly where we're going. I'm taking you to the Nyota Society." He clapped. "They can't wait to meet you, Taran. And you—" Cormac slid to my brother.

"Forgive me. I'm—"

"Velez," Cormac finished—a knowing smile lighting an almost mischievous glint in his eyes. "And your brother, Atlas. The Society welcomes you too."

The hand Velez held out snatched back. "How do you know that?"

Cormac shrugged. "The Society knows a lot of things about a lot of things. But this isn't a safe place to talk. Come. I've finished my shopping. Unless there's something you need?"

Velez and I shared a silent communication.

"Before we go anywhere," I began. "Let's be clear. Do you have what I'm looking for?"

His easy smile went nowhere. "Of course. I wouldn't waste your time. We have exactly what you're looking for." Cormac set off.

My feet followed him of their own accord. Wobbling on the ice, I tried to keep up. "Aren't you going to ask if I have what you want?"

He tapped his nose. "I already know you have it, Taran."

Right. If he knows I'm the dragon thief and that Velez is sharing a soul with his brother. Of course he can find out if I'm a liar or have the money to pay him.

"That's going to take some getting used to," I muttered.

I pitched forward but Velez was already there. Taking my hand, he linked his arm through mine and drew me close. He bore a hole in the back of Cormac's head that he either didn't notice, or was doing a great job ignoring. We didn't need to share a silent communication, because I already knew.

He didn't trust him.

"Where are we going?" I asked. "Do you not have it with you?"

"We're not far, and no." Cormac skated around a cocoa stall, leading us through the wafting heavenly scents of chocolate and vanilla. "I couldn't carry such a thing in my pocket."

"Is it big?"

"Very."

Now Velez and I shared a look. Zaeah help me, why didn't I consider the claw could be from a fully grown celestial dragon—which could make it six feet wide and tall. We couldn't sneak such a thing through the city back to Tulsi's house without being notice, and we no longer had dear Akasha to make it look like a loaf of bread.

What do we do? his eyes shouted.

We'll figure something out. One thing at a time.

Blowing out a breath, he nodded. Of course he understood me. The only person who understood my mind better was—

Dominic.

Visions of him tumbled through my head—so fast and heart-pounding, I wondered if a mind mage lingered nearby, torturing me.

I felt his lips on my skin, nipping the sensitive spot under my ear before I thought to ask. I sat next to him, his arm heavy and secure around my shoulders as he passed me all the best bits on his plate before I finished mine. I was both lost and safe under the pelts in the icy cold cabin—limbs tangled with his while his calloused fingers drew characters on my chest—each filthier than the last. My giggles warmed our little, private space. Never thought the first words I learned to spell would be cock, hard, sweet, pussy, and love, but I wouldn't trade him for a less perverted teacher for all the money in the land.

Dominic loved me. He loved me completely, wholly, without reservation or judgement. I had something people wait their entire lives for, and I threw it away with one single letter.

"Ains."

Something in his voice stopped my ruminating.

"Look."

Cormac skated straight and true away from the market and up a side street leading away from the cathedral, clock tower, and Tulsi's home. Calixto was a town separated by more than gender. Anybody with eyes could see that this side of the cathedral was where the rich lived.

The three of us skated past bigger and bigger wooden homes, and grander and grander mansions. The people we wove around looked the part of wealthy Edjerians with expensive pelt coats, fur-lined boots studded with diamonds, and gold chains braided through their hair and beards.

I wouldn't have figured this was the Nyota's part of town. Cormac's clothes were as plain and simple as ours.

"Will you tell us more about the Society?" I called against the wind.

"Inside," he replied. "They watch close those they think don't belong."

Good point, I thought, not missing the sideways glances of the royals and nobles. I thought the tradition of weighing themselves down in so many jewels they couldn't stand up straight was silly, but it did have the added twist of separating the haves and the have-nots with one glance.

We soon arrived in front of a black wrought-iron gate. I stood on the tips of my skates, peering over a deliberately placed half wall to see the mansion. From the outside, it looked similar to Tulsi's place but on the grandest scale. Wooden frame, awnings over all the windows and doors, two stories of wealth dusted in a fine layer of snow, and it all surrounded by a frozen black sea.

Cormac opened the gate to let us in. We didn't move.

"Where is everyone?" I eyed all the darkened windows. "Are we going to walk inside and find out the Nyota Society is you and your mother?"

He barked a laugh. "There you go again. You make me laugh, Taran. I'll be sad to see you go after you've gotten what you need."

I still didn't move. "That didn't answer my question."

"No, Taran." Amusement laced his voice, heavy on my fake name. "We are a real society, the members make up more than me, and doesn't include my mother. Come inside. We've been waiting for you."

Velez tightened his grip on me. It wasn't that I sensed anything off or dangerous about Cormac. The fact remained he had his chance to turn me over to the general, and he didn't take it. What was the point of dragging me all the way out here to betray me?

What was the point of Junia betraying you and killing Akasha? She died that day right alongside the Watchers and Awnan, and for what?

"Okay, let's go." I didn't come all the way out here and give up so much to quit when we were so close. "But don't try anything, Cormac."

"My wish is to help you on your path to truth." His smile was starting to unsettle me. "I won't try to do anything else. As your servant guide to enlightenment, you can trust me completely."

Velez grimaced. "You're real weird, man."

He hummed. "As weird as the guy sharing a body with a Druk who was a hundred years old at birth?"

"Weirder."

"Touché," Cormac returned, chuckling.

He took off, their verbal sparring over. Velez and I followed at a slower pace.

Cormac was at the top of the stairs with his hand on the knob when we hit the top step. We took off our skates and closed the distance to the door—bodies tensing at the same time. These people knew so much about us while we knew nothing. What were we about to walk into?

Cormac swept open the door, and a wall of sound knocked us flat.

"Welcome," Cormac said, walking in backwards. "To the Nyota Society."

Why hadn't I noticed until then that his grin... was a smirk.

We walked inside, jaws pulling lower with each step. The mansion only appeared empty from the outside. Heavy black drapes covered every window. I suspected they were magicked to keep in light and sound. They wouldn't want this neighborhood of rich snobs to be disturbed by the party.

We stepped down into a sunken living space, descending into the paradise, or punishment, beyond the veil. It was hard to tell.

Everywhere we looked, naked bodies jumped, twisted, wined, ground, and writhed on each other. No, not naked. Their single claim to coverings was masks dipped in midnight and studded with glittering diamonds.

Stars.

I wondered if the same mage who conjured the lights in the square was somewhere nearby. Glowing, dusky orbs illuminated every corner of the room, and all the activities going on in those corners. A band played a low, seductive tune on a platform covered with snake dancers. Beautiful, haunting, enchanting, head-scrambling music, I felt my hips begin to sway.

Shaking my head, I flung away and nearly fell on a fountain spouting a dark, purplish liquid from a dozen spigots. Members drank from it with their heads thrown back and their mouths open. One woman drank from the fountain while a man feasted on her—his head bobbing between her legs.

What he was doing was no less scandalous than absolutely everyone. All over the room, someone was inside someone else, or bent over and begging for more. Piles of cushions scattered about the rim of the circular space, and each was occupied by an amorous twosome, threesome, foursome, and so many -somes, I didn't know where the pussies began and the cocks ended.

I jumped behind Velez when snaking fingers came for me.

"I thought you said you weren't hedonists," I snapped at Cormac. "So much for truth."

"We're not hedonists." Two masked women and a man latched on to him. They danced and rubbed all over him, undressing him before our eyes. "You just caught us on a rare night. Sister Jolena wished for a night of total debauchery, where we could all let loose and tap into our primal selves. Sister's wish was true, so it was granted."

"Is this really the best time to be calling these people your brothers and sisters!"

Cormac cracked up as his dick fell out of his pants. "You are a treat, Ainsley Boreen."

I clenched my teeth. We were finally done with the fake names and bullshit. He knew all about me.

"I didn't know it, but my deepish wish was to meet you."

There he went again with his strange, but sincere flirting. Just being around the guy threw me off-center, and it wasn't because he was standing in front of me half-hard and getting jerked off the rest of the way.

"Okay," I cried, cracking my neck to look up at the ceiling. "Please, let's skip all this and go straight to the trade. You've got the claw. I've got payment. We should've been done already."

"I'm afraid I've got nothing to do with the trade." He paused to give the man hanging on him a passionate, eyebrow-burning kiss. He broke away gasping. "It was only my job to get you here. It's Vania that you're—here to—" They were getting more insistent in pumping his cock, and his reddening face showed the effort of holding back.

"To see," he grunted. "She's down that hallway."

A point was all he was allowed before they picked him up and carried him away. I didn't look to see if Velez was behind me. I beat it down the east hallway as quickly as the shoving bodies and groping fingers would let me.

I put a pillow over my head every time Poet and Maili had sex in the bunk next to me. There was nothing about my blushing and stuttering like a maiden whenever I was in the same room as people having sex that said I could handle walking into an orgy. I could barely handle sex with Dominic without getting nervous and stuttery.

"What the hell is this place?" Velez caught up, then pulled me along, tugging me away faster. "How is there a mansion in the middle of the city where people in diamond masks drink, dance, and fuck every night, and no one knows? Tulsi spoke like they were just a bunch of sidewalk sisters, yelling about their order at anyone who'd hear them."

I stumbled after him, eyes snapping this way and that, taking everything in. A parade of faces that were serious, smiling, sultry, and all the expressions in between covered both sides of the walls—so many, the portrait frames were nailed butting against the other.

Members of the society. More than the four dozen or so reveling in the front room, so they had to be members from throughout the years. "Does seem like a hard secret for so many people to keep," I whispered, head spinning. "She said they offer to lead people to their deepest wish, but she had no idea that meant they had a celestial dragon claw. Why does no one know?"

"Do I really have to say it?"

We burst out of the hallway and stumbled off another step. Righting myself, my gaze landed on a pair of slippered feet. The most delicate, fine sapphire satin dipped in diamonds, and wrapped around slim legs. I followed till it ended at her midriff.

There were no more clothes to admire. Barring silver, diamond-studded chains hugging her throat, and falling in a gleaming waterfall around her breasts, she wore nothing on top.

Thick, ebony hair shorn close to her scalp, giving all an unobstructed view of the silver crown reflecting me. She was beautiful with fallen-leaf eyes; full, smirking lips; an impish nose, and a brown dusting across her cheeks that added mystery to an already unforgettable face. The woman studied me just as intensely as she leaned back on her throne.

Ornate silver, royal-blue upholstery, intricate designs fashioned out of the metal. There was nothing else to call it but a throne, and nothing else to call that place but a throne room.

A line of muscled, half-naked men stood at attention on both sides of the wall, not including the two silent and chiseled figures standing behind her.

Heavy drapes covered ceiling-high windows, though these were deep, verdant green. A beautiful story recited in its stitching—depicting a beautiful maiden and handsome man, dancing around a clear blue lake. Heavy chandeliers reached down to the top of our heads. Plush cushioned stools lined two rows leading up to her—a comfy place for her subjects to kneel. Expensive carpets, towering sculptures, antique weapons covering the walls, and opulence everywhere my eyes could see.

I stood inside the throne room of the king general of the five kingdoms, and this was still the grandest place I'd ever been.

"Ainsley Boreen."

It took me a moment to realize the soft, throaty purr came from her.

"What a treat this is."

I stepped back, staying close to the hallway, and my escape. "You have to forgive me. I'd greet you, but I have no idea who you are."

She chuckled. "No reason you should. I am Vania of House Izarra. Welcome to the Nyota Society."

"Pleasure to meet you. Lovely place you have. How long has the Society been here?"

She stared at me—silent.

I waited an unnaturally long beat, then discomfort overtook me. "Look, I'm sure you want to get back to the party, so let's do this. I'm told you have the claw of a celestial dragon. I'm here to trade you that claw for an item worth one million ryus."

Her brow quirked up. "An item worth one million ryus? I don't recall that language being used in your notice. What is this... item?"

She said item like most people said old shit-covered boots.

"Show me the claw," I replied, "and I'll show you my item."

Vania smiled. "No."

"No?"

"No."

I waited for more. None came.

Sharing a look with Velez, we shared another silent talk on what to do next.

"Do you have a celestial dragon claw?" I asked.

"I do."

"And are you willing to give it to me—no questions asked, no strings—if I pay you?"

"No."

Frustration clenched my jaw. "What do you mean no?" I gritted.

Vania was laughing at me. She didn't need to do it out loud for me to know. "I mean, I will have questions. A great many questions, and you will answer them if you desire my claw. One cannot enter the path of the light of truth, if they cower in the shadow of scrutiny."

"I'm not sure that even made sense."

One of her guards came alive. Frowning, he made like he was going to advance on me. A single hand raise sent him back into position.

"Be that as it may," she continued. "If we're to proceed, you will answer this: what item do you possess that is supposedly worth one million ryus?"

I glanced at Velez, who nodded. Reaching into my many layers, I pulled out the pouch I'd been carrying with me since the night my mother gave it to me. Honestly, this wasn't for my quest. She just wanted me to have it because, as she put it, there were very few problems that the right amount of coin can't buy you out of.

I tipped the pouch onto my palm, feeling the weighty smack of the diamond leaving its prison.

Vania's impassive mask blew to pieces. Her brows shot up her forehead, lips parting as she rose from her throne.

"A diamond the size of a baby's head," I dropped. "An item worth one million gold ryus, wouldn't you say?"

"That's—!" She sucked in a breath and composed herself. "I'd say that's worth quite a bit more than a million."

I shrugged. "Pickpockets deal in small coins. I don't know what diamonds are worth."

She gaped at me. "How did you come to possess such a thing without knowing its worth? Did you steal it?"

"No. It was a gift."

Actually, it was a gift to Meriall. A potential earth slayer suitor showered her in diamonds, trying to impress her. Vania's mind might shatter to pieces if I told her Meriall had a table centerpiece full of diamonds even bigger than the one in my hands. They were nothing more than decoration to her.

Vania fiddled with one of the diamond chains hanging between her breasts, throat bobbing. There was another thing pickpockets deal in—greed. She wanted my *item*.

"I'm to believe *you* will hand that over—no questions asked, no strings attached—and all you want in return is the claw?"

I nodded. "Do we have a deal?"

Her gaze flicked over my head. I looked but nothing was there. "We have a deal," she replied, reclaiming her throne. "Bring the claw."

Four men broke off from their station and headed past us. We watched her while we waited. She watched the diamond.

"Prepare yourself," she suddenly said, breaking the silence. "I am nothing like the queens you've known."

"What are you talking—?" A faint squeaking tickled my ear, turning my head around.

The diamond slipped through numb fingers.

"Mother Zaeah," Velez breathed and Atlas finished. His brother claimed his space before the exclamation left his mouth. His slack jaw carried none of his usual arrogance or flirtation.

Her attendants brushed past us, carefully lifting the cart over the step and wheeling it past. Our eyes connected.

Encased in glass was a being unlike anything I'd ever seen. Swirling, moving spots of bright, twinkling light shimmered within the dark blue liquid satin that was her body. Long, curving horns flapped in her breeze-less prison—nothing like the hard, lethal horns I knew. Something thin and pure white flowed from her impossible body, pooling beneath shimmering claws. She looked in my eyes, and the pain in them made me want to cry and throw up.

I did both.

"What have you done?" I rasped, choking. "What have you done!"

The attendants wheeled the celestial dragon to the foot of their queen. Alive, tortured, trapped, suffering.

Vania barely glanced at the creature. "I do not appreciate your tone, or your addition to my carpeting. It's a good thing your payment will more than cover a replacement."

"Pay— Payment?" My legs gave out, dropping me in Atlas's quick and waiting arms. "What have you done? Why? Why?"

"You'd do well to calm down, Ainsley Boreen. We told you we had a celestial dragon claw. It was your assumption that the claw was a fossil." She swept her hand over the trapped creature. It was then I realized the white liquid was blood. "Go ahead and take what you came here for. If it is your true wish, you shall have it. The creature cannot resist granting a wish, even to its own detriment."

"Take what I— Are you insane!"

A chill blew through the room and ripped through my clothes. Right through. I flung them off, tearing off my jackets and scarves, and eyes widening to find the insides iced over.

An ice mage.

"I am not insane, dragon thief. Far from it." Vania stepped off her throne. My hackles went up when she placed a hand on the glass case. Hard as it was to tell, I swore the dragon's did too. "I take no pleasure in hurting this beautiful creature. I too struggled over what to do when I found it—"

"Her!"

She inclined her head—ever the calm, impassive queen. "Her. I struggled over what to do when I found her. But then, without realizing what I said, I picked her up and whispered, 'I wish I knew what to do.'" Vania's eyes shone. "And then I did.

"Just like that. In the blink of a moment, I knew exactly what to do, and the answer was to bring her here, keep her secret, and share her power only with those committed to truth and desire in their purest form. The answer... was the Nyota Society."

Atlas's grip was iron around me—shielding me. "You are some kind of crazy bitch, lady."

Her guards snapped to. Their hands came up, ready and waiting to attack on her sign. Her sign was to wave them off.

"Am I, Atlas Stoneslayer? That's mighty hypocritical coming from you." She was smiling. How dare she fucking smile! "I think we both know if you'd been the one to find her those twenty years ago, you'd have done the same. Actually, with your perverse tastes, you'd have done worse."

"Twenty years?" I repeated. I didn't have anything left in my stomach to throw up, but my heaving belly tried. "You've kept her imprisoned for twenty years?"

"How is that possible?" Atlas asked. "How old are you?"

Vania sniffed, raising her chin. "Age is meaningless when one of your true wishes is to remain young and vibrant forever. Besides, how old I am isn't relevant. I'd say it all has to do with how old you are, Boreen?"

"How old I am?" Suddenly, I was yelling. "What the fuck are you talking about! Who cares how old I am? Let her go." I shook the diamond at her. "If that's worth more than a million, have it all and free her!"

Her eyes followed the shaking diamond like a pendulum. She wanted it. Badly. "You will take the claw and no more. Even if I wished to free her, I couldn't. I've wished for too many things that have made that impossible. That she can't leave this place, be freed, or bonded. I've wished anybody who steps outside the door loses the ability to talk about her. I've wished that she remains in this case and under my control forever." Vania lightly shrugged. "So take the claw or don't take the claw, but I will have my payment."

My lips peeled back from my teeth. "You're not getting this. This ends today. Your torture of that poor, beautiful dragon is over."

"Is it?" Her voice slithered through the room. "Go ahead. Try it."

I rose, eyes narrowing to slits. "Gladly. Atlas, now!"

He flung his hands up, and the ground rumbled. "Argh—!"

"I wish you couldn't use stone magic."

Atlas collapsed like a puppet with its strings cut. His shout died in his throat—as quick and quiet as the ground ceased rumbling. Shaking, Atlas punched the ground again, and again, and again.

Nothing happened. He barely ruffled the rug.

"What did you do to him?" I rushed her, fists raised.

"I wish you couldn't move."

I dropped like a bag of rocks—body bouncing off the rug. My limbs sunk in and burrowed to stay. They wouldn't move. My mind refused to send the command to try.

"Now that that's over." My eyes rolled in their head, following Vania back up to her throne. "We can have a civilized conversation. But first, fetch me my diamond."

I was helpless to stop the guard picking the diamond off the floor and bringing it to her. "Why are you doing this? You must know it's wrong."

She clicked her tongue. "One of you, pick her up. I can't speak to her when she's talking to the floor."

"Back off!" It was Atlas who crawled over and picked me up. He settled me on his lap, cradling me like the helpless baby I'd become.

"I know a great many things, Ainsley Boreen, daughter of Titana, prophesied child, and future queen of the six kingdoms." Vania turned the diamond in the light, marveling under its glittering brilliance. "That's why she didn't see my jaw grow even more slack. "Oh yes, I know all about you. My greatest wish above all was knowledge, and thus she gave it to me."

"How do you have a living, breathing celestial dragon locked up in this hellhole, and no one knows?" Atlas snapped. "They fall to the earth in an explosion that's seen for miles around. Celestial dragons returning cannot be kept secret. No matter how many times an old, sad crone wished it so."

"I'm not old!" she shrieked, red blooming in her pale cheeks. "And you should not be so confident in your ignorance."

"I'm confident I know a con artist when I see one." He snorted. "That creature isn't even real. One of the half-naked bastards is an illusion mage. The other is a bone mage. They help you make this little pantomime real, so you and your friends can keep stealing to fund your drunken orgies." He laughed while her snarl deepened. "Don't get me wrong. I respect it, but you chose the wrong mark, old lady. Hand over the diamond, and let us go."

Surprise bloomed in my chest. Was Atlas right? Was this all a horrible illusion to trick me into handing them one million ryus?

My gaze grasped on to the dragon's.

No.

"—no trick," Vania was saying. "The star dragon fell to earth twenty years ago. After two thousand years, who is to say if anyone but a handful of people knew what it meant when they saw the being streak across the sky. But what I do know is that even if they did, they weren't in a position to do anything about it. Not like I was that snowy, winter day I went out to pick inkberries.

"Because on that night, the people of Adalinda went inside and locked their doors in observance of the blood moon, obeying the tradition of sitting in quiet contemplation with Tenille until the sun rose. It was also the night—"

"I was born," I whispered through numb lips.

"Yes." Vania looked away from the diamond to turn that shrewd gaze on me. "You're special, Ainsley Boreen. If your impossible birth wasn't proof enough. The fact that a being extinct for two thousand years returned to the world to mark the day you entered it is... incredible. Everything I've learned about you since only confirms it.

"That's why... I want you to take the claw."

What did she say?

"When I saw the notice for the reward, I wished for the knowledge of why you truly wanted a celestial dragon claw." She leaned forward, eyes huge. "She showed me so much more than I could comprehend. Imprisoned gods, war through the realms, blood, pain, enslavement, the end of everything, and the rise of something…" Vania shuddered. "Horrible. A fate that once put in motion, will bring about destruction no living being can survive.

"You must succeed, daughter of Titana. You must *take the claw*."

"I will gladly take her from this place right now," I slurred. My jaw did not want to form the words. "Free her, and we'll leave."

"Don't be ridiculous." She snorted, leaning back. "If you fail, the Nyota Society will need our prize more than ever. She is our assurance of survival. But I do not wish you to fail. Her claws, scales, and parts of her still grant wishes when separated from her body."

It sickened me to think how she knew that.

"All you have to do is wish for it, and the means to save us all, in this realm and the next, is yours. As a show of good faith, I wish that you could move."

My body returned to me before she finished waving her hand. I shot to my feet, and froze. I didn't know what to do. I couldn't begin to think of a word to say. My mind twisted and spun, and all the time, the dragon watched me.

"No," I croaked. "No, no! None of this makes sense. I see the greed in your eyes, *Queen Vania*." I said the title like she said item. "You didn't bring me here because you want me to succeed. You want the money. Those desperate fingers are holding so tight to that diamond, they're going to break."

Her nostrils flared. "Do not dare suggest I'm a liar. I have committed to the path of truth, and the desires it reveals along the way. I never said I didn't want the reward," she replied. "The creature is not all-powerful. She can grant many wishes, but there are limits. She cannot create something from nothing.

"If I wish for coin, jewels, riches, or wealth, it's taken from someone else and given to me. But the thing about royals, they don't like to lose a single coin." She looked away. "He sent riders, Watchers, Renders, and every tracker in Edjer to hunt down the person who stole his coin. We were almost caught. We never made that mistake again."

Atlas laughed. "A con woman always has a plausible explanation. But if Ainsley can use that claw to save the realms, doesn't it follow that you could too?" He cocked his head, wings rippling. "But you don't, because she can't. Nothing but lies out of that wrinkled mouth."

She bared her teeth like Reyna before a kill. Atlas was striking a nerve, and they both knew it. "It does follow, you ignorant soul parasite. I can't wish for any and everything. I can only wish for the desires true to my heart. Knowledge, youth, beauty, power. I've never wanted to be a hero or a savior of nations, and won't waste time pretending otherwise, because she'll know.

"One doesn't wish for a fertile womb when they don't want children. They don't wish to fly when they fear heights. She ignores an insincere wish. But she's forced to grant a true one," Vania said. "As such, I punish anyone who approaches her with lies and frivolities. She has served the Nyota Society faithfully for twenty years. She deserves more than the constant, inane babbling of fools who don't know what they want."

"How generous of you," I shrieked. "Let's all throw a parade for Queen Vania, ruler of inane fools. Huzzah, huzzah!"

I was hysterical and knew it. I couldn't help myself. I felt crazy and out of control. It was like I walked into a room and found a broken and battered child locked in a cage with everyone around her crowing about how her agony made their lives better. It felt that way, because that's exactly what was happening. If Vania wished the dragon would stop growing to keep her under control, it meant she found this poor, helpless nestling—just born. Brand new to the world.

Then threw her in a cage and tortured her for decades.

I can't believe I once thought us superior to Druks. We're no better to the dragons. We just find other ways to steal from them.

Keely's voice floated through my mind, and I cried.

"Oh, cease your dramatics," Vania snapped. "Why can't you see what I'm giving you? It's not my desire to free gods or win wars, but it is yours. With her claw, not only will you do so, but you can right every wrong in your life. The claw may be needed for the ritual to bring down the walls, but what's to stop you fulfilling your own desires before you do." Passion leeched into her voice and pulled her off the throne. "Ainsley, you could wish General Roark and High Queen Kisandra dead."

I choked on a sob. "Excuse me?"

"It's true. My heart isn't full of hatred for them, but yours is. More than any person alive," she hissed. "Hatred is desire by another name. If you wish them dead, she will make it so. Wherever they stand, the creature will snatch their souls and send them beyond the veil."

"She can bring people back from the veil too."

My body went rigid. "Don't."

"But she can," she said softly, fervor lighting those cold eyes. "Those children from the orphanage. The tumbler you're so fond of, and that sister of the order— What was her name? Ah yes. Sister Aven."

Her name was an arrow through my chest.

"With one sentence, you can correct the tragedy of their deaths, and return them to the great and peaceful life you fought to give them."

"Stop it!" I screamed, clapping my hands over my ears. "You don't get to do this, you piece of shit. You're not using my family to convince me to become as vile and evil as you—exploiting that poor dragon for my own gain. The only thing I wish is for her to be free.

"I wish you free," I cried.

The dragon gazed at me from within her prison, her black, bottomless eyes trapping me drowning me. But she didn't move. The glass cage didn't break.

"Come now, stupid girl." Vania's voice grated on my soul. "I told you that wouldn't work. No wish made in this place can negate my own. I wished for that too," she whispered, winking.

I couldn't look away. Pressure built in my throat, squeezing the air from my lungs, but the little dragon wouldn't let me look away. "This is wrong," I croaked. "You know it is, and—and you have true wealth now! Sell that diamond for millions of ryus, and then buy whatever the fuck you desire. Just let her go."

"This is not a negotiation. It's a choice. You take the claw and leave this place—accepting you will forget about my prize the moment you walk through the door—or these men toss you out like trash, and you still forget about my prize. Either way, there's no ending that results in you stealing *my* dragon, dragon thief.

"Make your choice."

Atlas shot between us, blocking that smile within a smirk. "Ainsley, she's fucking with your head. We both know nothing she's saying adds up. She has her stupid diamond, but she's still trying to manipulate you into wishing for the claw—"

"Because I don't wish for the future I've seen to come to pass!"

"—because she's playing you," he growled. "There must be some kind of catch. A trick to these wishes. Maybe she *wished* that anyone who uses the dragon's power in this place becomes her slavish, empty-headed servant." He snapped a wing at the motionless guards. "This has to be a trap to claim one million ryus... and a dragon thief."

I backed away, head whipping this way and that. Was this true? Was Vania plotting to put me in a glass case right next to the celestial dragon?

"Enough," Vania barked. "It is that hypocritical beast who lies and manipulates. I've spoken nothing but the truth. I want you to save us, Ainsley. I know you can do so. *Take the claw.*"

Atlas spun on her. "Don't you dare speak to her. You overplayed your hand, old hag. Let the desperation show. That little dragon can't make diamonds, but she can bring people back from beyond the veil? Ha!"

A vein throbbed between Vania's smooth, unlined brow. "What is so humorous, parasite? Of course it's possible to bring someone back from the veil. Why... just ask the heir to the six kingdoms how often she's done it." She latched on to me. "Go on, Princess. Wish for your family back. Wish for your friend. Wish for that poor sensory mage, Akasha, to return."

"Be quiet," Atlas growled.

"Her death was tragic," Vania plowed on. "Senseless. Evil. You can undo it all with a few words."

"Shut the fuck up. Leave her alone!"

"You could wish to finally have control over your power and bonds." Vania's voice rose over Atlas's. "Wielding your ability at its fullest without fear of losing your mind. Wouldn't that solve everything?"

"You're not fooling anyone except the mirror, dusty old crone," Atlas sliced in. "No one with a brain would believe anything could be so easy. It doesn't work that way. Not even with magic. Just because I say I wish the curse was broken, doesn't mean—"

Atlas blew off his feet—thrown across the room by an invisible force. He tumbled head over wing, crashing into the wall.

But my eyes weren't on him.

"Velez?"

Velez staggered on the spot—eyes huge and jaw working. He turned... and locked on to Atlas across the room.

"Brother?"

I gasped, hands clapping over my mouth.

Atlas slowly got to his feet. He stared at Velez like he'd never seen him before. In a very true way, he never had.

"Velez... is that you?"

They pressed their fingers to the left sides of their foreheads at the same time. Was that where they always felt their brother's presence? Waiting in the light and warm until it was their turn to live?

Atlas took a step. Velez took two. In a blink, they were running.

They threw their arms around each other—laughing, jumping, pounding each other's backs... crying.

"We're free." Velez grasped his brother's face, smashing their forehead together. "We're free, brother."

I stood frozen to the spot. What did this mean? Atlas believed all this to be lies and tricks. He denounced the woman as an old fraud, but to look at him then, hugging his brother, his deepest wish had come true. And he didn't care about anything else.

"Do you see?"

Her voice slithered in my ear. "I offer you everything you want. All you need to do is take it."

I swallowed hard. "You don't know what I want. You know nothing about me, and no information you wished up can change that."

"I'm the only one who knows you, Ainsley Boreen." She moved into my line of sight, dragging my gaze off Velez and Atlas. "I know your truest and deepest wish. Dominic Roark."

"Stop."

"He doesn't know, does he?" She wouldn't stop, and the dragon wouldn't look away. "He doesn't know why you pushed him away, even though the answer is obvious even to people who can't use wish magic?"

"I said stop!"

"A mother would do anything for her children, and to give you full control of your power, Mother Fate killed Dominic Roark."

My nails pierced my palm, staining the tips red. "Enough!"

"But that was his fate, wasn't it?" Her tone turned malicious. Taunting. "He was supposed to die that day in the snow, and you were meant to come into your full power on that very same day. Instead, here you are months and months later, unable to summon so much as a candle flame's worth of hellfire.

"With every day that passes and your ability remains out of reach, you grow more terrified that Mother Fate will come for Dominic again... and give you a death you'll finally be strong enough to avenge. Whatever it takes to free her trapped children."

I shook, lips trembling. "You don't know what you're talking—"

"I am the only one who knows," she roared. "I see all. I know all. You keep pushing him away because you pray that if you convince Mother Future you don't love him that much, she won't take him from you like she took your family and closest friend. Admit it!"

"What do you want from me!" I screamed, grabbing my head. "Why are you doing this!"

"Because you have to win this fight and be less of a sanctimonious bitch while you do it!" Vania wasn't looking very much like the cold, impassive beauty then. Anger made her face splotchy and lips thin. "You can't succeed as you are. You're weak," she spat. "Your every action is pushing you further off the path you must walk, because you're letting fear and hatred cloud your mind.

"I've said it many times. My wish is for you to succeed, and you can't save the future if you're stuck in the past." Taking control of herself, she cleared her throat—easing down on her throne. "So, Ainsley Boreen, heir to the six kingdoms. Take the claw. Wish your family and friends back to life. Wish the general and high queen dead. Wish for full and complete control of your power and mind, then walk life's path with Dominic Roark once again.

"Wish for your every true desire," she said, "then save us all."

I stared at her for a long time, mind whirling. How could I deny what I heard? Vania knew secrets I hadn't revealed to anyone. How could I ignore what I'd seen with my own eyes? A curse that's plagued my brothers and countless more for centuries was lifted with a single misspoken sentence.

The wish magic was real... and I could get everyone back.

Rosaleen. Sister Aven. The children. Akasha. My father.

I could destroy the high queen and the general without risking my friends anymore, and I could get control of my power and be with Dominic again. These people were all committed to the truth, and I didn't know why. It was terrible having her rip open my chest and expose my deepest fear about Mother Future. It was the fate of the man I loved for him to die, so I'd become her weapon of vengeance.

Then he almost died again when I rescued the unique mages from the estate in the woods. Then again when he was thrown into the Everlasting Flame. She kept trying to take him away from me. How else could I protect the love of my life except by breaking his heart?

No more. You can be happy. I looked to Atlas and Velez. *We all can be happy, healthy, alive, and in love. All I have to do...*

My eyes connected with the little dragon. She hadn't looked away from me since they brought her into the room. All I had to do was rip a body part off this precious and rare creature, very likely the last of her kind, and then abandon her to Vania's mercy. In exchange, I'd get everything I ever wanted, and the people I loved would get a second chance.

Pain and longing pumped through my chest. I ached to talk with Rosaleen, laugh with Sister Aven, and play with my brothers and sisters again. And I... Fuck's sake, I wanted to be with Dominic so badly, I am with him every night in my dreams, and every day in my memories. My heart couldn't let him go, and it never would.

"But I—"

"I wish our family was alive."

That didn't come from me.

"Velez!" I whirled on him. "What are you doing? We—!"

"Heavens, are you two still bickering?"

My mind went white. Slowly, achingly, I turned. Sister Aven smiled at me.

"You're both adults, and the closest of friends—though you deny it. I'd have thought you'd have outgrown all this arguing by now."

Breath trapped in my lungs. It was her. Sister Aven stood before me as whole and healthy as the day I left for dragon rider training, wearing an easy smile on her lips, and the red-green-blue-and-white habit of the Holy Order of Tenille.

She held her arms out to me, as she did every time she saw me. According to her, I gave the best hugs. "Hello, dear. I take it you've got a lot to fill me in on."

"Me too."

I twisted around, jaw falling as Rosaleen walked up.

"What the hell happened?" she asked. A smirk danced on her full, bee-stung lips. "One minute I'm shouting at you in the throne room, and the next I'm here in..." She looked around. "Another throne room? And— Oh my goodness, what are you?" she cried, seeing the celestial dragon. "I'm definitely missing something."

"Wow." Pema went streaking across the carpets, throwing herself against the glass cage. "She's so pretty."

"Wow." "What is it?" "Is it a dragon?" "Course it's not a dragon, dummy. Dragons don't look like that." "Don't call me a dummy!"

I choked. Falling to my knees, I couldn't suck in a breath, or get out a word as the children ran all over the place. Pressing their noses to the cage. Poking the still guards. Oohing over the expensive things. And giggling at the half-naked Vania. They were everywhere... and they were alive.

"Velez!" Ilemka jumped into his arms. "I missed you so much." She punched him dead in the chest, tearing out a groan. "Why did you leave us!"

"I don't know." I couldn't tell if he was crying or laughing. It must be both. "But I'll never do it again."

My heart broke as he squeezed her tight, but his didn't. I could see in his eyes as the kids climbed all over Atlas, poking and tugging on his wings—Velez's heart had never been so full.

They were here. My borrowed family. All of them. The only one missing was the one I never met. My father. And that would only take one wish.

"Ains, what are you doing?" Rosaleen picked me up by the shoulders.

I cried out at the feel of her hands on me, her familiar sweet scent surrounding me, and her *you're so weird* grin that she flashed me almost every single day since the day we met.

"You're real..."

She snorted. "Of course I'm real. Are you okay? Why are you looking at me like that?"

"Because, I suspect"—Sister Aven took me in her arms—"we've been away longer than we know." She kissed my forehead. "I'm sorry, my sweet Ainsley. However long we've been gone. We're back now, and we're not going anywhere."

"They won't," Vania said. "As long as the dragon remains with me, your family will be with you for the rest of your days. You can be happy, Ainsley. *They* can be happy. Isn't that what you've always wanted?"

I barely heard her over my sobs. I hugged Sister Aven so tight, I was breaking her in half.

I couldn't believe she was here. Holding me. Saying all the comforting words she'd always say.

"It can all be yours," Vania said softly. "All you have to do is wish."

She didn't have to keep pushing. I knew exactly what to do. Honestly, my decision was made from the moment I saw Sister Aven.

"Okay." I straightened, wiping my face. "You win. I'll do it."

"Excellent." Satisfaction laced Vania's voice. "Now let's move on from this business. I have a party to attend. Wish for the claw and be on your way."

Closing the distance, I placed my hands on the glass cage. "I'm sorry," I whispered. "You and I are a lot alike. We're both impossible things that demanded to be born, then the world spent every day making us pay for it."

"That's enough," Vania said sharply. Her shadow fell over us. "Make your wish and leave."

"You deserve better than all of this. But then... I did too."

I steeled my heart as I backed away. Atlas and Velez were silent figures behind me. They were shouting loudest of all that this was bullshit and

I couldn't trust her, and now they were quiet. Because they knew exactly what I was going to do.

All life had done to me was take, take, take. I was born to make the wishes of gods and goddesses come true. It was my turn to be happy.

It was my wishes that should come true.

I took a deep breath, let it out slow, then spoke with a certainty that echoed through my bones. "I wish that you had my thief magic."

"What? No!"

The dragon reared up like a hissing cat—back arched and all limbs going rigid. She roared.

I blew off my feet, crashing into Atlas and Velez. The ground pitched and rumbled beneath our shoes—toppling kneeling stands, shaking tapestries off the wall, and knocking over that stupid throne. Rosaleen, Sister Aven, and the children went flying to all corners of the room.

"No!" Vania screamed, scrambling to right herself. "What have you done!" Her guards rushed to help her. "Get off me, idiots. Do something. Don't let her get away!"

They sprung into action—flinging water, sand, fire, air, stone, and all the blessings of Tenille at the cage. It smashed into the glass, and ricocheted in every direction.

"Look out!" I tackled Atlas, throwing him to the floor as a ball of fire cut through the spot he'd been kneeling in. It struck the man coming up behind him.

"Ahh! Ahhh!" The guard fell screaming and burning.

The sound of shattering glass broke through the bellows. She burst through the cage, growing to overtake the cart, and splintering it to pieces under her weight.

"Ainsley? Ainsley, what's happening!" Rosaleen tried to run to me. "Help!"

"No! I wish you didn't have her magic." Ice shards flew from Vania's palm, impaling the dragon's stomach. "I wish you were imprisoned in a cage!"

"ARRGH!" Her roar rattled my bones.

"We have to go." I grabbed Atlas's arm, dragging him onto his feet. "We have to go now!"

"Wait." Atlas threw himself over me, reaching for Velez. Their fingers connected, then Velez ripped away.

Piercing ice shards tore through his chest, and flung him against the wall—impaling him to the wood. Atlas's bellowed snarl stood my hairs on end.

"Brother!"

Magic flew around the room. A whirling torrent of elements that battered and beat at me—ripping my clothes, soaking me, and singeing my skin with every lash of flame that got too close. The dragon's head struck the ceiling, and she kept growing. A twenty-year-old dragon couldn't fit in a room like this. Neither would she.

"Atlas, please," I cried, shoving against him. "We can't stay!"

Cracks spiderwebbed across the ceiling. Chunks of masonry broke off, coming down like deadly rain. Sister Aven was struck, knocking her over and pinning her leg.

"Ainsley!" She reached for me as I finally got Atlas on his feet. "Help me, please."

Heart-wrenching wails shredded my throat. It was happening again. All around me, my family was dying.

I couldn't see. A flurry of snow swept through the throne room—plunging us in a blizzard worse than the never-ending one that trapped us in the cabin all those months ago.

My teeth clacked together. Tears turned to ice on my cheeks. My coats and scarves whipped through the space, leaving me exposed to the cold. I shuffled through the rising snow—strength leeching away faster than warmth.

"I wish I had my magic back! I wish Ainsley Boreen was dead! I wish you couldn't fight back! I wish you couldn't—"

"ARRGH!"

The raging slurry cleared for the barest possible second, and I locked eyes with Vania's, before the dragon crushed her underfoot.

Hands suddenly seized me under the arms. Atlas lifted me and took off, flying through the ice, rage, and death.

"Ainsley, wait," Rosaleen's voice pierced me. "Don't leave us. We need your help. Come back!"

Atlas broke through the ceiling as the dragon did, soaring through the sky as the mortar and stone crashed down on them—her roar nowhere as loud as their screams.

Chapter Seventeen

Atlas dropped out of the air, falling behind a familiar stack of fish carts.

A few feet away in the square, people ran around shouting and hollering about the destroyed mansion on Hemel Street, the search for survivors, and what was that creature that flew away from the wreckage?

"Okay, I think we're safe here." Atlas peered around the wood. "No one's looking for the speck in the sky that could've been a Druk. The first celestial dragon sighting in two thousand years trumps that."

I huddled against the wall, shivering. It was so cold. No one had ever been this cold—inside and out.

"We should be able to make our way back to Tulsi's soon. First, we—Hey." He finally looked at me. "Ainsley, are you—? Oh shit, you must be freezing." His wings folded over us, encasing me in their surprising warmth. "Is that—?"

I launched at him. Throwing my arms around his neck, I buried my face in his chest and sobbed.

"I'm sorry. I'm so sorry." He grunted under my strangling grip. "I couldn't do it. I had to free her, Atlas. It wasn't real. I know you hate me but—"

"No," he sliced in. "I don't hate you, Ainsley. I... I heard it too. Right at the end, she gave herself away when she said *as long as the dragon remains with me, your family will be with you for the rest of your days.*

"The wrinkled old con woman was doing so well until that slipup. The wishes only hold as long as she has complete control over the poor creature. If they can be taken away, it means—"

"They were never really there," I whispered.

He heaved a sigh. "If that wasn't enough, the children weren't afraid of me. They never knew who I was. All they saw was a big, scary Druk. They should've run screaming behind Sister Aven's skirts, but that would hardly be my wish come true."

I nodded along, face soaked. Atlas had noticed all the things I did. He knew I made the only choice there was. "Velez?" I croaked. "Is he okay?"

"He's fine." Atlas tapped the side of his head. "He's still in the light and warm. Safe and sound. I don't think he ever left. B-but I have to say—" His voice cracked. "Even though I knew it wasn't real. Even though it couldn't be— To look upon my brother's face for the first time. To believe for a moment that we were finally free…" Atlas trailed off, his jaw clenched so tight it could break.

"It's no wonder to me those people couldn't leave that place. They just stayed holed up in that mansion, spending every day with those illusions, and happy because there was nothing real out here, that's better than the fantasy in there." His eyes clouded, gazing up at the stars. "I don't know anyone who could walk away from everything they've ever wanted… except for you.

"You're the strongest person I know, Ainsley Shadowslayer. You…" He shook his head. "You just are."

"Thank you." My voice was so small, I wasn't sure he heard me. "But I don't feel very strong right now."

"That's okay." He held me close. "You can cry, Ainsley. As much and as long as you need to. I'm not going anywhere."

That was all the permission I needed. I broke down, crying hard on his sleeve. Searing pain went through my skull. "Ah! Ahhh!" Screams ripped from my lips.

"Dammit, woman, don't cry that loud." Atlas snapped his wings tighter around us. "Are you trying to get us caught?"

I flung back, clutching my head as agony tore a hole in my mind and filled it with fire. There was only one thing in the world that caused this pain.

"*Thank you*," she whispered in my mind as our bond formed. Unbreakable and forever. "*Dragon mother.*"

Shakily, I pushed up. Atlas's shaking and asking if I was okay faded in the background.

I stared at the shimmering glow in the sky—knowing it was her like I knew my own name. "You're welcome, Celine." I opened my palm. A beautiful, impossible celestial dragon claw glittered back at me—lighter than water. "Thank you, my beauty."

***

Velez and I were a silent pair, weaving through the back streets of Calixto in the early hours of the morning. Just in case, we didn't want to take the direct route back to Tulsi's home. Although, it was less about the people who weren't following us, and more about us... just needing to walk.

I shivered in my stolen coats, pulling them tighter around me.

"So..." Velez strolled next to me, hands in his pockets and chin tucked low in his hood. "You did it. You got the claw of a celestial dragon, and bonded with her in the process. Every time I think I've seen you do the most amazing thing anyone has ever done, you go and top it."

I chuckled soft. "Thanks."

"You okay?"

A beat stretched into a full minute, then I nodded. "I'm okay. Seeing them like that was..." I shook my head. "But it wasn't real. No more than a dream mage's creations are real. Wherever they really are beyond the veil, they're safe and happy. I realized that last night when she was tempting me with those illusions. It was more important to me that they were happy and together where they were than living in pretend with me.

"One day, I'll cross the veil and we'll spend the rest of eternity laughing, joking, and playing together. That's what I want. It's my true wish," I said. "Vania was right about that one thing. Now that I know what I truly want, there's no point wishing for less or something else. I want to be with our family again for real, and one day I will be. That's good enough for now."

"Atlas was right." His smile warmed my heart. "You are strong."

"All right, all right," I said, shoving his shoulder. "Don't get all soft on me. I'm still the dummy, Pain-in-the-Ains you know and love."

He laughed. "Good. Don't go changing on me too much, little sister."

"I'll try."

We lapsed into a comfortable silence as we turned the last corner headed to Tulsi's house.

"What should we do now?" Velez spoke up. "Should we say goodbye to Tulsi, then leave for Nehebkau? Or do you want a day of hot cocoa and letting her stuff you with food before we throw ourselves in it again?"

"We can't delay too long," I admitted. "Celine's free. She ended all the wishes she was forced to grant, including the one that anyone who leaves Vania's can't talk about her. The Watchers are swarming all over the wrecked mansion by now. They're talking to survivors who'll tell them the dragon thief was there. They'll say Celine took off never to return.

"The general will figure I have the claw or it's far out of my reach. Either way, there's no reason for me to stay here. He's going to move on to the Infinity Tree. We have to get there first."

Velez nodded along. "Agreed."

"But."

"But?" he repeated, frowning. "What but?"

"But there's something I need to do first." The first real smile in days stretched my lips. "Get my fucking fiancé back."

"Now that's the little sister I know." He spun me laughing off my feet, hugging me tight. "It's about time. If you moped for another day, I was going to track him down and bring you both together myself."

"Ugh. Hearing Vania say it out loud made me realize how stupid I was being. I was so afraid of losing him, I gave him up."

"That's absolutely fucking stupid."

"Shut up," I cried, swatting his arm. "I know, okay. Mother Future is going to do whatever she wants to do, but as long as I've got my power, I'll snatch him back from the veil however many times I have to. Dominic and I were meant to be together, so that's what we're going to do."

Velez hugged me close, smooshing my face in his chest. "I'm happy for you."

A noise pricked my ear. I strained to turn my head. Out of the corner of my eyes, a shadow moved.

"I'm less happy for you," Atlas said, taking over. "You're making a huge mistake choosing your tiny-dick, cheese-breath general spawn over the true love of your life."

Even with alarm bells ringing in my head, he could make me roll my eyes.

"But I'll accept it for now since I have a lifetime to woo you away from that mistake."

Thud.

I stiffened. No mistake. There was definitely someone there. "Atlas, be quiet for a minute and—"

"If we'd had a chance to make love, you'd have seen—"

Hands seized and pulled me away. I went flying through the air, only for an unseen force to catch and lower me safely to the ground. I was blinking at the threads suddenly around my wrists when a black streak burst out of the alley, and punched Atlas in the face.

I cried out as he went down, and didn't get back up.

"Make love to the fucking sidewalk, you flying piece of shit!" Dominic tore off his hood. "You won't touch my wife even after I'm dead."

"Dominic?" I kept blinking but he was still standing there—pissed as shit. "Is this real? Did I accidentally tap into Celine's magic? Tell me you're real."

"Of course I'm real. What the hell are you talking about?"

Oh yes. That *I love you but you're nuts* tone was pure Dominic.

"Dom." Shaking off the threads, I ran to him. "I can't believe you're here. Why did you hit Atlas?"

"Why did you leave me this shit!" Dominic whipped out the letter, pulling me up short.

"Ah." I winced. "So you read it."

"Yeah. I read it." The man practically vibrated with rage. "*I'm sorry, Dom, it's over. I've fallen in love with Atlas and I'm marrying him. Please don't follow me. I don't love you anymore.*"

Hearing the words out loud twisted my stomach. "I'm so sorry. I didn't mean any of it. None of it's true—"

"I knew it wasn't true," he exploded. "No way in hell you'd leave me for that fuck. You hate that aggressive, flowery, flirty garbage. You roll your eyes every time he opens his mouth."

Dominic did know me better than anyone.

"You left me this and ran out because after Akasha died, and we got hurt, you convinced yourself it was too dangerous for us to be around you." The letter went up in a flash of hellfire. "Didn't work."

I glanced down at the unconscious Atlas. "But if you know that, why did you hit him?"

Dominic's eyes narrowed to slits. "Because there's no way that flying piece of shit and his twin parasite bastard didn't prod you on the way to making that terrible decision. They've both wanted rid of us from the start."

I took his face in my hands, so happy his rage couldn't burst it. "I love you," I whispered. "I'll never leave you again."

Something flickered in his amber pools, letting an emotion that was far from anger through. "You might," he gruffed, body untensing. "But I'll follow you then too, so it won't last."

"Wait. How did you find me this time?"

Keely poked her head out from around the corner. Poet was right behind her.

They were both whole and perfect. Not so much as a blemish remained from their brush with death.

"That would be me," Keely sang. "You're an escape risk, so I tied a thread around you ages ago to link us together. It took a while to follow it with the way it looped all around the city, but we got here in the end."

My brows blew up my forehead. "You tied a tracking thread around me? Not sure how to feel about that."

"Stop leaving us and we won't need to," Poet deadpanned.

"I'd like to point out that one of those times, you sent me away."

He inclined his head. "Fair point."

"But I'm not going anywhere," I said, lacing my fingers through Dominic's. "You're my one true wish, baby. Why would I ever leave you?"

Dom cocked a brow. "One true wish? Look, Princess, don't try that flowery flirty stuff on me either. I'm still mad at you. I love you, but you don't know what waking up, finding you gone, and that letter in my hand did to me. I need time to get past it."

"I understand." I wrapped his arms around my waist, pulling him in close. "But I have a feeling you won't need much time. You're going to forgive me pretty soon."

Skepticism crumpled his forehead even while his body responded naturally, molding to mine. "Why am I doing that?"

"Because, fiancé, no more waiting. No more excuses. We're getting married the second I get you in front of a sister of the order. The next time you shout at Atlas to stay away from your wife, you'll be talking about me."

Dominic gaped at me so long, I thought I broke him. "Okay, you're right," he said slowly. "I forgive you."

Laughing, I rose on tiptoe and crushed my mouth on his. The world spun, then I was up against the wall, sinking in the spicy, sweet scent of Dominic as he exploded the heat between us—devouring me without a care to who was watching.

Our tongues tangled, lips clashed, hands roamed, and moans got louder, drowning out Keely and Poet's whistling and hollering. No one existed except me and him.

Breaking away, he pressed his forehead against me—rubbing his nose on mine till I giggled. "I love you," he whispered.

"I love you too."

"But the twin shits aren't invited to our wedding."

I snorted holding back a laugh. "You might want to invite them since they'll have to be your witnesses. Keely and Poet will be taken. By me," I said to their astonished faces. "If you'll accept."

Keely held her hand to her heart, eyes shining. "Ainsley, I... I'd be honored."

"I'd love to," Poet said. "Thank you."

Dominic set me back on my feet, much more mussed and ravished than when he picked me up. "What about your mother?" he asked. "She can be one of your maiden witnesses. That way I can take Poet and any old random guy we pick up off the street. Literally anyone."

I gave him a look as I bent down to prod Atlas. "We're not having any old random person at our wedding. Besides, my mother can't do it because she'll be marrying us. She's a sister of the order."

"What? She is?"

"Crazy, right?" I tossed my head. "Meriall has had quite a life. You couldn't even begin to guess. Just wait until you hear the story of how she met my father."

"That is a story I'd like to hear."

I shot to my feet, whipping around as five figures entered the alley.

"But first, I must say I'm disappointed you didn't consider your own father as one of your witnesses." General Roark towered over Maili and

Ormr—his smirk ten times wider and smug than theirs could ever be. "Hello, son."

"How?" Dominic grabbed and put me behind him before I could blink. Another blink and Poet and Keely were in front of me too. Fire ropes, hellfire balls, and threads surrounded us. "How did you find us!"

"I'm afraid the credit for that goes to Badr." He gestured to the pompous windbag of a fool that was with him the day I literally ran into him. "It is my pleasure to introduce to you the first of his aberrant kind. A bloodline mage."

Badr lifted his chin, beaming pride. It was only then I noticed the gleam of gold peeking through his coat sleeve.

"All he needs is a drop of someone's blood, and he can track down every one of their children, descendants, and blood relatives. It's truly amazing," Roark said, sounding sincere. "Thanks to him, I've also made the discovery that I have five other children I never knew about. It seems a few of my wives saw fit to give birth in secret and give them away."

I scoffed. "That makes sense," I said, straining to see over Dominic's shoulder. "You're a terrible fucking father. I'd hide those kids from you too."

"I wouldn't have thought you the judge on good or bad fathers," Roark drawled. "You have neither."

"You're not taking her, Father." Dominic gathered hellfire around him, burning so hot, Keely and Poet had to back away. "But I dare you to try."

"Save your puffery, boy, you impress no one here," Roark snapped. "You can have a fight if you wish, but it will be decisively one-sided. Meet another member of the high queen's aberrant army."

He pointed to the other silent woman in their party. She couldn't have been a native Edjerian. She covered herself in more coats than me. Eyes were all I could make out.

"I have no idea what you'd call her magic, but I do know"—he whipped out his sword and sliced right through Maili—"that it allows all physical and magical attacks to pass harmlessly through whoever she wishes."

"Impossible," I breathed.

But it was true. Child Maili stood there with not a scratch on her.

"Do not waste your time fighting." Roark pulled off his gloves. "It takes an immense amount of my magical strength to push my power out of my body and wither someone I'm not touching. I've been saving that strength for weeks in anticipation of this day." He slid off Dominic... on to Keely. "Surrender, put on your manacles, and the girl lives for another day."

Ormr was already pulling the golden manacles from the folds of their coat. "I'll do you one better. Surrender, put on the manacles, and tell us where and how to free Kenna and Cadmus," they said. "Then the thread aberrant gets to live another day."

Poet and Keely shared panicked looks. No attack or punch would touch them. Running away would get us nowhere with a bloodline mage on our tails. How would we get out of this?

Touching Dominic's shoulder, I squeezed between them and planted myself before my siblings and the general. Looking him in the eye, I said, "No."

His lip twitched. "Excuse me?"

"You heard me. No," I said clearly. "We're not surrendering. We're not going anywhere with you."

"You don't seem to understand. There's nowhere for you to go. There's nowhere to run. This ends in that girl's death, and you in chains. Surrender."

"Nope," I sang. "Because you don't seem to understand that your little habit of announcing the magic and ability of every unique mage you forcibly collect just makes it easier for me to know exactly who to do this to."

I snapped my fingers. Badr's shadow peeled off the ground and seized the surprised mage from behind. They both disappeared leaving behind the faint echo of a scream.

"What was that!" Maili screamed.

"Where did he go?" Ormr demanded. "How did she do that!"

"Shadow magic," Roark barked without skipping a beat. "The Stryker boy's stolen dragon. Stop her quickly! Don't let her get away!"

Vines and wind scythes sliced through the air, heading straight for us. I snapped my fingers, and we were gone.

***

The shadows released us in the middle of the forest. Ossian Forest.

I was home.

My dragons sunned their scales, bathed in the river, growled at the light poking through the leaves, and munched on a half-eaten cow. Even Valor was here, lying belly-up under the sun. All we were missing was Tizor and Celine. Tizor remained with his hatchlings, and Celine was staying in the sky. She needed a break from humans. I suspected it'd be a long time before she ever touched ground again. Maybe never.

Hello, my beauties.

Five heads snapped up.

Reyna burst out of the river. She tore up the shore clawing out and bounding over to me. I braced myself for her head-smacking brand of a hug.

"*How have you done this?*" Reyna asked. "*Tell me. I order you.*"

I laughed. "I don't know why people call me the queen of the kingdoms. It's clearly you."

Reyna sat back on her haunches—head high and chest out. If she was a bird, she'd be preening. "*I accept the title.*"

"You're talking to her, aren't you?"

I turned to my staring friends. Atlas would be staring too if he wasn't still unconscious in the safe place I put him downwind. The last thing he needed after getting punched in the face is getting eaten by dragons.

"Plus, you got rid of the bloodline mage, and got us out of there with a snap of your fingers," Keely said. "Did you do it? You learned to control your magic?"

Smiling, I nodded. "Well, at least kind of. Maybe it was being near Celine, or maybe she gifted me the knowledge like she did the claw, but while I was in that horrible mansion, I finally figured out my ball of thread."

"Ainsley, that's amazing."

Dominic and Poet exchanged confused looks. They didn't get the reference.

"I had everything all wrong." I stroked Reyna's snout. "I thought because I'm a weapon of vengeance, it meant I needed hate and anger to channel my power, but that's not what Kai said. He told me I couldn't use my power if I didn't have someone to avenge. He meant someone I loved."

Dominic stepped forward, reaching for my hand. "Me?"

"Yeah," I whispered. "You. And Sister Aven. And Rosaleen. And the children. That day in the hut, I wasn't thinking about anything other than how much I loved and missed you—and just like that, we made hellfire together.

"Those four months I roamed the kingdoms. It was love of my family, my dragons, and the children I was finding and protecting that drove me. And all those years ago, Zalina summoned Titana to avenge her family. The people she loved. It was a broken heart that fueled her, much like Gaius Daoud after he lost his wife and daughter.

"You don't avenge a person if you never loved them, and you damn sure don't become a weapon of vengeance if you weren't loved in return."

"Love." Dom's fingers skated over my cheek—soft and sweet. "Sounds about right."

"So," Poet broke in. "You just think about how much you love Dom, then you kill a bunch of people?"

I gave him a look. "It's not that simple. If it was, I'd have figure this out a long time ago. I think about how much I love Dom a million times a day."

"Hmm. I change my mind," Dominic said. "I do like this flowery flirty stuff."

"Behave." I poked him. "No, Poet, it's more that I have to be open to it. Have full faith in myself, my loves, and my want to make sure no one who hurts them ever draws breath. The slightest doubt or break in concentration, and the walls close down."

I looked away. "After we escaped with Vania, I did something I didn't think I'd ever do. I stopped thinking about how much I missed my family and hated the people who took them away, and I... just thought about how much I loved them, and that I couldn't wait to see them again beyond the veil. That's when Celine spoke to me."

"That's incredible," Poet said. "Who's Celine?"

"Oh, right. I forgot to tell you. I bonded with a celestial dragon." I beamed at their hanging jaws. "We were born on the same day. Her name's Celine. She's not a big fan of humans, and she's absolutely beautiful."

Growling, Reyna snapped the air above my head.

"Not more beautiful than you, Reyna."

A sharp spike went through my skull. "Ah! You're both equally beautiful," I cried to the petty creatures. "I have no favorites."

Reyna snorted. "*I am your favorite. I demand no less. Say it.*" Another snap. "*Say I'm your favorite. I order it.*"

I groaned. Titana, save me, why in the world did I miss this?

Reyna stuck her haunches in my face, then lumbered to the water.

"That didn't look like it went well." Amusement laced Dominic's tone.

"It didn't." I fell against his chest. Dominic wrapped me up safe and warm immediately. "I wanted to say that I'm doing what you said. Not holding back the tide. I'm putting obstacles in its way.

"Kai built the walls in my mind. I bring them down, but there's always something in the way. The first time we kissed. The first time we tumbled. The first day Velez arrived at the orphanage. Laughing with my brother till we cried. All my happiest memories with the people I love." I smiled up at him. "They keep me sane, Dom. You do."

"Sounds about right, since you did the opposite. You knocked down all my walls, Princess. I'm an out-of-control, obsessed mess who can't think of anything other than how much I need to be with you."

"Oh, Dom—"

"Ugh." Poet heaved. "Take it back. Please, take it back. No more of this flowery flirty stuff. I haven't been eating enough on this damn mission for you guys to bring my meager meals back up again."

Keely smacked her hands on her hips. "Fucking hell, Poet. Have a heart. They're finally back together and getting married after everything that's happened. You could at least fake being happy for your best friends."

"How could they be my best friends, milady? Obviously, you're my best friend. That's why you're always on my ass!"

"You wish I was on your ass!"

Poet stormed off to Valor, and of course Keely went tearing off after him. The familiar bickering filled the forest.

"How has that not happened yet?" I whispered through clenched teeth.

Dominic heaved a sigh. "After Keely woke up from Mireu's healing, she told him he kissed her in the heat of the moment because he thought he was going to die. It didn't mean anything."

"She told him it didn't mean anything? Oooh, ouch."

"Oh, yeah." He shook his head. "Poet just said okay, but they've been snapping at each other worse than ever since." Dominic kissed my forehead. "You should teach them how to open themselves to love."

"It'd take a swarm of dragons to pry the stubbornness out of those two," I muttered. "But I do need to tell you, I'm not at my full ability. I've learned to open the bonds again, but channeling so much of their magic that I take on dragon form? I don't know how to do that on purpose, or even how to try. I think about draining them dry like that—"

"—and it feels wrong because you love them," he finished. "The doubt creeps in and the bond closes you out, responding to your hesitation. That's tough, baby, but now that we know how it works, we can practice and train until you feel comfortable. We may even be able to find a way you can take on full form without draining them like overturned buckets."

"I'm so glad you're here."

Our lips met, sharing tiny, sweet kisses.

Dominic winked. "Where to next, boss?"

"Calixto." I saw the look on his face. "I know, I know. But we left the Everlasting Flame at Tulsi's house. I have the well water with me, but the Flame I can't exactly carry around in my pocket unless I want it to catch fire. The only good news is that your father caught us before we got to her home. I'd never forgive myself if we led him to her door."

"What about the bloodline mage? Where is he, by the way?"

I grinned. "I dropped him on top of a mountain."

"You did what?"

"Not a snowy mountain," I said, shrugging. "The air is thin, but it's warm. And, the mountain is covered in fruit trees, so he'll have plenty to eat on the long way down. That'll give us time to find the Infinity Tree, get the bark, and make it back to Itzala before the general finds him and they catch up with us."

Dominic leaned back, holding my shoulders. "That could be sooner than we think. Those manacles will have means of tracking the unique mages. They might already know where he is, and a rider only has to hop on their dragon and pick him up."

"I'm ready when you are."

Dominic snapped to. "Poet, Keely, we're going back to Calixto. Dragons, we won't be long." He marched off, ever the soldier. "After this, we go straight to Nehebkau and track down the Infinity Tree. The general knows what we're after. Nehebkau is where he'll be too.

"The flying piece of shit fucked off somewhere to die," he announced. "He's an earth Druk, so the mud and manure will claim him. No need to go back for his body."

My gusty sigh shook the leaves. Keely was right. Those three were never going to like each other.

"Ready?" he asked me.

Nodding, I dove back into the place I created in my mind—filled with the happy memories of my loves, and the bonds with my dragons. Suoh's wasn't so much an entry behind a wall as it was a trapdoor tucked away in a dark, shadowed corner. I opened the hatch and dove in, sinking into the world of shadows, and taking my friends with me.

I dropped us straight in Tulsi's living room, surprising a cup of cocoa out of her hands. After saying our goodbyes properly, and entrusting the Flame into Poet's care, we returned to Ossian Forest and found an awake Atlas rubbing his jaw.

"I thank you for returning to me, my light of the morning." Atlas kicked off with his nonsense at first sight. "It's unfortunate you brought that violent, insane brute along, but it's okay. The more he makes a jealous ass of himself, the closer he drives you to me."

Hellfire balls appeared in the air. They rained down on a wall of stone erected before the snarl came out of Dominic's mouth.

Keely, Poet, and I walked away, leaving them to it.

"Why did you bring us back here?" Poet asked. "We don't have much time. We need to get to Nehebkau."

"We need a plan," I said. "The well, the Flame, the celestial dragon. We walked into all of those situations thinking we had it all figured out, then discovered the hard way we didn't have a fucking clue. Not this time.

"Poet, you said your family has an estate in Nehebkau and you spent every winter there. Do you know the legend of the Infinity Tree?"

"Every Nehebkan does," he admitted. "No one knows how it came to be, but it's said deep in the Shahina Forest, there's a tree that's stood since before Parthelan made man. According to legend, the bark is medicinal. If you brew it in a tea, it'll cure you of any illness. Even death."

Keely stood up straight. "Death? You're not serious."

"Very serious," he replied. "I had a friend in the neighboring estate. We played together every winter when I returned home. Then in my tenth year, I came back to find him dying."

We were rapt. "What happened?" I asked.

"Don't know. He threw up everything he ate and drank, including water. None of the healers could figure it out. Odion was wasting away before our eyes, and there was nothing we could do about it. One morning, we woke up and his mother was gone."

"She went to find the Infinity Tree," I said.

Poet nodded. "It was a grueling trek. Shahina Forest isn't like this one. It's a magical forest. No one knows if it was cultivated by an earth mage or a curse mage cursed the land, but the trees move," he said to our shock. "Paths and landmarks disappear. Fresh water becomes salt at the first sip. The trees lean in close together to block out the sun. It's a forest that doesn't like visitors, or letting them leave. I don't know of a single person who's gone into the forest and made it out... except for Odion's mother.

"She came back—battered, bleeding, dehydrated—but clutching the bark. They made the tea, gave it to Odion, and he kept it down. The next morning, he was sitting up in bed, scarfing down everything in sight. The washed-out skeleton that was in his bed the day before was replaced by my friend. He looked like nothing ever happened to him.

"I went away, then came back the next day to play, and they were gone."

"Gone?" I repeated. "Gone where?"

"The entire family was taken, arrested, and executed after one of the household staff reported on them. Odion was killed too."

I choked. "What! Why?"

Poet's fist balled. "It's against Nehebkan law to search for the Infinity Tree. The bark doesn't just cure illnesses. It also keeps you alive much longer than bonding with a dragon can. They say it could keep you alive forever."

"Infinity," Keely whispered.

"Yes." Poet shuffled away, turning his back on us. "Something like that is just too irresistible. People went on treks to find the tree. It became almost a rite of passage. Most of them were never seen again.

"That was just the people who took the peaceful approach. Others tried magically burning and cutting down everything in their way." He scoffed. "That is until the forest fought back. Poison got into the soil and groundwater. Our crops rotted in the fields and Nehebkau fell into a five-year famine. After that..."

"They outlawed the search for the Infinity Tree and harshly punished anyone who didn't obey," I finished. "But why the entire family? Why little Odion? Titana, bless me, she was just trying to save her son's life."

"That's why." Poet's voice was flat. Dead. "When you're that desperate and love someone that much, you don't care what the consequences are. You'll do whatever you have to. But, if they also execute the person you saved, then it's an option of letting them die. Or killing them. The law gives them no way out."

"Poet..." Keely said softly. She reached out for him. "You lost your childhood friend. Why didn't you tell me about this?"

"My parents forbade me at the time." His voice was gruff. "There are consequences for people who know and don't report. My dad was trying to protect me, but more than that, I... couldn't. Not for a long time."

"You can talk to me now." She pushed through the gulf, resting her head on Poet's shoulder. "I'm here. I'll listen."

"Will you, Keels? Last I checked, you and I don't do honest conversations." Shaking her off, he stormed away.

"Poet, wait—!"

I touched her arm, gently holding her back. "Give him a minute to cool down. It's not you he's angry with."

"Yes," she whispered. "It is."

I didn't know what to say. Keely was such a good friend to me. I should've had words to comfort her, but I didn't know how to be there for her any more than she and Poet knew how to be there for each other.

"You and Poet will find your way to each other in the end."

Keely's head snapped up, eyes wide.

"When the time is right and you're both ready." I squeezed her hands tight. "You will. I know it."

Her eyes filled. Breaking away, she roughly rubbed them—clearing her throat.

See? You said the wrong thing.

I backed away, leaving her be.

A hand suddenly grabbed my fingers and squeezed them. "Thank you."

Keely let go and was gone before I got another word out. I smiled at her back. Maybe I did remember how to be a sister.

I relaxed under a tree, deep in conversation with Dominic and how we'd get to the Infinity Tree, while Poet and Keely had a minute to themselves.

"We have to fly," he said. "Going through will take too long, and kill us. Going over the forest is the only choice. The five of us will split up and search more ground. Same thing when one spots the tree. They'll take its bark from above. No one risks touching the forest floor."

"I agree," I said, head bobbing. "I assume because of the law, no one tries to go after the tree on dragon-back. Kind of hard to hide a twenty-foot-tall dragon. But that's our best chance. We just don't have the time to search a magical, vindictive, human-hating forest, and I'm not risking your lives to try."

"We can do this, Ains." Dominic tickled up my spine. Tangling in my hair, he tugged soft but sudden on the nape of my neck, making me moan.

Poet and Keely had been walking up to us. They both stopped.

"Uhh..." Poet turned away. "We can give you both a minute if you need to make up for lost time."

Heat exploded in my cheeks. The handsome jerk knew what his strangely intimate hair-pulling did to me.

"It'd take a lot longer than a minute."

"Dom," I cried. "Stop."

"Yes, Dom, stop," Velez said, joining us in the clearing. "All that bragging is obvious overcompensating."

"All the sex you're not having with a female population disgusted by you is obvious jealousy."

Velez smirked. "I do just fine, General Spawn. I can't play your Daddy-was-mean-and-damaged-me card, but most women like that I'm not a broken, weepy mess."

"Hmm," I hummed, getting to my feet. "I feel like I took a bit of a hit with that insult too."

"No, Ains, you're great. You've got terrible taste in men." He grinned. "But you're great."

"Thanks?" Velez opened his mouth to say something else to Dominic. "Nope, you're both done. You're not allowed to talk to each other until you figure out a way to be friends."

"Never going to happen."

"No, thanks."

"Then you're never going to talk," I gritted through clenched teeth. "Now come on. We're all going to Akpan. Dragons too. It's a small town bordering the Shahina Forest. I've never been, so I can't shadow-travel there. Suoh will have to take us. Be prepared for panic when we all suddenly appear."

"But one advantage of small towns like this," Poet spoke up. "They only have one Watcher assigned to their home, and most times not even that much. The magic ability will be low for commoners, and no one wants anything to do with people going into the Shahina Forest, so they'll look the other way."

"Exactly," I said. "I don't want to tempt Mother Future into a challenge, but this might actually be simple. We fly over, find the Infinity Tree, get the bark, and head straight for Itzala. After everything we've been through, the end is finally in sight."

Keely hugged me from the side. "We lost a friend along the way..." We had a quiet moment for Akasha. "But we made it here. Together. We're going to finish this together." Her smile swept over us. "You're all the bravest, most honorable men and woman in Adalinda. I'm so thankful I've gotten to know and fight alongside you."

"I can't say it better than that, so I won't try," Poet said. "It's been an honor."

"Thank you." Dominic tangled in my hair, soft and stroking. "All of you, for helping me protect the woman I love. I can never repay you."

"Dom." There went my blush. "It's not about me."

"Yes, it is. To me, you're everything."

I hid my face in his neck—so happy I could cry.

Clearing my throat, I held my hands out for Dominic and Keely. "Let's go get that bark."

One jump to travel to Suoh and the dragons, then Suoh took over. Holding tight to my grumpy boy, we grinned at each other over his scales. We did it. The end was in sight.

Ossian Forest winked out and Akpan unfolded all around us.

"Ahhh!"

I threw myself against Suoh, scream catching behind my teeth. The woman ran through the spot I was standing in, hitting me with her pack and not bothering to look back to see if I was okay.

Coughing, I doubled over, taken down by a fit. My eyes stung and burned, refusing to let me see the horror my ears were hearing.

We arrived in the small village. Fragments of memory of my time wandering the kingdoms without my mind, recalled the beauty of Nehebkau. The Steel Kingdom. There wasn't a place to look that didn't boast the fine workmanship of decades of master artisans. Steel carriages shaped like headless swans rolled through the street. Homes built with unbreakable bones rose two or three stories, then topped with a steepled roof.

I'd been looking forward to seeing this unique country again through my own eyes.

"Hurry! Leave the rest and get in!" A man picked up a woman stumbling out of her home, weighted down with five packs. He tossed her in the carriage and they took off, narrowly running over a dozen people in their haste.

People were running, screaming, throwing themselves on the ground and wailing, and above it all, the air burned. Slowly, I turned around.

"No!" Poet fell to his knees. "What have they done!"

It wasn't what they'd done. It was what were they doing.

I clapped my hand over my mouth, horror dropping me to my own knees as the Royal Riders dominated the sky, directing their dragons to set fire to Shahina Forest.

Everything was burning. The inferno engulfed every tree, leaf, vine, and twig, and I swear I heard them all screaming.

"They can't do this," Poet roared. "The forest will punish us. It'll poison our water, rot our crops, and kill the livestock. They're killing Nehebkau. They're killing us all! They sacrifice an entire kingdom to stop one person?" Poet's agony broke my heart. "How could the High Council allow this?"

"They didn't," Dominic said. Flames reflected in his eyes. "Guys, I... I don't think the High Council is in charge anymore. The representatives of all five kingdoms, working together to ensure balance and fairness to all? They'll never be in charge again."

Terrible realization dawned and my stomach heaved. "Because High Queen Kisandra is, and she'd allow this," I said. "She'd want this. The death of Nehebkau... would be a bonus."

Poet whirled on me, eyes crazy with tears and rage. He looked like he wanted to shout nothing so horrible could be true, but he couldn't. The truth was burning right before his eyes.

"Ainsley..."

"Yes?"

Poet looked me dead in the face. "Let's kill that fucking bitch."

"Gladly." I seized him, hugging him tight.

Dominic and Velez came up behind, grasping his shoulders. We comforted him even though we couldn't. What could anyone do or say that'd make the destruction of your home and legacy any better?

"How?"

A small voice lifted our heads. Keely gazed at us, face wet.

"The Infinity Tree is in there somewhere burning. It'll be nothing but a scorched stump when the fire burns out," she cried. "We failed, guys. We lost. After everything... it ends here."

"Keely." Velez stepped toward her. "Don't say that. We'll figure something—"

"What are we going to figure out!" she screamed, blowing us back. "We abandoned our families. We were tortured. Akasha died. We were poisoned. Dominic burned alive. All of that to get here, and it was for nothing! The only thing we have to show for ourselves is the death of an entire kingdom! Not even the usurper accomplished that."

I flinched. "Keely, I know this is horrible, but we've accomplished so much more than that. We freed the unique mages who were caught, captured, and held at the general's estate. We discovered the truth of what happened to Princess Inaya. We freed the Everlasting Flame and earned the gratitude of every fire dragon in Adalinda.

"We rescued Celine from a nightmare, and we did it together," I said, reaching out for their hands. "Two Ghidorians, one half Nehebkan, a Druk's daughter, and two cursed Nevaehans. All of us from different places. All of us with different stories. Rich, poor, commoner, orphan, dragon slayer, dragon rider.

"Together, all of us were such a threat—so unstoppable—Queen Kisandra committed this horrible, insane tragedy to get in our way, and in doing so, she's made more enemies than I can name—further weakening the crumbling support under her.

"She won't come back from what she's done here today, but we will. When we lead an army of the gods against the mad queen, rip her from the throne, and build this in its place," I said, squeezing Dominic and Keely. "Us. A kingdom of people working together, accepting each other, fighting for each other. Actually, make that six kingdoms."

Keely fell quiet under the hazy, smoke-filled devastation. "But how?" she whispered. "We can't complete the ritual now. You said without it, the dragon slayers will never be strong enough to face everything Kisandra and General Roark are going to throw at us. We can't face *this* without an army."

I gazed upon the dragon riders destroying their own country.

"I haven't given up," I stated, lifting my chin. "This ritual hasn't been done before. We believed the power of the four elements would give us our best chance, but three could still work." A coughing fit took me. This wasn't the place to have a discussion, but it also didn't feel right to leave as quickly as we blundered in. How could I? Nehebkau was dying because of me.

"I won't let this ritual fail." My eyes watered from so much more than the smoke. "We've all sacrificed too much, and now Nehebkau is sharing in that sacrifice. It won't be in vain. If the claw, Flame, and water don't work by itself, then I think I know something that will." I met each of their eyes in turn. "Are you still with me?"

"Yes," said Velez.

"To the end," said Poet.

"Of course," Keely said.

Dominic kissed my fingertips. "Always."

We broke our circle, but didn't move.

"Shouldn't we do something?" Keely's voice wavered. "Stop them somehow?"

"We're too late," Dominic replied, knuckles whitening in his clenched grip. "The fire's already raging out of control, and it's not magical fire, so Ainsley can't steal it. We'd need every water mage in Adalinda to put this out... and the forest would still be dead."

"At least we should stop them," Velez cried, throwing a hand out at the dragon riders. "They can't just do shit like this and get away with it."

"Those aren't unbonded Watchers," Dominic said. "If we fight, we're facing dragon and rider. We swore at the start of this we wouldn't kill any dragons. The dragons want Ainsley to succeed. These guys are just following their riders' lead. And the riders are following Kisandra's orders."

"Stop talking about what we can't do and talk about what we can," Poet snapped. "We have to do something!"

"I'll do something." Atlas pushed between us, marching up to the inferno.

"Ahh! A Druk!"

Atlas sent the villagers running faster than the flames. A fire would only burn them. A Druk would slice their stomachs open, spill out their guts, and eat them. Or so the stories said.

Atlas dropped to the ground. Digging his fingers in the dirt, his wings snapped out wide and he roared.

The earth began to rumble. I pitched headfirst into Poet's back, taking us both down. Dominic tried to help me up, then he went down too.

"Is he causing a fucking earthquake?" Keely shouted over the earth's groaning. "How does that help anyone!"

My eyes went round.

The whole of Tenille's domain split, cleaving Nehebkau away from Shahina Forest. A wall of stone tore from the ground, rising higher... higher... and higher. Atlas arched his back, bellowing like he was pulling the stone from the core of the world with his bare hands alone.

The wall grew over top of the trees, trapping all but the smoke behind.

I ran to him as the wall morphed, changed, and swirled—forming a design? No— A face.

Many faces, I realized as Nia's smile appeared in the stone, followed by her sweet, cherubic face and dozens of tiny braids that framed it. Flowing out on both sides of her, the rest of my family who were waiting for their statues, soared high into the air—covering the shouts and roars of the dragon rider bondeds, and filling the horizon with sweet, smiling children.

"Argh!" Atlas shot back and fell hard on his wings. Face red and pouring sweat, he looked like he'd just done battle with all two dozen of those dragon riders, and the victory was short-lived.

"Atlas," I cried, dropping to my knees. I placed his head on my lap. "You did too much."

"I did it all," he croaked, head lolling to the side. "That's it. I'm drained of magic. I'm sorry."

My face was wet. "Why are you sorry, dummy?"

All around, villagers stopped their rushing, running, and screaming. The stone contained the fire. It wouldn't save them from the forest's curse, but it gave them time to pack their homes and leave with dignity. It wouldn't save Nehebkau, but it was more than their sovereign, High Queen Kisandra, would do for them.

"I wanted to... honor them all for... you." His lids were getting heavy. "Sister Aven's statue... I'll need days to recover—"

"Shh. You have days to recover." I closed his eyes for him. They didn't open again. "Besides, I have a special place in mind for Sister Aven's statue."

A hand covered my shoulder. "We should go, baby. I'm sorry, but we don't know when that bloodline mage will be found and rescued. We need to be on the right side of the Dark Border when that happens."

"Yes. We have to go."

I said it, but I didn't move just yet. This was it. The end of my journey of the impossible, and the beginning of a rebellion. A prison break. A war. A prophecy.

I left Itzala as a scared and confused girl, desperate not to mess up and let everyone down. I returned as the heir of the six kingdoms. Princess Ainsley. Titana's daughter.

Queen of Adalinda.

Chapter Eighteen

"Are you nervous?" *Kiss.*

I could only shake my head until my face stuck against my arm and hid there. Dominic continued on with his business, unconcerned.

"I know you got the ritual from Osman, not Junia, but it's hard to trust anything she touched." *Kiss.* "They gave us two weeks and we've returned early." Dominic kissed the freckle on the underside of my breast again. He seemed particularly interested in worshipping that spot with attention. It was both arousing and ticklish. I couldn't stop shivering, or blushing.

Kiss. "Maybe we take that time to do our own research on forbidden magics and this ritual. Make sure we get it right." Dominic finally stopped teasing the poor thing and closed his mouth over my nipple, sucking hard.

I hissed sweet, delicious pleasure—moans echoing through the trees. It was good to be home in the Gaia Curves, although stranger to call it home, and stranger that no other word felt right.

We returned the day before, and found nothing as we left it. While we'd been away, the dragon slayers took advantage of most of the dragons being gone to turn a camp for refugees into a home. Gone were the simple dirt huts. In their place were proper houses, a meeting hall, a kitchen, a mess hall, and even a library.

The children frolicked through the newly laid streets, chasing after Tizor's scampering nestlings, and most surprisingly of all, Nada joined Tizor in his vigilant watch over my own nestlings. It was the biggest shock when the flying carriage dropped down, and there she was, grooming her claws in the sun while children climbed on her back.

Apparently, she smelled them cooking goat one evening and flew in, demanding some. My thought that she was just like Reyna didn't go over well with her sister.

Through all the hugs, congratulations, chats, and well-wishes, Dominic and I grinned whenever our eyes met. That morning, we stole away into the trees, taking nothing but a blanket.

"I wish we could— Oohh." Dominic nipped a burning trail from one nub to the other.

Truthfully, it hadn't been long since that night in the inn, but it felt like the opposite. The gulf that stretched between us when I pushed him away, then off a cliff with that letter—turned the days into years. Being with Dominic in that moment was like coming home in its own beautiful way.

"Meriall is gathering the dragon slayers from all the nations," I said.

Dominic pressed kisses like raindrops down through the valley of my breasts—light and tickling.

"Some refused to give up their dragon-stolen ability, but most have pledged to follow the savior—me—wherever I lead. As soon as the ritual's complete, the Five have promised to free all ten thousand dragons. Those dragons have been locked away for too long. I can't ask them to wait any longer."

"Not even to make sure we're not missing anything?"

Only Dominic and I could argue while having sex. Still, I smiled. This felt good. Familiar. *Right.*

"Osman knows, and he'll be there. He's nothing like Junia was. He wants to help us."

Dominic kissed the apex of my thighs, tugging a sharp intake of breath from me. That breath was shamed by a moan as he swiped a tongue through my folds, and plundered his prize like a starving man at a feast.

We bucked, writhed, and molded together—becoming one like we always would and were destined to be.

The trees spun. I giggled to suddenly find myself upright and on his lap.

Dominic threw his head back, and his bronze skin caught the sun. He was the most handsome man I'd ever seen. His warm, syrupy eyes always glinted with mischief. His hard, scarred body drew me like a bee to honey. I just wanted to touch him, kiss him, run my hands all over him, tracing the difficult years of his life under my tender hands, and letting him know those years were over. I loved him.

Dominic pushed inside me with a hard snap of his waist. The familiar, wonderful fullness between my legs ripped a growl from my teeth.

"Still got a little dragon in you, baby." Dominic kissed me hard and passionate—tongues tangling and lips smashing. "Why is that so fucking sexy?"

"Because I'll be violently and possessively defending your seed for the rest of your days." I laughed. "You're more into that than you want to admit."

"Oh, I'll admit it." He rocked back and forth, bouncing me up and down on his pole like a seesaw. "I'm into it. I'm loving this *he's mine* energy coming off you."

My already hard nipples were about to pop off and roll away, they couldn't handle what he did to me any more than I could. My whole body was about to burst.

"Makes me feel very special to belong to the queen of the six kingdoms. Even more to be her husband." His bottom lifted off the blanket and took me with him. He straight hammered my pussy like there was a tricky little nail in there. He'd put it in its place if it was the last thing he'd do.

How could he talk right then let alone do it coherently? My moans were screams bouncing off the barks and escaping up through the leaves, telling the heavens of my love and need for Dominic Roark.

"Even more to call this beautiful, smart, strong, perfect woman my wife."

"Dom," I cried, throwing my arms around his shoulders. "I love YOU!"

I meant to say that last word and ended up screaming it. Dominic struck that spot and the world upended, tossing me off and dropping me into a realm of pure heat and pleasure. Light magic exploded in my mind, painting my world in starbursts of golds and reds.

Dominic gripped my hips, fingers digging permanent marks of possession as he followed, hoarsely yelling his climax.

We both collapsed in a heap of tangled limbs, kissing, and laughing. There was nothing more fun and relaxing than making love with Dominic. It was the one thing I didn't know I wanted. A true wish. To be with someone who filled every moment with happiness. There was no one I felt safer with.

"How was that, wife?" He nipped my chin. "Better than the life-changing night of orgasmic passion you shared with Atlas after you, and I quote, dumped my ass and dumped me hard."

I winced. "Ridiculous fool. I'm glad we can laugh about this now."

"Oh, yes. It was quite funny when I lit his ass on fire. The only one who got dumped hard was him in the nearest stream. Keely saved his life, for reasons unknown."

"Any chance you two will stop trying to rile up and kill each other?"

"I'm certain we'll stop when one of us is dead."

Chuckling, I tucked my head under his chin. "I'm too blissed out right now to scold you."

Dominic and I lay on the blanket, surrounded by wildflowers. A cool breeze whispered through the meadow, tickling our heated skin and inviting the primroses and daisies to dance.

Lava pockets heated the air, making the Gaia Curves feel like summer. Was there a more beautiful place to live? Would any Adalindian other than us have a chance to know this land beyond the Dark Border and appreciate it for the untapped, natural beauty it is?

"Hey," I said, finger-walking across his chest. "Want to see something pretty?"

"Yes, please." He flipped me over and headed down.

"Behave," I cried, laughing. "That's not what I meant. Here, look."

I waved my hand, slow and steady. As it fell back on the blanket, the flowers came alive. Flying free of their earthly binds, they swirled around us in a cyclone of color—purples, reds, golds, and blues. The rainbow army of Tenille dropped their kisses on our skin as we laughed in delight.

Their teasing done, they floated away—gently falling around like rain.

"Wow, Ains, that was amazing. Was that wind magic?"

"You'd think so, but no. It was earth magic. I borrowed a little from Cadmus."

He shook his head, eyes blown. "But I thought you could only do vine magic with his power?"

"That was just me limiting myself by what I saw Maili do, but Cadmus's magic is so much more than that. My magic is so much more."

Kai's words echoed in my mind. *"You'll plumb the deepest depths of what a goddess of fury and vengeance can do, because believe me, you haven't begun to tap into your potential."*

"I am so much more."

Dominic cupped my cheek. "You're incredible, Ainsley, and you were before any of this. I knew from the day you picked yourself off the ground, and limped back to the dragon who threw you—determined not to give up. I knew I was looking at my future."

I kissed the tip of his nose, smile playing at the corner of my lips. "That makes me feel kind of bad, because I had no such warm and fuzzy inklings about you. I thought you were a jerk."

He cracked up—head thrown back and free like I'd never seen him when other people were around. I gave my love the same feeling. With me, he was safe and happy.

"Will you let me show you something too?" Getting on his feet, he held his hand out to me. "It's not far."

"Okay."

We dressed, then he led me away. The two of us slipped through the trees.

"I've been working on this since we've been back, so it's not finished yet," he said. "I messed up with the gravestones. I was so stupid. I'm still sorry for that."

I blinked at the back of his head. Why was he bringing this up? "Dom, I was never mad at you. It came from a sweet place. I knew that then and now."

"I messed up and hurt you, Ains. I can promise you this for the future. I may mess up once but I'll never repeat my mistakes." Dominic stopped before hanging moss. Pulling it back, he stepped aside. "It's not as good as that flying piece of shit but... I hope you like it."

Ducking under the moss, I stepped into a small clearing with a bench. A ray of sunlight shone on something sitting before the little wooden seat. What was it?

I approached, heart clenching as it came into view. A statue.

Not stone. I couldn't be sure what kind of metal was shining in the sun, but I could be sure of what the metal made. Two little girls holding hands, one with wavy hair and an impish smile, the other's hair straight and her nose scrunched up—the cutest thing about me, according to Dominic.

They were me and Rosaleen. Two little kids. Two best friends. Ready to take on an unfair world... together.

I fell to my knees, clapping my hands over my mouth. "Oh, Dom..."

"You don't like it? Ains, I'm sorry." He rushed to grab it. "I'll get rid of it, I—"

"No." I grasped his hands, gently pulling him down next to me. "I love it. It's perfect."

"Is it?" I wasn't used to this side of him. Nervous and vulnerable. It made me love him more. "I'm no sculptor. I messed up on the eyes and mouths, and I couldn't make it nearly as big as that bastard."

The corner of my mouth curled up. "I thought Velez was that bastard?"

"They're both bastards."

Shaking my head, I dropped it on his shoulder. "I don't know about that, but I do know you're perfect. This is perfect. It looks just like us. I can't believe you envisioned little Rosie so correctly after seeing her the once."

"Twice," he said softly. "The day she stood before the queen of Adalinda and a room full of screaming, hateful royals, and all she cared about was protecting you."

My lips trembled.

"She was loyal to the very last, Ainsley. Seeing what she did showed me I've never had a real friend in my life, because *she* is what a great friend is. She encouraged you to go to training. She put you on the path to discovering your birthright. She told you to seduce me—may the gods bless her. There wouldn't be me and you without Rosaleen.

"Of course I know that brave woman's face. I'll never forget her."

My heart burst with love for him. There were so many things I wanted to say to his beautiful speech, but mine failed me. All I could do was bury my face in his shoulder—shedding tears for my friend who was all of that and more.

Rosaleen Orosco, the bravest woman in Adalinda. That sounded right to me.

"Did you make the bench too?" I asked. "I didn't know you knew how."

"I don't," he confessed. "I begged it off of one of the earth dragon slayers. Since I couldn't make it bigger, I thought at least I can make it private. Give you this calm, quiet place to remember your friend."

I placed my hand were theirs met. "This is the best gift anyone's ever given me."

We were quiet for a long time. Sitting in that peaceful place, we remembered those we lost. I wasn't sure who Dominic was thinking of, but I had a feeling he was looking on them as fondly as I did of Rosaleen. This wasn't a sad place or a sad day. We loved and were loved in return. How could that ever be sad?

The sun was setting by the time we returned to the resettlement camp. My dragons were chiming their irritation and bloodlust very clear. Didn't seem wise to delay.

We broke through the trees, landing on Meriall in conversation with Atlas.

The dragons would never kill my mother, and they were beginning to warm up to Atlas after he risked his life saving me and the Everlasting Flame, but having two Druks that close to them was testing their patience.

"—shared a passionate, steamy kiss under the moonlight. It was beautiful, Meriall. We fell in love." Atlas heaved a sigh. "But as you know, your daughter has a pitying, charitable heart."

"Does she?"

"Oh, yes. Dominic wailed and cried and got violent." He shrugged shoulders and wings. "After such a pathetic, embarrassing display, she snapped that she'd take him back to get him to stop bawling."

"I see," Meriall replied, spotting us over his shoulder.

"You don't see. No one has ever seen a grown man fall apart like that. He was pounding and kicking the ground. At one point, he shit his pants."

Meriall stifled a laugh, fighting to keep a straight face. "Oh no, poor Dominic was really hurting."

Poor Dominic was wound tighter than a bowstring. Like the dragons, he was summoning indomitable will to hold back from killing Atlas.

"You say that because you have the same charitable, pitying heart, Meriall. In the end, I gave her my blessing to marry the sad, little man. The bonds of matrimony shall never come between true love. We will happily continue our affair after the wedding."

"Atlas!" I snapped.

He whirled around, eyes huge. "Ainsley," he gasped. "Oh my— I didn't know you were both there! Oh, forgive me, my love. Now he knows our plan."

"Atlas," I forced through clenched teeth. "You know you're an idiot, so I'm not going to dignify your nonsense right now."

"I love you too, my morning berry."

"Fuck's sake! Would you switch places with Velez? Having two dragon slayers nearby is too much for the dragons."

He bowed low. Velez rose up in his place.

"Ainsley," Meriall greeted, fighting to contain her laughter. "Forgive me for coming. I don't mean to stress your dragons, but we need to talk."

I looked to Dominic.

"It's okay," he said. "I won't kill anyone while you're gone."

Meriall and I walked off.

"But," Dominic continued, "we'll discuss that passionate, steamy kiss when you get back."

We walked off quicker. Meriall stopped holding it back and laughed freely. "I see that Atlas has been a challenge."

"No," I barked. "Blistering boils on your genitals are a challenge. Atlas Stoneslayer is every nightmare come to life."

"He certainly kept my hands full as a borrowed mother. Even though they both say it's due to the curse, Atlas was a babe born into a grown man's body. He had the freedom to drink, carouse, and get into mischief, because he had the body and mind to get away with it. All the things a child needs to learn, he never had the chance to." She sighed. "The cruel thing is, when age finally does give him wisdom and patience, he'll be too young to use that gift as well."

I took that in. Meriall had wisdom. She was right. They saw his selfishness and immaturity as a curse, but what else was one supposed to be when he was born with the freedom that comes with adulthood? No one made him sit at the table until he finished his meal, do chores, be inside before the sunset, or taught him to handle the whims and urges that came with a grown person's body.

Atlas had been cast a terrible hand. Whoever created the Gemini curse must've been really, really pissed off.

"Will you still care for him when he becomes a teenager, then a child, then a baby?" I asked.

"I will. Atlas and Velez are family. I could do nothing else." Both her hands closed over mine. "It's also my deepest wish to help care for your babes. Family, my precious one. How long I have waited for this one."

I swallowed hard, emotion tickling my throat. Words couldn't capture how long I'd been waiting too. "Does this mean you'll marry us?"

"You never had to ask. Of course I will."

My tears wiped away, bringing back my beaming happiness. "Is that what you came here to tell us? Are we performing the ceremony now? Oh, gosh. Oh, gods," I cried, twisting this way and that. "I don't have a red dress yet, and oh— I'll need a red dress and suit for Poet and Keely too. Can we get someone to erect the tent? And I want my dragons there, so I'll make sure they can handle being that close to you. And—"

"Wait, slow down, my love," she said. "That isn't why I'm here. I came because... it's time."

I stilled. "Time? As in, time for the ritual?"

"Yes."

I stepped back, rubbing my hands on my pants, touching my hair, fixing my clothes unnecessarily. "The Four accepted the water, Flame, and claw as real?"

"They have."

"They've summoned all the willing dragon slayers?"

"And unwilling," she said, blowing my eyes wide. "We're a democratic society. We believe in the people having a choice, but the future of slayer nation is on the line, and the Four now believe more than ever that you'll lead us into the bright future of the six kingdoms. The Well of Sorrows was a legend. Celestial dragons were no more. The Flame couldn't be reached. This was known and accepted by all, and you proved them wrong in less than two weeks.

"The Four will allow no one to stand in the way of your vision. Everyone flies here," she said, gesturing past the mountains. "When night falls, we will cease to be dragon slayers, and greet the new day as god slayers."

I nodded slow, breaths coming faster than normal. This is what I wanted. What I worked for. Sacrificed for. It was time to free my godly mother, and pry Kisandra's and the general's grips off of Adalinda.

"There is something else you need to know."

I lifted my head. "What is it?"

"General Roark is coming with an army of twenty thousand Ryuku warriors," she dropped. "They're coming straight for the Gaia Curves. They're coming here."

"What! How do you know this?"

"We have seven spies among the Ryuku. All seven reported their new orders." She pinched the bridge of her nose. I could tell with one look that it'd been a long day for her. "Roark has a unique mage. A tracker. They say he's frighteningly good at tracking people down, and he's found Dominic Roark."

"The bloodline mage." I spat the words. "I didn't kill him because Roark enslaved him with those manacles same as the others, but dumping him on top of a mountain clearly wasn't enough."

"He isn't our problem right now. Becoming strong enough to face the Ryuku is."

"How much time do we have?"

"We don't know," she replied. "The squads were simply told to be ready to leave at a moment's notice. Since they're ready, we need to be as well. The ritual will commence tonight, in an hour's time. Will you be ready?"

"Yes," I said before she finished the question. "I have to send the dragons away first, then prepare an area for the ritual. Dominic and Osman will help me. I'll be ready."

"Excellent. Are you certain it won't be an issue that you couldn't get to the Infinity Tree?"

"I have something else to take its place. We'll be okay."

"All right." Clapping her hands on my shoulder, she took a deep breath, and smiled as she let it out. "My precious girl. I admit, I'm scared for what happens next. I've been a dragon slayer for so long. But tonight, I get to step into a new future... with you. That is worth any and everything I must give up on the way."

I bit my lip. I didn't want to do something embarrassing—like cry. "Can I ask you something?"

"Anything."

"Do you have any idea why the Four is really going along with all this?"

Her smile wiped away. Holding my gaze, she replied, "No."

Velez did say it. Meriall was a straightforward and honest person. She did me the decency of not pretending she didn't know what I was talking about.

"I have no idea what their ulterior motive is, although like you, I'm certain they have one."

I considered that, mind churning. "Are you certain that they at least don't want to conquer Adalinda, and have it and the dragons under their control?"

"I'm certain that if they try... I'll rip their heads off and feed it up the asses they used for their thinking when they made up that idiotic plan."

I couldn't help but grin. "Guess that's good enough for me."

She pressed a soft kiss on my forehead. "Good luck. I'll be back soon."

Meriall left to marshal the forces that'd be descending on this place. She had her job. I had mine.

Over the next hour, Osman, Dominic, and I rode my dragons to the other side of the mountains—far from the resettlement camp. The dragons returned to camp, and we stayed. My borrowed wind magic shaved the tall grass. Dominic's magic burned the symbols into the earth. I knew not what any of it meant, but Osman and Dominic had ancient language lessons I never did. They told me that basically, they were symbols of destruction.

"That's what we're doing," Osman said. "It's like any wall. If you want to bring it down, you have to tear it down. We're tearing down the walls between realms, and I cannot begin to think of what the lasting consequences will be."

"Why did anyone create such a ritual in the first place?" I asked.

"That's where the text got muddled." Osman spoke to me and consulted his notes while he followed behind Dominic, making sure everything was correct. "One theory was that a besotted young mage fell in love with a goddess, and wanted to tear down the walls so they could be together. Another theory is that an older, dying mage believed if he could bring down the walls and cross, he'd find the key to becoming a god and living forever.

"The backstory isn't certain, but the result is"—Osman's gaze pinned me—"the ritual worked. They brought down the walls, and lost their mind."

"What?" Dominic's hellfire extinguished in a flash. "Lost their mind? You conveniently left out that detail till the end!"

"What? No," Osman cried. "I told Ainsley it ended badly for the first mage, and that's why it's forbidden. I swear I did."

"He did." Carefully, I set the water, Flame, and claw at the north, south, and east points on the circle. "Kai told me the gods live within the eternal nothingness. Humans can't handle seeing it. They lose their minds."

"Then why the fuck are we doing this!"

"Because," I returned, planting my hands on my hips. "I'm going to do something so amazing, so outstanding, so surprising, no one else could've thought of it."

"What's that?"

I gave him a look. "Close my eyes."

"Haha. Very funny, Princess, but I'm serious. All I care about is you making it out of this."

"I will. This will work, Dominic. Everything has come together too perfectly for it not to."

"That's what scares me," he said, setting his palms aflame. "How perfectly this all came together."

***

If I thought that the end of the matter, I was mistaken. Dominic battered Osman with questions for the entire hour. The guy kept looking at me for help, but there was nothing I could do. Dominic went along with the plan because he loved and trusted me. Now it was real. His future wife was about to perform a ritual that drove its creator to insanity. Even the random street person he wanted to invite to our wedding would be worried about me.

As the hour came to a close, I watched the Druks fly in from all directions—their multicolored wings and scales lighting up in the setting sun.

"What do you think of all this, my beauties?" I whispered. "We never really got a chance to talk about it."

"*You do what is right, dragon mother,*" Tizor replied. "*This is the necessary path. There couldn't be another.*"

"It is?" I had to admit that answer surprised me. "How do you know?"

"*The abominations have stolen, slaughtered, and desecrated the dragonkin. Today, they free the captured dragons and return the lost souls to Mother Zaeah—granting them peace. This is necessary. This is right.*"

Reyna, Cadmus, Celine, Kenna, Mireu, and Suoh chimed in agreement.

"Do you mean it's right because it's right for the dragonkin?" I asked. "Or it's right because this will work, and we'll win the war against the queen and approaching army?"

"*The dragonkin,*" they all said at once.

"*We know not if your circles and burnt grass will create more like the dragon mother,*" Kenna said.

"*Why would we?*" Cadmus asked. With more control, I was getting better at hearing their voices one at a time. "*No one in dragonkin history has attempted something on the scale you are.*"

"*You will likely fail,*" Suoh stated. "*This is silly human nonsense, and silly human nonsense never turns out the way you want. Why you wasted our time and yours on this foolishness is the real question. Now you've woken me up to ask pointless questions? You will bring me an ox to apologize!*"

I sighed. "I'm sorry, my shadow love, I'll bring you two oxen."

The rest were nicer about it than Suoh, but they said much the same things. They didn't have a clue what was about to happen. This was new territory for all of us—dragon, human, and god alike.

The Five were the last to arrive. They dropped down just outside the edge of the circle.

"We're ready," Ramses said. "Begin."

I inclined my head. There wasn't much more to say. We all knew what we were here to do.

Turning my back, I moved to the western point of the circle. A symbol marked my spot, and down I went, kneeling on it and the final rays of the setting sun. Dominic was close, standing by the northern symbol. Osman by the southern symbol, and Keely, Poet, and Atlas by the east.

We told Poet and Keely they didn't have to come, but they arrived with Atlas. They wouldn't be anywhere else, they told us. They would see this through to the end.

I released a long breath, calming my racing heart. "This is it," I whispered. "The fall of the dragon slayers, and the rise of the god slayers. So it begins."

So I began. Lapsing in ancient Adalindian, I started the chant. I didn't understand everything I was saying. According to Dominic, it was a song. A song of destruction, endings, beginnings, transformation, and favor.

"Wall of the realms," I called, switching into new Adalindian. "We destroy you. We crumble your foundation, and blow apart your barriers. No longer shall you keep us from our gods. Wall of the veil prison, we raze you to the ground and free those who must be free.

"Humbly we ask your favor and boldly we move forward without it. For what we must destroy, we will give. We sacrifice to you these one hundred and fifty thousand dragon souls. Let them be released from their human binds. Let them pass on to Mother Zaeah. Take," I said, "so they'll destroy."

I fell quiet, dropping my forehead to the earth. I waited.

And waited.

And waited.

"That's it?" Ramses's voice grated on my ears. "It's not working. I knew we couldn't continue with a component of the ritual missing. We wasted precious time on this, and now the general and his army are on our doorstep! Why did we entertain this girl—?"

The ground exploded.

Shooting up, I twisted around. The eastern, northern, and southern points came alive, throwing my friends and Dominic back. Columns of fire, water, and star magic blasted through the sky. Revealing light swept over the many scared and awed faces.

Then the columns moved.

They fell like water from an upright spigot, sweeping over the crowd. Screams erupted through the Gaia Curves as flames consumed Atlas, water blasted my mother, and starlight suffocated the Five. Everywhere, everyone—burning, drowning, and suffocated as power I couldn't begin to comprehend took back what was stolen.

It was nearly impossible to describe the sight before me. I knew when I looked back on this day, there'd be nothing but a white space where the memory used to be. How could one hold the image in their minds of wings burning away, scales melting, claws falling off and evaporating on the wind. Before my eyes, the dragon slayers were undone.

My mother ceased her screaming. Her head threw back as if trying to escape from her body. She bent like an arrow—chest pointed to the sky. Lips parting, I watched rapt as a small, black orb floated out of her heart. Ever so slowly it glided into the circle, and fell upon the symbol for offering.

My gift to witness that amazing sight was followed by many more. Dragon souls floated into the air, painting the world in their ethereal beauty.

Ramses cried on his knees, overwhelmed by the same emotion that brought everyone, including me, to tears. Suddenly, there were no more cruel and terrifying Druks before me. There were only people. All too soon, the final soul descended onto the circle, and with its departure to where it belonged, the columns righted themselves and shrank to burning, gushing, and swirling pillars just higher than Atlas's true height.

There was no denying it. The ritual was working. The walls were coming down. There was only one more column needed.

"Forgotten gods," I shouted. "We build a bridge to you. Down will come the walls. Powerless, it falls before the might of the Everlasting Flame, the despair of the Well of Sorrows, the beauty of the celestial dragon... and the impossibility of the Druk's daughter."

"What?" Dominic broke in. "Ains, what does that mean?"

I couldn't look at him. I couldn't allow him to stop me.

"Forgotten gods, I give you the final sacrifice." Reaching into the folds of my dress, I pulled out the dagger.

"Hey! What are you doing with that!"

"No child could be more impossible than one of a Druk."

This was always the only way. It took the impossible to break down the realm walls. Impossible was me.

"The godling," I blared over his shouting. Heavy footfalls came for me. "The impossible child. The weapon of fury and vengeance. The daughter of Titana. By her power I am made strong. For your freedom, I am weakened."

I raised the knife over my head. I sensed more than saw Dominic. He swiped for the blade, and I ducked—rolling away and out of the circle. Spinning fast, I brought the knife down.

"Ainsley, don't!"

Vicious pain tore through my arm. It hurt horribly for a cut no bigger than a spoon's head.

While Dominic looked on in confused shock, I held my bleeding wound over the circle. With each drop, it burned brighter.

"I thought... I thought you were..."

"Going to stab myself through the heart or something?" I was outside the circle and could speak to him. "You've got to learn to trust me, my love. I can hardly complete the ritual if I'm dead. Besides, if a couple of drops from the well was enough, why wouldn't a couple drops of my blood do too?"

Strength whooshed out of him. He dropped beside me, took my injured hand, and ripped his tunic for binding. He tended to me as my column grew. Not the representation of the dirt, trees, and soil it was meant to be, I was no less awed by the beaming ray of ruby light.

The columns moved once more. Falling in on the circle, they came together like standing cards. Swirling, mixing, becoming one—our heads snapped back in unison as the lone column shot into the sky.

"Ainsley," Osman yelled over the din. "It's time! You have to do it now!"

"Okay, okay," I cried, head bobbing hard. This was it. If that torrent of fire, water, celestial, and blood magic broke through the walls of the realm and prison, we'd find out then. If I failed, we would harshly discover that too.

Dominic laced his fingers through mine. He met my eyes, and nodded. *You can do this.*

"Titana, goddess of vengeance, I release you from your prison!"

Boom!

The ground heaved us off her back. Dominic and I tumbled head over heels. We skidded to a rough stop as laughter filled the air.

Titana rose to full height, throwing her hands in the air and laughing raucously. My eyes burned in her godly radiance—a being of pure fire, poison, and revenge. She broke apart into tiny orbs and blasted from the circle.

My mother blew off her feet, a beam striking her through the heart. Nerilla of the Five struck the ground beside her—chosen by Titana. All over, shouts and cries went up as the revenge goddess chose her vessels.

"Keep going," Osman bellowed.

Shaking myself, I crawled back to the circle, shouting as I went. "Leander, god of friendship, I release you from your prison!"

A young, peaceful-looking man appeared in the circle—arriving with none of his sister's fanfare. Meeting my eyes, he looked at me, and smiled.

I blinked and he was gone, breaking to pieces to spread his soul among the worthy.

"Maximus, god of war, I release you from your prison. Dara, goddess of love, I release you from your prison. Engel, god of fortune, I release you from your prison." One by one, they came by my call. One by one, the former Druks fell—brought to their knees and backs by godly power.

"It's working!" Dominic laughed in delight, hugging me close. "You're doing it, Ains!"

I could've laughed too if I wasn't rattling off names and power as quickly as the dragons gave them to me. They remembered the old gods. Truly, they never forgot.

"Goddess of forgetfulness. God of peace. Goddess of justice. Goddess of truth. God of terror." My heart thumped hard when the last god arrived. He no longer wore Inaya's face, but I knew as I looked into it, I was gazing at the god who lurked at the bottom of the Well of Sorrows.

He lurked there no more.

"G-goddess of nightmares." I forced myself to continue. "I release you from your prison. God of wealth—"

"*Dragon mother!*" Tizor's shout ripped through my skull.

I screamed, clutching my head.

"Ainsley? Ains, what's wrong?"

Dominic's voice faded. Drowned out by jarring, jangling voices in my head.

"*Hurry!*" "*Flee!*" "*Dominic's sire attacks!*" "*Sire has Tizor.*" "*Sire has the nestlings.*" "*Back away!*" "*Flee before me.*" "*Release me!*" "*Run, dragon mother.*"

"*RUN!*"

"My dragons!" I shot up, bolting from the circle. The bridge between realms whooshed out of existence.

"What's going on?" Ramses demanded. "You can't be finished? I haven't been chosen. I have no power!"

I barely heard him. They were all shouting at once. I couldn't hold back the voices—rage and bloodlust made them stronger.

"Ainsley, why did you do that?" Osman cried. "That was your only chance. You—"

One clear and urgent thought came through.

"General Roark is attacking," I roared, blowing their complaints down their throats. "He's at the resettlement camp! He'll be here in seconds. We have to—"

A hole punched through my mind, blowing a crater in my soul that physically knocked my head to the side. I never thought about how it would feel... when one of my dragons died.

"Tizor!"

My beauty. My death dragon. My proud and wonderful father. Dead.

I screamed.

"Ainsley, what's going on!"

Poet, Keely, Osman, Dominic, Atlas, and my mother rushed me. Meriall caught me when I fell.

"Don't pelt her with questions," Meriall snapped. "Give her room! Ainsley's told us what happened. General Roark is on the other side of the mountain, attacking the settlement camp.

"Everyone," she bellowed. "Get in formation. Attack is imminent."

"What formation?" someone shouted back. "We can't fly!"

"I don't know what my power is."

"I need to get back to my family."

A swarm of panic, complaining, and worry blew back on us. Their own way of fighting, flying, and striking fear into the hearts of riders was over. Their new way hadn't been discovered yet.

"We have to get over the mountain," Keely cried. "Ainsley, I'm sorry, but can you call upon the dragons? As many as possible. They're not Druks anymore. The dragons will fight with them."

Poet grasped Keely's shoulder, skin ashen in the moonlight. "It's too late for that," he rasped, firmly putting her behind him. "Much too late."

"What are you talking about?" I broke free of Meriall's grip and forced myself up. My skull was a nest of agony. I clutched the back of my head as though it was bleeding, but it wasn't. This wound was on the inside.

I grabbed Atlas's pant leg, straining to pull up the rest of the way. My dragons were roaring in my skull. My Tizor was gone. The ritual was only half complete, and the god slayers weren't ready to fight. As perfectly as everything went right, that's how spectacularly it all fell apart.

Thunder rumbled the sky.

No, not thunder. Dragons.

They soared over the mountains, winging fast for us, and leading the charge on a dragon not his—was General Roark.

"Ainsley Boreen!" Roark boomed over the plains. "Because of you, I was forced to sacrifice Tizor. Because of *you*!"

It was impossible. The man didn't know feeling, emotion, or love. It couldn't be... but I heard it.

His voice was choked—heavy and warped by tears. General Ladon Roark was crying—

"Because he sacrificed what he loved..." I whispered, horror strangling my neck with the god of terror's fist. "In a ritual."

"Die, Druk's spawn!" Roark raised his fist to the sky, clutching something much bigger than a dagger. "Calthoon, god of the veil, imbibe me with the power to serve your will."

"Is that a scythe?" Dominic said. "Why the fuck does he have that?"

"Run," I screamed, repeating the word my dragons were all bellowing in my mind. "Everybody, run away!"

Roark sliced his scythe through the air. Poet, Keely, and Atlas turned to dust.

Screams and wails flooded the plains as the cascading tide of death browned the grass, killed the trees, struck the birds from the sky, and kept killing—striking down half our force where they stood.

Chaos ripped our people apart. They ran into every direction—flinging around magic they didn't understand or control. A purple cloud struck Osman in the back, and he burst into a hundred bubbles.

Gone.

Dominic grasped my arms, eyes bulging with an emotion I rarely saw in him. *Fear.*

"Ains, use your shadow magic. Get out of here now!"

"But—but—" My head whipped around. "Where's Velez? Where's my mother?"

"I'll find them." He pushed me back. "Just go, and remember I'll always love—"

"Die."

The scythe fell.

Chapter Nineteen

Dominic, Keely, Poet, Atlas, Meriall, and I stood in a smoke-filled room.

Or was it a room? I couldn't see where the wall began and the ceiling ended. I couldn't see walls at all.

"Where are we?" Atlas asked.

"You needn't ask," Velez replied. Even in this place, they were cursed. "There is only one place we could be."

"Are you saying...?" Keely's voice wavered. "We died?"

Silence fell over us in the oppressively silent space. I knew I died. Only death could be this quiet.

"How did he do it?" Meriall gazed down at her shaking hands. She felt behind her as if she wanted—hoped—that her wings would be there. "It happened so fast."

"I'll tell you what happened." My voice was flat. Dead. "The general performed a ritual of his own. He killed Tizor to call upon the power of Calthoon."

"Genius, wasn't it?"

I spun around as four figures emerged from the smoke.

"Mother would've had another one of her fits if we stopped you directly, but it's not against the rules for your enemy to beg for our help of his own free will."

I studied the speaker, brows crumpling.

He was gorgeous. Long, wavy raven locks tickled the tops of his shoulder. Honey eyes; pointed nose; strong jaw; small mouth with a huge, beaming smile. He was as gorgeous as the woman standing next to him was beautiful. I'd almost say they were twins, if not for the bluish-green scales covering her from head to toe.

Wait? Scales?

I flicked to the other two, studying them hard.

The tallest one stood off to the side, examining something under his nails, and not sparing us so much as a look. His bald head shone, and bored face never knew a smile, but none of that made him any less handsome than—

"Parthelan," I breathed. "Mother Zaeah. Tenille."

The bored man flicked to me when I said Tenille, then flicked away. I still wasn't interesting.

"Calthoon."

The god of death before me was nothing like the terrifying, silent skeleton that tried to pull us through the veil. This guy... looked more like a kid.

Well, a teenager to be more precise. If I passed him on the street and didn't know I was looking at an immortal god, I put him at a year or two younger than me. A simple black tunic, black pants, and black boots. The non-descript attire went with a non-descript face.

Another thing that would've happened if I passed him on the street, is I would've forgotten about him the second he was out of my sight. Nothing about his average nose, average mouth, and small brown eyes was worth recalling.

"Hello, Ainsley Boreen," greeted Parthelan. "My mother's chosen."

Swallowing, I lifted my chin. I reached back and Meriall was already there, taking my hand. Dominic held tight to the other. Poet grabbed his shoulder, then laced his fingers through Keely's. Keely pulled Velez in close.

We stood before them—all of us. Together.

"You don't look like what I expected," I said.

"Actually, we do. A mortal mind cannot handle seeing a god in their true form, so you've shrunk and molded us into forms more appealing to you." Parthelan's tone was conversational. Some would say kind. "Humans didn't exist when we were born. Why would we look like them?"

"Fair point." I kept the lightness in my voice.

Ten thousand years, and Kai ran away at the slightest chance they'd find him talking to me. If he feared them, it'd be wise for me to fear them too. They were the most powerful beings in the universe. My smart mouth could take a day off.

"Do you know why you're here, Ainsley Boreen?"

My mother's grip on me tightened.

"Because I brought down the walls between realms, freed the gods, and fulfilled the prophecy?"

"No."

"Excuse me?"

"No," he repeated clearly. "That's not why you're here. How could that be the reason when you've committed no such crimes?"

I exchanged looks with my friends, family, and love. "I don't understand."

"You didn't bring down the walls between realms. Such a thing would be a cataclysmic disaster. Your entire world would fall into the eternal nothingness, and you'd all die," he dropped. "You, Ainsley, merely slipped through a crack in the walls. What you actually destroyed, was the gate around my siblings' prison when you freed them.

"But, wait." He tapped his chin. "Did you?"

"Yes," I cried. "I saw it. I couldn't save them all, but the ones I did were free."

"A god is both free and confined. They have always been both in and out of the prison, but because they weren't worshipped, they were weak. Worthless." Parthelan's friendly atmosphere was dripping away. "When you released them from the prison, they were still too weak to walk the world. That is why I admit your plan was genius.

"Let them scatter pieces of themselves within the souls of one hundred and fifty thousand humans. Those humans will go on to wield their power and sing their praises, slowly but surely returning the forgotten gods to the human consciousness.

"Too bad Ladon Roark killed all one hundred and fifty of those humans, returning their souls, and the gods within them, right back here."

"No!"

"Yes," he hissed. "Prophecy decidedly not fulfilled, my little traitorous niece."

"I'm a traitor? You're the jealous, pathetic, crybaby whiner who locked your family away because you weren't getting enough attention!"

Fuck holding back my smart mouth. We worked so hard, sacrificed so much, and with one powerful gift to a homicidal monster, it all washed away in a blink.

"Jealous, pathetic, crybaby whiner," Parthelan slowly repeated. "That as may be, but I'm the jealous, pathetic, crybaby whiner who decides your fate."

"Hey," Dominic barked. "Don't you dare threaten—"

Parthelan snapped his fingers. "Do not interrupt. This is a family matter."

Dominic's mouth kept moving but nothing came out.

Tenille cracked his jaw yawning. Zaeah and Calthoon remained silent and watching. No one would intervene. This was actually between me and Parthelan.

"You think because my sister spun some sob story in your ear that you've gotten the full picture? These decisions were made for reasons you couldn't possibly understand." Yes, his friendliness was fading fast. "How dare you interfere!"

"I didn't interfere," I said, holding his gaze steady. "Your mommy did."

Whether I controlled their forms or not, I was certain the tic in his jaw when I invoked Mother Future came entirely from him.

"She doesn't like how you play with your brothers and sisters, so she sent me to teach you a lesson."

He straightened, staring his nose down at me. "And what lesson would that be?"

"That it doesn't matter if you were born a hundred-year-old man, or an all-powerful god. There's always someone out there who'll tan your backside when you've gone too far."

Someone made a small noise.

Was that Mother Zaeah? And did she... laugh?

To look at her impassive face, it was hard to tell, but Parthelan glared at her—lips peeled back and revealing almost dragon-like, razor-sharp teeth. Maybe they were twins.

"Enough of this," Parthelan snapped. "You're dead. Your fate rests in my hands now, not Mother's. Whatever lesson there is to be learned, looks like I'll be teaching it to you."

I backed away, taking my loved ones with me. "You don't decide my fate. Calthoon does."

"Deciding the right punishment for you, daughter of Titana, was difficult." He continued like I hadn't spoken. "Hardship has made you stronger. Wisdom took away your fear of death. You're even happy to be in this place, and unconcerned with facing me, because you do it with the people you love at your side.

"Let's change that."

"What—?"

The hands holding mine disappeared.

I spun around. Dominic was gone. Meriall was gone. Keely, Poet, and Velez—gone.

"What have you done with them? Bring them back!"

"I heard your little speech in Calixto," he plowed on, again pretending I hadn't spoken. "Your one true wish is for your family and friends to be safe and happy beyond the veil until you can all be together again.

"They will be safe, but I doubt the little orphan children and spoiled royals will be happy spending the rest of eternity in the prison you thought too good for my brothers and sisters."

"No! Leave them alone." I ran at him, and ran, and ran. The distance between us didn't close an inch. "Punish me," I screamed. "Lock me away. I'll do anything. Just free them, please, Calthoon."

I beseeched the death god. "You'd never let innocent souls be treated this way. Stand up to your brother! Stop this, please!"

Parthelan stepped in front of him. "Don't worry, daughter of failures, you'll have your chance to continue pointlessly begging his favor. You will not be imprisoned with your family. You'll stay with us, where I can keep an eye on you until the end of all time."

Golden manacles clamped my wrists, ankles, and neck.

"You'll be our servant, our pet, our entertainment, and our example," he hissed. "But what you'll never be is a hero. And what you'll never do... is see Dominic Roark again."

"No! Don't do this!"

He snapped his fingers, and we were gone.

***

Keep In Touch

Join R.A. Vincent's mailing list for news, teasers, and more:
https://www.subscribepage.com/ravincentpage
Join R.A. Vincent's Facebook Reader Group:
https://www.facebook.com/groups/ravincentbooklovers

ABOUT THE AUTHOR

R.A Vincent is a lover of all things enemies to lovers. From fantasy romance to contemporary romance, she loves saucy heroines, bold alpha males, and weaving a tale where both get their happy ever after.